# A CENTURY OF
# FANTASY
# 1980-1989

EDITED BY
ROBERT SILVERBERG

## THE GREATEST STORIES
## OF THE DECADE

MJF BOOKS
NEW YORK

Published by MJF Books
Fine Communications
Two Lincoln Square
60 West 66th Street
New York, NY 10023

Library of Congress Catalog Card Number 96-78810
ISBN 1-56731-156-3

Copyright © 1996 Agberg, Ltd. and Tekno-Books

Manufactured in the United States of America on acid-free paper

MJF Books and the MJF colophon are trademarks of Fine Creative Media, Inc.

10   9   8   7   6   5   4   3   2   1

## A Century of Fantasy: 1980–1989
Edited by Robert Silverberg

# Introduction

*by Robert Silverberg*

The early Seventies had put fantasy on the commercial publishing map in the United States with the overwhelming success of the paperback reprint of the Tolkien trilogy. *The Lord of the Rings*, selling by the millions, demonstrated that what had been thought to be a quaint little sub-genre admired only by its small group of special admirers was, in the chaotic era of the Vietnam War and the whimsical counterculture that sprang up in opposition to it, a major force in popular literary entertainment. The immense and steadily growing audience that had devoured—and virtually memorized—the three long novels of Professor Tolkien demanded more of the same kind of thing, and publishers were only too happy to comply.

By the end of that decade, Tolkien's esoteric *Silmarillion* had joined the original three novels (and their prequel, *The Hobbit*) on the best-seller lists. Robert E. Howard's long series of novels about the mighty-thewed hero Conan of Cimmeria, systematically reissued in many paperback volumes, found its own enthusiastic readership. The Fafhrd and Gray Mouser novels of Fritz Leiber, a somewhat more sophisticated representative of the sword-and-sorcery form, also won a large public. So did Andre Norton's Witch World books. The Ballantine Adult Fantasy series, edited by Lin Carter, made the classic work of such superb fantasists as E.R. Eddison, Lord Dunsany, William Morris, and Mervyn Peake available to the mass-market audience. Roger Zelazny launched his Amber series and Katherine Kurtz her Deryni novels. Stephen R. Donaldson achieved near-Tolkien-sized success with *Lord Foul's Bane*, the first of his Thomas Covenant books, and Terry Brooks began his well-received Shannara series.

Thus the groundwork for the great fantasy boom was laid, all through the Seventies. And in the Eighties came the payoff: a vast surge of fantasy novels, short-story anthologies, and magazines, covering the whole literary spectrum from the utterly forgettable to the wondrously memorable. Fantasy fiction, once the shy stepsister of science fiction in American publishing, now became a mighty publishing phenomenon in its own right.

In the book field in the new decade, the Zelazny and Kurtz series continued, as did those of Donaldson and Brooks, and were joined by many other novels in what had already become the almost inevitable multi-volume format. David Eddings, whose Belgariad books had reached wide popularity in the Seventies, now commenced a new long saga, the Malloreon. Gene Wolfe's *The Shadow of the Torturer* of 1980 launched a four-volume set that ingeniously occupied the borderland between science fiction and fantasy. Michael Moorcock did a great deal of remarkable work, both in several fantasy series that he had established and in stand-alone books like *The War Hound and the World's Pain*. And there were dozens or perhaps hundreds of other novels from writers new and old, good, bad, indifferent, nearly all of them linked in groups of (usually) three.

Short fantasy fiction, which had led an exiguous existence all through the previous five decades, now enjoyed a flourishing renaissance too. *The Magazine of Fantasy and Science Fiction*, founded in 1949, had been the only newsstand magazine in the United States during that era that ran any substantial proportion of fantasy in its pages which had survived more than a few years; during the Eighties it moved on successfully into another decade of valuable contribution to the field. It was joined, for a time, by *Rod Serling's Twilight Zone Magazine*, which featured both fantasy and horror, and by other magazines of smaller circulation like *Whispers, Weirdbook, Dragonfields, Noctulpa*, and *Fantasy Tales*. At the same time, the new sustainability of fantasy in the paperback field led to a great outpouring of anthologies of original stories—*Swordswomen and Sorceresses, Other Edens, Full Spectrum, Arabesques, Elsewhere, Heroic Visions, Imaginary Lands*, and on and on and on. For a time, too, there were the popular "shared world" books, in which a number of authors wrote stories set in a single commonly-agreed-upon background: among them were *Thieves World, Heroes in Hell*, and *Tales of the Witch World*.

Out of all this wealth of material of the Eighties I have attempted to choose a sampling of the best short fiction, stories that demonstrate a notably Eighties take on the traditional themes of fantasy. Curiously, the fantasy-only specialists that came forth during the period are poorly represented: Ellen Kushner is the only writer that qualifies for that label. This is due, mainly, to the preference of the new fantasists for writing novels, and very long novels at that. Most of the contributors here are, in fact, equally adept at fantasy and science fiction: I speak primarily, though not exclusively, of Ursula K. Le Guin, James Tiptree, Jr., Joe Haldeman, Michael Bishop, and George R.R. Martin. Some, like Greg Bear, Larry Niven, and Isaac Asimov, are so firmly identified with science fiction that to find them here may be surprising to some, but each of them has dabbled with satisfying results in fantasy. To my regret, such established masters as Fritz Leiber, Michael Moorcock, Poul Anderson, and Ray Bradbury are missing from the table of contents: though all of them did commendable work in the decade, even finer material of theirs can be found in anthologies dealing with other periods of fantasy, and it seemed best to showcase here, in the main, the writers whose stories helped to shape and define the fantasy fiction of the fertile and exciting decade of the Eighties.

# ROGER ZELAZNY

## "The George Business"

*One of the modern giants of fantasy and science fiction, Roger Ze-lazny (1937–1995) began writing science fiction in 1962 and earned immediate acclaim as one of the best and brightest of science fiction's New Wave. He established an early reputation as a writer of outstanding short and novel-length fiction, and by 1968 had won Hugo Awards for* This Immortal *and* Lord of Light, *and Nebula Awards for "He Who Shapes" and "The Doors of His Face, the Lamps of His Mouth." The Hugo-nominated "A Rose for Ecclesi-astes," also published in this interval, was eventually voted into the Science Fiction Hall of Fame by the Science Fiction Writers of America. In 1970, he published* Nine Princes in Amber, *a multi-layered mythic fantasy novel. This proved the first of ten novels in his celebrated Chronicles of Amber, a series that has made an in-delible impact on the writing of heroic fantasy. He has also written the Wizard World world diptych (comprised of* Madwand *and* Changeling), *two fantasy novels centered around a rogue thief hero,* Dilvish the Damned *and* The Changing Land, *and the fantasy satire* A Night in the Lonesome October. *His short fiction can be found in the collections* Four for Tomorrow *and* The Doors of His Face, the Lamps of His Mouth, and Other Stories. *His novel* Damnation Alley *was adapted for film in 1977.*

# The George Business

## by Roger Zelazny

eep in his lair, Dart twisted his green and golden length about his small hoard, his sleep troubled by dreams of a series of identical armored assailants. Since dragons' dreams are always prophetic, he woke with a shudder, cleared his throat to the point of sufficient illumination to check on the state of his treasure, stretched, yawned and set forth up the tunnel to consider the strength of the opposition. If it was too great, he would simply flee, he decided. The hell with the hoard; it wouldn't be the first time.

As he peered from the cave mouth, he beheld a single knight in mismatched armor atop a tired-looking gray horse, just rounding the bend. His lance was not even couched, but still pointing skyward.

Assuring himself that the man was unaccompanied, he roared and slithered forth.

"Halt," he bellowed, "you who are about to fry!"

The knight obliged.

"You're the one I came to see," the man said. "I have—"

"Why," Dart asked, "do you wish to start this business up again? Do you realize how long it has been since a knight and dragon have done battle?"

"Yes, I do. Quite a while. But I—"

"It is almost invariably fatal to one of the parties concerned. Usually your side."

"Don't I know it. Look, you've got me wrong—"

"I dreamt a dragon dream of a young man named George with

whom I must do battle. You bear him an extremely close resemblance."

"I can explain. It's not as bad as it looks. You see—"

"*Is* your name George?"

"Well, yes. But don't let that bother you—"

"It *does* bother me. You want my pitiful hoard? It wouldn't keep you in beer money for the season. Hardly worth the risk."

"I'm not after your hoard—"

"I haven't grabbed off a virgin in centuries. They're usually old and tough, anyhow, not to mention hard to find."

"No one's accusing—"

"As for cattle, I always go a great distance. I've gone out of my way, you might say, to avoid getting a bad name in my own territory."

"I know you're no real threat here. I've researched it quite carefully—"

"And do you think that armor will really protect you when I exhale my deepest, hottest flames?"

"Hell, no! So don't do it, huh? If you'd please—"

"And that lance . . . You're not even holding it properly."

George lowered the lance.

"On that you are correct," he said, "but it happens to be tipped with one of the deadliest poisons known to Herman the Apothecary."

"I say! That's hardly sporting!"

"I know. But even if you incinerate me, I'll bet I can scratch you before I go."

"Now that would be rather silly—both of us dying like that—wouldn't it?" Dart observed edging away. "It would serve no useful purpose that I can see."

"I feel precisely the same way about it."

"Then why are we getting ready to fight?"

"I have no desire whatsoever to fight with you!"

"I'm afraid I don't understand. You said your name is George, and I had this dream—"

"I can explain it."

"But the poisoned lance—"

"Self-protection, to hold you off long enough to put a proposition to you."

Dart's eyelids lowered slightly.

"What sort of proposition?"

"I want to hire you."

"Hire me? Whatever for? And what are you paying?"

"Mind if I rest this lance a minute? No tricks?"

"Go ahead. If you're talking gold your life is safe."

George rested his lance and undid a pouch at his belt. He dipped his hand into it and withdrew a fistful of shining coins. He tossed them gently, so that they clinked and shone in the morning light.

"You have my full attention. That's a good piece of change there."

"My life's savings. All yours—in return for a bit of business."

"What's the deal?"

George replaced the coins in his pouch and gestured.

"See that castle in the distance—two hills away?"

"I've flown over it many times."

"In the tower to the west are the chambers of Rosalind, daughter of the Baron Maurice. She is very dear to his heart, and I wish to wed her."

"There's a problem?"

"Yes. She's attracted to big, brawny barbarian types, into which category I, alas, do not fall. In short, she doesn't like me."

"That *is* a problem."

"So, if I could pay you to crash in there and abduct her, to bear her off to some convenient and isolated place and wait for me, I'll come along, we'll fake a battle, I'll vanquish you, you'll fly away and I'll take her home. I am certain I will then appear sufficiently heroic in her eyes to rise from sixth to first position on her list of suitors. How does that sound to you?"

Dart sighed a long column of smoke.

"Human, I bear your kind no special fondness—particularly the armored variety with lances—so I don't know why I'm telling you this. . . . Well, I do know, actually. . . . But never mind. I could manage it, all right. But, if you win the hand of that maid, do you know what's going to happen? The novelty of your deed will wear off after a time—and you know that there will be no encore. Give her a year, I'd say, and you'll catch her fooling around with one of those brawny barbarians she finds so attractive. Then you must either fight him and be slaughtered or wear horns, as they say."

George laughed.

"It's nothing to me how she spends her spare time. I've a girl-friend in town myself."

Dart's eyes widened.

"I'm afraid I don't understand. . . ."

"She's the old baron's only offspring, and he's on his last legs. Why else do you think an uncomely wench like that would have six suitors? Why else would I gamble my life's savings to win her?"

"I see," said Dart. "Yes, I can understand greed."

"I call it a desire for security."

"Quite. In that case, forget my simple-minded advice. All right, give me the gold and I'll do it." Dart gestured with one gleaming vane. "The first valley in those western mountains seems far enough from my home for our confrontation."

"I'll pay you half now and half on delivery."

"Agreed. Be sure to have the balance with you, though, and drop it during the scuffle. I'll return for it after you two have departed. Cheat me and I'll repeat the performance, with a different ending."

"The thought had already occurred to me.—Now, we'd better practice a bit, to make it look realistic. I'll rush at you with the lance, and whatever side she's standing on I'll aim for it to pass you on the other. You raise that wing, grab the lance and scream like hell. Blow a few flames around, too."

"I'm going to see you scour the tip of that lance before we rehearse this."

"Right.—I'll release the lance while you're holding it next to you and rolling around. Then I'll dismount and rush toward you with my blade. I'll whack you with the flat of it—again, on the far side—a few times. Then you bellow again and fly away."

"Just how sharp is that thing, anyway?"

"Damned dull. It was my grandfather's. Hasn't been honed since he was a boy."

"And you drop the money during the fight?"

"Certainly.—How does that sound?"

"Not bad. I can have a few clusters of red berries under my wing, too. I'll squash them once the action gets going."

"Nice touch. Yes, do that. Let's give it a quick rehearsal now and then get on with the real thing."

"And don't whack too hard. . . ."

That afternoon, Rosalind of Maurice Manor was abducted by a green-and-gold dragon who crashed through the wall of her chamber and bore her off in the direction of the western mountains.

"Never fear!" shouted her sixth-ranked suitor—who just happened to be riding by—to her aged father who stood wringing his hands on a nearby balcony. "I'll rescue her!" and he rode off to the west.

8

Coming into the valley where Rosalind stood backed into a rocky cleft, guarded by the fuming beast of gold and green, George couched his lance.

"Release that maiden and face your doom!" he cried.

Dart bellowed, George rushed. The lance fell from his hands and the dragon rolled upon the ground, spewing gouts of fire into the air. A red substance dribbled from beneath the thundering creature's left wing. Before Rosalind's wide eyes, George advanced and swung his blade several times.

". . . and that!" he cried, as the monster stumbled to its feet and sprang into the air, dripping more red.

It circled once and beat its way off toward the top of the mountain, then over it and away.

"Oh George!" Rosalind cried, and she was in his arms. "Oh, George . . ."

He pressed her to him for a moment.

"I'll take you home now," he said.

That evening as he was counting his gold, Dart heard the sound of two horses approaching his cave. He rushed up the tunnel and peered out.

George, now mounted on a proud white stallion and leading the gray, wore a matched suit of bright armor. He was not smiling, however.

"Good evening," he said.

"Good evening. What brings you back so soon?"

"Things didn't turn out exactly as I'd anticipated."

"You see far better accoutered. I'd say your fortunes had taken a turn."

"Oh, I recovered my expenses and came out a bit ahead. But that's all. I'm on my way out of town. Though I'd stop by and tell you the end of the story.—Good show you put on, by the way. It probably would have done the trick—"

"But—?"

"She was married to one of the brawny barbarians this morning, in their family chapel. They were just getting ready for a wedding trip when you happened by."

"I'm awfully sorry."

"Well, it's the breaks. To add insult, though, her father dropped dead during your performance. My former competitor is now the new baron. He rewarded me with a new horse and armor, a gratuity and a scroll from the local scribe lauding me as a dragon slayer. Then he hinted rather strongly that the horse and my new reputation could take me far. Didn't like the way Rosalind was looking at me now I'm a hero."

"That is a shame. Well, we tried."

"Yes. So I just stopped by to thank you and let you know how it all turned out. It would have been a good idea—if it had worked."

"You could hardly have foreseen such abrupt nuptials.—You know, I've spent the entire day thinking about the affair. We *did* manage it awfully well."

"Oh, no doubt about that. It went beautifully."

"I was thinking . . . How'd you like a chance to get your money back?"

"What have you got in mind?"

"Uh—When I was advising you earlier that you might not be happy with the lady, I was trying to think about the situation in human terms. Your desire was entirely understandable to me otherwise. In fact, you think quite a bit like a dragon."

"Really?"

"Yes. It's rather amazing, actually. Now—realizing that it only failed because of a fluke, your idea still has considerable merit."

"I'm afraid I don't follow you."

"There is—ah—a lovely lady of my own species whom I have been singularly unsuccessful in impressing for a long while now. Actually, there are an unusual number of parallels in our situations."

"She has a large hoard, huh?"

"Extremely so."

"Older woman?"

"Among dragons, a few centuries this way or that are not so important. But she, too, had other admirers and seems attracted by the more brash variety."

"Uh-huh. I begin to get the drift. You gave me some advice once. I'll return the favor. Some things are more important than hoards."

"Name one."

"My life. If I were to threaten her she might do me in all by herself, before you could come to her rescue."

"No, she's a demure little thing. Anyway, it's all a matter of timing. I'll perch on a hilltop nearby—I'll show you where—and signal you when to begin your approach. Now, this time I have to win, of course. Here's how we'll work it. . . ."

\*　　\*　　\*

George sat on the white charger and divided his attention between the distant cave mouth and the crest of a high hill off to his left. After a time, a shining winged form flashed through the air and settled upon the hill. Moments later, it raised one bright wing.

He lowered his visor, couched his lance and started forward. When he came within hailing distance of the cave he cried out:

"I know you're in there, Megtag! I've come to destroy you and make off with your hoard! You godless beast! Eater of children! This is your last day on earth!"

An enormous burnished head with cold green eyes emerged from the cave. Twenty feet of flame shot from its huge mouth and scorched the rock before it. Dart halted hastily. The beast looked twice the size of Dart and did not seem in the least retiring. Its scales rattled like metal as it began to move forward.

"Perhaps I exaggerated. . . ." George began, and he heard the frantic flapping of giant vanes overhead.

As the creature advanced, he felt himself seized by the shoulders. He was borne aloft so rapidly that the scene below dwindled to toy size in a matter of moments. He saw his new steed bolt and flee rapidly back along the route they had followed.

"What the hell happened?" he cried.

"I hadn't been around for a while," Dart replied. "Didn't know one of the others had moved in with her. You're lucky I'm fast. That's Pelladon. He's a mean one."

"Great. Don't you think you should have checked first?"

"Sorry. I thought she'd take decades to make up her mind—without prompting. Oh, what a hoard! You should have seen it!"

"Follow that horse. I want him back."

They sat before Dart's cave, drinking.

"Where'd you ever get a whole barrel of wine?"

"Lifted it from a barge, up the river. I do that every now and then. I keep a pretty good cellar, if I do say so."

"Indeed. Well, we're none the poorer, really. We can drink to that."

"True, but I've been thinking again. You know, you're a very good actor."

"Thanks. You're not so bad yourself."

"Now supposing—just supposing—you were to travel about. Good distances from here each time. Scout out villages, on the continent and in the isles. Find out which ones are well off and lacking in local heroes. . . ."

"Yes?"

". . . And let them see that dragon-slaying certificate of yours. Brag a bit. Then come back with a list of towns. Maps, too."

"Go ahead."

"Find the best spots for a little harmless predation and choose a good battle site—"

"Refill?"

"Please."

"Here."

"Thanks. Then you show up, and for a fee—"

"Sixty-forty."

"That's what I was thinking, but I'll bet you've got the figures transposed."

"Maybe fifty-five and forty-five then."

"Down the middle, and let's drink on it."

"Fair enough. Why haggle?"

"Now I know why I dreamed of fighting a great number of knights, all of them looking like you. You're going to make a name for yourself, George."

# JOE HALDEMAN

## "Lindsay and the Red City Blues"

*Joe Haldeman (1943- ) began publishing science fiction in 1969, following a two-year tour of duty in Vietnam, and achieved notoriety five years later with his first novel,* The Forever War, *a futuristic extrapolation of the dehumanizing potential of warfare. He followed this with the highly regarded* Mindbridge *and* All My Sins Remembered, *novels that further established his reputation as a writer with a strong moral vision. Several of his novels are genre splices, including the technothriller* Tools of the Trade *and his borderline science fiction-espionage novels* Attar's Revenge *and* War of Nerves. *He has won both the Hugo and Nebula Awards for his short fiction, a sampling of which can be found in his collection* Infinite Dreams *and* Dealing in Futures. *His recent novels include* The Hemingway Hoax, *expanded from his Nebula Award-winning novella, and the non-genre work* 1968. *His contributions as an anthologist have ranged from the humorous science fiction compilation* Cosmic Laughter *to* Study War No More.

# Lindsay and the Red City Blues

*by Joe Haldeman*

---

he ancient red city of Marrakesh," his guidebook said, "is
the last large oasis for travelers moving south into the
Sahara. It is the most exotic of Moroccan cities, where
Arab Africa and Black Africa meet in a setting that has
changed but little in the past thousand years."

In midafternoon, the book did not mention, it becomes so hot
that even the flies stop moving.

The air conditioner in his window hummed impressively but neither moved nor cooled the air. He had complained three times and
the desk clerk responded with two shrugs and a blank stare. By
two o'clock his little warren was unbearable. He fled to the street,
where it was hotter.

Scott Lindsay was a salesman who demonstrated chemical
glassware for a large scientific-supply house in the suburbs of
Washington, D.C. Like all Washingtonians, Lindsay thought that a
person who could survive summer on the banks of the Potomac
could survive it anywhere. He saved up six weeks of vacation time
and flew to Europe in late July. Paris was pleasant enough, and
the Pyrenees were even cool, but nobody had told him that on August first all of Europe goes on vacation; every good hotel room has
been sewed up for six months, restaurants are jammed or closed,
and you spend all your time making bad travel connections to
cities where only the most expensive hotels have accommodations.

In Nice a Canadian said he had just come from Morocco, where it

14

was hotter than hell but there were practically no tourists, this time of year. Scott looked wistfully over the poisoned but still blue Mediterranean, felt the pressure of twenty million fellow travelers at his back, remembered Bogie, and booked the next flight to Casablanca.

Casablanca combined the charm of Pittsburgh with the climate of Dallas. The still air was thick with dust from high-rise construction. He picked up a guidebook and riffled through it and, on the basis of a few paragraphs, took the predawn train to Marrakesh.

"The Red City," it went on, "takes its name from the color of the local sandstone from which the city and its ramparts were built." It would be more accurate, Scott reflected though less alluring, to call it the Pink City. The Dirty Pink City. He stumbled along the sidewalk on the shady side of the street. The twelve-inch strip of shade at the edge of the sidewalk was crowded with sleeping beggars. The heat was so dry he couldn't even sweat.

He passed two bars that were closed and stepped gratefully into a third. It was a Moslem bar, a milk bar, no booze, but at least it was shade. Two young men slumped at the bar, arguing in guttural whispers, and a pair of ancients in burnooses sat at a table plying a static game of checkers. An oscillating fan pushed the hot air and dust around. He raised a finger at the bartender, who regarded him with stolid hostility, and ordered in schoolboy French a small bottle of Vichy water, carbonated, without ice, and, out of deference to the guidebook, a glass of hot mint tea. The bartender brought the mint tea and a liter bottle of Sidi Harazim water, not carbonated, with a glass of ice. Scott tried to argue with the man but he only stared and kept repeating the price. He finally paid and dumped the ice (which the guidebook had warned him about) into the ashtray. The young men at the bar watched the transaction with sleepy indifference.

The mint tea was an aromatic infusion of mint leaves in hot sugar water. He sipped and was surprised, and perversely annoyed, to find it quite pleasant. He took a paperback novel out of his pocket and read the same two paragraphs over and over, feeling his eyes track, unable to concentrate in the heat.

He put the book down and looked around with slow deliberation, trying to be impressed by the alienness of the place. Through the open front of the bar he could see across the street, where a small park shaded the outskirts of the Djemaa El Fna, the largest open-air market in Morocco and, according to the guidebook, the most exciting and colorful; which itself was the gateway to the mysterious labyrinthine medina, where even this moment someone was being murdered for his pocket change, goats were being used in ways of which Allah did not approve, men were smoking a mixture of camel dung and opium, children were merchandised like groceries; where dark men and women would do anything for a price, and the price would not be high. Scott touched his pocket unconsciously and the hard bulge of the condom was still there.

The best condoms in the world are packaged in a blue plastic cylinder, squared off along the prolate axis, about the size of a small matchbox. The package is a marvel of technology, held fast by a combination of geometry and sticky tape, and a cool-headed man, under good lighting conditions, can open it in less than a minute. Scott had bought six of them in the drugstore in Dulles International, and had only opened one. He hadn't opened it for the Parisian woman who had looked like a prostitute but had returned his polite proposition with a storm of outrage. He opened it for the fat customs inspector at the Casablanca airport, who had to have its function explained to him, who held it between two dainty fingers like a dead sea thing, and called his compatriots over for a look.

The Djemaa El Fna was closed against the heat, pale-orange dusty tents slack and pallid in the stillness. And the trees through which he stared at the open-air market, the souk, they were also covered with pale dust; the sky was so pale as to be almost white, and the street and sidewalk were the color of dirty chalk. It was like a faded watercolor displayed under too strong a light.

"Hey, mister." A slim Arab boy, evidently in his early teens, had slipped into the place and was standing beside Lindsay. He was well scrubbed and wore Western-style clothing, discreetly patched.

"Hey, mister," he repeated. "You American?"

"Nu. Eeg bin Jugoslav."

The boy nodded. "You from New York? I got four friends New York."

"Jugoslav."

"You from Chicago? I got four friends Chicago. No, five. Five friends Chicago."

"Jugoslav," he said.

"Where in U.S. you from?" He took a melting ice cube from the ashtray, buffed it on his sleeve, popped it into his mouth, crunched.

"New Caledonia," Scott said.

"Don't like ice? Ice is good this time day." He repeated the process with another cube. "New what?" he mumbled.

"New Caledonia. Little place in the Rockies, between Georgia and Wisconsin. I don't like polluted ice."

"No, mister, this ice okay. Bottle-water ice." He rattled off a stream of Arabic at the bartender, who answered with a single harsh syllable. "Come on, I guide you through medina."

"No."

"I guide you free. Student, English student. I take you free, take you my father's factory."

"You'll take me, all right."

"Okay, we go now. No touris' shit, make good deal."

Well, Lindsay, you wanted experiences. How about being knocked over the head and raped by a goat? "All right, I'll go. But no pay."

"Sure, no pay." He took Scott by the hand and dragged him out of the bar, into the park.

"Is there any place in the medina where you can buy cold beer?"

"Sure, lots of place. Ice beer. You got cigarette?"

"Don't smoke."

"That's okay, you buy pack up here." He pointed at a gazebo-shaped concession on the edge of the park.

"Hell, no. You find me a beer and I might buy you some cigarettes." They came out of the shady park and crossed the packed-earth plaza of the Djemaa El Fna. Dust stung his throat and nostrils, but it wasn't quite as hot as it had been earlier; a slight breeze had come up. One industrious merchant was rolling up the front flap of his tent, exposing racks of leather goods. He called out "Hey, you buy!" but Scott ignored him, and the boy made a fist gesture, thumb erect between the two first fingers.

Scott had missed one section of the guidebook: "Never visit the medina without a guide; the streets are laid out in crazy, unpredictable angles and someone who doesn't live there will be hopelessly lost in minutes. The best guides are older men or young Americans who live there for the cheap narcotics; with them you can arrange the price ahead of time, usually about 5 dirham ($1.10). *Under no circumstances* hire one of the street urchins who pose as students and offer to guide you for free; you will be cheated or even beaten up and robbed."

They passed behind the long double row of tents and entered the medina through the Bab Agnou gateway. The main street of the place was a dirty alley some eight feet wide, flanked on both sides by small shops and stalls, most of which were closed, either with curtains or steel shutters or with the proprietor dozing on the stoop. None of the shops had a wall on the side fronting the alley, but the ones that served food usually had chest-high counters. If they passed an open shop the merchant would block their way and importune them in urgent simple French or English, plucking at Scott's sleeve as they passed.

It was surprisingly cool in the medina, the sun's rays partially blocked by wooden lattices suspended over the alleyway. There was a roast-chestnut smell of semolina being parched, with accents of garlic and strange herbs smoldering. Slight tang of exhaust fumes and sickly-sweet hint of garbage and sewage hidden from the sun. The boy led him down a side street, and then another. Scott couldn't tell the position of the sun and was quickly disoriented.

"Where the hell are we going?"

"Cold beer. You see." He plunged down an even smaller alley, dark and sinister, and Lindsay followed, feeling unarmed.

They huddled against a damp wall while a white-haired man on an antique one-cylinder motor scooter hammered by. "How much farther is this place? I'm not going to—"

"Here, one corner." The boy dragged him around the corner and into a musty-smelling, dark shop. The shopkeeper, small and round, smiled gold teeth and greeted the boy by name, Abdul. "The word for beer is 'bera,' he said. Scott repeated the word to the fat little man and Abdul added something. The man opened two beers and set them down on the counter, along with a pack of cigarettes.

It's a new little Arab, Lindsay, but I think you'll be amused by its presumption. He paid and gave Abdul his cigarettes and beer. "Aren't you Moslem? I thought Moslems didn't drink."

"Hell yes, man." He stuck his finger down the neck of the bottle and flicked away a drop of beer, then tilted the bottle up and drained half of it in one gulp. Lindsay sipped at his. It was warm and sour.

"What you do in the States, man?" He lit a cigarette and held it awkwardly.

Chemical glassware salesman? "I drive a truck." The acrid Turkish tobacco smoke stung his eyes.

"Make lots of money."

"No, I don't." He felt foolish saying it. World traveler, Lindsay, you spent more on your ticket than this boy will see in his life.

"Let's go my father's factory."

"What does your father make?"

"All kinds things. Rugs."

"I wouldn't know what to do with a rug."

"We wrap it, mail to New Caledonia."

"No. Let's go back to—"

"I take you my uncle's factory. Brass, very pretty."

"No. Back to the plaza, you got your cig—"

"Sure, let's go." He gulped down the rest of his beer and stepped back into the alley, Scott following. After a couple of twists and turns they passed an antique-weapons shop that Scott knew he would have noticed, if they'd come by it before. He stopped.

"Where are you taking me now?"

He looked hurt. "Back to Djemaa El Fna. Like you say."

"The hell you are. Get lost, Abdul. I'll find my own way back." He turned and started retracing their path. The boy followed about ten paces behind him, smoking.

He walked for twenty minutes or so, trying to find the relatively broad alleyway that would lead back to the gate. The character of the medina changed: there were fewer and fewer places selling souvenirs, and then none; only residences and little general-merchandise stores, and some small-craft factories, where one or two men, working at a feverish pace, cranked out the items that were sold in the shops. No one tried to sell him anything, and when a little girl held out her hand to beg, an old woman shuffled over and slapped her. Everybody stared when he passed.

Finally he stopped and let Abdul catch up with him. "All right, you win. How much to lead me out?"

"Ten dirham."

"Stuff it. I'll give you two."

Abdul looked at him for a long time, hands in pockets. "Nine dirham." They haggled for a while and finally settled on seven dirham, about $1.50, half now and half at the gate.

They walked through yet another part of the medina, single file through narrow streets, Abdul smoking silently in the lead. Suddenly he stopped.

Scott almost ran into him. "Say, you want girl?"

"Uh . . . I'm not sure," Scott said, startled into honesty.

He laughed, surprisingly deep and lewd, "A boy, then?"

"No, no." Composure, Lindsay. "Your sister, no doubt."

"*What?*" Wrong thing to say.

"American joke. She a friend of yours?"

"Good friend, good fuck. Fifty dirham."

Scott sighed. "Ten." Eventually they settled on thirty-two, Abdul to wait outside until Scott needed his services as a guide again.

Abdul took him to a caftan shop, where he spoke in whispers with the fat owner, and gave him part of the money. They led Lindsay to the rear of the place, behind a curtain. A woman sat on her heels beside the bed, patiently crocheting. She stood up gracelessly. She was short and slight, the top of her head barely reaching Scott's shoulders, and was dressed in traditional costume: lower part of the face veiled, dark blue caftan reaching her ankles. At a command from the owner, she hiked the caftan up around her hips and sat down on the bed with her legs spread apart.

"You see, very clean," Abdul said. She was the skinniest woman Scott had ever seen naked, partially naked, her pelvic girdle prominent under smooth brown skin. She had very little pubic hair and the lips of her vulva were dry and grey. But she was only in her early teens, Scott estimated; that, and the bizarre prospect of screwing a fully clothed masked stranger stimulated him instantly, urgently.

"All right," he said hoarse. "I'll meet you outside."

She watched with alert curiosity as he fumbled with the condom package, and the only sound she made throughout their encounter was to giggle when she fitted the device over his penis. It was manufactured to accommodate the complete range of possible sizes, and on Scott it had a couple of inches to spare.

This wonder condom, first-class special-delivery French letter is coated with a fluid so similar to natural female secretions, so perfectly intermiscible and isotonic, that it could fool the inside of a vagina. But Scott's ran out of juice in seconds, and the aloof lady's physiology didn't supply any replacement, so he had to fall back on saliva and an old familiar fantasy. It was a long dry haul, the bedding straw crunching monotonously under them, she constantly shifting to more comfortable positions as he angrily pressed his weight into her, finally a draining that was more hydrostatics than passion which left him jumpy rather than satisfied. When he rolled off her the condom stayed put, there being more lubrication inside it than out. The woman extracted it and, out of some obscure motive, twisted a knot in the end and dropped it behind the bed.

When he'd finished dressing, she held out her hand for a tip. He laughed and told her in English that he was the one who ought to be paid, he'd done all the work, but gave her five dirham anyhow, for the first rush of excitement and her vulnerable eyes.

Abdul was not waiting for him. He tried to interrogate the caftan dealer in French, but got only an interesting spectrum of shrugs. He stepped out onto the street, saw no trace of the little scroundrel, went back inside and gave the dealer a five while asking the way to Djemaa El Fna. He nodded once and wrote down on a slip of paper in clear, copybook English.

"You speak English?"

"No," he said with an Oxford vowel.

Scott threaded his way through the maze of narrow streets, carefully memorizing the appearance of each corner in case he had to backtrack. None of the streets was identified by name. The sun was down far enough for the medina to be completely in shadow, and it was getting cooler. He stopped at a counter to drink a bottle of beer, and a pleasant lassitude fell over him, the first time he had not felt keyed-up since the Casablanca airport. He strolled on, taking a left at the corner of dye shop and motor scooter.

Halfway down the street, Abdul stood with seven or eight other boys, chattering away, laughing.

Scott half-ran toward the group and Abdul looked up, startled, when he roared "You little bastard!"—but Abdul only smiled and muttered something to his companions, and all of them rushed him.

Not a violent man by any means, Scott nevertheless suffered enough at the hands of this boy, and he planted his feet, balled his fists, bared his teeth and listened with his whole body to the sweet singing adrenalin. He'd had twelve hours of hand-to-hand combat instruction in basic training, the first rule of which (*If you're outnumbered, run*) he ignored; the second rule of which (*Kick, don't punch*) he forgot, and swung a satisfying roundhouse into the first face that came within reach, breaking lips and teeth and one knuckle (he would realize later); then assayed a side-kick to the groin, which only hit a hip but did put the victim out of the fray; touched the ground for balance and bounced up, shaking a child off his right arm while swinging his left at Abdul's neck, and missing; another side-kick, this time straight to a kidney, producing a good loud shriek; Abdul hanging out of reach, boys all over him, kicking, punching, finally dragging him to his knees; Abdul stepping forward and kicking him in the chest, then the solar plexus; the taste of dust as someone keeps kicking his head; losing it, losing it, fading out as someone takes his wallet, then from the other pocket, his traveler's checks, Lindsay, tell them to leave the checks, they can't, nobody will, just doing it to annoy me, fuck them.

It was raining and singing. He opened one eye and saw dark brown. His tongue was flat on the dirt, interesting crunchy dirt-taste in his mouth, Lindsay, reel in your tongue, this is stupid, people piss in this street. Raining and singing, I have died and gone to Marrakesh. He slid forearm and elbow under his chest and pushed up a few inches. An irregular stain of blood caked the dust in front of him, and blood was why he couldn't open the other eye. He wiped the mud off his tongue with his sleeve, then used the other sleeve to unstick his eyelid.

The rain was a wrinkled old woman without a veil, patiently sprinkling water on his head, from a pitcher, looking very old and sad. When he sat up, she offered him two white tablets with the letter "A" impressed on them, and a glass of the same water. He took them gratefully, gagged on them, used another glass of water to wash them farther down. Thanked the impassive woman in three languages, hoped it was bottled water, stood up shakily, sledgehammer headache. The slip of paper with directions lay crumpled in the dust, scuffed but still legible. He continued on his way.

The singing was a muezzin, calling the faithful to prayer. He could hear others singing, in more distant parts of the city. Should he take off his hat? No hat. Some native were simply walking around, going about their business. An old man was prostrate on a prayer rug in the middle of the street; Scott tiptoed around him.

He came out of the medina through a different gate, and the Djemaa El Fna was spread out in front of him in all its early-evening frenzy. A troupe of black dancers did amazing things to machine-gun drum rhythms; acrobats formed high shaky pyramids, dropped, re-formed; people sang, shouted, laughed.

He watched a snake handler for a long time, going through a creepy repertoire of cobras, vipers, scorpions, tarantulas. He dropped a half-dirham in the man's cup and went on. A large loud group was crowded around a bedsheet-size game board where roosters strutted from one chalked area to another, pecking at a vase of plastic flowers here, a broken doll there, a painted tin can or torn deck of playing cards elsewhere; men lying down incomprehensible bets, collecting money, shouting at the roosters, baby needs a new pair of sandals.

Then a quiet, patient line, men and women squatting, waiting for the services of a healer. The woman being treated had her dress tucked modestly between her thighs, back bared from shoulders to buttocks, while the healer burned angry welts in a symmetrical pattern with the smoldering end of a length of clothesline, and Scott walked on, charmed in the old sense of the word, hypnotized.

People shrank from his bloody face and he laughed at them, feeling like part of the show, then feeling like something apart, a visitation. Drifting down the rows of merchants: leather, brass, ceramics, carvings, textiles, books, junk, blankets, weapons, hardware, jewelry, food. Stopping to buy a bag of green pistachio nuts, the vendor gives him the bag and then waves him away, flapping; no pay, just leave.

Gathering darkness and most of the merchants closed their tents but the thousands of people didn't leave the square. They moved in around men, perhaps a dozen of them, who sat on blankets scattered around the square, in the flickering light of kerosene lanterns, droning the same singsong words over and over. Scott moved to the closest and shouldered his way to the edge of the blanket and squatted there, an American gargoyle, staring. Most of the people gave him room but light fingers tested his hip pocket; he swatted the hand away without looking back. The man in the center of the blanket fixed on his bloody stare and smiled back a tight smile, eyes bright with excitement. He raised both arms and the crowd fell silent, switched off.

A hundred people breathed in at once when he whispered the first words, barely audible words that must have been the Arabic equivalent of "Once upon a time." And then the storyteller shouted and began to pace back and forth, playing out his tale in a dramatic staccato voice, waving his arms, hugging himself, whispering, moaning—and Lindsay followed it perfectly, laughing on cue, crying when the storyteller cried, understanding nothing and everything. When it was over, the man held out his cap first to the big American with the bloody face, and Scott emptied his left pocket into the cap: dirham and half-dirham pieces and leftover francs and one rogue dime.

And he stood up and turned around and watched his long broad shadow dance over the crowd as the storyteller with his lantern moved on around the blanket, and he spotted his hotel and pushed toward it through the mob.

It was worth it. The magic was worth the pain and humiliation.

He forced himself to think of practical things, as he approached the hotel. He had no money, no credit cards, no traveler's checks, no identification. Should he go to the police? Probably it would be best to go to American Express first. Collect phone call to the office. Have some money wired. Identity established, so he could have the checks replaced. Police here unlikely to help unless "tipped."

Ah, simplicity. He did have identification; his passport, that he'd left at the hotel desk. That had been annoying, now a lifesaver. Numbers of traveler's checks in his suitcase.

There was a woman in the dusty dim lobby of the hotel. He walked right by her and she whispered "Lin—say."

He remembered the eyes and stopped. "What do you want?"

"I have something of yours." Absurdly, he thought of the knotted condom. But what she held up was a fifty-dollar traveler's check. He snatched it from her; she didn't attempt to stop him.

"You sign that to me," she said. "I bring you everything else the boys took."

"Even the money?" He had over five hundred dirhams' cash.

"What they gave me, I bring you."

"Well, you bring it here, and we'll see."

She shook her head angrily. "No, I bring *you*. I bring you . . . *to* it. Right now. You sign that to me."

He was tempted. "At the caftan shop?"

"That's right. Wallet and 'merican 'spress check. You come."

The medina at night. A little sense emerged. "Not now. I'll come with you in the morning."

"Come now."

"I'll see you here in the morning." He turned and walked up the stairs.

Well, he had fifty out of the twelve hundred dollars. He checked the suitcase and the list of numbers was where he'd remembered. If she wasn't there in the morning, he would be able to survive the loss. He caressed the dry leather sheath of the antique dagger he'd bought in the Paris flea market. If she was waiting, he would go into the medina armed. It would simplify things to have the credit cards. He fell asleep and had violent dreams.

\*     \*     \*

He woke at dawn. Washed up and shaved. The apparition that peered back from the mirror looked worse than he felt; he was still more exhilarated than otherwise. He took a healing drink of brandy and stuck the dagger in his belt, in the back so he wouldn't have to button his sport coat. The muezzin's morning wail stopped.

She was sitting in the lobby's only chair, and stood when he came down the stairs.

"No tricks," he said. "If you have what you say, you get the fifty dollars."

They went out of the hotel and the air was almost cool, damp smell of garbage. "Why did the boys give this to you?"

"Not *give*. Business deal, I get half."

There was no magic in the Djemaa El Fna in the morning, just dozens of people walking through the dust. They entered the medina and it was likewise bereft of mystery and danger. Sleepy collection of closed-off shopfronts, everything beaded with dew, quiet and stinking. She led him back the way he had come yesterday afternoon. Passing the alley where he had encountered the boys, he noticed there was no sign of blood. Had the old woman neatly cleaned up, or was it simply scuffed away on the sandals of negligent passersby? Thinking about the fight, he touched the dagger, loosening it in its sheath. Not for the first time, he wondered whether he was walking into a trap. He almost hoped so. But all he had left of value was his signature.

Lindsay had gotten combat pay in Vietnam, but the closest he'd come to fighting was to sit in a bunker while mortars and rockets slammed around in the night. He'd never fired a shot in anger, never seen a dead man, never this never that, and he vaguely felt unproven. The press of the knife both comforted and frightened him.

They entered the caftan shop, Lindsay careful to leave the door open behind them. The fat caftan dealer was seated behind a table. On the table were Lindsay's wallet and a china plate with a small pile of dried mud.

The dealer watched impassively while Lindsay snatched up his wallet. "The checks."

The dealer nodded. "I have a proposition for you."

"You've learned English."

"I believe I have something you would like to buy with those checks."

25

Lindsay jerked out the dagger and pointed it at the man's neck. His hand and voice shook with rage. "I'll cut your throat first. Honest to God, I will."

There was a childish giggle and the curtain to the "bedroom" parted, revealing Abdul with a pistol. The pistol was so large he had to hold it with both hands, but he held it steadily, aimed at Lindsay's chest.

"Drop the knife," the dealer said.

Lindsay didn't. "This won't work. Not even here."

"A merchant has a right to protect himself."

"That's not what I mean. You can kill me, I know, but you can't force me to sign those checks at gunpoint. *I will not do it!*"

He chuckled. "That is not what I had in mind, not at all. I truly do have something to sell you, something beyond worth. The gun is only for my protection; I assumed you were wise enough to come armed. Relinquish the knife and Abdul will leave."

Lindsay hesitated, weighing obscure odds, balancing the will to live against his newly born passion. He dropped the dagger.

The merchant said something in Arabic while the prostitute picked up the knife and set it on the table. Abdul emerged from the room with no gun and two straight wooden chairs. He set one next to the table and one behind Lindsay, and left, slamming the door.

"Please sign the check you have and give it to the woman. You promised."

He signed it and asked in a shaking voice, "What do you have that you think I'll pay twelve hundred dollars for?"

The woman reached into her skirts and pulled out the tied-up condom. She dropped it on the plate.

"This," he said, "your blood and seed." With the point of the dagger he opened the condom and its contents spilled into the dirt. He stirred them into mud.

"You are a modern man—"

"What kind of mumbo jumbo—"

"—a modern man who certainly doesn't believe in magic. Are you Christian?"

"Yes. No." He as born Baptist but hadn't gone inside a church since he was eighteen.

He nodded. "I was confident the boys could bring back some of your blood last night. More than I needed, really." He dipped his thumb in the vile mud and smeared a rough cross on the woman's forehead.

"I can't believe this."

"But you can." He held out a small piece of string. "This is a symbolic restraint." He laid it over the glob of mud and pressed down on it.

Lindsay felt himself being pushed back into the chair. Cold sweat peppered his back and palms.

"Try to get up."

"Why should I?" Lindsay said, trying to control his voice. "I find this fascinating." Insane, Lindsay, voodoo only works on people who believe in it. Psychosomatic.

"It gets even better." He reached into a drawer and pulled out Lindsay's checkbook; opened it and set it in front of Lindsay with a pen. "Sign."

Get up get up. "No."

He took four long sharp needles out of the drawer, and began talking in a low monotone, mostly Arabic but some nonsense English. The woman's eyes drooped half-shut and she slumped in the chair.

"Now," he said in a normal voice, "I can do anything to this woman, and she won't feel it. You will." He pulled up her left sleeve and pinched her arm. "Do you feel like writing your name?"

Lindsay tried to ignore the feeling. You can't hypnotize an unwilling subject. Get up get up get up.

The man ran a needle into the woman's left triceps. Lindsay flinched and cried out. Deny him, get up.

He murmured something and the woman lifted her veil and stuck out her tongue, which was long and stained blue. He drove a needle through it and Lindsay's chin jerked back onto his chest, tongue on fire, bile foaming up in his throat. His right hand scrabbled for the pen and the man withdrew the needles.

He scrawled his name on the fifties and hundreds. The merchant took them wordlessly and went to the door. He came back with Abdul, armed again.

"I am going to the bank. When I return, you will be free to go." He lifted the piece of string out of the mud. "In the meantime, you may do as you wish with this woman; she is being paid well. I advice you not to hurt her, of course."

Lindsay pushed her into the back room. It wasn't proper rape, since she didn't resist, but whatever it was he did it twice, and was sore for a week. He left her there and sat at the merchant's table, glaring at Abdul. When he came back, the merchant told Lindsay to gather up the mud and hold it in his hand for at least a half hour. And get out of Marrakesh.

Out in the bright sun he felt silly with the handful of crud, and ineffably angry with himself, and he flung it away and rubbed the offended hand in the dirt. He got a couple of hundred dollars on his credit cards, at an outrageous rate of exchange, and got the first train back to Casablanca and the first plane back to the United States.

Where he found himself to be infected with gonorrhea.

And over the next few months paid a psychotherapist and a hypnotist over two thousand dollars, and nevertheless felt rotten for no organic reason.

And nine months later lay on an examining table in the emergency room of Suburban Hospital, with terrible abdominal pains of apparently psychogenic origin, not responding to muscle relaxants or tranquilizers, while a doctor and two aides watched in helpless horror as his own muscles cracked his pelvic girdle into sharp knives of bone, and his child was born without pain four thousand miles away.

# CHARLES DE LINT

## "A Pattern of Silver Strings"

*Canadian Charles de Lint (1951- ) began publishing fantasy fiction in 1979 and has emerged as one of the most distinctive voices in contemporary fantasy. Although the themes of his novels have ranged from the alternate world fantasy of* Yarrow *to the near-future science fiction of* Svaha, *he is best known for his modern urban fantasies, such as* Jack the Giant-Killer, *a reworking of the classic fairy tale, and its sequel* Drink Down the Moon. *He is the author of more than a score of novels, including* Moonheart: A Romance, Ascian in Rose, Westlin Wind *and* Ghostwood, *which comprise the* Spirit Walk *series. His rich and polished short fiction has appeared in numerous anthologies and has been gathered in the World Fantasy Award-nominated omnibus* Dreams Underfoot. *As Samuel Key, he has written the horror novels* Angel of Darkness, From a Whisper to a Scream, *and* I'll Be Watching You. *He also writes a regular book review column for* The Magazine of Fantasy and Science Fiction.

# A Pattern of Silver Strings

*by Charles de Lint*

---

*For Mary Ann*

Nagakaramu
Kokoro mo shirazu
Kurokami no
Midarete kesa wa
Mono wo koso omoe

Lady Horikawa

[Will he always love me?
I cannot read his heart.
This morning my thoughts
Are as disordered
As my hair.]

Meran Gwynder was the daughter of an oak king and the wife of a harper, though neither her royal green blood nor her marriage seemed very real to her just now. Loss filled her heart and she could find no way to deal with it. The sadness of what seemed a broken trust shared an uneasy rule with her unending questions. If she could know why . . .

"He left without a word," she said.

Bethowen the hillwife clicked her teeth in reply, though whether the sound was meant to be sympathetic or was only a habit, remained debatable. They sat on a hilltop, under the guardianship of an old longstone, with the stars glimmering pale in the night skies above and the fire between them throwing strange shadows that seemed to echo the whisper of the wind as it braided the hill's grasses. Stirring the fire with a short stick, Bethowen looked through the glitter of sparks at her guest.

Meran had nut-brown skin and brown-green hair. She was slim, but strong-limbed. Her eyes were the liquid brown of an otter's. The hillwife could see none of this in the poor light. Those images she drew up from her memory. What she saw was a troubled woman, her features strained and wan in the firelight. At the oak-maid's knee the striped head of Old Badger looked up to meet the hillwife's eyes.

"Men will do that," Bethowen said at last. "It's not a new thing, my dear."

"Not him."

"What makes me wonder," the hillwife continued as though she'd never been interrupted, "is what brings one of the treefolk so far from her tree." Ogwen Wood was a good two hours south and west across the dark hills, a long distance for an oakmaid.

"My tree fell in a storm years ago—you never heard? I should— *would* have died but for him. As the green blood spilled, he drew me back. With his harpmagic. With his love."

"And you have no more need of your tree?"

"He made me charms. Three talismans."

Meran could see his quick sure hands working the oakwood as surely as though he were beside her now. First he made a pendant, shaped like an oak leaf, and that she wore under her tunic, close to her heart. Then a comb, fine-toothed and decorated with acorn shapes, and that she wore in her hair to keep the unruly locks under control. Lastly a flute that she kept in a sheath hanging from her shoulder. Oak was not the best of woods for such an instrument, but his harpmagic had instilled in it a tone and timbre that the natural wood lacked.

"He built us a new home of sod and stone and thatch and there we lived as we had before. Until this morning . . ."

"When you awoke and found him gone," Bethowen finished for her. "But he journeys often, doesn't he, this husband of yours?

*31*

Roadfaring and worldwalking from time to time. I have heard tales . . ."

"And well you might. But you don't understand. He left without a word. I woke and he was gone. Gone." She tugged at the edge of her cloak with unhappy fingers and looked up to meet the hillwife's bright eyes. "He left Telynros behind."

"Telynros?"

"His harp. The roseharp."

Telynros was a Tuathan gift, an enchanted instrument that plainly bore the touch of the old gods' workmanship. Silverstringed and strangely carved, it had, growing from the wood where forepillar met the curving neck, a living blossom. A grey rose.

"Please," Meran said, "tell me where he has gone."

Bethowen nodded. "I can try, my dear. I can only try."

From the unrolled cloth that lay at her knee, she chose a pinch of flaked alder bark and tossed it into the flames with a soft-spoken word. The fire's hue changed from red-gold to blue. Muttering under her breath, she added a second pinch and the blue dissolved into violet.

"Look into the flames," she said. "Look and tell me what you see."

"Only flames. No, I see . . ."

An oak tree strained at its roots, green-leafed boughs reaching for . . . something. There was a sense of loss about that tree, an incompleteness that reflected in the pattern of its boughs. Under the spread of its leafed canopy, half covered in autumn leaves, stood a harp.

"My tree," Meran whispered. "But it's . . ." She shook her head. "My tree standing in my father's wood as ever it did. And that is Telynros, his harp. Bethowen?"

"It is the present you see," the hillwife replied. "But a view of it that we already know, not what you seek."

Sighing, Bethowen closed her eyes. Deep inside, where the herenow curled around her thoughts, she drew on the heart of her strength. Her taw, the inner silence that is the basis for all magic, rose sure and firm like a well-remembered tune. When she spoke a word, the air crackled about her and a pale green rune hovered in the air above the fire. Sinking, it slowly became a part of the flames.

Meran leaned closer to the fire. The scent of wildflowers was strong in the air. The vision in the flames remained. Only its per-spective changed. First the harp grew large and larger still, until all she could see was the silvery glisten of its strings, then between them, amidst eddying rivers of mist that hid more than they showed, she saw him, saw his face. Her heart grew tight in her breast.

"Cerin," she breathed. There was both hope and loss in her voice.

He stood on the ramparts of an old ruined fortress, the grey stoneworks stark against a spill of dusky hills and the tendrils of mist. Beside him was a tall man clad all in black—tunic, trousers, boots and jacket. The man in black had a strangely shaped lute hanging from a shoulder strap. Its shining wood was of the darkest ebony. Even the strings were black. Meran shivered and looked away.

"Who is he with?" she asked.

Bethowen shrugged.

"Where are they, then?"

"In this world, but not."

Bethowen passed her hands above the fire and the flames stirred the image into a new shape. The two men still stood on the ramparts, but now the fortress was changed. Gone were the ruined walls and tottering high towers. Stone was fashioned cunningly to stone, wall to towers to inner keep until the whole of it seemed the fashioning of master stoneworkers. Brave pennants fluttered in a breeze that blew across the sudden green hills.

"This is what he sees," the hillwife said.

She spoke a last word and the vision was lost in mists once more. Harpstrings, silver and taut, took shape amidst the swirl of mist, then a harp, half covered with leaves, and above it a yearning oak keeping watch. Then there was only the fire and its red-gold flames.

"Where is that keep?" Meran asked.

"North of Abercorn and far from your father's wood. Across the Dolking Downs. Too far for an oakmaid. In the old days they named it Taencaer and it prospered. Now it is a nameless ruin where no one goes."

"I must go to him."

"Too far," Bethowen said.

"But still I must go." Meran bit at her lip, finding the next ques-tion, for all that it burned inside her, difficult to frame into words. It was not the question so much as what the answer to it might be.

"Is he . . . is he enspelled?" she asked.

Bethowen shrugged. "I have shown you all that the flames have to show, my dear. More I cannot do. For your sake, I hope . . ." The hillwife shut her mouth and entwined her knobby fingers together on her lap. She hoped what? That all was well? If all was well the oak king's daughter would not be here asking her questions.

"You must take care," she began, but stopped again. Hers was only the gift of farseeing and a few remedial cures. Advice had never been her province. To each their own wisdom. But this oak-maid, so determined, as stubborn as the badger that bided by her knee, as much a part of the Middle Kingdom as the ensorcered keep she meant to visit . . . what advice had the hills for her? None, save caution and, to one so headstrong, that would only be so much mouthing in the wind.

"He is enspelled," Meran said.

He had to be. He would never just leave her. But the fear, once having risen whisperingly inside her, couldn't be shunted aside. Like a serpent's insidious hiss it worried at all she'd ever held as certainty.

Is our love such a frail thing that I should question it like this? She demanded of herself.

He left, the whisperer replied slyly. Without a word.

He was enspelled! she insisted. He'd never be gone otherwise.

Men will do that, the inner voice replied, repeating Bethowen's earlier words, but mockingly, without the sense of comfort that one woman might offer to another.

Fiercely Meran shook her head. She thought of the roseharp's strings and the dead leaves entwined amidst them. She turned her gaze northward and followed the line of the hills with her eyes.

"Thank you," she murmured to the hillwife, her thoughts already far away, already planning her journey.

Fighting down the draw of her dead oak that still called to her for all the charms she carried with her, she left the hilltop. Old Badger trailed at her heels.

"Luck go with you," Bethowen said, but there was no one left to answer. Only the night remained, with its voiceless stars and the crackle of the flames.

Those same stars looked down on what was once named Taencaer, the old hillfort that straddled the border between Abercorn and Staynes. But where they saw the keep for the impoverished memory that it was, with leaning stone-cracked towers and debris rounding the once-straight planes of its walls, the two men who stood atop its ramparts saw it as it had been in longyears past, a bustling keep filled with the retainers of the old king's court, the last bastion of man before the grim wastes of the wild northlands. Where the hawk in the deserted west tower and the rodents that made their nests in the courtyards below heard only the wind and the stirrings of dead grasses as they rasped against the weathered stones, the two men heard music drifting lazily from the inner keep, the voices of stableboys and maids gossiping in the courtyard, horses stamping in the stables, the creak of the wooden pulley as water was drawn from the well, and the hundred other sounds of an occupied keep.

One of the men was a black-haired tinker, brown-skinned and dark-eyed. His name was Jeth Tewdol. He leaned against the old stone of the ramparts and eyed his prisoner with amusement, his lean fingers straying from time to time to the strings of his lute. The occasional snatch of music that answered had a sardonic quality to it that matched the dark cunning of his eyes for mood.

The other was Cerin called the Songweaver, the husband of Meran Gwynder and a harper, though he was far from his wife and had no instrument at hand to show his calling. There was more grey than brown in his beard and his braided hair was greyer still. He was thin and his face seemed a map of lines, like the many roads he'd journeyed, but where the tinker's dark eyes reflected without depth, his were clear and tarn-deep, more the eyes of a young man for all his body's apparent age.

Staring across the darkened hills, Cerin worried at the why and where of his situation. It was a strange thing to go abed in your own house, with your wife at your side, and wake in a strange keep, who knew where, a prisoner. The sun had arisen and set once since then and still he was here. Try as he might, there was no way free of it. His captor's lutemagic bound him as surely as though he were chained, sapping his will, refusing him the chance to raise his own magics.

For he had magics, only they were denied him, here in this strangely familiar place. His taw, the inner quiet where his power had its birth, was silent, but silent with a silence of absence, not the silence that was like music, that was his strength. What he needed was his harp, but Telynros too was denied him.

Ordinarily there was a bond that joined them so that, no matter what the distance between them, he could call the roseharp to him, or him to it. But when he reached out to it, the lutemagic thickened about him and he heard no scatter of welcoming notes, no greeting. Nothing. With the roseharp in hand he could have surmounted his captor's spells, the clear notes cutting through his unseen fetters like an otter cutting through water. But as it was . . .

And Meran. What was she to think, waking and finding him gone?

As though reading Cerin's thoughts, Jeth Tewdol grinned. He pulled a flask from the pocket of his jacket and took a long swig before offering it to his prisoner.

Cerin shook his head. "I think not."

"Afraid it's a faery drink?" the tinker asked. "That if you take a sip you'll be bound here forever?"

"Something binds me already, tinker."

"Why, so it does."

Jeth Tewdol drew chords from his lute and Cerin's head swam with sharp pains that came like dagger blows on the heels of the dark music. He staggered and leaned against the stonework for balance, his lips drawn back as he fought the pain.

"A reminder," the tinker said with a smile. His hands fell away from his instrument.

As the last note faded, Cerin's breath returned to him in ragged gasps. The pains faded into a dull ache and were gone. All save the memory of them.

"You've only the one more night of my company, Songweaver," Jeth Tewdol added. "And then?" He grinned. "Why, then you're free to go as you will, where you will. Home to your woman of wood, if you want. If she'll still have you."

For all that he controlled the situation, the tinker took a step back at the sudden fire in his prisoner's eyes.

"No," he said, holding up his hands in a disarming manner. "You mistake me. I haven't harmed her, nor will I." His moment of unease dissolved as though it had never been and he made himself comfortable on the stoneworks, enjoying himself again. "This is the why of it," he explained. "Have you heard in your travels of Taencaer, the old king's keep?"

Cerin looked around with a new insight. The sharp edges of the keep wavered for a moment, as though the deepseeing of his magic had returned to him. The sounds that rose up from the courtyard and inner keep were now like the wind playing through ruined stonework. Then that moment was gone and all was as it had been, except that Cerin knew now where he was: in ruined Taencaer, where ghosts were said to play with the wind and the spirits of the dead slept lightly if they slept at all. The hillfort had been brought back to a semblance of life through the tinker's lutemagic, the same lutemagic that kept him from gathering his taw and putting an end to his captivity. Recognizing the fort and the hills beyond, he wondered how many he would know amongst the ghosts that the tinker had woken.

"What of it?" he asked. The where he was he understood now, but not the why.

"They had a contest here, in days long gone. Barden and musicians came from many lands to compete in it."

"I know," Cerin said. "Tasanin was the last to win it—a young fiddler from Yern."

The tinker regarded him strangely. Something in his prisoner's voice brought him up sharply, but Cerin, for all the furor of his thoughts, kept a bland expression on his face.

"How could you know that?" Jeth Tewdol asked.

"I was here that day."

"But that was . . . long ago."

Cerin smiled, enjoying the tinker's disconcertment. "I know. But still I was here and remember it."

"Songweaver," Jeth Tewdol said. "That's your name? Not a title?" At Cerin's nod a queasy feeling went through the tinker. It had been one man through the centuries bearing that name, not wearing it as a title? For a long moment he said nothing, then a new gleam entered his eyes.

"That makes it even better," he said. "That contest will be held again tomorrow night—for the first time in many a year—and I mean to win it. It was for that reason that I raised the dead of Taencaer. I mean to win the contest and take the title of Songweaver from you. But now . . . now I take more than a title. I take your name and all the magic in it."

"Contests mean nothing," Cerin said. "They are for youths who have yet to prove something to themselves, not for men such as you and I. And my name, like the roseharp, was a gift of the Tuathan. You cannot take it from me."

Jeth Tewdol touched his lute and an eerie note sang forth. "You needn't sound so smug, Songweaver. I too have a god-gifted instrument, though mine was given to me by the Daketh."

Cerin looked from the lute that the tinker claimed came from the Tuathan's dark cousins, to the man's brown face.

"How so?" he asked. "Why were you gifted?"

"Through no special effort on my part," Jeth Tewdol said. "Would you know the tale? I can see by your eyes you would—for all that you shake your head. Then listen and marvel, you who have lived down through the longyears. We are more alike than I thought, for I see now that as you are, so must I be, for are we not both god-gifted?

"My instrument came to me in such a fashion: I was traveling through the Kierlands—do you know them? They're unfriendly dales in the best of times, but for a tinker there's none worse. It was winter and I sought lodgings, but was turned away from every inn until I took refuge in the one place no man could, or would, deny me—a ruined fane in the north marches. There was little enough there, but the walls that remained were enough to shelter me from the wind's cold bite, and what with this and that—a stolen haunch of a wild fowl from the last inn I'd tried, a small fire that spluttered and spat more than it gave off heat, and a thread-bare cloak—I made do. A piteous picture, don't you think?

"I gave no thought to ghosts or the like—knew nothing of them save from my own people's roadtales. I fell asleep knowing nothing of the history of those ruins. That I found out later. Once it was a Tuathan fane, desecrated in years long gone, and now a place of dark shadows where the Daketh's power was strong. I slept and dreamt that they came to me, those dark gods, came to me who was nothing. I remember cowering from them, yet accepting their presence as we will do in a dream. They saw something in me—my bitterness, perhaps?—and fanned it to life with promises.

" 'What would you have?' they asked me.

"I remember thinking of the instrument my father had left me— a poor old flute that I sold for a week's lodgings and meals a year or so before. I'd never've done it, but I was desperate. The innkeeper had the city guard waiting at this door if I couldn't pay him some-thing.

"Well, I thought of it, and remembered its warmth and comfort. You must know what I mean, Songweaver. When all's wrong in your world, a snatch of music can still lift your spirits. So I opened my mouth to ask for another like it, but when I spoke, all that came out was one word: 'Power.'

"The Daketh laughed—such a sound!

" 'Then power you shall have,' they said and were gone.

"When I woke, my fire was gone out and the wind was howling. I recalled my dream and found, lying next to me, this." The tinker tapped his lute. "They left me this instrument and its magics, yes, and the skill to use both. Why? Who can say? On a whim, perhaps? It makes little difference to me, for I'll tell you this, Songweaver. Innkeepers no longer look at my darkened skin and bid me begone. With the lutemagic I could tumble their walls down about their ears and they know it. They see it in my eyes, sense the lute's power. Ah, isn't she a beauty?"

Cerin nodded obligingly.

"And it's with it that I'll take your name."

"I do not engage in contests," Cerin replied.

"Are you afraid to lose?"

"Win or lose, it means nothing. I take my music as I find it. Whether you are the better musician or not, does not invalidate my own skill. And my name is still my name."

"And yet there will be a contest and you will play in it. And when the king's barden name me the winner, I will be the Songweaver and you will be nothing."

Cerin shrugged. If the tinker wished a contest, so be it. If he named himself Songweaver, there was little he could do about that either. A name was only a name. It had power, as all names must, but only if it was a true name. The tinker deluded himself if he thought otherwise.

"I have no instrument," he said.

Jeth Tewdol smiled. "I have one for you. A harp—the like of which you've never seen before."

And indeed he hadn't.

When the tinker brought the harp to him, Cerin could only stare. The soundbox was cracked. The supports, forepillar and curving neck both, were warped. The tuning pins had no hold in them so that a string wouldn't stay in tune, while the strings themselves were discolored with rust and buzzed when he tried one.

"Well?" the tinker asked.

Cerin looked from harp to man and answered softly. "A fine instrument, Jeth Tewdol, and I thank you for its use. If you will allow me to . . . accustom myself to it?"

"By all means." The tinker laughed. "I will leave you to your task. Only, Songweaver. Do us both a favour. Don't try to escape."

He tapped his lute meaningfully, with all the subtlety of a bit actor in a mummer's play.

"I am yours to command," Cerin said.

"So you are. Why, so you are!"

Chuckling to himself, the tinker wandered off, plucking a tune from his lute. When he was gone, Cerin leaned against the stoneworks and eyed his borrowed harp for long moments. Then, sighing, he began to take out the tuning pins, one by one.

Rubbing dust and stone powder onto then, he fitted each back in place, testing them for give and how they'd hold for tuning. Some still fitted so loosely that he had to add slivers of wood to achieve the desired tightness. When he was done with them, he polished the strings themselves, working every fleck of rust out of them until they gleamed as bright as his roseharp's. He ignored the warpage and the soundbox's cracks. There was nothing he could do for them except rub the wood until it regained some of its lost luster.

He thought of Meran as he worked and wished there was some way he could get word to her so that she'd not think he was hurt or dead, or worse, that he'd left her. What *would* she think? The shock of waking alone and finding him gone . . . Frowning, he rubbed the wood all the harder, trying not to think of it.

At last he was done and he could test the instrument. The tuning pins held, for what it was worth, but the tone was abysmal, without projection. The bass strings still buzzed, though they could perhaps be fixed. Holding the harp on his lap, he closed his eyes and concentrated on Telynros, hoping that the tinker's guard might have dropped or the lutemagic fallen away enough for him to reach the roseharp with his need, but it was no use. He called up the grey rose and the silver strings, but only mists answered.

Weary, he went to find a place to sleep for the day. Finding it, he lay long awake, thinking of his wife and their home, and what the tinker would do with him when the contest was done. Surely he would not simply set him free? He would fear Cerin's reprisal, as well he might. But worry though he did, if there was a solution to his problem, Cerin couldn't see it.

Dawn found Meran many leagues north of Ogwen Wood and the longstone where Bethowen the hillwife kept her seeing-flames. Her legs ached, from ankle to calf especially, and she longed to rest.

But there was still so far to go. And when she got there . . . What if he wasn't there? What if he was, but he'd gone of his own volition?

"I'm tired," she said, kneeling in the coarse grass. "Ah, but I'm tired."

Old Badger rubbed up against her and she ruffled his thick neck fur. She watched the sun rise, saw the hills unfolding for bleak miles north. Her dead oak called to her, stronger than before, for she'd never been this far from her father's wood. Rubbing her pendant, feeling the oak grain between her fingers, she tried to ignore the insistent summons to return, but it stayed with her, a constant need that sapped her determination, weakening her when she needed all her strength.

"I don't know if I can run that far, Old Badger. I don't know if it's in me."

But it had to be. As surely as though she felt Cerin's arm around her shoulders, she knew he needed her. Or was it her own need that drove her? She frowned, not liking this turn her thoughts kept taking. He was enspelled, she told herself yet again, and wished the voice inside her, whispering otherwise, would go away. She would continue. She'd run until her legs collapsed under her and then she'd run some more. Unless . . .

She smiled suddenly, wondering why she hadn't thought of it earlier. Drawing her flute from its sheath, she looked along its length, seeing Cerin's handiwork in its every curved inch. Then she slipped the instrument and, gazing skyward, began to play.

For a moment she thought she heard a harp answer, accompanying her as it had so many times before, then she knew that it was only her need that heard it. She shook off the feeling and concentrated on her playing. Her fingers moved in a slow dance across the wood and clear notes rang in the air. For a long time it was the only sound the hills heard. Then, far off in the distance, there was an answer—a deep-throated whistling call. A black speck grew larger in the sky and larger still, until a greatowl dropped groundward on silent wings.

Like calls to like, the old tales say. So an oakmaid's playing drew one of her skykin to her. The greatowl's wingspread spanned sixteen feet and his torso was as long as a man's. Landing, he ruffled his feathers and became a man, tall and round-eyed, with feathers streaming down to his shoulders in place of hair. Meran drew her flute back from her lips and laid it across her knees.

"Thairn," she said in greeting, her voice warm. They were old friends, these two.

"Your song was sad enough to make the wind weep, Meran. Why did you call me?"

Listening to her reply, he cocked his head like the great bird in whose shape he was more comfortable.

"I can bear one of you," Thairn said, looking from her to Old Badger when she was done.

Meran sheathed her flute and bent down to kiss Old Badger's brow.

"That will be enough," she said.

Thairn nodded and took his skyshape again. He lowered his neck to help her get a better purchase and she mounted awkwardly, afraid to pull the feathers too hard lest they loosen and come away in her hand. Once she was settled, Thairn rose effortlessly into the morning air and hovered.

"Goodbye, Old Badger!" Meran called down. "Wish me luck!"

Thairn's long wings plied the air and they were off, swifter than ever Meran's legs could have taken her. Behind, Old Badger whined, looking this way and that. Then he set off, doggedly following the bird and its rider. When they were only a speck in the distance and finally gone from sight, still he followed, his short legs churning, his body moving in a strange flowing motion that looked for all the world like a furry carpet come to life and floating a few inches off the ground as it followed the contours of the terrain.

The distance sped by under Thairn's tireless flight. Burrowing her face in his soft neck feathers, Meran stared ahead, northward, until just before the coming of twilight, she saw the fortress in the distance. By the time they reached its ruined walls, the night had fallen. Thairn coasted in and landed near the gates. Disembarking, Meran stretched, trying to work the stiffness out of her muscles.

"Thank you, Thairn," she said.

The greatowl took manshape again.

"I'll come with you," he said.

Meran shook her head. "Please. I have to go by myself." She didn't want to have to explain about the whisper that had kept up its constant nagging the whole of the journey north. All she knew was that she wanted to see Cerin on her own in case . . . in case . . . She bit at her lip and savagely pushed the thought away.

"You're certain?" Thairn asked.

"I'm certain."

She waited until he'd changed back to a greatowl and his wings had lifted him into the dark skies again before she turned to make for the gate. As she reached it, the whole fortress seemed to waver in her sight. She blinked and rubbed at her eyes. In place of the ruin were solid walls, rearing high, lit by torchlight. Where the gateway had been empty, two guards now stood.

"Your business?" one of them demanded.

"I . . ."

The guard looked at the flute sheath hanging from her shoulder. "Are you here for the musician's contest?"

"The . . .? Yes. Yes, I am!"

Musician's contest? Was it for this that her husband had left her? To take part in some mad contest? The whispering grew stronger in her mind and, feeling sick, she didn't have the strength to force it away.

"They're just finishing up," the guard said. "In the main hall. You'd better hurry."

Nodding her thanks, feeling more numb than real, Meran stepped through the gates and made her way across the inner courtyard. A musician's contest? Why had he come to it? Without his harp, even! As if he cared for such things in the first place. Contests were for people who needed titles, he'd told her often enough, not for anyone who cared about their music. Then she heard someone playing a harp, a strange harried sound as though the player were exhausted or drunk, and she recognized her husband's playing in the phrasing of the notes.

He *was* here! Part of this contest, and playing badly. Unsure if she was angry or sad, or perhaps some painful combination of the two emotions, she made for the door.

Disconcerting as the gathered dead were, what interested Cerin most was that there were more contestants than simply the tinker and himself. He wondered why. Long tables ran the length of the hall, except for the cleared space before the dais where the king and his retinue sat. And though he knew the people gathered here were only shades of the dead, he saw no mouldering corpses or gaunt bony shapes wrapped in their death palls. Instead they appeared as real as the tinker that walked at Cerin's side. They joined the other contestants, three men and a woman, at a table set aside for them to the left of the cleared space.

"The rules are simple," Jeth Tewdol told him. "Musicianship is judged by those three," he indicated the dais where the king's barden sat with fiddle, harp and flute respectively on their knees. Cerin didn't recognize any of them, though he knew the king. He looked away at the dead king's mocking smile. There had been no love between them when the king was alive.

"But the judging," the tinker was explaining, "is also measured on how well you appeal to the less tutored—those gathered here to listen. Thunderous applause is what you're seeking, Songweaver. If you wish to keep your name." He glanced down at Cerin's instrument and grinned. "I wish you the best of luck."

One by one the contestants played and, living or dead though they might be (Cerin was no longer sure), they were all skilled musicians. He found himself enjoying their strange tunes and tried to remember this flourish or that decoration for future reference. *If* Jeth Tewdol was going to allow him a future. Then it was the tinker's turn.

He bowed, first to the king's dais, then to the crowd that filled the hall to overflowing. Giving Cerin a wink, the tinker began to play.

There was no doubting his skill. Why on top of that he needed to be named the best, Cerin couldn't understand. He played with a dark grace. Moody tunes grew out of his fey instrument that sent shivers up the spines of his listeners and their feet to tapping the weird rhythms. When his last note died away, a long silence filled the hall. Then it was shattered as the people roared, clapping their hands and stamping their feet. They banged their mugs on the tables, whistled shrilly and generally raised a hullabaloo. Beaming, the tinker returned to the contestants' table.

"Now it is your turn," he said.

Cerin nodded, rising as his name was called.

"Lastly, Cerin called the Songweaver, Harper from Ogwen Wood."

As Cerin took his place, settling the tinker's harp on his lap, a murmur went through the crowd. There were faces he knew amongst them—the faces of folk long dead—and they recognized him and his name, though there wasn't one that had a friendly smile for him. Looking down at his instrument, he sighed. It's not the harp, it's the player, he told himself. And it matters not whether you win or lose, just let it be done.

He was tempted to play badly, just to let the tinker win, but knew he couldn't. Whatever he might think of contests or his present situation, he had the pride of his art to consider as well. When he played, he always played his best, whether it be for a king in his court or a shepherd in his cot. Tonight could be no different else he'd lost his name in truth, though not in the way that the tinker meant he should lose it. Turning so that he could watch Jeth Tewdol, he began to play.

He started with a familiar air, fingers curled like a hawk's talons as they plucked sweet notes from the shabby instrument on his lap. It was a simple piece but, in his hands, for all the drawbacks of the instrument, he breathed new life into it; gave it a deepness so that for all that his listeners had heard it played a thousand times before, in his hands it sounded like a newly-composed piece. He grinned at Jeth Tewdol as he began a second time, enjoying despite himself the look on the tinker's face. But his amusement didn't last long.

Seven bars into the tune, he saw Jeth Tewdol caress a string of his lute and the harp Cerin played rang discordantly. He tried to remedy the turn his music had taken, but the more he tried, the worse it sounded. The damage was done. Titters started up at the back of the hall and his neck reddened, but try though he did, he could no longer control the instrument. For every true note he fingered, the lutemagic awoke a dozen discords. At last he let his hands fall from the strings and he bent his head under the laughter of the gathered dead. And laughing loudest of all was Jeth Tewdol.

"Ha!" he cried. "I've won! See him now, he who was once called the Songweaver!"

Cerin's face burned. He knew he could play better, knew the flaws heard by these people were none of his doing, but knew as well that as far as they were concerned, he was worse than a novice player. They had wanted to see him fail and cared not how that failure was brought about. He could hold the truth of his own skill in his heart, but it did little to diminish the weight of the ridicule he bore. This was like his worst nightmares as a fledgling harper come to life. How often hadn't he woken bolt upright in his bed, sticky with sweaty fear, the dregs of a dream thudding in his heart? He'd be before a crowd, playing his best, and then it would all go wrong, and instead of applause, he received jeering and laughter. Like now.

Slowly he rose to his feet and, clutching his harp tight against his chest, made his way back to his seat. There was no use protesting, no use in doing anything except seeing this thing through to its end. And perhaps, in some measure, he deserved to be treated in this way, taken down a notch. He didn't believe in contests, no. But perhaps all his noble wordage as to why merely covered up the fact that he thought himself above them. Just as when he'd been playing and he'd mocked the tinker—something he'd never done to another musician no matter how good or bad his playing. Who was better? Was it because perhaps Jeth Tewdol *was* better? Why should it matter? It never had before. But just now, with the jeering and catcalls still loud in his ears and the tinker's grinning face so near his own, it seemed to matter more than anything else ever had before.

"We have little love for the living," the dead king said as the noise finally fell away. His voice boomed hollowly through the hall. "But, in truth, Jeth Tewdol, you have provided an entertainment this evening that we'll not soon forget. To see the Bright Gods' champion brought so low! Ha! Arise and accept from me now the winner's cup!"

"See?" the tinker said to Cerin. "It's done."

As he rose to collect his reward, Cerin caught at his arm.

"Am I free to go now?" he asked.

Jeth Tewdol shrugged. "Perhaps." He ran a finger along one of his lute's dark strings and Cerin shivered as the lutemagic bit at him. "There's still the matter of a name to settle between us. We can scarce have two Songweavers wandering the world, now can we?"

He laughed at the impotent rage in Cerin's eyes and turned away. Laying his instrument on the dais before the king, he went to where the king's harper held the winning cup. But before his hand touched it, the clear sound of flute-playing spoke across the hall.

As one, all heads turned to the door to see the woman with her green-brown hair and her cloak like leaves who lipped her flute. Her fingers fluttered across the holes of the instrument as though she were caressing a lover and there came forth such a sound! The low notes thrummed like a bear's honeyed breath, the high ones skirled and pierced the sky with sudden stars.

"Who?" the tinker cried, but none save Cerin and the king's harper heard him. The rest were too entranced by her playing to heed him.

"At last contestant it seems," the king's harper said.

"Meran!" the Songweaver cried.

Her playing was like the woods in summer, full and merry, deep with old tree secrets, yet held an underpining sweet sorrow, for, like music, the seasons change, summer to autumn to winter and round again to spring. Her music told the tale of that cycle, now joyful, now sad. And, by the faces of those who listened, such a music had never been heard in that hall before.

Jeth Tewdol's features contorted with rage. He leapt for his lute to stop her music, but Cerin was there first. The harper's boot crushed the hellish instrument before ever the tinker could lay a hand on it. With the sound of a great wind, the glamour of Taencaer fled, ghosts and all. The three of them stood in a ruined hall, the stars showing through the roofless heights above them. And still Meran played. Jeth Tewdol spun away from Cerin's grasp and made for her.

But as the tinker scrabbled across the rubble, he forgot who his prisoner was, the power Cerin wielded that had been denied him. Still seething from the ridicule he'd undergone, concerned for his wife, no longer restrained, Cerin reached out to Telynros, his thoughts leaping the distance between the ruins of Taencaer and the cottage where his roseharp awoke with music as it stood by the hearth, though no hand touched its strings. A moment it played on its own, then the harp was in Cerin's hands and its music rushed forward to accompany the sound of Meran's flute.

Across the ruined hall, harper and flautist met each other's gaze. Meran brought her flute from her lips and held it at her side, her fingers whitening as she squeezed it. She tried to focus on her husband's face, but her vision swam.

She didn't know what had possessed her to play in the doorway as she had, unless it be that those people had mocked her love and she meant to show them that it was wrong to do so. She'd not played to be a part of the contest. Rather she'd only tried, through her music, to reach out and touch the audience, show them that ridicule was cruel, hoped to awaken some compassion in their dead hearts. Blinking now, she saw only the vision from Bethowen's seeing-flames—the pattern of silver strings and the dead leaves that half covered the instrument, the mists aswirl, and then, at last, her husband's face.

The sly whisperer inside her was laid to rest at last as she looked into his eyes. But a new fear rose to take its place. He played Telynros savagely and the dark-clothed man that was between them jerked to the music, helpless as a marionette. Cerin's eyes were dark with a wild anger, as though he didn't know what he was doing, or worse, that he knew all too well.

"Cerin!" she cried. "Cerin!"

His anger seemed to blind him, for there was no flicker of recognition in his eyes when she called his name, no lessening of that terrible harping. She opened her mouth to call again, then lifted her flute to her lips and sent her own music skirling through the maelstrom of the roseharp's notes, weaving and binding them. As their musics joined, she came to understand what drove him. It was not so much his ordeal that burned in him, as what he'd found in himself.

A new tone entered her playing and it pierced his anger with its reason.

No one can be perfect, love, it seemed to say. Yet remember that he drove you to it and learn the lesson of it. Don't become what he is. Where is the gentle man I love? Where is the Songweaver amid such anger?

Slowly his rage faded. Telynros's grim notes dissolved into echoes and Cerin slumped to his knees, hugging his roseharp to him. He stared at the tinker's still form, sick at what he'd done. But as he watched, Jeth Tewdol raised himself painfully and sat up against a block of weather-roughened stonework, lifted, it seemed, by the flute music that still rang sweetly through the hall, healing all hurts. Then it too died and Meran picked her way across. She paused by the tinker and looked down at him.

"Why?" she asked. "By my father's Oak, why?"

Jeth Tewdol lifted his gaze. "I am a tinker," he said bitterly.

"That is not reason enough."

"The Dark Gods gave me an instrument that made me a prince of players—I who was nothing before they gifted me, a two-copper pretender of a musician, a tinker welcomed more often with a cuff in the face and a curse. The Daketh gave me power. They delight in torment, so should I not offer it to them in payment? Is that reason enough? They . . ." He shook his head. "How could you understand?"

Meran regarded him silently for long moments, then handed him her flute.

"Then I gift you with this," she said. "Will you now take delight in bringing joy to people?"

"I . . ." The tinker looked at the flute, remembering its sweet tone when she'd played it. His fingers trembled as he took it in his hands, running his fingers along the smooth length of its wood. For long moments, now he was silent. When he spoke again, his voice had a different tone to it. Gone was the mockery and self-assurance.

"I . . . I know it's the player, not the instrument that makes a musician. Your husband . . . even on that box with strings I gave him to use . . . he was still the better player. I can't accept this. I . . ." His eyes glistened with unshed tears. "I don't deserve it."

"Still you don't understand," Meran said softly. "It's the music that matters, not who's better or worse."

"But . . . I . . . What will you use?"

Meran looked to Cerin and smiled. "Perhaps my husband will make me another. There's still some of the old tree left."

Jeth Tewdol could find no more words. He simply leaned against the stone, holding the flute as though it were the greatest treasure the world had to offer. Watching them, hearing his wife speak, Cerin felt the tightness in his chest ease and he could breathe again. He thought to himself that he should still be angry, but searching inside, all he could find was pity. Shaking his head, he stood and then Meran came to him, lifting her face to be kissed.

"Such a spell you wove!" he said with a smile. "Who's the Song-weaver now?"

She grinned. "You are, silly! Who else?"

"Perhaps," he said as he kissed her.

Meran looked at his harp and, remembering the pattern the strings had made in the seeing-flames, reached out to touch one. A tiny bell-like note rang forth.

"Maybe I'll take up the harp then," she said, "and maybe not. But right now there's an Old Badger stuck somewhere between here and home, and a night's sleep that we never saw completed."

"So there is." He looked over her shoulder to the tinker. Jeth Tewdol raised his gaze from the flute to meet Cerin's eyes.

"If I said I was sorry . . ." the tinker began, but Cerin shook his head.

"We both learned something tonight, Jeth. I as much as you. If you're ever 'round Ogwen Wood, visit us, will you? Only come when we're awake."

Cerin's smile awoke a tentative answer on the tinker's lips.

"If you'll have me," he said slowly, "I'd be honored to come."

"Good. Till then . . ."

Cerin set the roseharp to ringing with deep chords and an amber hue surrounded Meran and him.

"Thank you!" the tinker called.

From the amber glow he heard a chorus of farewells. When the harping died away and the amber hue was gone, Jeth Tewdol sat alone amidst the ruined stoneworks of Taencaer. Rising he went to the ramparts to watch the dawn pink the sky above the eastern hills. He thought for a moment of the Daketh instrument that lay broken below him, then shook his head and lifted Meran's flute to his lips. He was out of practice, so the sound that came forth was awkward and breathy, but the tinker smiled.

# MICHAEL BISHOP

## "The Quickening"

*Although generally considered a science fiction writer, Michael Bishop (1945- ) has made a career out of crossing back and forth between the horror, fantasy and science fiction genres.* His novels A Funeral for the Eyes of Fire, The Secret Ascension, *and the Nebula Award-winning* No Enemy But Time *deploy the traditional science fiction themes of interplanetary adventure, alternate universes and time travel for stories that pose questions regarding human identity and social responsibility.* Who Made Stevie Crye? *is a horror novel with darkly comic overtones, and* Unicorn Mountain *a moving fantasy parable about coming to terms with terminal illness. For his World Fantasy Award-nominated novel* Brittle Innings, *he reworked the Frankenstein theme for an odyssey of self-discovery set in the world of minor league baseball. Some of his best short fiction has been collected in* Blooded on Arachne, One Winter in Eden *and* At the City Limits of Fate. *"The Quickening" was nominated for a Hugo Award and won the Nebula Award.*

# The Quickening

*by Michael Bishop*

*L*awson came out of his sleep feeling drugged and disoriented. Instead of the susurrus of traffic on Rivermont and the early-morning barking of dogs, he heard running feet and an unsettling orchestration of moans and cries. No curtains screened or softened the sun that beat down on his face, and an incandescent blueness had replaced their ceiling. "Marlena," Lawson said doubtfully. He wondered if one of the children was sick and told himself that he ought to get up to help.

But when he tried to rise, scraping the back of his hand on a stone set firmly in mortar, he found that his bed had become a parapet beside a river flowing through an unfamiliar city. He was wearing, instead of the green Chinese-peasant pajamas that Marlena had given him for Christmas, a suit of khaki 1505s from his days in the Air Force and a pair of ragged Converse sneakers. Clumsily, as if deserting a mortuary slab, Lawson leapt away from the wall. In his sleep, the world had turned over. The forms of a bewildered anarchy had begun to assert themselves.

The city—and Lawson knew that it sure as hell wasn't Lynchburg, that the river running through it wasn't the James—was full of people. A few, their expressions terrified and their postures defensive, were padding past Lawson on the boulevard beside the parapet. Many shrieked or babbled as they ran. Other human shapes, dressed not even remotely alike, were lifting themselves bemusedly from paving stones, or riverside benches, or the gutter beyond the sidewalk. Their grogginess and their swiftly congealing fear, Lawson realized, mirrored his own: like him, these people were awakening to nightmare.

Because the terrible fact of his displacement seemed more important than the myriad physical details confronting him, it was hard to take in everything at once—but Lawson tried to balance and integrate what he saw.

The city was foreign. Its architecture was a clash of the Gothic and the sterile, pseudoadobe Modern, one style to each side of the river. On this side, palm trees waved their dreamy fronds at precise intervals along the boulevard, and toward the city's interior an intricate cathedral tower defined by its great height nearly everything beneath it. Already the sun crackled off the rose-colored tower with an arid fierceness that struck Lawson, who had never been abroad, as Mediterranean. . . . Off to his left was a bridge leading into a more modern quarter of the city, where beige and brick-red highrises clustered like tombstones. On both sides of the bridge buses, taxicabs, and other sorts of motorized vehicles were stalled or abandoned in the thoroughfares.

Unfamiliar, Lawson reflected, but not unearthly—he recognized things, saw the imprint of a culture somewhat akin to his own. And, for a moment, he let the inanimate bulk of the city and the languor of its palms and bougainvillea crowd out of his vision the human horror show taking place in the streets.

A dark woman in a sari hurried past. Lawson lifted his hand to her. Dredging up a remnant of a high-school language course, he shouted, "*¿Habla Español?*" The woman quickened her pace, crossed the street, recrossed it, crossed it again; her movements were random, motivated, it seemed, by panic and the complicated need to *do* something.

At a black man in a loincloth farther down the parapet, Lawson shouted, "This is Spain! We're somewhere in Spain! That's all I know! Do you speak English? Spanish? Do you know what's happened to us?"

The black man, grimacing so that his skin went taut across his cheekbones, flattened himself atop the wall like a lizard. His elbows jutted, his eyes narrowed to slits. Watching him, Lawson perceived that the man was listening intently to a sound that had been steadily rising in volume ever since Lawson had opened his eyes: the city was wailing. From courtyards, apartment buildings, taverns, and plazas, an eerie and discordant wail was rising into the bland blue indifference of the day. It consisted of many strains. The Negro in the loincloth seemed determined to separate these and pick out the ones that spoke most directly to him. He tilted his head.

"Spain!" Lawson yelled against the uproar. "*¡España!*"

The black man looked at Lawson, but the hieroglyph of recognition was not among those that glinted in his eyes. As if to dislodge the wailing of the city, he shook his head. Then, still crouching lizard-fashion on the wall, he began methodically banging his head against its stones. Lawson, helplessly aghast, watched him until he had knocked himself insensible in a sickening, repetitive spattering of blood.

But Lawson was the only one who watched. When he approached the man to see if he had killed himself, Lawson's eyes were seduced away from the African by a movement in the river. A bundle of some sort was floating in the greasy waters below the wall—an infant, clad only in a shirt. The tie-strings on the shirt trailed out behind the child like the severed, wavering legs of a water-walker. Lawson wondered if, in Spain, they even had waterwalkers. . . .

Meanwhile, still growing in volume, there crooned above the highrises and Moorish gardens the impotent air-raid siren of 400,000 human voices. Lawson cursed the sound. Then he covered his face and wept.

## II.

The city was Seville. The river was the Guadalquivir. Lynchburg and the James River, around which Lawson had grown up as the eldest child of an itinerant fundamentalist preacher, were several thousand miles and one helluva big ocean away. You couldn't get there by swimming, and if you imagined that your loved ones would be waiting for you when you got back, you were probably fantasizing the nature of the world's changed reality. No one was where he or she belonged anymore, and Lawson knew himself lucky even to realize where he was. Most of the dispossessed, displaced people inhabiting Seville today *didn't* know that much; all they knew was the intolerable cruelty of their uprooting, the pain of separation from husbands, wives, children, lovers, friends. These things, and fear.

The bodies of infants floated in the Guadalquivir; and Lawson, from his early reconnoiterings of the city on a motor scooter that he had found near the Jardines de Cristina park, knew that thousands of adults already lay dead on streets and in apartment buildings—victims of panic-inspired beatings or their own traumatized hearts. Who knew exactly what was going on in the morning's chaos? Babel had come again and with it, as part of the package, the utter dissolution of all family and societal ties. You couldn't go around a corner without encountering a child of some exotic ethnic caste, her face snot-glazed, sobbing loudly or maybe running through a crush of bodies calling out names in an alien tongue.

What were you supposed to do? Wheeling by on his motor scooter, Lawson either ignored these children or searched their faces to see how much they resembled his daughters.

Where was Marlena now? Where were Karen and Hannah? Just as he played deaf to the cries of the children in the boulevards, Lawson had to harden himself against the implications of these questions. As dialects of German, Chinese, Bantu, Russian, Celtic, and a hundred other languages rattled in his ears, his scooter rattled past a host of cars and buses with uncertain-seeming drivers at their wheels. Probably he too should have chosen an enclosed vehicle. If these frustrated and angry drivers, raging in polyglot defiance, decided to run over him, they could do so with impunity. Who would stop them?

Maybe—in Istanbul, or La Paz, or Mangalore, or Jönköping, or Boise City, or Kaesŏng—his own wife and children had already lost their lives to people made murderous by fear or the absence of helmeted men with pistols and billy sticks. Maybe Marlena and his children were dead. . . .

I'm in Seville, Lawson told himself, cruising. He had determined the name of the city soon after mounting the motor scooter and going by a sign that said *Plaza de Toros de Sevilla*. A circular stadium of considerable size near the river. The bullring. Lawson's Spanish was just good enough to decipher the signs and posters plastered on its walls. *Corrida a las cinco de la tarde.* (Garcia Lorca, he thought, unsure of where the name had come from.) *Sombra y sol.* That morning, then, he took the scooter around the stadium three or four times and then shot off toward the center of the city.

Lawson wanted nothing to do with the nondescript highrises across the Guadalquivir, but had no real idea what he was going to do on the Moorish and Gothic side of the river, either. All he knew was that the empty bullring, with its dormant potential for death, frightened him. On the other hand, how did you go about establishing order in a city whose population had not willingly chosen to be there?

Seville's population, Lawson felt sure, had been redistributed across the face of the globe, like chess pieces flung from a height. The population of every other human community on Earth had undergone similar displacements. The result, as if by malevolent design, was chaos and suffering. Your ears eventually tried to shut out the audible manifestations of this pain, but your eyes held you accountable and you hated yourself for ignoring the wailing Arab child, the assaulted Polynesian woman, the blue-eyed old man bleeding from the palms as he prayed in the shadow of a department-store awning. Very nearly, you hated yourself for surviving.

Early in the afternoon, at the entrance to the Calle de las Sierpes, Lawson got off his scooter and propped it against a wall. Then he waded into the crowd and lifted his right arm above his head.

"I speak English!" he called. "*¡Y hablo un poco Español!* Any who speak English or Spanish please come to me!"

A man who might have been Vietnamese or Kampuchean, or even Malaysian, stole Lawson's motor scooter and rode it in a wobbling zigzag down the Street of the Serpents. A heavyset blond woman with red cheeks glared at Lawson from a doorway, and a twelve- or thirteen-year-old boy who appeared to be Italian clutched hungrily at Lawson's belt, seeking purchase on an adult, hoping for commiseration. Although he did not try to brush the boy's hand away, Lawson avoided his eyes.

"English! English here! *¡Un poco Español también!*"

Farther down Sierpes, Lawson saw another man with his hand in the air; he was calling aloud in a crisp but melodic Slavic dialect, and already he had succeeded in attracting two or three other people to him. In fact, pockets of like-speaking people seemed to be forming in the crowded commercial avenue, causing Lawson to fear that he had put up his hand too late to end his own isolation. What if those who spoke either English or Spanish had already gathered into survival-conscious groups? What if they had already made their way into the countryside, where the competition for food and drink might be a little less predatory? If they had, he would be a lost, solitary Virginian in this Babel. Reduced to sign language and guttural noises to make his wants known, he would die a cipher. . . .

"*Signore*," the boy hanging on his belt cried. "*Signore*."

Lawson let his eyes drift to the boy's face. "*Ciao*," he said. It was the only word of Italian he knew, or the only word that came immediately to mind, and he spoke it much louder than he meant.

The boy shook his head vehemently, pulled harder on Lawson's belt. His words tumbled out like the contents of an unburdened closet into a darkened room, not a single one of them distinct or recognizable.

"English!" Lawson shouted. "English here!"

"English here, too, man!" a voice responded from the milling crush of people at the mouth of Sierpes. "Hang on a minute, I'm coming to you!"

A small muscular man with a large head and not much chin stepped daintily through an opening in the crowd and put out his hand to Lawson. His grip was firm. As he shook hands, he placed his left arm over the shoulder of the Italian boy hanging on to Lawson's belt. The boy stopped talking and gaped at the newcomer.

"Dai Secombe," the man said. "I went to bed in Aberystwyth, where I teach philosophy, and I wake up in Spain. Pleased to meet you, Mr.—"

"Lawson," Lawson said.

The boy began babbling again, his hand shifting from Lawson's belt to the Welshman's flannel shirt facing. Secombe took the boy's hands in his own. "I've got you, lad. There's a ragged crew of your compatriots in a poolhall pub right down this lane. Come on, then, I'll take you." He glanced at Lawson. "Wait for me, sir. I'll be right back."

Secombe and the boy disappeared, but in less than five minutes the Welshman had returned. He introduced himself all over again. "To go to bed in Aberystwyth and to wake up in Seville," he said, "is pretty damn harrowing. I'm glad to be alive, sir."

"Do you have a family?"

"Only my father. He's eighty-four."

"You're lucky. Not to have anyone else to worry about, I mean."

"Perhaps," Dai Secombe said, a sudden trace of sharpness in his voice. "Yesterday I would not've thought so."

The two men stared at each other as the wail of the city modulated into a less hysterical but still inhuman drone. People surged around them, scrutinized them from foyers and balconies, took their measure. Out of the corner of his eye Lawson was aware of a moonfaced woman in summer deerskins slumping abruptly and probably painfully to the street. An Eskimo woman—the conceit was almost comic, but the woman herself was dying and a child with a Swedish-steel switchblade was already freeing a necklace of teeth and shells from her throat.

Lawson turned away from Secombe to watch the plundering of the Eskimo woman's body. Enraged, he took off his wristwatch and threw it at the boy's head, scoring a glancing sort of hit on his ear.

"You little jackal, get away from there!"

The red-cheeked woman who had been glaring at Lawson applied her foot to the rump of the boy with the switchblade and pushed him over. Then she retrieved the thrown watch, hoisted her skirts, and retreated into the dim interior of the café whose door she had been haunting.

"In this climate, in this environment," Dai Secombe told Lawson, "an Eskimo is doomed. It's as much psychological and emotional as it is physical. There may be a few others who've already died for similar reasons. Not much we can do, sir."

Lawson turned back to the Welshman with a mixture of awe and disdain. How had this curly-haired lump of a man, in the space of no more than three or four hours, come to respond so lackadaisically to the deaths of his fellows? Was it merely because the sky was still blue and the edifices of another age still stood?

Pointedly, Secombe said, "That was a needless forfeiture of your watch, Lawson."

"How the hell did that poor woman get here?" Lawson demanded, his gesture taking in the entire city. "How the hell did any of us get here?" The stench of open wounds and the first sweet hints of decomposition mocked the luxury of his ardor.

"Good questions," the Welshman responded, taking Lawson's arm and leading him out of the Calle de las Sierpes. "It's a pity I can't answer 'em."

## III.

That night they ate fried fish and drank beer together in a dirty little apartment over a shop whose glass display cases were filled with a variety of latex contraceptives. They had obtained the fish from a *pescadería* voluntarily tended by men and women of Greek and Yugoslavian citizenship, people who had run similar shops in their own countries. The beer they had taken from one of the classier bars on the Street of the Serpents. Both the fish and the beer were at room temperature, but tasted none the worse for that.

With the fall of evening, however, the wail that during the day had subsided into a whine began to reverberate again with its first full burden of grief. If the noise was not quite so loud as it had been that morning, Lawson thought, it was probably because the city contained fewer people. Many had died, and a great many more, unmindful of the distances involved, had set out to return to their homelands.

Lawson chewed a piece of *adobo* and washed this down with a swig of the vaguely bitter *Cruz del Campo* beer.

"Isn't this fine?" Secombe said, his butt on the tiles of the room's one windowsill. "Dinner over a rubber shop. And this a Catholic country, too."

"I was raised a Baptist," Lawson said, realizing at once that his confession was a *non sequitur*.

"Oh," Secombe put in immediately. "Then I imagine you could get all the rubbers you wanted."

"Sure. For a quarter. In almost any gas-station restroom."

"Sorry," Secombe said.

They ate for a while in silence. Lawson's back was to a cool plaster wall; he leaned his head against it, too, and released a sharp moan from his chest. Then, sustaining the sound, he moaned again, adding his own strand of grief to the cacophonous harmonies already afloat over the city. He was no different from all the bereaved others who shared his pain by concentrating on their own.

"What did you do in . . . in Lynchburg?" Secombe suddenly asked.

"Campus liaison for the Veterans Administration. I traveled to four different colleges in the area straightening out people's problems with the GI Bill. I tried to see to it that—Sweet Jesus, Secombe, who cares? I miss my wife. I'm afraid my girls are dead."

"Karen and Hannah?"

"They're three and five. I've taught them to play chess. Karen's good enough to beat me occasionally if I spot her my queen. Hannah knows the moves, but she hasn't got her sister's patience—she's only three, you know. Yeah. Sometimes she sweeps the pieces off the board and folds her arms, and we play hell trying to find them all. There'll be pawns under the sofa, horsemen upside down in the shag—" Lawson stopped.

"She levels them," Secombe said. "As we've all been leveled. The knight's no more than the pawn, the king no more than the bishop."

Lawson could tell that the Welshman was trying to turn aside the ruinous thrust of his grief. But he brushed the metaphor aside: "I don't think we've been 'leveled,' Secombe."

"Certainly we have. Guess who I saw this morning near the cathedral when I first woke up."

"God only knows."

"God and Dai Secombe, sir. I saw the Marxist dictator of . . . oh, you know, that little African country where there's just been a coup. I recognized the bastard from the telly broadcasts during the purge trials there. There he was, though, in white ducks and a ribbed T-shirt—terrified, Lawson, and as powerless as you or I. He'd been quite decidedly leveled; you'd better believe he had."

"I'll bet he's alive tonight, Secombe."

The Welshman's eyes flickered with a sudden insight. He extended the greasy cone of newspaper from the *pescadería*. "Another piece of fish, Lawson? Come on, then, there's only one more."

"To be leveled, Secombe, is to be put on a par with everyone else. Your dictator, even deprived of office, is a grown man. What about infant children? Toddlers and preadolescents? And what about people like that Eskimo woman who haven't got a chance in an unfamiliar environment, even if its inhabitants don't happen to be hostile? . . . I saw a man knock his brains out on a stone wall this morning because he took a look around and knew he couldn't make it here. Maybe he thought he was in Hell, Secombe. I don't know. But his chance certainly wasn't ours."

"He knew he couldn't adjust."

"Of course he couldn't adjust. Don't give me that bullshit about leveling!"

Secombe turned the cone of newspaper around and withdrew the last piece of fish. "I'm going to eat this myself, if you don't mind." He ate. As he was chewing, he said, "I didn't think that Virginia Baptists were so free with their tongues, Lawson. Tsk, tsk. Undercuts my preconceptions."

"I've fallen away."

"Haven't we all."

Lawson took a final swig of warm beer. Then he hurled the bottled across the room. Fragments of amber glass went everywhere. "God!" he cried. "God, God, God!" Weeping, he was no different from three quarters of Seville's new citizens-by-chance. Why, then, as he sobbed, did he shoot such guilty and threatening glances at the Welshman?

"Go ahead," Secombe advised him, waving the empty cone of newspaper. "I feel a little that way myself."

## IV.

In the morning an oddly blithe woman of forty-five or so accosted them in the alley outside the contraceptive shop. A military pistol in a patent-leather holster was strapped about her skirt. Her seeming airiness, Lawson quickly realized, was a function of her appearance and her movements; her eyes were as grim and frightened as everyone else's. But, as soon as they came out of the shop onto the cobblestones, she approached them fearlessly, hailing Secombe almost as if he were an old friend.

"You left us yesterday, Mr. Secombe. Why?"

"I saw everything dissolving into cliques."

"Dissolving? Coming together, don't you mean?"

Secombe smiled noncommittally, then introduced the woman to Lawson as Mrs. Alexander. "She's one of your own, Lawson. She's from Wyoming or some such place. I met her outside the cathedral yesterday morning when the first self-appointed muezzins started calling their language-mates together. She didn't have a pistol then."

"I got it from one of the Guardia Civil stations," Mrs. Alexander said. "And I feel lots better just having it, let me tell you." She looked at Lawson. "Are you in the Air Force?"

"Not anymore. These are the clothes I woke up in."

"My husband's in the Air Force. Or was. We were stationed at Warren in Cheyenne. I'm originally from upstate New York. And these are the clothes *I* woke up in." A riding skirt, a blouse, low-cut rubber-soled shoes. "I think they tried to give us the most serviceable clothes we had in our wardrobes—but they succeeded better in some cases than others."

" 'They'?" Secombe asked.

"Whoever's done this. It's just a manner of speaking."

"What do you want?" Secombe asked Mrs. Alexander. His brusqueness of tone surprised Lawson.

Smiling, she replied, "The word for today is Exportadora. We're trying to get as many English-speaking people as we can to Exportadora. That's where the commercial center for American servicemen and their families in Seville is located, and it's just off one of the major boulevards to the south of here."

On a piece of paper sack Mrs. Alexander drew them a crude map and explained that her husband had once been stationed in Zaragoza in the north of Spain. Yesterday she had recalled that Seville was one of the four Spanish cities supporting the American military presence, and with persistence and a little luck a pair of carefully briefed English-speaking DPs (the abbreviation was Mrs. Alexander's) had discovered the site of the American PX and commissary just before nightfall. Looting the place when they arrived had been an impossibly mixed crew of foreigners, busily hauling American merchandise out of the ancient buildings. But Mrs. Alexander's DPs had run off the looters by the simple expedient of revving the engine of their commandeered taxicab and blowing its horn as if to announce Armageddon. In ten minutes the little American enclave had emptied of all human beings but the two men in the cab. After that, as English-speaking DPs all over the city learned of Exportadora's existence and sought to reach it, the place had begun to fill up again.

"Is there an air base in Seville?" Lawson asked the woman.

"No, not really. The base itself is near Morón de la Frontera, about thirty miles away, but Seville is where the real action is." After a brief pause, lifting her eyebrows, she corrected herself: "Was."

She thrust her map into Secombe's hands. "Here. Go on out to Exportadora. I'm going to look around for more of us. You're the first people I've found this morning. Others are looking too, though. Maybe things'll soon start making some sense."

Secombe shook his head. "Us. Them. There isn't anybody now who isn't a 'DP,' you know. This regrouping on the basis of tired cultural affiliations is probably a mistake. I don't like it."

"You took up with Mr. Lawson, didn't you?"

"Out of pity only, I assure you. He looked lost. Moreover, you've got to have companionship of *some* sort—especially when you're in a strange place."

"Sure. That's why the word for today is Exportadora."

"It's a mistake, Mrs. Alexander."

"Why?"

"For the same reason your mysterious 'they' saw fit to displace us to begin with, I'd venture. It's a feeling I have."

"Old cultural affiliations are a source of stability," Mrs. Alexander said earnestly. As she talked, Lawson took the rumpled map out of Secombe's fingers. "This chaos around us won't go away until people have settled themselves into units—it's a natural process, it's beginning already. Why, walking along the river this morning, I saw several groups of like-speaking people burying yesterday's dead. The city's churches and chapels have begun to fill up, too. You can still hear the frightened and the heartbroken keening in solitary rooms, of course—but it can't go on forever. They'll either make connection or die. I'm not one of those who wish to die, Mr. Secombe."

"Who wishes that?" Lawson put in, annoyed by the shallow metaphysical drift of this exchange and by Secombe's irrationality. Although Mrs. Alexander was right, she didn't have to defend her position at such length. The map was her most important contribution to the return of order in their lives, and Lawson wanted her to let them use that map.

"Come on, Secombe," he said. "Let's get out to this Exportadora. It's probably the only chance we have of making it home."

"I don't think there's any chance of our making it home again, Lawson. Ever."

Perceiving that Mrs. Alexander was about to ask the Welshman why, Lawson turned on his heel and took several steps down the alley. "Come on, Secombe. We have to try. What the hell are you going to do in this flip-flopped city all by yourself?"

"Look for somebody else to talk to, I suppose."

But in a moment Secombe was at Lawson's side helping him

decipher the smudged geometries of Mrs. Alexander's map, and the woman herself, before heading back to Sierpes to look for more of her own kind, called out, "It'll only take you twenty or so minutes, walking. Good luck. See you later."

Walking, they passed a white-skinned child lying in an alley doorway opening onto a courtyard festooned with two-day-old washing and populated by a pack of orphaned dogs. The child's head was covered by a coat, but she did appear to be breathing. Lawson was not even tempted to examine her more closely, however. He kept his eyes resolutely on the map.

## V.

The newsstand in the small American enclave had not been looted. On Lawson's second day at Exportadora it still contained quality paperbacks, the most recent American news and entertainment magazines, and a variety of tabloids, including the military paper *The Stars and Stripes*. No one knew how old these publications were because no one knew over what length of time the redistribution of the world's population had taken place. How long had everyone slept? And what about the discrepancies among time zones and the differences among people's waking hours within the same time zones? These questions were academic now, it seemed to Lawson, because the agency of transfer had apparently encompassed every single human being alive on Earth.

Thumbing desultorily through a copy of *Stars and Stripes*, he encountered an article on the problems of military hospitals and wondered how many of the world's sick had awakened in the open, doomed to immediate death because the care they required was nowhere at hand. The smell of spilled tobacco and melted Life Savers made the newsstand a pleasant place to contemplate these horrors; and, even as his conscience nagged and a contingent of impatient DPs awaited him, Lawson perversely continued to flip through the newspaper.

Secombe's squat form appeared in the doorway. "I thought you were looking for a local roadmap."

"Found it already, just skimmin' the news."

"Come on, if you would. The folks're ready to be off."

Reluctantly, Lawson followed Secombe outside, where the raw

Andalusian sunlight broke like invisible surf against the pavement and the fragile-seeming shell of the Air Force bus. It was of the Bluebird shuttle variety, and Lawson remembered summer camp at Eglin Air Force Base in Florida and bus rides from his squadron's minimum-maintenance ROTC barracks to the survival-training camps near the swamp. That had been a long time ago, but this Bluebird might have hailed from an even more distant era. It was as boxy and sheepish-looking as if it had come off a 1954 assembly line, and it appeared to be made out of warped tin rather than steel. The people inside the bus had opened all its windows, and many of those on the driver's side were watching Secombe and Lawson approach.

"Move your asses!" a man shouted at them. "Let's get some wind blowing through this thing before we all suffo-damn-cate."

"Just keep talking," Secombe advised him. "That should do fine."

Aboard the bus was a motley lot of Americans, Britishers, and Australians, with two or three English-speaking Europeans and an Oxford-educated native of India to lend the group ballast. Lawson took up a window seat over the hump of one of the bus's rear tires, and Secombe squeezed in beside him. A few people introduced themselves; others, lost in fitful reveries, ignored them altogether. The most unsettling thing about the contingent to Lawson was the absence of children. Although about equally divided between men and women, the group contained no boys or girls any younger than their early teens.

Lawson opened the map of southern Spain he had found in the newsstand and traced is finger along a highway route leading out of Seville to two small American enclaves outside the city, Santa Clara and San Pablo. Farther to the south were Jerez and the port city of Cádiz. Lawson's heart misgave him; the names were all so foreign, so formidable in what they evoked, and he felt this entire enterprise to be hopeless. . . .

About midway along the right-hand side of the bus a black woman was sobbing into the hem of her blouse, and a man perched on the Bluebird's long rear seat had his hands clasped to his ears and his head canted forward to touch his knees. Lawson folded up the map and stuck it into the crevice between the seat and the side of the bus.

"The bottom-line common denominator here isn't our all speaking English," Secombe whispered. "It's what we're suffering."

Driven by one of Mrs. Alexander's original explorers, a doctor from Ivanhoe, New South Wales, the Bluebird shuddered and lurched forward. In a moment it had left Exportadora and begun banging along one of the wide avenues that would lead it out of town.

"And our suffering," Secombe went on, still whispering, "unites us with all those poor souls raving in the streets and sleeping facedown in their own vomit. You felt that the other night above the condom shop, Lawson. I know you did, talking of your daughters. So why are you so quick to go looking for what you aren't likely to find? Why are you so ready to unite yourself with this artificial family born out of catastrophe? Do you really think you're going to catch a flight home to Lynchburg? Do you really think the bird driving this sardine can—who ought to be out in the streets plying his trade instead of running a shuttle service— d'you really think he's ever going to get back to Australia?"

"Secombe—"

"Do you, Lawson?"

Lawson clapped a hand over the Welshman's knee and wobbled it back and forth. "You wouldn't be badgering me like this if you had a family of your own. What the hell do you want us to do? Stay here forever?"

"I don't know, exactly." He removed Lawson's hand from his knee. "But I do have a father, sir, and I happen to be fond of him. . . . All I know for certain is that things are *supposed* to be different now. We shouldn't be rushing to restore what we already had."

"Shit," Lawson murmured. He leaned his head against the bottom edge of the open window beside him.

From deep within the city came the brittle noise of gunshots. The Bluebird's driver, in response to this sound and to the vegetable carts and automobiles that had been moved into the streets as obstacles, began wheeling and cornering like a stock-car jockey. The bus clanked and stuttered alarmingly. It growled through an intersection below a stone bridge, leapt over that bridge like something living, and roared down into a semi-industrial suburb of Seville where a Coca-Cola bottling factory and a local brewery lifted huge competing signs.

On top of one of these buildings Lawson saw a man with a rifle taking unhurried potshots at anyone who came into his sights. Several people already lay dead.

And a moment later the Bluebird's front window shattered, another bullet ricocheted off its flank, and everyone in the bus was either shouting or weeping. The next time Lawson looked, the bus's front window appeared to have woven inside it a large and exceedingly intricate spider's web.

The Bluebird careened madly, but the doctor from Ivanhoe kept it upright and turned it with considerable skill onto the highway to San Pablo. Here the bus eased into a quiet and rhythmic cruising that made this final incident in Seville—except for the evidence of the front window—seem only the cottony aftertaste of nightmare. At last they were on their way. Maybe.

"Another good reason for trying to get home," Lawson said.

"What makes you think it's going to be different there?"

Irritably Lawson turned on the Welshman. "I thought your idea was that this change was some kind of *improvement*."

"Perhaps it will be. Eventually."

Lawson made a dismissive noise and looked at the olive orchard spinning by on his left. Who would harvest the crop? Who would set the aircraft factories, the distilleries, the chemical and textile plants running again? Who would see to it that seed was sown in the empty fields?

Maybe Secombe had something. Maybe, when you ran for home, you ran from the new reality at hand. The effects of this new reality's advent were not going to go away very soon, no matter what you did—but seeking to reestablish yesterday's order would probably create an even nastier entropic pattern than would accepting the present chaos and working to rein it in. How, though, did you best rein it in? Maybe by trying to get back home . . .

Lawson shook his head and thought of Marlena, Karen, Hannah; of the distant, mist-softened cradle of the Blue Ridge. Lord. That was country much easier to put in tune with than the harsh, white-sky bleakness of this Andalusian valley. If you stay here, Lawson told himself, the pain will *never* go away.

They passed Santa Clara, which was a housing area for the officers and senior NCOs who had been stationed at Morón. With its neatly trimmed hedgerows, tall aluminum streetlamps, and low-roofed houses with carports and picture windows, Santa Clara resembled a middle-class exurbia in New Jersey or Ohio. Black smoke was curling over the area, however, and the people on the streets and lawns were definitely not Americans—they were transplanted Dutch South Africans, Amazonian tribesmen, Poles, Ethiopians, God-only-knew-what. All Lawson could accurately deduce was that a few of these people had moved into the vacant houses—maybe they had awakened in them—and that others had aimlessly set bonfires about the area's neighborhoods. These fires, because there was no wind, burned with a maddening slowness and lack of urgency.

"Little America," Secombe said aloud.

"That's in Antarctica," Lawson responded sarcastically.

"Right. No matter where it happens to be."

"Up yours."

Their destination was now San Pablo, where the Americans had hospital facilities, a library, a movie theater, a snackbar, a commissary, and, in conjunction with the Spaniards, a small commercial and military airfield. San Pablo lay only a few more miles down the road, and Lawson contemplated the idea of a flight to Portugal. What would be the chances, supposing you actually reached Lisbon, of crossing the Atlantic, either by sea or air, and reaching one of the United States's coastal cities? One in a hundred? One in a thousand? Less than that?

A couple of seats behind the driver, an Englishman with a crisp-looking moustache and an American woman with a distinct Southwestern accent were arguing the merits of bypassing San Pablo and heading on to Gibraltar, a British possession. The Englishman seemed to feel that Gibraltar would have escaped the upheaval to which the remainder of the world had fallen victim, whereas the American woman thought he was crazy. A shouting match involving five or six other passengers ensued. Finally, his patience at an end, the Bluebird's driver put his elbow on the horn and held it there until everyone had shut up.

"It's San Pablo," he announced. "Not Gibraltar or anywhere else. There'll be a plane waitin' for us when we get there."

## VI.

*Two* aircraft were waiting, a pair of patched-up DC-7s that had once belonged to the Spanish airline known as Iberia. Mrs. Alexander had recruited one of her pilots from the DPs who had shown up at Exportadora; the other, a retired TWA veteran from Riverside, California, had made it by himself to the airfield by virtue of a prior acquaintance with Seville and its American military installations. Both men were eager to carry passengers home, one via a stopover in Lisbon and the other by using Madrid as a stepping-stone to the British Isles. The hope was that they could transfer their passengers to jet aircraft at these cities' more cosmopolitan airports, but no one spoke very much about the real obstacles to success that had already begun stalking them: civil chaos, delay, inadequate communications, fuel shortages, mechanical hangups, doubt and ignorance, a thousand other things.

At twilight, then, Lawson stood next to Dai Secombe at the chain-link fence fronting San Pablo's pothole-riven runway and watched the evening light glimmer off the wings of the DC-7s. Bathed in a muted dazzle, the two old airplanes were almost beautiful. Even though Mrs. Alexander had informed the DPs that they must spend the night in the installation's movie theater, so that the Bluebird could make several more shuttle runs to Exportadora, Lawson truly believed that he was bound for home.

"Good-bye," Secombe told him.

"Good-bye? . . . Oh, because you'll be on the other flight?"

"No, I'm telling you good-bye, Lawson, because I'm leaving. Right now, you see. This very minute."

"Where are you going?"

"Back into the city."

"How? What for?"

"I'll walk, I suppose. As for why, it has something to do with wanting to appease Mrs. Alexander's 'they,' also with finding out what's to become of us all. Seville's the place for that, I think."

"Then why'd you even come out here."

"To say good-bye, you bloody imbecile." Secombe laughed, grabbed Lawson's hand, shook it heartily. "Since I couldn't manage to change your mind."

With that, he turned and walked along the chain-link fence until he had found the roadway past the installation's commissary. Lawson watched him disappear behind that building's complicated system of loading ramps. After a time the Welshman reappeared on the other side, but, against the vast Spanish sky, his compact striding form rapidly dwindled to an imperceptible smudge. A smudge on the darkness.

"Good-bye," Lawson said.

That night, slumped in a lumpy theater chair, he slept with

nearly sixty other people in San Pablo's movie house. A teenage boy, over only a few objections, insisted on showing all the old movies still in tins in the projection room. As a result, Lawson awoke once in the middle of *Apocalypse Now* and another time near the end of Kubrick's *The Left Hand of Darkness*. The ice on the screen, dunelike *sastrugi* ranged from horizon to horizon, chilled him, touching a sensitive spot in his memory. "Little America," he murmured. Then he went back to sleep.

## VII.

With the passengers bound for Lisbon, Lawson stood at the fence where he had stood with Secombe, and watched the silver pinwheeling of propellers as the aircraft's engines engaged. The DC-7 flying to Madrid would not leave until much later that day, primarily because it still had several vacant seats and Mrs. Alexander felt sure that more English-speaking DPs could still be found in the city.

The people at the gate with Lawson shifted uneasily and whispered among themselves. The engines of their savior airplane whined deafeningly, and the runway seemed to tremble. What woebegone eyes the women had, Lawson thought, and the men were as scraggly as railroad hoboes. Feeling his jaw, he understood that he was no more handsome or well-groomed than any of those he waited with. And, like them, he was impatient for the signal to board, for the thumbs-up sign indicating that their airplane had passed its latest rudimentary ground tests.

At least, he consoled himself, you're not eating potato chips at ten-thirty in the morning. Disgustedly, he turned aside from a jut-eared man who was doing just that.

"There're more people here than our plane's supposed to carry," the potato-chip cruncher said. "That could be dangerous."

"But it isn't really that far to Lisbon, is it?" a woman replied. "And none of us has any luggage."

"Yeah, but—" The man gagged on a chip, coughed, tried to speak again. Facing deliberately away, Lawson felt that the man's words would acquire eloquence only if he suddenly volunteered to ride in the DC-7's unpressurized baggage compartment.

As it was, the signal came to board and the jut-eared man had no chance to finish his remarks. He threw his cellophane sack to the ground, and Lawson heard it crackling underfoot as people crowded through the gate onto the grassy verge of the runway.

In order to fix the anomaly of San Pablo in his memory, Lawson turned around and walked backward across the field. He saw that bringing up the rear were four men with automatic weapons—weapons procured, most likely, from the installation's Air Police station. These men, like Lawson, were walking backward, but with their guns as well as their eyes trained on the weirdly constituted band of people who had just appeared, seemingly out of nowhere, along the airfield's fence.

One of these people wore nothing but a ragged pair of shorts, another an ankle-length burnoose, another a pair of trousers belted with a rope. One of their number was a doe-eyed young woman with an exposed torso and a circlet of bright coral on her wrist. But there were others, too, and they all seemed to have been drawn to the runway by the airplane's engine whine; they moved along the fence like desperate ghosts. As the first members of Lawson's group mounted into the plane, even more of these people appeared—an assembly of nomads, hunters, hodcarriers, fishers, herdspeople. Apparently they all understood what an airplane was for, and one of the swarthiest men among them ventured out onto the runway with his arms thrown out imploringly.

"Where you go?" he shouted. "Where you go?"

"There's no more room!" responded a blue-jean-clad man with a machine gun. "Get back! You'll have to wait for another flight!"

Oh, sure, Lawson thought, the one to Madrid. He was at the base of the airplane's mobile stairway. The jut-eared man who had been eating potato chips nodded brusquely at him.

"You'd better get on up there," he shouted over the robust hiccoughing of the airplane's engines, "before we have unwanted company breathing down our necks!"

"After you." Lawson stepped aside.

Behind the swarthy man importuning the armed guards for a seat on the airplane, there clamored thirty or more insistent people, their only real resemblance to one another their longing for a way out. "Where you go? Where you go?" the bravest and most desperate among them yelled, but they all wanted to board the airplane that Mrs. Alexander's charges had already laid claim to; and most of them could see that it was too late to accomplish their purpose without some kind of risk-taking. The man who had been shouting in English, along with four or five others, broke into an assertive dogtrot toward the plane. Although their cries continued to be modestly beseeching, Lawson could tell that the passengers' guards now believed themselves under direct attack.

A burst of machine-gun fire sounded above the field and echoed away like rain drumming on a tin roof. The man who had been asking, "Where you go?," pitched forward on his face. Others fell beside him, including the woman with the coral bracelet. Panicked or prodded by this evidence of their assailants' mortality, one of the guards raked the chain-link fence with his weapon, bringing down some of those who had already begun to retreat and summoning forth both screams and the distressingly incongruous sound of popping wire. Then, eerily, it was quiet again.

"Get on that airplane!" a guard shouted at Lawson. He was the only passenger still left on the ground, and everyone wanted him inside the plane so that the mobile stairway could be rolled away.

"I don't think so," Lawson said to himself.

Hunching forward like a man under fire, he ran toward the gate and the crude mandala of bodies partially blocking it. The slaughter he had just witnessed struck him as abysmally repetitive of a great deal of recent history, and he did not wish to belong to that history anymore. Further, the airplane behind him was a gross iron-plated emblem of the burden he no longer cared to bear—even if it also seemed to represent the promise of passage home.

"Hey, where the hell you think you're goin'?"

Lawson did not answer. He stepped gingerly through the corpses on the runway's margin, halted on the other side of the fence, and, his eyes misted with glare and poignant bewilderment, turned to watch the DC-7 taxi down the scrub-lined length of concrete to the very end of the field. There the airplane negotiated a turn and started back the way it had come. Soon it was hurtling along like a colossal metal dragonfly, building speed. When it lifted from the ground, its tires screaming shrilly with the last series of bumps before take-off, Lawson held his breath.

Then the airplane's right wing dipped, dipped again, struck the ground, and broke off like a piece of balsa wood, splintering brilliantly. After that, the airplane went flipping, cartwheeling, across the end of the tarmac and into the desolate open field beyond, where its shell and remaining wing were suddenly engulfed in flames. You could hear people frying in that inferno; you could smell gasoline and burnt flesh.

"Jesus," Lawson said.

He loped away from the airfield's fence, hurried through the short grass behind the San Pablo library, and joined a group of those who had just fled the English-speaking guards' automatic-weapon fire. He met them on the highway going back to Seville and walked among them as merely another of their number. Although several people viewed his 1505 trousers with suspicion, no one argued that he did not belong, and no one threatened to cut his throat for him.

As hangdog and exotically nondescript as most of his companions, Lawson watched his tennis shoes track the pavement like the feet of a mechanical toy. He wondered what he was going to do back in Seville. Successfully dodge bullets and eat fried fish, if he was lucky. Talk with Secombe again, if he could find the man. And, if he had any sense, try to organize his life around some purpose other than the insane and hopeless one of returning to Lynchburg. What purpose, though? What purpose beyond the basic, animal purpose of staying alive?

"Are any of you hungry?" Lawson asked.

He was regarded with suspicious curiosity.

"Hungry," he repeated. "¿*Tiene hambre?*"

English? Spanish? Neither worked. What languages did they have, these refugees from an enigma? It looked as if they had all tried to speak together before and found the task impossible—because, moving along the asphalt under the hot Andalusian sun, they now relied on gestures and easily interpretable noises to express themselves.

Perceiving this, Lawson brought the fingers of his right hand to his mouth and clacked his teeth to indicate chewing.

He was understood. A thin barefoot man in a capacious linen shirt and trousers led Lawson off the highway into an orchard of orange trees. The fruit was not yet completely ripe, and was sour because of its greenness, but all twelve or thirteen of Lawson's crew ate, letting the juice run down their arms. When they again took up the trek to Seville, Lawson's mind was almost absolutely blank with satiety. The only thing rattling about in it now was the fear that he would not know what to do once they arrived. He never did find out if the day's other scheduled flight, the one to Madrid, made it safely to its destination, but the matter struck him now as of little import. He wiped his sticky mouth and trudged along numbly.

# VIII.

He lived above the contraceptive shop. In the mornings he walked through the alley to a bakery that a woman with calm Mongolian features had taken over. In return for a daily allotment of bread and a percentage of the goods brought in for barter, Lawson swept the bakery's floor, washed the utensils that were dirtied each day, and kept the shop's front counter. His most rewarding skill, in fact, was communicating with those who entered to buy something. He had an uncanny grasp of several varieties of sign language, and, on occasion, he found himself speaking a monosyllabic patois whose derivation was a complete mystery to him. Sometimes he thought that he had invented it himself; sometimes he believed that he had learned it from the transplanted Sevillanos among whom he now lived.

English, on the other hand, seemed to leak slowly out of his mind, a thick, unrecoverable fluid.

The first three or four weeks of chaos following The Change had, by this time, run their course, a circumstance that surprised Lawson. Still, it was true. Now you could lie down at night on your pallet without hearing pistol reports or fearing that some benighted freak was going to set fire to your staircase. Most of the city's essential services—electricity, water, and sewerage—were working again, albeit uncertainly, and agricultural goods were coming in from the countryside. People had gone back to doing what they knew best, while those whose previous jobs had had little to do with the basics of day-to-day survival were now apprenticing as bricklayers, carpenters, bakers, fishers, water and power technicians. That men and women chose to live separately and that children were as rare as sapphires, no one seemed to find disturbing or unnatural. A new pattern was evolving. You lived among your fellows without tension or quarrel, and you formed no dangerously intimate relationships.

One night, standing at his window, Lawson's knee struck a loose tile below the casement. He removed the tile and set it on the floor. Every night for nearly two months he pried away at least one tile and, careful not to chip or break it, stacked it near an inner wall with those he had already removed.

After completing this task, as he lay on his pallet, he would often hear a man or a woman somewhere in the city singing a high, sweet song whose words had no significance for him. Sometimes a pair of voices would answer each other, always in different languages. Then, near the end of the summer, as Lawson stood staring at the lathing and the wall beams he had methodically exposed, he was moved to sing a melancholy song of his own. And he sang it without knowing what it meant.

The days grew cooler. Lawson took to leaving the bakery during its midafternoon closing and proceeding by way of the Calle de las Sierpes to a bodega across from the bullring. A crew of silent laborers, who worked very purposively in spite of their seeming to have no single boss, was dismantling the Plaza de Toros, and Lawson liked to watch as he drank his wine and ate the breadsticks he had brought with him.

Other crews about the city were carefully taking down the government buildings, banks, and barrio chapels that no one frequented anymore, preserving the bricks, tiles, and beams as if in the hope of some still unspecified future construction. By this time Lawson himself had knocked out the rear wall of his room over the contraceptive shop, and he felt a strong sense of identification with the laborers craftily gutting the bullring of its railings and barricades. Eventually, of course, everything would have to come down. Everything.

The rainy season began. The wind and the cold. Lawson continued to visit the sidewalk café near the ruins of the stadium; and because the bullring's destruction went forward even in wet weather, he wore an overcoat he had recently acquired and staked out a nicely sheltered table under the bodega's awning. This was where he customarily sat.

One particularly gusty day, rain pouring down, he shook out his umbrella and sat down at this table only to find another man sitting across from him. Upon the table was a wooden game board of some kind, divided into squares.

"Hello, Lawson," the interloper said.

Lawson blinked and licked his lips thoughtfully. Although he had not called his family to mind in some time, and wondered now if he had ever really married and fathered children, Dai Secombe's face had occasionally floated up before him in the dark of his room. But now Lawson could not remember the Welshman's name, or his nationality, and he had no notion of what to say to him. The first words he spoke, therefore, came out sounding like dream babble, or a voice played backward on the phonograph. In order to say hello he was forced to the indignity, almost comic, of making a childlike motion with his hand.

Secombe, pointing to the game board, indicated that they should play. From a carved wooden box with a velvet lining he emptied the pieces onto the table, then arranged them on both sides of the board. Chess, Lawson thought vaguely, but he really did not recognize the pieces—they seemed changed from what he believed they should look like. And when it came his turn to move, Secombe had to demonstrate the capabilities of all the major pieces before he, Lawson, could essay even the most timid advance. The piece that most reminded him of a knight had to be moved according to two distinct sets of criteria, depending on whether it started from a black square or a white one; the "rooks," on the other hand, were able, at certain times, to *jump* an opponent's intervening pieces. The game boggled Lawson's understanding. After ten or twelve moves he pushed his chair back and took a long, bittersweet taste of wine. The rain continued to pour down like an endless curtain of deliquescent beads.

"That's all right," Secombe said. "I haven't got it all down yet myself, quite. A Bhutanese fellow near where I live made the pieces, you see, and just recently taught me how to play."

With difficulty Lawson managed to frame a question: "What work have you been doing?"

"I'm in demolition. As we all will be soon. It's the only really constructive occupation going." The Welshman chuckled mildly, finished his own wine, and rose. Lifting his umbrella, he bid Lawson farewell with a word that, when Lawson later tried to repeat and intellectually encompass it, had no meaning at all.

Every afternoon of that dismal, rainy winter Lawson came back to the same table, but Secombe never showed up there again. Nor did Lawson miss him terribly. He had grown accustomed to the strange richness of his own company. Besides, if he wanted people to talk to, all he needed to do was remain behind the counter at the bakery.

## IX.

Spring came again. All of his room's interior walls were down, and it amused him to be able to see the porcelain chalice of the commode as he came up the stairs from the contraceptive shop.

The plaster that he had sledgehammered down would never be of use to anybody again, of course, but he had saved from the debris whatever was worth the salvage. With the return of good weather, men driving oxcarts were coming through the city's backstreets and alleys to collect these items. You never saw anyone trying to drive a motorized vehicle nowadays, probably because, over the winter, most of them had been hauled away. The scarcity of gasoline and replacement parts might well have been a factor, too—but, in truth, people seemed no longer to want to mess with internal-combustion engines. Ending pollution and noise had nothing to do with it, either. A person with dung on his shoes or front stoop was not very likely to be convinced of a vast improvement in the environment, and the clattering of wooden carts—the ringing of metal-rimmed wheels on cobblestone— could be as ear-wrenching as the hum and blare of motorized traffic. Still, Lawson liked to hear the oxcarts turn into his alley. More than once, called out by the noise, he had helped the drivers load them with masonry, doors, window sashes, even ornate carven mantles.

At the bakery the Mongolian woman with whom Lawson worked, and had worked for almost a year, caught the handle of his broom one day and told him her name. Speaking the odd, quicksilver monosyllables of the dialect that nearly everyone in Seville had by now mastered, she asked him to call her Tij. Lawson did not know whether this was her name from before The Change or one she had recently invented for herself. Pleased in either case, he responded by telling her his own Christian name. He stumbled saying it, and when Tij also had trouble pronouncing the name, they laughed together about its uncommon awkwardness on their tongues.

A week later he had moved into the tenement building where Tij lived. They slept in the same "room" three flights up from a courtyard filled with clambering wisteria. Because all but the supporting walls on this floor had been knocked out, Lawson often felt that he was living in an open-bay barracks. People stepped over his pallet to get to the stairwell and dressed in front

77

of him as if he were not even there. Always a quick study, he emulated their casual behavior.

And when the ice in his loins finally began to thaw, he turned in the darkness to Tij—without in the least worrying about propriety. Their coupling was invariably silent, and the release Lawson experienced was always a serene rather than a shuddering one. Afterward, in the wisteria fragrance pervading their building, Tij and he lay beside each other like a pair of larval bumblebees as the moon rolled shadows over their naked, sweat-gleaming bodies.

Each day after they had finished making and trading away their bread, Tij and Lawson closed the bakery and took long walks. Often they strolled among the hedge-enclosed pathways and the small wrought-iron fences at the base of the city's cathedral. From these paths, so overwhelmed were they by buttresses of stones and arcaded balconies, they could not even see the bronze weathervane of Faith atop the Giralda. But, evening after evening, Lawson insisted on returning to that place, and at last his persistence and his sense of expectation were rewarded by the sound of jackhammers biting into marble in each one of the cathedral's five tremendous naves. He and Tij, holding hands, entered.

Inside, men and women were at work removing the altar screens, the metalwork grilles, the oil paintings, sections of stained-glass windows, religious relics. Twelve or more oxcarts were parked beneath the vault of the cathedral, and the noise of the jackhammers echoed shatteringly from nave to nave, from floor to cavernous ceiling. The oxen stood so complacently in their traces that Lawson wondered if the drivers of the carts had somehow contrived to deafen the animals. Tij released Lawson's hand to cover her ears. He covered his own ears. It did no good. You could remain in the cathedral only if you accepted the noise and resolved to be a participant in the building's destruction. Many people had already made that decision. They were swarming through its chambered stone belly like a spectacularly efficient variety of stone-eating termite.

An albino man of indeterminate race—a man as pale as a termite—thrust his pickax at Lawson. Lawson uncovered his ears and took the pickax by its handle. Tij, a moment later, found a crowbar hanging precariously from the side of one of the oxcarts. With these tools the pair of them crossed the nave they had entered and halted in front of an imposing mausoleum. Straining against the cathedral's poor light and the strange linguistic static in his head, Lawson painstakingly deciphered the plaque near the tomb.

"Christopher Columbus is buried here," he said.

Tij did not hear him. He made a motion indicating that this was the place where they should start. Tij nodded her understanding. Together, Lawson thought, they would dismantle the mausoleum of the discoverer of the New World and bring his corrupt remains out into the street. After all these centuries they would free the man.

Then the bronze statue of Faith atop the belltower would come down, followed by the lovely belltower itself. After that, the flying buttresses, the balconies, the walls; every beautiful, tainted stone.

It would hurt like hell to destroy the cathedral, and it would take a long, long time—but, considering everything, it was the only meaningful option they had. Lawson raised his pickax.

# GEORGE R. R. MARTIN

## "Remembering Melody"

*It is impossible to pigeonhole the work of George R. R. Martin (1948- ) to any one genre. He won his first Hugo Award for his 1974 science fiction story "A Song for Lya," and the Hugo and Nebula Award for the science fiction-horror hybrid "Sandkings." He is also a recipient of the Horror Writers of America Bram Stoker Award for his tale "The Pear-Shaped Man." His short fiction collections include* A Song for Lya and Other Stories, Sandkings, Nightflyers *and* Portraits of His Children, *and his novels, the vampire tale* Fevre Dream *and the apocalyptic thriller* The Armageddon Rag. *His work for television includes contributions to the revived "The Twilight Zone" and "Beauty and the Beast." Since 1987, he has edited the* Wild Cards *series of mosaic novels whose shared-world concept he created.*

# Remembering Melody

### by George R. R. Martin

ed was shaving when the doorbell sounded. It startled him so badly that he cut himself. His condominium was on the thirty-second floor, and Jack the doorman generally gave him advance warning of any prospective visitors. This had to be someone from the building, then. Except that Ted didn't know anyone in the building, at least not beyond the trade-smiles-in-the-elevator level.

"Coming," he shouted. Scowling, he snatched up a towel and wiped the lather from his face, then dabbed at his cut with a tissue. "Shit," he said loudly to his face in the mirror. He had to be in court this afternoon. If this was another Jehovah's Witness like the one who'd gotten past Jack last month, they were going to be in for a very rough time indeed.

The buzzer sounded again. "Coming, dammit," Ted yelled. He made a final dab at the blood on his neck, then threw the tissue into the wastebasket and strode across the sunken living room to the door. He peered through the eyehole carefully before he opened. "Oh, hell," he muttered. Before she could buzz again, Ted slid off the chain and threw open the door.

"Hello, Melody," he said.

She smiled wanly. "Hi, Ted," she replied. She had an old suitcase in her hand, a battered cloth bag with a hideous red-and-black plaid pattern, its broken handle replaced by a length of rope. The last time Ted had seen her, three years before, she'd looked terrible. Now she looked worse. Her clothes—shorts and a tie-dyed T-shirt—were wrinkled and dirty, and emphasized how gaunt she'd become. Her ribs showed through plainly; her legs were pipestems. Her long stringy blond hair hadn't been washed recently, and her face was red and puffy, as if she'd been crying. That was no surprise. Melody was always crying about one thing or another.

"Aren't you going to ask me in, Ted?"

Ted grimaced. He certainly didn't *want* to ask her in. He knew from past experience how difficult it was to get her out again. But he couldn't just leave her standing in the hall with her suitcase in hand. After all, he thought sourly, she was an old and dear friend. "Oh, sure," he said. He gestured. "Come on in."

He took her bag from her and set it by the door, then led her into the kitchen and put on some water to boil. "You look as though you could use a cup of coffee," he said, trying to keep his voice friendly.

Melody smiled again. "Don't you remember, Ted? I don't drink coffee. It's no good for you, Ted. I used to tell you that. Don't you remember?" She got up from the kitchen table and began rummaging through his cupboards. "Do you have any hot chocolate?" she asked. "I like hot chocolate."

"I don't drink hot chocolate," he said. "Just a lot of coffee."

"You shouldn't," she said. "It's no good for you."

"Yeah," he said. "Do you want juice? I've got juice."

Melody nodded. "Fine."

He poured her a glass of orange juice and led her back to the table, then spooned some Maxim into a mug while he waited for his kettle to whistle. "So," he asked, "what brings you to Chicago?"

Melody began to cry. Ted leaned back against the stove and watched her. She was a very noisy crier, and she produced an amazing amount of tears for someone who cried so often. She didn't look up until the water began to boil. Ted poured some into his cup and stirred in a teaspoon of sugar. Her face was redder and puffier than ever. Her eyes fixed on him accusingly. "Things have been real bad," she said. "I need help, Ted. I don't have anyplace to live. I thought maybe I could stay with you awhile. Things have been real bad."

"I'm sorry to hear that, Melody," Ted replied, sipping at his coffee thoughtfully. "You can stay here for a few days, if you want. But no longer. I'm not in the market for a roommate." She always made him feel like such a bastard, but it was better to be firm with her right from the start.

Melody began to cry again when he mentioned roommates. "You

used to say I was a *good* roommate," she whined. "We used to have fun, don't you remember? You were my friend."

Ted set down his coffee mug and looked at the kitchen clock. "I don't have time to talk about old times right now," he said. "I was shaving when you rang. I've got to get to the office." He frowned. "Drink your juice and make yourself at home. I've got to get dressed." He turned abruptly and left her weeping at the kitchen table.

Back in the bathroom, Ted finished shaving and tended to his cut more properly, his mind full of Melody. Already he could tell that this was going to be difficult. He felt sorry for her—she was messed up and miserably unhappy, with no one to turn to—but he wasn't going to let her inflict all her troubles on him. Not this time. She'd done it too many times before.

In his bedroom, Ted stared pensively into the closet for a long time before selecting the gray suit. He knotted his tie carefully in the mirror, scowling at his cut. Then he checked his briefcase to make sure all the papers on the Syndio case were in order, nodded, and walked back into the kitchen.

Melody was at the stove, making pancakes. She turned and smiled at him happily when he entered. "You remember my pancakes, Ted?" she asked. "You used to love it when I made pancakes, especially blueberry pancakes, you remember? You didn't have any blueberries, though, so I'm just making plain. Is that all right?"

"Jesus," Ted muttered. "Dammit, Melody, who said you should make *anything?* I told you I had to get to the office. I don't have time to eat with you. I'm late already. Anyway, I don't eat breakfast. I'm trying to lose weight."

Tears began to trickle from her eyes again. "But—but these are my special pancakes, Ted. What am I going to do with them? What am I going to *do?*"

"Eat them," Ted said. "You could use a few extra pounds. Jesus, you look terrible. You look like you haven't eaten for a month."

Melody's face screwed up and became ugly. "You bastard," she said. "You're supposed to be my *friend.*"

Ted sighed. "Take it easy," he said. He glanced at his watch. "Look, I'm fifteen minutes late already. I've got to go. You eat your pancakes and get some sleep. I'll be back around six. We can have dinner together and talk, all right? Is that what you want?"

"That would be nice," she said, suddenly contrite. "That would be real nice."

"Tell Jill I want to see her in my office, right away," Ted snapped to the secretary when he arrived. "And get us some coffee, will you? I really need some coffee."

"Sure."

Jill arrived a few minutes after the coffee. She and Ted were associates in the same law firm. He motioned her to a seat and pushed a cup at her. "Sit down," he said. "Look, the date's off tonight. I've got problems."

"You look it," she said. "What's wrong?"

"An old friend showed up on my doorstep this morning."

Jill arched one elegant eyebrow. "So?" she said. "Reunions can be fun."

"Not with Melody they can't."

"Melody?" she said. "A pretty name. An old flame, Ted? What is it, unrequited love?"

"No," he said, "no, it wasn't like that."

"Tell me what it was like, then. You know I love the gory details."

"Melody and I were roommates back in college. Not just us—don't get the wrong idea. There were four of us. Me and a guy named Michael Englehart, Melody and another girl, Anne Kaye. The four of us shared a big run-down house for two years. We were—friends."

"Friends?" Jill looked skeptical.

Ted scowled at her. "Friends," he repeated. "Oh, hell, I slept with Melody a few times. With Anne, too. And both of them balled Michael a time or two. But when it happened, it was just kind of—kind of *friendly*, you know? Our love lives were mostly with outsiders. We used to tell each other our troubles, swap advice, cry on one another's shoulders. Hell, I know it sounds weird. It was 1970, though. I had hair down to my ass. Everything was weird." He sloshed the dregs of his coffee around in the cup and looked pensive. "They were good times, too. Special times. Sometimes I'm sorry they had to end. The four of us were close, really close. I loved those people."

"Watch out," Jill said, "I'll get jealous. My roommate and I cordially despised each other." She smiled. "So what happened?"

Ted shrugged. "The usual story," he said. "We graduated, drifted apart. I remember the last night in the old house. We smoked a ton of dope and got very silly. Swore eternal friendship. We weren't ever going to be strangers, no matter what happened, and if any of us ever needed help, well, the other three would always be there. We sealed the bargain with—well, kind of an orgy."

Jill smiled. "Touching," she said. "I never dreamed you had it in you."

"It didn't last, of course," Ted continued. "We tried, I'll give us that much. But things changed too much. I went on to law school, wound up here in Chicago. Michael got a job with a publishing house in New York City. He's an editor at Random House now, been married and divorced, two kids. We used to write. Now we trade Christmas cards. Anne's a teacher. She was down in Phoenix the last I heard, but that was four, five years ago. Her husband didn't like the rest of us much, the one time we had a reunion. I think Anne must have told him about the orgy."

"And your houseguest?"

"Melody," he sighed. "She became a problem. In college, she was wonderful: gutsy, pretty, a real free spirit. But afterwards, she couldn't cut it. She tried to make it as a painter for a couple of years, but she wasn't good enough. Got nowhere. She went through a couple of relationships that turned sour, then married some guy about a week after she'd met him in a singles bar. That was terrible. He used to get drunk and beat her. She took about six months of it, and finally got a divorce. He still came around to beat her up for a year, until he finally got frightened off. After that, Melody got into drugs—bad. She spent some time in an asylum. When she got out, it was more of the same. She can't hold a job or stay away from drugs. Her relationships don't last more than a few weeks. She's let her body go to hell." He shook his head.

Jill pursed her lips. "Sounds like a lady who needs help," she said.

Ted flushed and grew angry. "You think I don't know that? You think we haven't tried to help her? *Jesus!* When she was trying to be an artist, Michael got her a couple of cover assignments from the paperback house he was with. Not only did she blow the deadlines, but she got into a screaming match with the art director. Almost cost Michael his job. I flew to Cleveland and handled her divorce for her, gratis. Flew back a couple of months later and spent quite a while there trying to get the cops to give her protection against her ex-hubby. Anne took her in when she had no place to live, got her into a drug rehabilitation program. In return,

Melody tried to seduce her boyfriend—said she wanted to *share* him, like they'd done in the old days. All of us have lent her money. She's never paid back any of it. And we've listened to her troubles, God but we've listened to her troubles. There was a period a few years ago when she'd phone every week, usually collect, with some new sad story. She cried over the phone a lot. If *Queen for a Day* was still on TV, Melody would be a natural!"

"I'm beginning to see why you're not thrilled by her visit," Jill said dryly. "What are you going to do?"

"I don't know," Ted replied. "I shouldn't have let her in. The last few times she's called, I just hung up on her, and that seemed to work pretty well. Felt guilty about it at first, but that passed. This morning, though, she looked so pathetic that I didn't know how to send her away. I suppose eventually I'll have to get brutal and go through a scene. Nothing else works. She'll make a lot of accusations, remind me of what good friends we were and the promises we made, threaten to kill herself. Fun times ahead."

"Can I help?" Jill asked.

"Pick up my pieces afterwards," Ted said. "It's always nice to have someone around afterwards to tell you that you're not a son-of-a-bitch even though you just kicked an old dear friend out into the gutter."

He was terrible in court that afternoon. His thoughts were full of Melody, and the strategies that most occupied him concerned how to get rid of her most painlessly, instead of the case at hand. Melody had danced flamenco on his psyche too many times before; Ted wasn't going to let her leech off him this time, nor leave him an emotional wreck.

When he got back to his condo with a bag of Chinese food under his arm—he'd decided he didn't want to take her out to a restaurant—Melody was sitting nude in the middle of his conversation pit, giggling and sniffing some white powder. She looked up at Ted happily when he entered. "Here," she said. "I scored some coke."

"*Jesus,*" he swore. He dropped the Chinese food and his brief-case, and strode furiously across the carpet. "I don't *believe* you," he roared. "I'm a *lawyer*, for Chrissakes. Do you want to get me disbarred?"

Melody had the coke in a little paper square and was sniffing it from a rolled-up dollar bill. Ted snatched it all away from her, and she began to cry. He went to the bathroom and flushed it down the toilet, dollar bill and all. Except it wasn't a dollar bill, he saw as it was sucked out of sight. It was a twenty. That made him even angrier. When he returned to the living room, Melody was still crying.

"Stop that," he said. "I don't want to hear it. And put some clothes on." Another suspicion came to him. "Where did you get the money for that stuff?" he demanded. "Huh, *where?*"

Melody whimpered. "I sold some stuff," she said in a timid voice. "I didn't think you'd mind. It was good coke." She shied away from him and threw an arm across her face, as if Ted was going to hit her.

Ted didn't need to ask whose stuff she'd sold. He knew; she'd pulled the same trick on Michael years before, or so he'd heard. He sighed. "Get dressed," he repeated wearily. "I brought Chinese food." Later he could check what was missing and phone the insurance company.

"Chinese food is no good for you," Melody said. "It's full of monosodium glutamate. Gives you headaches, Ted." But she got to her feet obediently, if a bit unsteadily, went off towards the bathroom, and came back a few minutes later wearing a halter top and a pair of ratty cutoffs. Nothing else, Ted guessed. A couple of years ago she must have decided that underwear was no good for you.

Ignoring her comment about the monosodium glutamate, Ted found some plates and served up the Chinese food in his dining nook. Melody ate it meekly enough, drowning everything in soy sauce. Every few minutes she giggled at some private joke, then grew very serious again and resumed eating. When she broke open her fortune cookie, a wide smile lit her face. "Look, Ted,'" she said happily, passing the little slip of paper across to him.

He read it. OLD FRIENDS ARE THE BEST FRIENDS, it said. "Oh, shit," he muttered. He didn't even open his own. Melody wanted to know why. "You ought to read it, Ted," she told him. "It's bad luck if you don't read your fortune cookie."

"I don't want to read it," he said. "I'm going to change out of this suit." He rose. "Don't do anything."

But when he came back, she'd put an album on the stereo. At least she hadn't sold that, he thought gratefully.

"Do you want me to dance for you?" she asked. "Remember how I used to dance for you and Michael? Real sexy. . . . You used to tell me how good I danced. I could of been a dancer if I'd wanted." She did a few dance steps in the middle of his living room, stumbled, and almost fell. It was grotesque.

"Sit down, Melody," Ted said, as sternly as he could manage. "We have to talk."

She sat down.

"Don't cry," he said before he started. "You understand that? I don't want you to cry. We can't talk if you're going to cry every time I say anything. You start crying and this conversation is over."

Melody nodded. "I won't cry, Ted," she said. "I feel much better now than this morning. I'm with you now. You make me feel better."

"You're *not* with me, Melody. Stop that."

Her eyes filled up with tears. "You're my friend, Ted. You and Michael and Anne, you're the special ones."

He sighed. "What's wrong, Melody? Why are you here?"

"I lost my job, Ted," she said.

"The waitress job?" he asked. The last time he'd seen her, three years ago, she'd been waiting tables in a bar in Kansas City.

Melody blinked at him, confused. "Waitress?" she said. "No, Ted. That was before. That was in Kansas City. Don't you remember?"

"I remember very well," he said. "What job was it you lost?"

"It was a shitty job," Melody said. "A factory job. It was in Iowa. In Des Moines. Des Moines is a shitty place. I didn't come to work, so they fired me. I was strung out, you know? I needed a couple days off. I would have come back to work. But they fired me." She looked close to tears again. "I haven't had a good job in a long time, Ted. I was an art major. You remember? You and Michael and Anne used to have my drawings hung up in your rooms. You still have my drawings, Ted?"

"Yes," he lied. "Sure. Somewhere." He'd gotten rid of them years ago. They reminded him too much of Melody, and that was too painful.

"Anyway, when I lost my job, Johnny said I wasn't bringing in any money. Johnny was the guy I lived with. He said he wasn't gonna support me, that I had to get some job, but I couldn't. I *tried*, Ted, but I couldn't. So Johnny talked to some man, and he got me this job in a massage parlor, you know. And he took me down there, but it was crummy. I didn't want to work in no massage parlor, Ted. I used to be an art major."

"I remember, Melody," Ted said. She seemed to expect him to say something.

Melody nodded. "So I didn't take it, and Johnny threw me out. I had no place to go, you know. And I thought of you, and Anne, and Michael. Remember the last night? We all said that if anyone ever needed help . . ."

"I remember, Melody," Ted said. "Not as often as you do, but I remember. You don't ever let any of us forget it, do you? But let it pass. What do you want this time?" His tone was flat and cold.

"You're a lawyer, Ted," she said.

"Yes."

"So, I thought—" Her long, thin fingers plucked nervously at her face. "I thought maybe you could get me a job. I could be a secretary, maybe. In your office. We could be together again, every day, like it used to be. Or maybe—" She brightened visibly. "—maybe I could be one of those people who draw pictures in the courtroom. You know. Like of Patty Hearst and people like that. On TV. I'd be good at that."

"Those artists work for the TV stations," Ted said patiently. "And there are no openings in my office. I'm sorry, Melody. I can't get you a job."

Melody took that surprisingly well. "All right, Ted," she said. "I can find a job, I guess. I'll get one all by myself. Only—only let me live here, okay? We can be roommates again."

"Oh, Jesus," Ted said. He sat back and crossed his arms. "No," he said flatly.

Melody took her hand away from her face and stared at him imploringly. "Please, Ted," she whispered. "Please."

"No," he said. The word hung there, chill and final.

"You're my *friend*, Ted," she said. "You *promised*."

"You can stay here a week," he said. "No longer. I have my own life, Melody. I have my own problems. I'm tired of dealing with yours. We all are. You're nothing but problems. In college, you were fun. You're not fun any longer. I've helped you and helped you and helped you. How goddam much do you want out of me?" He was getting angrier as he talked. "Things change, Melody," he said brutally. "People change. You can't hold me forever to some dumb promise I made when I was stoned out of my mind back in college. I'm not responsible for your life. Tough up, dammit. Pull yourself together. I can't do it for you, and I'm sick of all your shit. I don't even like to see you anymore, Melody, you know that?"

She whimpered. "Don't say that, Ted. We're friends. You're special. As long as I have you and Michael and Anne, I'll never be alone, don't you see?"

"You *are* alone," he said. Melody infuriated him.

"No, I'm not," she insisted. "I have my friends, my special friends. They'll help me. You're my *friend*, Ted."

"I used to be your friend," he replied.

She stared at him, her lip trembling, hurt beyond words. For a moment he thought that the dam was going to burst, that Melody was finally about to break down and begin one of her marathon crying jags. Instead, a change came over her face. She paled perceptibly, and her lips drew back slowly, and her expression settled into a terrible mask of anger. She was hideous when she was angry. "You bastard," she said.

Ted had been this route too. He got up from the couch and walked to his bar. "Don't start," he said, pouring himself a glass of Chivas Regal on the rocks. "The first thing you throw, you're out on your ass. Got that, Melody?"

"You scum," she repeated. "You were never my friend. None of you were. You lied to me, made me trust you, used me. Now you're all so high and mighty and I'm nothing, and you don't want to know me. You don't want to help me. You never wanted to help me."

"I did help you," Ted pointed out. "Several times. You owe me something close to two thousand dollars, I believe."

"Money," she said. "That's all you care about, you bastard."

Ted sipped at his scotch and frowned at her. "Go to hell," he said.

"I could, for all you care." Her face had gone white. "I cabled you, two years ago. I cabled all three of you. I needed you, you promised that you'd come if I needed you, that you'd be there, you promised that and you made love to me and you were my friend, but I cabled you and you didn't come, you bastard, you didn't come, none of you came, none of you came." She was screaming.

Ted had forgotten about the telegram. But it came back to him in a rush. He'd read it over several times, and finally he'd picked up the phone and called Michael. Michael hadn't been in. So he'd reread the telegram one last time, then crumpled it up and flushed it down the toilet. One of the others could go to her this time, he remembered thinking. He had a big case, the Argrath Corporation patent suit, and he couldn't risk leaving it. But it had been a desperate telegram, and he'd been guilty about it for weeks, until he finally managed to put the whole thing out of his mind. "I was busy," he said, his tone half-angry and half-defensive. "I had more important things to do than come hold your hand through another crisis."

"It was *horrible*," Melody screamed. "I needed you and you left me all *alone*. I almost *killed* myself."

"But you didn't, did you?"

"I could have," she said, "I could have killed myself, and you wouldn't even of cared."

Threatening suicide was one of Melody's favorite tricks. Ted had been through it a hundred times before. This time he decided not to take it. "You could have killed yourself," he said calmly, "and we probably wouldn't have cared. I think you're right about that. You would have rotted for weeks before anyone found you, and we probably wouldn't even have heard about it for half a year. And when I did hear, finally, I guess it would have made me sad for an hour or two, remembering how things had been, but then I would have gotten drunk or phoned up my girlfriend or something, and pretty soon I'd have been out of it. And then I could have forgotten all about you."

"You would have been sorry," Melody said.

"No," Ted replied. He strolled back to the bar and freshened his drink. "No, you know, I don't think I would have been sorry. Not in the least. Not guilty, either. So you might as well stop threatening to kill yourself, Melody, because it isn't going to work."

The anger drained out of her face, and she gave a little whimper. "Please, Ted," she said. "Don't say such things. Tell me you'd care. Tell me you'd remember me."

He scowled at her. "No," he said. It was harder when she was piti-ful, when she shrunk up all small and vulnerable and whimpered instead of accusing him. But he had to end it once and for all, get rid of this curse on his life.

"I'll go away tomorrow," she said meekly. "I won't bother you. But tell me you care, Ted. That you're my friend. That you'll come to me. If I need you."

"I won't come to you, Melody," he said. "That's over. And I don't want you coming here anymore, or phoning, or sending telegrams, no matter what kind of trouble you're in. You understand? Do you? I want you out of my life, and when you're gone I'm going to forget you as quick as I can, 'cause lady, you are one hell of a bad memory."

Melody cried out as if he had struck her. *"No!"* she said. "No, don't say that, remember me, you *have* to. I'll leave you alone, I promise I will, I'll never see you again. But say you'll remember me." She stood up abruptly. "I'll go right now," she said. "If you want me to, I'll go. But make love to me first, Ted. Please. I want to give you something to remember me by." She smiled a lascivious little smile and began to struggle out of her halter top, and Ted felt sick.

He set down his glass with a bang. "You're crazy," he said. "You ought to get professional help, Melody. But I can't give it to you, and I'm not going to put up with this anymore. I'm going out for a walk. I'll be gone a couple of hours. You be gone when I get back."

Ted started for the door. Melody stood looking at him, her halter in her hand. Her breasts looked small and shrunken, and the left one had a tattoo on it that he'd never noticed before. There was nothing even vaguely desirable about her. She whimpered. "I just wanted to give you something to remember me by," she said.

Ted slammed the door.

It was midnight when he returned, drunk and surly, resolved that if Melody was still there, he would call the police and that would be the end of that. Jack was behind the desk, having just gone on duty. Ted stopped and gave him hell for having admitted Melody that morning, but the doorman denied it vehemently. "Wasn't nobody got in, Mr. Cirelli. I don't let in anyone without buzzing up, you ought to know that. I been here six years, and I never let in nobody without buzzing up." Ted reminded him forcefully about the Jehovah's Witness, and they ended up in a shouting match.

Finally Ted stormed away and took the elevator up to the thirty-second floor.

There was a drawing taped to his door.

He blinked at it furiously for a moment, then snatched it down. It was a cartoon, a caricature of Melody. Not the Melody he'd seen today, but the Melody he'd known in college: sharp, funny, pretty. When they'd been roommates, Melody had always illustrated her notes with little cartoons of herself. He was surprised that she could still draw this well. Beneath the face, she'd printed a message.

I LEFT YOU SOMETHING TO REMEMBER ME BY.

Ted scowled down at the cartoon, wondering whether he should keep it or not. His own hesitation made him angry. He crumpled the paper in his hand and fumbled for his keys. At least she's gone, he thought, and maybe for good. If she left the note, it meant that she'd gone. He was rid of her for another couple of years at least.

He went inside, tossed the crumpled ball of paper across the room towards a wastebasket, and smiled when it went in. "Two points," he said loudly to himself, drunk and self-satisfied. He went to the bar and began to mix himself a drink.

But something was wrong.

Ted stopped stirring his drink and listened. The water was running, he realized. She'd left the water running in the bathroom.

"Christ," he said, and then an awful thought hit him: maybe she hadn't gone after all. Maybe she was still in the bathroom, taking a shower or something, freaked out of her mind, crying, whatever. "*Melody!*" he shouted.

No answer. The water was running, all right. It couldn't be anything else. But she didn't answer.

"Melody, are you still here?" he yelled. "Answer, dammit!"

Silence.

He put down his drink and walked to the bathroom. The door was closed. Ted stood outside. The water was definitely running. "Melody," he said loudly, "are you in there? Melody?"

Nothing. Ted was beginning to be afraid.

He reached out and grasped the doorknob. It turned easily in his hand. The door hadn't been locked.

Inside, the bathroom was filled with steam. He could hardly see, but he made out that the shower curtain was drawn. The shower was running full blast, and judging from the amount of steam, it must be scalding. Ted stepped back and waited for the steam to dissipate. "Melody?" he said softly. There was no reply.

"Shit," he said. He tried not to be afraid. She only talked about it, he told himself; she'd never really do it. The ones who talk about it never do it, he'd read that somewhere. She was just doing this to frighten him.

He took two quick strides across the room and yanked back the shower curtain.

She was there, wreathed in steam, water streaming down her naked body. She wasn't stretched out in the tub at all; she was sitting up, crammed in sideways near the faucets, looking very small and pathetic. Her position seemed half-fetal. The needle spray had been directed down at her, at her hands. She'd opened her wrists with his razor blades and tried to hold them under the water, but it hadn't been enough; she'd slit the veins crosswise, and everybody knew the only way to do it was lengthwise. So she'd used the razor elsewhere, and now she had two mouths, and both of them were smiling at him, smiling. The shower had washed away most of the blood; there were no stains anywhere, but the second mouth below her chin was still red and dripping. Trickles oozed down her chest, over the flower tattooed on her breast, and the spray of the shower caught them and washed them away. Her hair hung down over her cheeks, limp and wet. She was smiling. She looked so happy. The steam was all around her. She'd been in there for hours, he thought. She was very clean.

Ted closed his eyes. It didn't make any difference. He still saw her. He would always see her.

He opened them again; Melody was still smiling. He reached across her and turned off the shower, getting the sleeve of his shirt soaked in the process.

Numb, he fled back into the living room. God, he thought, God. I have to call someone, I have to report this, I can't deal with this. He decided to call the police. He lifted the phone, and hesitated with his finger poised over the buttons. The police won't help, he thought. He punched for Jill.

When he had finished telling her, it grew very silent on the other end of the phone. "My God," she said at last, "how awful. Can I do anything?"

"Come over," he said. "Right away." He found the drink he'd set down, took a hurried sip from it.

Jill hesitated. "Er—look, Ted, I'm not very good at dealing with corpses. Why don't you come over here? I don't want to—well, you know. I don't think I'll ever shower at your place again."

"Jill," he said, stricken. "I need someone right now." He laughed a frightened, uncertain laugh.

"Come over here," she urged.

"I can't just *leave* it there," he said.

"Well, don't," she said. "Call the police. They'll take it away. Come over afterwards."

Ted called the police.

"If this is your idea of a joke, it isn't funny," the patrolman said. His partner was scowling.

"Joke?" Ted said.

"There's nothing in your shower," the patrolman said. "I ought to take you down to the station house."

"Nothing in the shower?" Ted repeated, incredulous.

"Leave him alone, Sam," the partner said. "He's stinko, can't you tell?"

Ted rushed past them both into the bathroom.

The tub was empty. Empty. He knelt and felt the bottom of it. Dry. Perfectly dry. But his shirt sleeve was still damp. "No," he said. "No." He rushed back out to the living room. The two cops watched him with amusement. Her suitcase was gone from its place by the door. The dishes had all been run through the dishwasher—no way to tell if anyone had made pancakes or not. Ted turned the wastebasket upside down, spilling out the contents all over his couch. He began to scrabble through the papers.

"Go to bed and sleep it off, mister," the older cop said. "You'll feel better in the morning."

"C'mon," his partner said. They departed, leaving Ted still pawing through the papers. No cartoon. No cartoon. No cartoon.

Ted flung the empty wastebasket across the room. It caromed off the wall with a ringing metallic clang.

He took a cab to Jill's.


It was near dawn when he sat up in bed suddenly, his heart thumping, his mouth dry with fear.

Jill murmured sleepily. "Jill," he said, shaking her.

She blinked up at him. "What?" she said. "What time is it, Ted? What's wrong?" She sat up, pulling up the blanket to cover herself.

"Don't you hear it?"

"Hear what?" she asked.

He giggled. "Your shower is running."

That morning he shaved in the kitchen, even though there was no mirror. He cut himself twice. His bladder ached, but he would not go past the bathroom door, despite Jill's repeated assurances that the shower was not running. Dammit, he could *hear* it. He waited until he got to the office. There was no shower in the washroom there.

But Jill looked at him strangely.


At the office, Ted cleared off his desk, and tried to think. He was a lawyer. He had a good analytical mind. He tried to reason it out. He drank only coffee, lots of coffee.

No suitcase, he thought. Jack hadn't seen her. No corpse. No cartoon. No one had seen her. The shower was dry. No dishes. He'd been drinking. But not all day, only later, after dinner. Couldn't be the drinking. Couldn't be. No cartoon. He was the only one who'd seen her. No cartoon. I LEFT YOU SOMETHING TO REMEMBER ME BY. He'd crumpled up her cable and flushed her away. Two years ago. Nothing in the shower.

He picked up his phone. "Billie," he said, "get me a newspaper in Des Moines, Iowa. Any newspaper, I don't care."

When he finally got through, the woman who tended the morgue was reluctant to give him any information. But she softened when he told her he was a lawyer and needed the information for an important case.

The obituary was very short. Melody was identified only as a "massage parlor employee." She'd killed herself in her shower.

"Thank you," Ted said. He set down the receiver. For a long time he sat staring out of his window. He had a very good view; he could see the lake and the soaring tower of the Standard Oil building. He pondered what to do next. There was a thick knot of fear in his gut.

He could take the day off and go home. But the shower would be running at home, and sooner or later he would have to go in there.

He could go back to Jill's. If Jill would have him. She'd seemed awfully cool after last night. She'd recommended a shrink to him as they shared a cab to the office. She didn't understand. No one would understand . . . unless . . . He picked up the phone again, searching through his circular file. There was no card, no number; they'd drifted that far apart. He buzzed for Billie again. "Get me through to Random House in New York City," he said. "To Mr. Michael Englehart. He's an editor there."

But when he was finally connected, the voice on the other end of the line was strange and distant. "Mr. Cirelli? Were you a friend of Michael's? Or one of his authors?"

Ted's mouth was dry. "A friend," he said. "Isn't Michael in? I need to talk to him. It's . . . urgent."

"I'm afraid Michael's no longer with us," the voice said. "He had a nervous breakdown, less than a week ago."

"Is he . . . ?"

"He's alive. They took him to a hospital, I believe. Maybe I can find you the number."

"No," Ted said, "no, that's quite all right." He hung up.

Phoenix directory assistance has no listing for Anne Kaye. Of course not, he thought. She was married now. He tried to remember her married name. It took him a long time. Something Polish, he thought. Finally it came to him.

He hadn't expected to find her at home. It was a school day, after all. But someone picked up the phone on the third ring. "Hello," he said. "Anne, is that you? This is Ted, in Chicago. Anne, I've got to talk to you. It's about Melody. Anne, I need help." He was breathless.

There was a giggle. "Anne isn't here right now, Ted," Melody said. "She's off at school, and then she's got to visit her husband. They're separated, you know. But she promised to come back by eight."

"Melody," he said.

"Of course, I don't know if I can believe her. You three were never very good about promises. But maybe she'll come back, Ted. I hope so.

"I want to leave her something to remember me by."

# ELLEN KUSHNER

## "The Unicorn Masque"

*Ellen Kushner (1955- ) broke into the fantasy field as editor of the* anthology Basilisk *in 1980. Four years later, she garnered critical acclaim for her first novel,* Swordspoint. *Her second novel,* Thomas the Rhymer, *won the World Fantasy Award for best novel of 1991. A Celtic fantasy derived from the traditional Scottish ballad of "True Thomas," it employs the structure of myth to elaborate a theme that dominates her work, the relationship of art to life. She collaborated with artist Richard W. Burhans on the evocative picture book* St. Nicholas and the Valley Beyond. *Her short fiction has appeared in several anthologies.*

# The Unicorn Masque

*by Ellen Kushner*

## I.

At the age of thirty-two, the queen was a dried rose. Although in her day she had numbered among the most valuable princesses on the marriage market, she had also been the most educated and the least beautiful. Contract after contract was dissolved before it could be consummated. Her younger sisters were married away to foreign powers, while she stayed at home to see her brother ascend the throne on their father's death, and descend it off the back of a rearing horse. The first five years of her reign had been marked by academic policies in council and dionysian splendors at court. It was in the dances, the gallant offerings of verse and song, that she found the attention and admiration denied her as a princess by all the marriage tokens courtesy had demanded be returned: the betrothal rings taken from her young hands, the portraits of foreign princes packed away.

After five years, though, the queen had begun to reconsider her state. Might the brilliant, posing revelry she delighted in be, not splendor, but merest frivolity? Frivolity lead to weakness—indeed, the mirror of history held it up as an early symptom of decay. It was true that she was surrounded by able counselors, but their wisdom would not live forever. She suddenly saw that she had been wrong to rush headlong into pleasure, leading the whole court with her as it was prone to do. So she curtailed the late-night revels that she might rise each morning at dawn to complete nine lines of translation before breakfast. Her constant entourage of beautiful, perfumed young men gave way to the ancient learned.

The court was amazed to find its favorite pastimes prohibited, its chiefest virtues in disgrace overnight. Its senior members took it in stride; they had lived through the rapid succession of three very different monarchs, and knew how to adapt. The country kept running much as before; only the fashions of whom to have to dinner changed: musicians were out, scholars were in. Soon books were replacing trinkets in the soft jeweled hands of courtiers. When the queen put off the gaudy gowns that had always outshone her, her faithful court apparelled itself with like sobriety. On this summer's royal progress through the north counties, though, the atmosphere relaxed as many of the younger set succumbed to bright and fanciful dress once more: time enough for drabness, they said, when school was called again in the fall.

Now the queen sat in her blue silk pavilion, shielded from the rays of the summer sun by three billowing walls weighted with her arms embroidered in gold. The fourth side was looped back, open to what breezes stirred the air. It was the queen's pleasure to keep this August's court on the broad summer lawns of her great lords' houses; there her retinue of nobles disported themselves at country pastimes while she assessed her lands and displayed her traditional right to beggar whom she chose in entertaining her. Despite her recent strictures, she continued to permit her liege lords to pay lavish tribute; they called her Divine Virgin, the Queen of Field and Grove, and presented musical masques, harvest fruits and their well-groomed children to her. It was one of these she awaited now: childless Lord Andreas' chosen heir, a youth reared abroad and newly come home to his guardian's estates. He was bound to be green; she only hoped he would not stammer, or trip.

They knew that he would not. There was less of chance involved than anyone could imagine in the young gentleman about to be presented to Her Grace. His noble patron put a final fret in the sober white frills around his neck, and stepped back for a look at their creation.

"Perfect," he wheezed, staring frankly at the poised and slender figure gilded like a confection by the shaft of sun coming through the mullion panes of the manor house.

The young man returned the look with a smile intended to make the marrow of any one's bones run quicksilver, and said, "Your servant, sir." If not the smile, then surely the voice; perfect, perfect, infinitely precious with the sense that either could be shattered with the proper blow—if one were wise enough to see past the sterling perfection, and fool enough to want to destroy it.

"It is time," said the tall lean man who had always been there, standing in his dark robes amongst the shadows by the window. "He doesn't need to be fussed over, I've promised you that. And you've had all summer to admire him; now let be."

"Yes," breathed the fleshy lord, squeezing his fat, ringed fingers together in such sinister anticipation that the fair young man threw back his head and laughed. The tall man's eyes slid to his employer's, meeting unquenchable satisfaction there. This arrogance suited him: nothing had been left to chance.

He walked across the green lawns past the clusters of nobles knowing all eyes were on him. The silk of the pavilion fluttered fitfully in the hot summer air. Inside it the Queen sat riffling in the hot summer air. Inside it the Queen sat riffling the pages of a book, formally oblivious to his approach until the bodyguard's pikes clashed together and apart to let the young man enter and kneel at her feet.

She was stunned at first by the blistering aureole over his bent head; then she realized that her eyes were only dazzled by the sun coming in the open tent-way, illuminating hair as light as mirrors.

He waited, head bowed before her, observing the court ways they had taught him with all their ancient formality, until he heard the queen say, "You are welcome." Then he raised his face to her.

The silk shaded her in a bath of color pure as cerulean moonlight. Slowly his eyes adjusted to distinguish her features. Her nose was sharp, her unpainted mouth small and pursed, like her father the king's. Narrow eyes of watery blue surveyed him under heavy half-moon lids. The jeweled clasps pinning her straight colorless hair flat on either side of her head only accentuated the harshness of her face. The only softness was in her cheeks, surprisingly full and round, and in the weakness of her chin. Against the sober, extravagant blue of her skirt, her pale hands, weighted with rings, restlessly toyed with a small book on her lap. Amber leather, stamped in gold. Quickly his eyes returned to his sovereign's face.

The queen caught her breath, then gave a small cough to cover it. She extended her hand for him to take; his limber fingers were smooth, with bones so fine she felt they might be hollow, like a bird's. The sculpted ridges of his lips touched the back of her hand, and then his eyes were again full on her.

"Sir, you are welcome," she said again; "I pray you rise and be seated."

He was modestly dressed in sober black, with white linen shirt ruffles crisp at wrist and throat. She watched him seat himself on a low stool across from her; his movements were lithe, his body as slender and tempered as wire.

He bore the queen's scrutiny calmly, with pride. He understood her expression, the cool reserve sheltering almost awed approval; understood and sympathized. He was flawless. Lord Pudge-Rings and his lean friend would have nothing but praise for him tonight.

"I am told," she said with pedantic formality, "that you spent many years abroad."

"Too many, madam, to please me." He smiled easily at her.

"You wished, then, to return?"

"Lady, it has been my dearest wish." Her eyes veiled slightly with reservation: she had a court full of men to spin her compliments. "Of course—" he laughed, his eyes dropping ruefully to his clasped hands—"one's dearest wish is always to go against one's elders, isn't it? They kept telling me how good it was for me to live abroad, so naturally I hated it." She nodded, thinking of all the hardships of duty. "My delicate health, they said, forbade travel, and my youth required stability." She could see them both, youth and recent illness, still in his face: the fine, girlish skin stretched over high-bred bones that had not yet hardened into maturity. "So I studied." He looked at her intently with eyes so blue that for a moment they were all she saw in the pale sculptured face that held them like jewels in a setting. "I resolved to do as much as I could with whatever they gave me, so that—" He stopped abruptly, eyes downcast, his skin colored a delicate rose. "Forgive me, Majesty. It cannot be of interest to Your Grace what—"

"Study, sir," she said softly, "is always of greatest interest to me. Pray go on."

"I read, then," he said, equally softly. "And played the lute. When they told me it might not be healthy for me to be so much indoors, I took up riding, and the bow, and spent hours at sword practice." He shifted in his seat, an unconsciously graceful movement. If he could move that way with a foil in his hands, he must be good.

"Do you plan to continue your studies now?"

"If I can get the books here. I have been through my lord's library, it is woefully out of date. . . ."

She noticed his eyes fixed hungrily on her lap and started, clutching the forgotten volume as she did so. The queen smiled to realize what he had been staring at, and held up the leather-bound book for him to see. "You must look at this, then: my own presentation copy of Dunn's new work on the movement of the heavens. It is only just printed, few others will have it." She patted her skirt. "Come, sit beside me and we shall read it." He rose and settled again, like a dancer, at her feet. All she could see of him now was the light sweep of hair, the dent of a smile partly obscured by the arc of his cheek. "They are all coming to the city now," she said eagerly: "the men of science, the philosophers . . . I plan to lower the taxes on printing . . . Ah, the country is all very well for quiet and study, but you must come to my city for the books and the minds . . . Now, then; here is the Preface."

He fixed his eyes on the page, printed with great carved capitals and wood-cut illustrations, and tried not to stray to the marginalia of her rounded fingertips and chewed-looking thumb . . . He knew nothing about Dunn, or books on the heavens. He must study now to seem informed, and to remember it perfectly. He must be perfect. There was still so much to be learned.

Candlelight glowed late into the night in one room of Lord Andreas' manor. The queen's "simple country supper," with its eight simultaneous courses, five wines and attending jugglers and minstrels, had been cleared away hours ago from the great hall, and the court had gone to its well-deserved rest in the various chambers appointed. Only in this small room were tapers lit, their flames polishing the wood-paneled walls to an amber gloss. Despite the warmth of the night heavy curtains were drawn across the windows. It was unlikely that anyone would come wandering down this far corridor and see the light under the door.

The lord of the manor and his lean confederate sat at a round, taper-studded table as the delicate blond man rehearsed to them the story of his day. He struck pose after pose without being aware of it, concluding with one arm outstretched, each finger precisely curled as though to allure his audience; "And so tomorrow I bid you a sweet farewell, and join the royal progress on its way back to court!"

A poised stillness followed. It was broken by the rhythmic thud of flesh against flesh: the fat man was clapping. When echoes began to fill the room, he stopped.

"Excellent," he said. "She'll take you."

"Oh, yes." The melodious voice almost crowed its well-bred triumph. "We are not to be parted, Her Grace and I."

"Perfect!" the lord wheezed. Infected by his enthusiasm, the young man flourished a royal obeisance. "My humble duty to your lordship. And now, pardon me, gentlemen." The bow extended itself to the black-robed one. "I fear I must retire; the court rides out early tomorrow."

But the fat lord's hand snaked out before he could turn away. Fleshy, surprisingly strong fingers gripped his chin. "No. We do not pardon you."

He knew better than to flinch. He forced himself to meet the glinting, tiny eyes and say politely, "How may I serve your lordship?"

The hand tightened on his jaw. He could smell the remnants of dinner on the man's breath. "You will obey me," Lord Andreas said. "You do not leave until I dismiss you."

"Of course, sir." He made sure the light, willing smile touched his eyes as well as his mouth. But the strong fingers flung his face aside.

"Don't try your tricks on me!" his patron growled. He raised his velvet-clad arm again. The young man spun away from the blow, his hand automatically reaching for a dagger at his hip.

"You are unarmed," the tall man observed placidly from his seat at the table. "Excellent reflexes." He continued amicably, overriding the threat of violence as though he had not seen it, "I was admiring the bow you just made. Would you mind telling me where you learned it?"

The young man lowered his empty hands. A test, he thought; it had only been another test. Lord Andreas, silent now, had subsided into a chair. He steadied his breathing, and prepared the familiar answer. "Abroad, sir, I had tutors—"

"No." The lines of the man's lean face shifted to condescending mockery. "You learned it here, remember?"

"Don't tell me," the fat lord chimed in with interest, "that you're beginning to believe your own stories?"

He held his temper tightly in his clenched hands, letting its heat keep him from the chill of fear. "Forgive me," he said with icy good manners. "I didn't know—"

Their laughter pierced him, striking like hammer-blows inside his head.

"No," the lean man said. "Of course you didn't. You don't really believe all those stories you told the queen?"

"Of course not," he snapped. "I know what's real and what isn't."

"Of course you do." The man's long hand reached out to a taper set on the table near him. For a moment his fingers hovered over the flame as if about to bestow a benediction; then he pinched out the candleflame between two bony fingertips. "So do I." Smoke trailed up from the black wick, dissolving into darkness. "Who are you—really?"

He felt the world lunge away from him in a belly-wrench of blackness—he flung his hands forward, and caught the smooth wood of the table's edge.

"Oh, dear lord!" Lord Andreas' voice echoed in his head. "He's not going to faint, is he?"

"No, of course not." The man stood up, his black robes falling about him in folds of deeper blackness. The young man shrank from his approach. He did not want to be touched by anyone; he wanted only to be alone in perfect darkness, curled in upon himself like a seashell . . . But the other man was only holding out a chair to him. Mutely he sank into it.

"He's exhausted," the man said over his head to Andreas. "He wants to be alone."

"He'll be alone soon enough," Lord Andreas said. "Let him be quiet for once, and listen to me." He heaved his bulk up from the table, and stood before the younger man. "Give me your hand," Andreas told him. He held his right hand up and watched it tremble. "No," said his patron; "the other one." His left hand bore a gold signet ring. It seemed to sink into the flesh of Andreas' fingers as they handled it. The nobleman smiled grimly. "I had this made for you, the day you were born. Do you remember?"

He had to lick his lips before he could answer. "Yes."

"It is yours, and yours alone. Remember. Now," Lord Andreas said, settling back against the table. He kept the young man's hand in his. "I am going to give you the advice any patron would give his ward upon his departure for the royal court. But in your case, it is not mere words—it must be followed to the letter. Do you hear me?" He nodded. "First of all, you are not to touch wine or spirits on any account. It will be noted, but you ought to be enough of a practiced liar by now to be able to make up excuses to fit any occasion. You may gamble with dice or cards all you like—I don't care how much money your run through, but I expect you will win more than you lose. Dress well, but not above your station: you're not to compete with the great lords' sons. They will be impressed with your swordsmanship—they ought to be!" his patron snorted. "You're better than all of them. If one of them should pick a quarrel for the pleasure of dueling with you, for god's sake don't kill him. If you should be wounded, you know you don't have to worry; just keep it covered until people forget so they don't miss the scar." Andreas ran his thumb over the smooth skin of the narrow wrist, which last week had been torn by steel. "I think that's all . . . Oh, yes—the usual warning, lest the ward's head be turned to ingratitude by the vices and splendors of the court: *We made you, and we can unmake you.*" The heavy fingers met sharply around the young man's hand. "Only in this case, my dear, it is not an empty threat."

He pulled together his returning strength to smile coolly up at the nobleman. "A threat indeed. I don't even know how you made me; what precisely should I fear in being unmade? I'm a better swordsman than any of you could set against me, and soon I shall have the favor of the crown. If you d—"

The thin man interrupted the exchange with a mournful sigh. "Bravado," he said. "You must have your little gestures. Appropriate, but scarcely wise." He touched the candlewick with his bare finger, and the flame leapt again into being, illuminating the harsh face from below.

The room was still, even the candle flames rose without a flicker into the hot, dark air. The young man tasted sweat on his upper lip, but did not move to wipe it away. "Ask me," the lean man said. "Ask me again."

The silver-blue eyes fixed helpless on their creator. "Who am I?"

"Yes . . ." Lord Andreas hissed in triumph, unable to restrain himself from joining in. "Who are you? Where did you come from? How did you gain all that expertise—with the sword, the lute, your own smooth muscles? You have no memory of any life but this—you might not even be human." The fair head jerked upward, and Andreas laughed. "Does that worry you. Does it, my dear?"

The thin man's eyes burned like pale agates. "You must be one of those people who never remember their dreams. But that doesn't mean you never had them. Dream again, my lovely; dream again before you question the gift I gave you. . . ."

The younger man wanted to profess his dislike of riddles, and his distrust of dreams. But the tall one rose, and his shadow rose with him, long and black climbing the wall, along with the candle-flame that became all he could see, a pillar of light. Out of it five fingers stretched, long and cool and dark, and touched his eyes, and he dreamed again—the old dream:

He was a woman, alone in a bare room weeping. It lasted only a moment, not enough time to know his name or face, or the cause of the tears; only the misery of being trapped by her own wishes, the four walls no refuge from what lay outside them when she herself was the room and the walls and the kernel of weakness and misery that refused to stop dreaming—

His hands were hot with tears. He opened his eyes to a world of indecipherable light; blinked, and sorted out the nimbus of each separate candle, and the white slashes of the two men's faces.

"It's all right now," the lean man said with alarming tenderness.

His eyes fell to his own hands, clasped on his lap. The gold ring on his forefinger glowed in a setting of tears like crystal. He turned his hand to see the light strike fire first from the tiny silver moon on one side, then from the ruby that was the sun. . . . In the center between them an etched figure danced, alone, one arm flung up toward the sun.

"Lazarus Merridon." He looked up, not sure which of them had addressed him. "Lazarus the Beggar," said the lean man. "Lazarus the New-Risen. A bit of local mythology. *Sol Meridionale:* brought forth at noon. If you're ever knighted you can use it as your motto."

"You see," said the nobleman; "you cannot fail us."

Lazarus rose to his feet, an elegant figure made all the more exquisite by the lineaments of exhaustion. Despite it all his voice was still bell-toned and honey-sweet. "And when I come to court," he asked, "what am I to do, besides gain a knighthood?"

"Anything you please, my dear," they said. "You cannot fail us."

## II.

Against all previous expectation, the court's return to its seat in the capital that autumn was anything but dull. Little piles of silver were already passing from hand to jeweled hand, honoring strong speculation on the queen's newest study partner. No one could get quite near enough the strange beauty to discover the definite end of his charms; all that could be ascertained was that he did seem to understand whatever it was she was studying. He also proved to be a fine musician and an admirable dancer; and that was really what saved them all in the end from what had hitherto promised to be the most tedious winter in living memory—periods of mourning excepted, of course.

It was the autumn hunt that had suggested it to him, or possibly a bit of exotica from one of her books: after all, she couldn't possibly disapprove of a masque based on a classical theme, and the Hunt of the Unicorn was the subject of innumerable pages of commentary. Odds were ridiculously high that the masque would be approved even before he had played her any of the exquisite music he had composed, since the central role of the captivating Virgin could only be enacted by the court's own Sovereign Lady (*and only virgin*, the snigger went). No one even bothered to wager on who would be Unicorn, and so they lost an interesting gamble, for the composer demurred, and the role went to the young Earl Dumaine—a pretty enough dancer, but everyone knew she had tired of him last year.

On the night of the masque the great hall shone with a forest. Its pillars were wreathed in living greens, while flowery carpets hid the floor. The Master of Revels had outdone himself in fantastical trees of paper, canvas, wood, satin . . . he had wanted live birds, but it was suggested that they might interfere with the music, and possibly the dancers, so he had to make do with elaborate arrays of feathers, with little jeweled eyes peeping out between the leaves.

The sides of the room were thick with courtiers who were not in the performance. Rehearsals had been going on for weeks behind closed doors; except for the subject matter, occasional public bickerings that broke out over costumes and precedence, and the stray tune that would at times escape someone's lips, no one else knew anything about the contents of the masque. They waited in eager anticipation, admiring the decor. The musicians, splendidly decked out in silver and green, were already seated on a dais trimmed with ribbons and boughs. Among them was Lazarus Merridon, holding the lute he would play. His cool eyes swept the audience; then he nodded to the sackbut player, and the notes of an ornamented hunting-call sounded through the hall. Immediately the watching courtiers stopped their gossip-ridden fidgeting to fix their eyes on the center of the room.

First came the dance of the Lovers, then the dance of the Hunters. Then the queen stepped forth, robed in virgin white, her pale hair streaming loose about her, her light eyes bright with excitement. And the Unicorn pranced out, capered with his ivory horn, earning applause for his spectacular leaps, until he danced his way to the seated maiden and, on a burst of cymbals, laid his glowing horn in her lap. . . . Wildly enthused, the hunter-lords broke into unprogrammed shouting as they burst from the undergrowth to slay the unfortunate Earl, whose new silk doublet was actually slashed by a few of the spears. At the center of their dance of death sat the queen with hair unbound, her face flushed, her eyes glittering.

All the nimble of the court found themselves whirling and jumping to the final wild music of victory. The hall was streaked with spinning velvet, silk and satin, the sharp glints of blue, red, green, rainbow jewels flashing from hair and breast, belt and hat and dagger. . . .

Above them, on the musicians' dais, Lazarus Merridon sat playing the lute, and smiled. In his mind, weaving in and out through the wild and measured rhythms of strings and brass and timpani, sounded the voice of the nameless man: *It's all right now.*

Lord Thomas Berowne would have been one of the masquers, being the younger son of a duke and owning an admirable pair of legs himself; but he had only just returned from a foreign embassage on the day of the performance. In the course of the afternoon, however, he had acquired all the gossip to be had about its originator, and he watched the lutenist carefully that night. Lord Thomas had only a rudimentary, nobleman's knowledge of music, but he knew a great deal about courts; thus he was not surprised at the news that followed the next afternoon. Being an extremely well-liked young man, and well-connected, he got it before most others, and managed to be the first to seek out Lazarus Merridon to congratulate him on his success.

Lazarus Merridon smiled, noting the scatter of costly rings on the young lord's hands. "My lord is too generous, truly. Once the music was written, my part was all idleness, while others did the work."

Lord Thomas laughed, as though he'd made a joke. "Oh, the masque, of course! But your real achievement is the royal summons, you know."

Lazarus blinked. He had only just received the summons himself. God, what a place! "Her Majesty's retiring, yes," he said politely. "I shall be deeply honored to be in attendance tonight."

Lord Thomas smiled at this stiffness with cheerful amusement. "You're used to the ways of courts, I see. Never trust anyone who knows too much about you, or who acts too interested. But your own lines of information must not be very well set up yet: anyone here can tell you I'm harmless. My family's too rich to need to make trouble for anyone." His smile sought the musician's eyes. "But I didn't come to gossip with you about the noble Berownes. I only wanted to pass on a little advice." Lord Thomas took his arm, walking familiarly with him down the gallery. It was an easy, comfortable hold. Lazarus tolerated it as he tolerated everything else the court had dealt him. "You see . . ." the young lord leaned his head of brown curls against the golden one—"I thought someone might as well tell you now. You're quite clearly the next royal favorite, and no one grudges you that—" *Don't you?* Lazarus Merridon thought scornfully. "—but you can't expect it to last, handsome stranger. It never does. You haven't been here long, you haven't seen the rest of them come and go the way some of us have."

*But,* thought the stranger, *have any of you ever seen my like before, Lord Thomas?* A wry smile touched his lips; misinterpreting it Berowne said, "Don't ever consider it. The last one who tried to touch her was sent off to command a troop in the Northern Wars, and hasn't been heard of since." There was a tone to his voice that had been lacking before, a sternness underlying the friendly banter. Lazarus glanced at him, but saw only bland amiableness on the round pleasant face. He suddenly wished for an excuse to leave, to escape the company of this friendly man and his enquiring eyes. "Oh, dear!" Lord Thomas cried in mock distress. "And have I managed to insult you, my silent Master Merridon?"

"Of course not, Lord Thomas."

They stopped before a large diamondpane window. "It would be unforgivably clumsy of me to insult a man I admire," said Berowne. The sun struck red lights off his hair as he stared out into the garden. "I do, you know. Ever since you joined us on Progress—"

"Were you—?" Lazarus began. There'd been so many of them then, each a name and a face and a title.

"Oh, you won't remember me," Thomas smiled easily, turning from the window; "I noticed you, though—there was a quietness about you, an otherness, as though you came from very far away . . . you were raised abroad, weren't you?"

For a moment his repertory of lies froze on his tongue. "Abroad, yes . . ." Then he recovered his aplomb, saying ruefully, "I didn't think it showed so much."

Thomas laughed. "Insulting you again, am I? No, it doesn't show, not now. Not that it matters," he added cheerfully. "If I could play and sing as you do, I wouldn't care if I had two heads and a tail! But I haven't any talent, alas, only lots of expensive clothing. . . ."

Lazarus said, despite himself, "I'm not what—not as good as you think I am."

"Aren't you?" the nobleman asked seriously. "Then I should like to meet your master."

His fair skin gave him away. Thomas saw the flush bleed across the musician's face, and immediately was all contrition, nimbly complimenting him on his fashionably pale complexion and diverting the conversation to his unusual ring.

Lazarus' long slender fingers lay loosely in the other man's soft, well-cared-for ones while Thomas scrutinized the gold signet. "That's fine work. Sun, moon . . . is that a man or a woman there between them?"

"I don't know," he said softly.

"It's nice." Lord Thomas smiled, releasing his hand. "You must come see my new paintings sometime; not now, though; you're about to be attacked by some new admirers." Surely enough, a pair of eager courtiers were making their purposeful way down the gallery. "I daren't stand between you and glory, my dear sir; I might get crushed. Master Merridon, good day—and good luck."

"My Lord." Lazarus bowed briefly, but was interrupted by a hand on his arm. "*Thomas*," the nobleman smiled. "If you think you can bring yourself to say it."

"Good day, Thomas." For an instant Lazarus met his eyes; then Berowne hurried off in the opposite direction as the two courtiers drew near.

He was relieved when evening came and he could withdraw from public attention to dress for the Retiring.

He arrived at the queen's apartments to find her sitting primly in her blue velvet chair, modestly wrapped in quilted satin and attending ladies. At the door he bowed, and again as he was bidden to enter; a third time before he approached, then he knelt to kiss her hand. When he rose, one of her women went back to brushing out her hair. It was long and fine, and clung to the brush like strands of cobweb. "Good evening, Lazarus," said the queen. She ignored the ministrations, smiling up at him with her pale, weak eyes. "Oh, please sit—there, in that chair; we're not so formal here at close of day. It is a time when I like the company of my friends."

He marveled at the thinness of her voice: one of the world's most powerful women, and she seemed as timid and brittle as a green girl. The fingers of one hand toyed with a golden tassel on her robe. Lazarus answered, "I am honored to be counted among them, Madam."

She leaned a little forward to focus her weak eyes on his face. "You *are* my friend. Your sweet voice and gentle music have lent grace to our court, and our studies together have given me great pleasure. Now I am able to give something to you." A small box was placed in her waiting hand. At a gesture from the queen he knelt before her. She lifted from the box a golden jewel glinting with gemstones, dripping with pearls. It was a unicorn, hung on a golden chair that splashed like water when she raised it. "Wear this for me," the queen said gravely, "in token of our friendship." He bent his head, and felt the heavy chain settle on his neck, weighting his shoulders. It was a princely gift.

Impulsively he twisted from his own finger a thin gold band set with a small ruby. "Madam, I have nothing so fine to offer in return. But if friendship will be content with tokens . . ."

The queen only stared at him.

"Have I offended, Madam?"

"No," she stammered; "no. It is a pretty ring. I—thank you." But still she held it in her hand, as though she feared it might break. Gently then he rose, and knelt down at her side, lifting her blue-veined hand to slip his ring onto her forefinger. "There." He smiled up into her face, his eyes deepened to summer—sky blue in the candlelight. "Now I am ever at your Grace's hand."

When she blinked bright drops stood on her short colorless lashes. "Thank you." She swallowed.

A lady murmured something about retiring. "Yes," said the queen, her voice still thin, "it is late."

Lazarus Merridon rose and bowed. "Then good night, Majesty."

"Good night." As he backed from the Presence, she recollected herself. "Oh—Lazarus. You will come tomorrow night, please—and bring your lute."

The court's attentions were, if anything, worse the second day. On the fourth and fifth they slacked off; those who desired to make their interest known to him had done so, and now they waited to see whether he were truly in. He was, and the seventh day brought him no rest at all from the favor-seekers, and, worse yet, people with long-term goals trying to convince him that they were his friends. He sought refuge in his own rooms with orders to his servant to admit no one, and slept, deep muffled sleep with no dreams. Waking, he would sort through and return most of the gifts the courtiers had left, and dress for those dinners he could not avoid without seeming churlish. He dressed soberly, in tribute to his rank and to the queen's current tastes; the only gaudy thing about him was the unicorn jewel, which had been designed for show and not for taste.

He could, of course, do nothing for them but be graceful and witty at their tables, favoring them with what prestige his presence lent. The queen did not summon him to talk of court positions; she spoke of books and music and, recently, of the fears she harbored: of assassination, of her two sisters, married abroad to kings. "They never liked me—but how they would like my throne. . . . My people love me, I know they do: they cheer as I pass by. But my younger sister always was a schemer—she seeks to suborn our loyal subjects to treason, for if I die her son inherits the throne. . . . she has spies, Lazarus. . . ." Then he would play the lute to her, as she lay back on many pillows in the great velvet bed of state, until she fell asleep, and her silent ladies blew the candles out.

He watched sourly for Thomas Berowne to come along with the rest of them, with more of his good advice and his friendly eyes; but the Duke's son was not among them—Too rich to need a favorite's favor, Lazarus told himself. When he encountered Lord Thomas about the palace, the young man only smiled pleasantly at him, and passed on.

The queen was more than usually melancholy, and did not wish to speak, so he sat and played to her while her ladies brushed and braided her hair for the night. She fretted under their care, turning her head so that her colorless hair escaped in cloud-snake wisps and had to be rebrushed, until she shook it out entirely and snapped to the hovering hands, "Be gone! I can attend myself."

The memories of the only other quarrels he had known made Lazarus nervous of this one; he kept his eyes on his fingers, his presence confined to the humming strings of the lute. Her ladies curtsied. They glanced at the gentleman from long, lowered eyes, waiting for him to stop playing and take his leave. He remained oblivious to their looks, though not to the tension they engendered; at last he looked up, only to hear the queen command, "Let him stay." She raised her voice again in the face of their dumb opposition, but the effect was childish, not regal: "Let him stay, I say! He is gentleman of the my court, he will not harm his sovereign. There is a guard outside the door," she added dryly; "I shall scream if I need help."

He slid his conspirator's grin to her amid the flutter of skirts, good-nights and trailing sleeves. When the great door closed on the last of them he said, "Your grace is very tartar tonight."

"I meant to be," she pouted. "Let them learn to obey me. I am their queen."

"And mine," he smiled, taking the hand that bore his ring. "How shall I serve my sovereign tonight?"

She pressed his hand, or gripped it, then released it just as suddenly and rose to walk about the dark and lofty room. Tall tapers threw her shadows long against the walls; they crossed and recrossed each other so that the pacing lady peopled the room with smoky dancers. Lazarus waited for her to speak, but she only moved from object to object, picking things up and putting them down, a hairbrush, a mirror. . . . Her long robe of claret velvet dragged sluggishly after her across the polished floor. He picked some random liquid notes from his instrument, but the queen whirled with a tiny cry. He put the lute down gently, knowing that no matter how awkward he felt, his movements would still express nothing but fluid ease. Watching him seemed to calm her. She came and stood at his side, looking down at the soft-fringed head made golden by candlelight, and said softly, "Lazarus."

He looked up. Her eyes were full of tears. The queen's sad gaze fell to where her small fingers twisted his ring around and around on her left hand. "Will you serve me in all things?"

"In all things, Highness."

She shook her head, lips pressed tight. "Not in duty, please, not now." He put up one hand to stop her nervous twisting of the ring, and was amazed at the fierceness of her grip. He asked. "In friendship, then?"

She nodded, full-eyed, not trusting herself to speak.

"In friendship I will serve you all I can." He took both her hands, and rose to draw her gently toward her chair. "Sit down, now, and tell me what I can do." But with a little cry she broke his grasp and clasped him to her.

Under his chin he smelt the clean smell of her hair. He put his arms around her to ease her trembling, but it didn't seem to help. Her hands were little fists, clenched into the small of his back. He felt a tickle of whispered breath close to his neck: "Please. Don't laugh."

"No, Highness."

She drew back enough to view his face fully. "Oh," the queen said softly. He didn't move. Her shaking fingers came up; their tips brushed his lips, then traced the sculpted ridges carefully so that he smiled, and they ran over the new shape as well. She returned him a dewy smile; then slowly, somberly she raised her face, her weak eyes still wide. When her mouth touched his her body shuddered. He kept his still, although he wanted to smile under her lips' rigidness. His own were soft, pliant . . . she felt them so and slowly let her own relax to meld with them. But when his mouth responded to hers she stiffened, and would have pulled away if he had not stilled it again.

Now her hand traced his jaw, dreamily curled the shell of his ear, parted and smoothed his feather-light hair. One fingertip lightly brushed a delicately-veined eyelid, and arced along the slender wing of brow above it. His eyes were closed. Stiff-fingered she untied his collar to rest her touch on the base of his throat, where the pulse beat against translucent skin between the rising muscles.

The jet buttons of his doublet gave her some trouble; but when he lifted his arms to assist, her fingers froze until they withdrew. She unlaced his outer sheeves, and he felt the cool linen of his shirt hanging loose about his arms.

He was pure white and golden in the candlelight, almost too perfect to be real: gilded ivory, a confection . . . but his chest rose and fell with his breathing, deep and not so regular as it had been, the only sound in the still room. She kissed the soft mouth again, forcing it taut against her lips. She pressed her body to his, and her throat made a sound. "Highness," his quiet voice said into her hair, "shall I?"

Soft skin brushed her cheek as she nodded. Soon she stood with her feet in a pool of crimson velvet, and her white gown floated up over her head . . . He lifted her at last in his strong slender arms, without words marveling at her frailty, at his own infinite knowledge of her desires and his tender exaltation in them. He moved to her will, and his own thoughts made no difference as the unicorn jewel swung through the air, glittering in the candle flames.

Lord Thomas Berowne strolled down a long sunlit gallery of the palace, on his way to the library. In one hand he carried a scarlet rose: no matter the season. Berowne's wealth and desire kept him surrounded by flowers. Courtiers were clustered up and down the gallery in bunches, their voices hushed and excited. As he passed them people looked up, then resumed their conversation. Thomas lifted the delicate blossom to his nose. Suddenly there was silence at the other end of the hallway. It rippled out before the slender man approaching like some courtly spring tide. Lazarus Merridon walked with a breathtakingly careless grace, courteously answering isolated greetings, ignoring the buzz that grew behind him as he passed. When he reached Lord Thomas, though, he hesitated. The young lord smiled. "Congratulations," he said, and offered him the rose.

"I never thought," she said, lying the curve of his arm in the dark, "that I would want to marry. Not once I was queen. And it doesn't matter that you are younger, and not of noble blood; I shall give you titles, and we will give my people an heir." She chuckled happily. "How my sister will be furious! There goes her hope of succession."

"You're not with child already!" he said, running his palm smoothly over her body.

She giggled. "No, silly man, how could I tell yet? But if we keep on like this, I will be. . . ."

The queen's chief lady was being rudely shaken. She peered through sleep-gummed lashes at the intruder, and made out the sharp, pale features of Master Lazarus Merridon, her lady's paramour.

"What time is it?"

"Midnight," he responded tersely. "Her Majesty's physician—you must fetch him at once!"

Lady Sophia pulled a dressing gown around her ample form; she was used to emergencies, and even to the ill manners of hysteria. "What is it?"

"I don't know!" He was dressed as scantily—as hastily—as decency would allow. "I don't know, she is in pain—"

"Probably a touch of bad meat," Lady Sophia said comfortably. "Put your clothes on, Master Merridon, and go back to your own bed; I'll see to her Grace's comfort."

But for days thereafter her Grace knew no comfort. It was rumored that her physicians suspected poison. All her food was tasted, and certain investigations made, to no effect. Lazarus remained in her chamber, to sit by her side and play the lute and hold her hand. After a time her pain subsided into weakness, and he came again at night to give her joy.

"Lazarus, if I die . . ."

"Shh, shh, you won't die, you're getting better." But two days later, she woke up screaming again.

"Lazarus." He looked up. Thomas Berowne's hand lay on his shoulder, his eyes full of concern. "Lazarus, you can't sit here before her door all night like a dog. Her Grace is asleep, they say she's resting comfortably. Come up to my rooms." The eyes crinkled. "My dear father sent me a cask of old claret, I'd like you to help us empty it."

They had told him not to drink, Those Two. But what else had they done to him? What else had they told him? To hell with them and all their mysteries. Just once let him be—let him pretend to be a man like other men, and seek relief like others. Just once. He said, "I'll come."

Around Lord Thomas' polished table, faces were blurring. Lazarus Merridon dealt another round of cards. "Pentacles lead."

"Dammyou, Merridon," a lordling slurred, "you're as fresh as—a cucumber."

"I've been matching you cup for cup," said Lazarus mildly. "What do you bid?"

His head was quite clear. Alchohol, it seemed, had no effect on him. Winning a minor fortune from the cream of the junior nobility did only a little to console him.

"Merridon, put down your card!"

He was putting it down. It was down.

"Well, Merridon?"

What was their hurry?

"Go ahead, pick one."

"Lazarus," Thomas said sharply, "are you all right?"

Of course he was all right. He was fine.

"Lazarus?"

"I'm fine."

"No, you're pale."

"I'm perfectly all right," he said. Why were they all moving so quickly? He reached for his cup, watching the light gleaming on the ring on his hand, bright ruby claret at the bottom of the cup. . . . What was wrong with them all, were they nervous? Tom's mouth moved like hummingbird wings. "Hadn't you better lie down?"

"I am fine," he said. "Look at my hand—" he held it out steadily, "and look at yours."

Earl Dumaine sloshed some claret into his cup. "Keep drinking, then."

"No," Tom said quickly. "You'd better go. You're utterly white. My man will see you to your rooms."

Lazarus lay on his bed, wide-eyed, watching the carved canopy above him. There really was nothing wrong; only it had taken a long time, walking back. When he blinked the canopy went into darkness, then reappeared. This was not drunkenness, this was something else. Those Two, they must have known this would happen. Why had they not told him? Wryly he thought, they could hardly have been afraid he'd not believe them. What did they want? What did they want of him? Fear was forming, a dark, slow tide at the back of his mind. He would give it no room for advancement. Now . . . what, so far, had he done? The masque, where the court had danced to his music—not enough . . . Gifts, favors he had received—not enough . . . He had lain with the queen of course; but she wasn't pregnant, and he doubted that she ever would be, by him: the genius of his black-robed creator could only extend so far. Why would they want him with her, if not to get her with child? Did they think if he wed her he would strive for their advancement?

The candle at his bedside had burned low. Numbly he realized that he had been thinking for over an hour. Too long. *Am I dying?* he thought suddenly. *Am I poisoned?* But none of the other card-players had been affected this way; they were just drunk. They might have drunk themselves into a stupor by now. He had heard that you could drink yourself to death. Drink could poison. *But I feel fine,* he thought, *just slow. I cannot get drunk, I cannot be poisoned. . . .*

He could not be poisoned. They had known this would happen, with wine, with any potent substance, and they had not told him. The queen was being poisoned, and he was immune. What poison had they taken together? But he had never reacted this way before. Of the poison they took together, he had never received his full share—It had come from him.

Lazarus Merridon turned slowly onto his side. It was ridiculous, a horrible notion. No one could do that, no one. It was unnatural, hideous, impossible. His candle flickered, guttered and went out. In the darkness he fell asleep.

"Master—" Lazarus jumped at the light touch on his arm. "I wouldn't have woken you, sir, but my lord sent orders the message was to be delivered at once."

It was breaking dawn. He sat up in bed and took the packet his man offered, and broke open the crimson wax that bore Andreas' seal. Several pieces of gold fell into his lap. They had been enclosed in a note from his patron:

*My dear boy—*

*Your timing is abominable. Desist at once, and have the decency to wait until after the marriage, or you will make things very difficult for us. Remember: we made you. Do not fail us.*

He looked at the note without seeing it, jingling the gold his patron had sent in his other hand. . . . He had been right. Now there was nothing to do but to fail them.

The gold in his hand would see him out of the country; if he kept on the move he could live for nearly a year on it together with his winnings of last night; by then—God. His winnings. He had left them piled high on the table in Thomas Berowne's room.

\*     \*     \*

Lazarus strode down the halls to Berowne's apartments. Light had just broken, only the palace servants were about. Lord Thomas' man protested that his master was not to be disturbed, but the pale gentleman brushed past him into the inner rooms.

Heavy curtains had been drawn over every possible source of light. Lazarus uncovered one window. He found the bed and pulled back its hangings. The curtain rings rattled on their rods, but the bed's occupant didn't stir.

"Thomas!"

Lord Thomas uncurled just enough to cast one eye up at his visitor. His head was rumpled and stubbled, and he stank of sour wine.

"Thomas, I need the money!"

"Who are you?" Lord Thomas managed to push out from some dimly-remembered area deep inside his throat.

"Lazarus Merridon; I need the money I won last night."

Thomas groaned, closed his eyes and listened to his head throb. "I put it somewhere. . . ."

Lazarus gripped his limp shoulder. "Please, Tom, it's important!"

"Where's the water?" Berowne croaked.

Lazarus cast about the room for it, and found an enameled pitcher and basin. Tom took a swig from the pitcher and poured the rest over his head. He rose reluctantly and limped over to a cabinet, returned to his bedside for the key, and finally presented Lazarus with a knotted linen handkerchief heavy with gold.

"Thank you."

"Not at all," grunted Lord Thomas, sinking back as far as the edge of the bed. "Always delighted to oblige." He pressed his fingers into his eyes. "Now, would you mind telling me why you are calling for such fantastic wealth at this hour of night?"

"It's morning." Lazarus paced up and down the dusky room, nervously tossing the bundle in his hand. "I must ride home at once," he lied. "There was an urgent message from my guardian—"

"Does the queen know?"

"No." He shrugged brusquely. "She'll be all right now."

Tom's mouth opened and closed. "Will she?" he said quietly.

The fierceness of his visitor nearly knocked him over. "Yes! Yes, she will—Tom, you must believe me." The fair man clutched at Berowne's hand.

"Lazarus." Thomas looked at him. "What am I going to tell her?"

The silvery eyes darkened with tears. "I don't know," Lazarus whispered. "Tell her—I could not help it." He lifted the unicorn medal on his chest. "I have it still. I will send it before I come again. Can you tell her that?"

Lord Thomas closed his eyes. "Anything. Anything you like."

"Thank you." Berowne only barely heard the whispered words as he fell back within the bedcurtains. It was early yet. . . . He never missed the fullblown rose plucked from one of his crystal vases, that the queen found beside her on the pillow when she woke.

# ALAN DEAN FOSTER

## "Instant with Loud Voices"

*Alan Dean Foster (1946- ) is equally prolific in the fields of fantasy and science fiction. His vast Humanx Commonwealth series, whose* many novels include Icerigger, The End of the Matter, *and* Flinx in Flux, *displays his ingenuity at imagining complex alien civilizations. He is also the author of* Spellsinger at the Gate, The Moment of the Magician, The Path of the Perambulator, *and other novels in the comic high-fantasy Spellsinger series. Foster's short fiction has been gathered in* With Friends Like These . . . , . . . Who Needs Enemies, *and* The Metrognome and Other Stories, *and his many film novelizations include* Star Wars, The Thing *and the* Alien *trilogy. He co-edited the light fantasy anthology* Smart Dragons, Foolish Elves, *and compiled* The Best of Eric Frank Russell.

# Instant With Loud Voices

### by Alan Dean Foster

ow the devil was he going to tell Hank Strevelle that his life's work wouldn't work? As he hurried down the brightly lit white corridor, Ken Jerome tried to compose the right words as well as himself.

The remote unit via which he'd run the final check hung loosely from his right hand. His lab coat fluttered from his shoulders. The corridor was a football field of eggshell white, the remote unit a rectangular ball, and he was running, running hard and uncertainly toward the wrong goal.

There was nothing wrong with the concept of the question. It was the figuring that troubled Jerome. That, and the fact that no one knew if a machine could be mentally overstressed.

He'd spent a last hectic week reprocessing, rechecking. Wilson at MIT had confirmed his calculations, but at this late stage even Wilson's prestige might not be enough to get the question aborted.

He rounded the last bend in the main corridor. The guard smiled as he held up a restraining hand. Jerome had to wait impatiently while his identity tag was checked against the records. He was panting heavily. Forty-nine unathletic years old, and it was a long time since he'd run this far with anything heavier than a new equation.

The guard was smiling at him with maddening politeness. He was a handsome young man, probably a moonlighting theater arts student waiting for some visiting producer or director to stumble over his cleft chin.

"Nice day, sir. You should slow down. You look a little flushed."

Wait till you hit the archaic side of forty, Jerome thought. But all he said as he retrieved his ident card was, "I expect I do." The guard stood aside as the diminutive engineer hurried through the double doors.

Down another corridor, this one narrower and underpopulated. Through another check station, four glass doors strong enough to have defeated Dillinger, and into The Room. The Room was the only one in the building. It *was* the building. It had been built to house a single important entity and its attendants. Jerome was one of the attendants. The entity was DISRA—Direct Information Systematic Retrieval and Analysis.

The Room was a modest three stories high and roughly the length and width of a football field (I must be going through male menopause, Jerome thought idly, to account for all these sports metaphors here lately). As human constructions went, it was not especially awesome. Nor was the physical appearance of DISRA overwhelming. What it represented was.

The flat sides of the three-story machine was transparent, allowing inspection of the exterior components. Yellow and white monitoring lights winked on and off, giving the epidermis of the machine the aspect of a captured night sky. They indicated to any knowledgeable onlooker that the computer was powered up and working on only minor problems.

If a similar machine had been built back in the 1950's it would have covered most of North America and still been inferior in capability to DISRA. Twenty years of effort, money and intelligence had gone into its construction. Jerome had been involved with the project for the last ten of those years.

Each year new techniques, new knowledge, were acquired and immediately integrated into the design of the machine. Its architect, Henry Strevelle, was no dogmatic, blind believer in his own omnipotence. He was as flexible as his creation and eager to adapt the best ideas of others into its framework.

If only he'll be flexible now, Jerome thought worriedly.

DISRA had been in operation for the past six years, answering questions, pondering hypotheses, dispensing immensely valuable opinions on everything from Keynesian versus Marxist economics to particle physics. When the Secondary Matrix was linked with the DISRA Prime two years ago, Catastrophe Theory had for the first time taken on the aspect of a real science. DISRA had shown itself capable of predicting major earthquakes as well as fish population stocks. Space probes of many nations and consortiums were now programmed with previously unimaginable accuracy.

Six months ago construction on DISRA Prime itself had concluded. After a month of testing, Hank Strevelle had begun the task of programming the complex for a single question.

And, Jerome knew, DISRA was too valuable to mankind for that question to be asked.

He found Strevelle conversing with two technicians. The world's greatest computer scientist was six-four, thin as an oxygen tank and nearly as pale as the enclosing walls. His hair was brushed straight back and gave him the look of a man always walking into the wind. Jerome envied him the hair as much as the brain beneath. We are all frail, he thought.

Strevelle looked away from the techs as Jerome came over. He smiled tolerantly. He knew what was coming. Jerome had been badgering him with it for weeks.

"Now Ken," he said, "you're not going to hit me with your pet peeve again, are you? Now, of all times?" He glanced at his wrist. "Five minutes to startup. Give me a break, will you?"

Jerome conducted his words by waving the remote. "I've spent all night and most of the morning hooked up with the Eastern Nexus. Everything confirms what I've been telling you since the fourth of the month. You put this question to DISRA and we're liable to lose the whole works. A computer can be overstressed. Not a normal computer, but nothing about DISRA is normal."

"You're a good man, Ken. Best theoretical engineer I ever worked with. You'll probably be chosen to run DISRA operations when I retire."

"I can't run what isn't there."

Strevelle let out a resigned sigh. "Look, there are two and a half decades of my life and most of my reputation in this cube of circuits and bubbles and agitated electrons." He jerked a thumb back at the softly humming machine. "D'you really think I'd risk all that if I believed there was the slightest chance of losing capacity, let alone more serious damage?

"The machine runs twenty hours each day, four down for repair and recheck. Half the world depends on it to make decisions, or at least to offer opinions. Even the Soviets want it kept functional.

125

They haven't experienced a single wheat or corn failure in the ten years they've been relying on DISRA's predictions."

"Wilson confirms my calculations."

For a moment the great man appeared uncertain. "Kenji Wilson, at MIT?" Jerome nodded. Strevelle mulled that over, then his paternal smile and eternal optimism reasserted themselves.

"Wilson's the best alive, Ken. I won't deny that. But he bases his calculus on DISRA's own information and DISRA doesn't seem disinclined to try the question. Besides which he doesn't know DISRA the way I do."

"Nobody alive does, Hank. You know that." He desperately tried another tack. "Look, if I can't get you to call this off, at least postpone it so I can refine the figures." He held up the remote, touched tiny buttons. A series of equations flashed across the small screen, hieroglyphs of a physics so advanced that fewer than a hundred minds in the world could comprehend it.

Strevelle shook his head. "I've seen your work for weeks, Ken. I don't buy it." He gestured toward the control booth, led Jerome toward it. "There are five senators there plus representatives from all over Europe and Asia. I can't put them off." His eyes gleamed from under brows tufted with fleece.

"You know what that group of senators promised me? That if we derive any kind of sensible answer to the question, anything at all, they're going to try and put through appropriations to double DISRA's capacity. *Double* it. I won't be around to see that happen, but I don't care. It'll be my legacy, the first computer that doesn't just approximate the ability of a human brain but equals or surpasses it."

"Run this program," Jerome said, "and you're liable not to *have* any legacy, Hank." I'm not saying it right, he told himself frustratedly. I'm not making my point strongly enough, emotionally enough. I'm a bland personality and I live with a calculator. Damn to the hundredth power! He's going to go through with it.

The equations weren't solid enough, he knew. Though given the glow of the great man's expression, Jerome wasn't sure the solidest math in the universe could have dissuaded him today. He resigned himself to the asking of the question.

Five senators. Jerome tried to tell himself that he was wrong, that Wilson was wrong. They could be. Certainly Strevelle knew what he was doing. They'd said DISRA couldn't be built and Strevelle had built it. He'd proven everyone wrong. Among his early detractors had been the youthful, brilliant theoretician named Kenneth Jerome.

I hope to God he proves me wrong again.

There were quiet greetings and introductions, idle conversation to cover nervousness. Only a couple of reporters had been allowed in, one from the *New York Times*, the other from *Der Spiegel*. Friends of Strevelle from the early days of derision and doubt. Now they would receive recompense for that early support. Strevelle never forgot a circuit, or a friend.

He folded himself into a chair next to the master control board, touched instrumentation, murmured to his ready associates. Jerome stood back among the curious. He was Strevelle's backup in case the great man had a stroke or forgot some item of programming. But Strevelle had the body of a man half his age and the mind of several. He would not collapse either physically or mentally.

"Quiet, please," a technician requested. The multilingual muttering in the booth faded to silence.

Strevelle thumbed a switch. "Condition?"

"Ready," replied a tech.

"Secondary, Matrix?"

"On-line," came the quiet announcement.

Strevelle was too prosaic to construct a dramatic gesture. He just touched the button.

Banks of monitors sang in unison behind the watchers. Beyond the angled glass, out in The Room, thousands of tiny indicator lights suddenly flared green, red, blue. The inspiration was wholly mechanical, but it had the look of a hundred Christmas trees suddenly winking to life simultaneously, and provoked appreciative murmurs of admiration from the non-scientists in the group.

There were eight DISRA-2's emplaced in major cities across the United States, four more in Europe, four again in Japan. The Japanese were not involved in the question because of time-sharing conflicts and other problems. Together, the sixteen constituted the Secondary Matrix. They would combine to ask the question which DISRA Prime would attempt to answer.

Six massive communications satellites were temporarily taken out of commercial service to shunt the constituents of the question to DISRA, shutting down half the communications of Europe and the continental United States for fully eight minutes. It was dark outside The Room and still not morning in London. The timing had been carefully planned to cause minimal disruption to the world's commerce.

Five months of laborious pre-programming now spewed in an electronic torrent from two continents into the waiting storage banks of DISRA Prime, filling them to capacity.

The eight minutes passed in tense silence. Jerome found that his palms were damp.

The digital clock on the wall marked time silently, continued past the eight minute mark as the technician on Strevelle's right said calmly, "Programming received."

In The Room DISRA glowed like some ponderous deep-sea monster, awaiting instructions. It's not human, Jerome reminded himself firmly. It's different, and in its limited way superior, but it's not human. Even Strevelle agrees to that.

Strevelle touched the button beneath the plate which read, "Process question," then sat back and lit a small, feminine cigar. The onlookers shuffled uneasily. A red light came on beneath another readout and the single word everyone was waiting for appeared there: WORKING.

Someone made a bad joke in French. A few people laughed softly. Everything was functioning properly. It was the import of the question that had been put to DISRA which was making them nervous, not any fear of mechanical failure.

DISRA worked on the question, digesting at incredible speed the immense volume of programming it had been fed. Normally, the most complicated inquiry took less than three minutes to solve. The digital on the wall counted.

Half an hour passed. The readout on the console glowed steadily red. WORKING. The lights behind the transparent panels of the machine flashed rapidly, efficiently. While they waited, the onlookers discussed science, politics, their personal travails and problems.

The power requirements for such processing were enormous, another reason for running the program at night. Demand in the city was way down. As it was, there was still barely enough power to meet the demand, but the local utilities had been notified well in advance and were prepared to deal with any possible blackouts. Extra power had been purchased from out-of-state utilities to help cope with the temporary drain.

Forty minutes. Jerome considered. Better that he be proven wrong, much better. Of course, even if he and Wilson were correct, nothing might happen. When it was all over he intended to be the first to congratulate Strevelle. Despite their disagreement in this, they were anything but rivals.

For the first time in several weeks his concern gave way to curiosity. After all, he was as interested as anyone else in the machine's answer.

To support DISRA's pondering, everything known or theorized about the Big Bang had been programmed into it. That included just about the entire body of physics, chemistry, astronomy and a number of other physical sciences, not to mention all of philosophy and more. All in support of one question.

When was the Big Bang and what, precisely, did it consist of?

An equation for the Creation, Jerome mused. There were a few who'd argued against asking the question, but they were in the minority and outvoted. Many prominent theologians had helped with the programming. They were as anxious for a reply as the astronomers. DISRA would answer first in figures, then in words.

Forty-five minutes. One of the technicians on Strevelle's right leaned suddenly forward but did not take his eyes from the console. "Sir?"

Strevelle glanced down at him. He'd gone through four of the small cigars and was on his fifth. "Trouble?"

"Maybe. I'm not sure. We're running at least two cyclings now, maybe more."

Jerome joined Strevelle at the technician's station. Cycling occurred when a component of a question could not be either solved or disregarded. Yet the machine was programmed to answer. Its design demanded an answer. If not shut down or if the programming was not canceled, the same information would be run over and over, at greater strength and drawing on greater reserves. It was a rare occurrence.

"Four sections cycling now, sir. If the figures are right." He looked anxiously up at Strevelle.

"Cancel it, Hank," Jerome urged him quietly. "While there's still time."

"Eight sections, sir." The technician no longer tried to hide his nervousness. "Ten. Twelve."

There were forty sections comprising DISRA Prime. Forty sections devoted to Direct Information Systematic Retrieval and Analysis. Strevelle said nothing, stared stolidly down at the console, then out at the working machine.

"We've still plenty of capacity. Let it cycle."

"Come on, Hank," Jerome muttered intensely. "It's not going to work. You've reached beyond the machine's capacity. I told you."

"Nothing's beyond DISRA's capacity. We've asked it a perfectly logical question and supplied it with sufficient information to answer. I expect an answer." He put both hands on the console and leaned forward, his nose nearly touching the slanting glass.

"Twenty sections," muttered the technician. All the other technicians were watching his station now. "Thirty . . . thirty-five. . . ." Behind them something was buzzing, louder than the crowd.

"Forty . . . all sections cycling, sir." The technician's voice had turned hoarse.

Out in The Room there was no sign anything out of the ordinary was taking place. On the console WORKING continued to glow its steady red.

Then someone turned a spotlight on Jerome's face and just as quickly turned it out. . . .

The glass had missed him. So had most of the flying scrap. One of the support beams had not.

Still, he was one of the first out of the hospital, and the arm was healing nicely. He didn't need it for a while anyway, since there was nothing to work on for at least a month. Strevelle was already drawing up his new plans, dictating them from his hospital bed.

The roof was mostly gone, blown skyward to fall back in or to dust the campus, but the reinforced concrete walls had held. They'd been designed to withstand Richter-scale-nine earthquakes and near nuclear explosions. A little internal blowup had strained but not shattered them.

In the remnants of The Room workmen were cleaning up the last of the debris while technicians were already discussing where to begin rebuilding. DISRA resembled a cake that had fallen in on itself. About seventy percent of the machine was completely gone, scattered across the surrounding community in tiny pieces or else vaporized during the overload. So rapid was the final cycling even the safeties had been overloaded. The city-wide blackout had lasted two hours.

Jerome strolled around The Room, picking his way carefully over the remaining debris, chatting with those technicians he knew. There was no air of depression about The Room. An experiment had failed, that was all. Time to rebuild and try it again.

A slight figure near one of the walls was neither workman nor tech. Jerome squinted, thought he recognized the man, and made his way across to him.

"Hello. Hernandez, isn't it? From the *Times*? You were in the booth with us when she blew."

The man turned away from his examination of the concrete, smiled from beneath an afterthought of a mustache and extended a hand. "Yes. You're Dr. Jerome, aren't you? I understand the old man's already planning DISRA Prime Two."

For some reason Jerome felt embarrassed. "Yes. He's incorrigible. But we have to have a DISRA. The Secondary Matrix can only handle so many of the lesser inquiries. The world needs its questions answered."

"But not today's." Hernandez chuckled. "The astronomers will have to wait at least another generation."

"For that question? I don't think the government will let them try it again. Too much money for too little return."

"Oh?" The reporter was jotting notes down on a small pad. He's old-fashioned, Jerome mused. An odd trait to find in a science reporter.

Hernandez noticed his stare. "Tape recorders aren't right for every situation. There are people working here and I don't want to bother them. You're not bothered?"

"No. Just sore. It could've been a lot worse. Ninety-five percent of the energy seemed to go skyward instead of sideways."

"I know. I put that in my article."

"So I heard. Thanks for your kindness. We're going to need all the help we can get, despite the need for a new DISRA. Our public image isn't exactly at its most polished right now."

"Doesn't matter. As you say, the world needs a DISRA, and the public hardly suffered." He waved his pen at the wall. "A few people thought DISRA was the mechanical equivalent of a human being."

"A few people believe in astrology, too. DISRA was a brilliant machine, but that's all. Its superiority was limited to a few specific areas."

"Of course." Hernandez made some more notations, then indicated the wall. His voice lost some of its usual reportorial smoothness.

"Have you noticed the lines and markings on the concrete?"

Jerome had not paid much attention to the scorching. His attention had been centered on the ruined machine in the middle of The Room. But the source of the marks was obvious enough.

"You remember that most of DISRA's exterior paneling was transparent," Jerome said. "When she blew, the intense light was slightly masked by dark circuitry." He tapped the wall. "So we got these negative images seared into the walls, sort of a flash blueprint."

"That's what I thought." Hernandez nodded slowly. "I've seen such things before, only the outline was human and not mechanical."

"Oh, you mean the Hiroshima silhouettes," Jerome said, "the outlines burnt into the streets and walls of people close to the bomb when it was dropped?"

"I wasn't thinking of them," the reporter murmured. He traced some of the circuit patterns with his pen. "These are much more detailed, more delicately shaded than just a plain outline."

"That's explainable." Jerome wondered what the reporter was driving at.

"You know," said Hernandez quietly, "there's intelligence, and there's intelligence. There are representations of man and representations of man. Sometimes you can ask too much of a man just as you can of a machine. It's taken us a long time to reach the stage where we could make a machine suffer like a man."

"If it suffered," said Jerome chidingly, "it didn't suffer like a man."

"I wonder," said the reporter.

"You said you've seen such markings before." Jerome tried to bring the conversation back to a sensible tack. "If not the Hiroshima markings, then where?"

Hernandez turned, sat down on a broken conduit and regarded the remnants of the machine the bulk of whose substance had vanished.

"On an old shroud, in Italy, in Turin. . . ."

# ROBERT SILVERBERG

## "Not Our Brother"

*One of the most prolific of all fantasy and science fiction writers,
Robert Silverberg (1935- ) won the Hugo Award for most promising
new author in 1956, and wrote scores of stories and novels in the
years that followed under his own name and a clutch of pseudonyms. With the publication of his novel* Thorns *in 1967, he was recognized as one of the leading science fiction writers of his
generation.* Downward to Earth, A Time of Changes, The Book of
Skulls, Shadrach in the Furnace, Dying Inside *and other of his
novels have been justly lauded for their portrayals of characters en-
during the dehumanizing circumstances of their environment with
dignity. He is a multiple recipient of the Hugo and Nebula Awards,
mostly for his short fiction, which has been collected in* Born with
the Dead, The Feast of Saint Dionysus, Stardance and Other Science Fiction Stories, *and* Beyond the Safe Zone: The Collected
Short Fiction of Robert Silverberg. *His 1980 novel* Lord Valentine's
Castle *inaugurated a multi-volume heroic fantasy series set in the
world of Majipoor. He is the author of numerous books of non-
fiction, and the editor of more than 60 anthologies of classic and
original science fiction and fantasy.*

# Not Our Brother

## by Robert Silverberg

alperin came into San Simón Zuluaga in late October, a couple of days before the fiesta of the local patron saint, when the men of the town would dance in masks. He wanted to see that. This part of Mexico was famous for its masks, grotesque and terrifying ones portraying devils and monsters and fiends. Halperin had been collecting them for three years. But masks on a wall are one thing, and masks on dancers in the town plaza quite another.

San Simón was a mountain town about halfway between Acapulco and Taxco. "Tourists don't go there," Guzmán López had told him. "The road is terrible and the only hotel is a Cucaracha Hilton—five rooms, straw mattresses." Guzmán ran a gallery in Acapulco where Halperin had bought a great many masks. He was a suave, cosmopolitan man from Mexico City, with smooth dark skin and a bald head that gleamed as if it had been polished. "But they still do the Bat Dance there, the Lord of the Ánimals Dance. It is the only place left that performs it. This is from San Simón Zuluaga," said Guzmán, and pointed to an intricate and astonishing mask in purple and yellow depicting a bat with outspread leathery wings that was at the same time somehow also a human skull and a jaguar. Halperin would have paid ten thousand pesos for it, but Guzmán was not interested in selling. "Go to San Simón," he said. "You'll see others like this."

"For sale?"

Guzmán laughed and crossed himself. "Don't suggest it. In

134

Rome, would you make an offer for the Pope's robes? These masks are sacred."

"I want one. How did you get this one?"

"Sometimes favors are done. But not for strangers. Perhaps I'll be able to work something out for you."

"You'll be there, then?"

"I go every year for the Bat Dance," said Guzmán. "It's important to me. To touch the real Mexico, the old Mexico. I am too much a Spaniard, not enough an Aztec; so I go back and drink from the source. Do you understand?"

"I think so," Halperin said. "Yes."

"You want to see the true Mexico?"

"Do they still slice out hearts with an obsidian dagger?"

Guzmán said, chuckling. "If they do, they don't tell me about it. But they know the old gods there. You should go. You would learn much. You might even experience interesting dangers."

"Danger doesn't interest me a whole lot," said Halperin.

"Mexico interests you. If you wish to swallow Mexico, you must swallow some danger with it, like the salt with the tequila. If you want sunlight, you must have a little darkness. You should go to San Simón." Guzmán's eyes sparkled. "No one will harm you. They are very polite there. Stay away from demons and you will be fine. You should go."

Halperin arranged to keep his hotel room in Acapulco and rented a car with four-wheel drive. He invited Guzmán to ride with him, but the dealer was leaving for San Simón that afternoon, with stops en route to pick up artifacts at Chacalapa and Hueycantenango. Halperin could not go that soon. "I will reserve a room for you at the hotel," Guzmán promised, and drew a precise road map for him.

The road was rugged and winding and barely paved, and turned into a chaotic dirt-and-gravel track beyond Chichihualco. The last four kilometers were studded with boulders like the bed of a mountain stream. Halperin drove most of the way in first gear, gripping the wheel desperately, taking every jolt and jounce in his spine and kidneys. To come out of the pink-and manicured Disneyland of plush Acapulco into this primitive wilderness was to make a journey five hundred years back in time. But the air up here was fresh and cool and clean, and the jungle was lush from recent rains, and now and then Halperin saw a mysterious little town half-buried in the heavy greenery: dogs barked, naked children ran out and waved, leathery old Nahua folk peered gravely at him and called incomprehensible greetings. Once he heard a tremendous thump against his undercarriage and was sure he had ripped out his oil pan on a rock, but when he peered below everything seemed to be intact. Two kilometers later, he veered into a giant rut and thought he had cracked an axle, but he had not. He hunched down over the wheel, aching, tense, and imagined that splendid bat mask, or its twin, spotlighted against a stark white wall in his study. Would Guzmán be able to get him one? Probably. His talk of the difficulties involved was just a way of hyping the price. But even if Halperin came back empty-handed from San Simón, it would be reward enough simply to have witnessed the dance, that bizarre, alien rite of a lost pagan civilization. There was more to collecting Mexican masks, he knew, than simply acquiring objects for the wall.

In late afternoon he entered the town just as he was beginning to think he had misread Guzmán's map. To his surprise it was quite imposing, the largest village he had seen since turning off the main highway—a great bare plaza ringed by stone benches, marketplace on one side, vast heavy-walled old church on the other, giant gnarled trees, chickens, dogs, children running about everywhere, and houses of crumbling adobe spreading up the slope of a gray flat-faced mountain to the right and down into the dense darkness of a barranca thick with ferns and elephant-ears to the left. For the last hundred meters into town an impenetrable living palisade of cactus lined the road on both sides, unbranched spiny green columns that had been planted one flush against the next. Bougainvillea in many shades of red and purple and orange cascaded like gaudy draperies over walls and rooftops.

Halperin saw a few old Volkswagens and an ancient ramshackle bus parked on the far side of the plaza and pulled his car up beside them. Everyone stared at him as he got out. Well, why not? He was big news here, maybe the first stranger in six months. But the pressure of those scores of dark amphibian eyes unnerved him. These people were all Indians, Nahuas, untouched in any important way not only by the twentieth century but by the nineteenth, the eighteenth, all the centuries back to Moctezuma. They had nice Christian names like Santiago and Francisco and Jesús, and they went obligingly to the iglesia for mass whenever they thought they should, and they knew about cars and transistor radios and

Coca-Cola. But all that was on the surface. They were still Aztecs at heart, Halperin thought. Time-travelers. As alien as Martians.

He shrugged off his discomfort. Here *he* was the Martian, dropping in from a distant planet for a quick visit. Let them stare: he deserved it. They meant no harm. Halperin walked toward them and said, *"Por favor, donde está el hotel del pueblo?"*

Blank faces. *"El hotel?"* he asked, wandering around the plaza. *"Por favor. Donde?"* No one answered. That irritated him. Sure, Nahuatl was their language, but it was inconceivable that Spanish would be unknown here. Even in the most remote towns *someone* spoke Spanish. *"Por favor!"* he said, exasperated. They melted back at his approach as though he were ablaze. Halperin peered into dark cluttered shops. *"Habla usted Español?"* he asked again and again, and met only silence. He was at the edge of the marketplace, looking into a chaos of fruit stands, taco stands, piles of brilliant serapes and flimsy sandals and stacked sombreros, and booths where vendors were selling the toys of next week's Day of the Dead holiday, candy skeletons and green banners emblazoned with grinning red skulls. *"Por favor?"* he said loudly, feeling very foolish.

A woman in jodhpurs and an Eisenhower jacket materialized suddenly in front of him and said in English, "They don't mean to be rude. They're just very shy with strangers."

Halperin was taken aback. He realized that he had begun to think of himself as an intrepid explorer, making his way with difficulty through a mysterious primitive land. In an instant she had snatched all that from him, both the intrepidity and the difficulties.

She was about thirty, with close-cut dark hair and bright, alert eyes, attractive, obviously American. He struggled to hide the sense of letdown her advent had created in him and said, "I've been trying to find the hotel."

"Just off the plaza, three blocks behind the market. Let's go to your car and I'll ride over there with you."

"I'm from San Francisco," he said. "Tom Halperin."

"That's such a pretty city. I love San Francisco."

"And you?"

"Miami," she said. "Ellen Chambers." She seemed to be measuring him with her eyes. He noticed that she was carrying a couple of Day of the Dead trinkets—a crudely carved wooden skeleton with big eyeglasses, and a rubber snake with a gleaming human skull of white plastic, like a cue ball, for a head. As they reached his car she said, "You came here alone?"

Halperin nodded. "Did you?"

"Yes," she said. "Came down from Taxco. How did you find this place?"

"Antiquities dealer in Acapulco told me about it. Antonio Guzmán López. I collect Mexican masks."

"Ah."

"But I've never actually seen one of the dances."

"They do an unusual one here," she said as he drove down a street of high, ragged, mud-colored walls, patched and plastered, that looked a thousand years old. "Lord of the Animals, it's called. Died out everywhere else. Pre-Hispanic shamanistic rite, invoking protective deities, fertility spirits."

"Guzmán told me a little about it. Not much. Are you an anthropologist?"

"Strictly amateur. Turn left here." There was a little street, an open wrought-iron gateway, a driveway of large white gravel. Set back a considerable distance was a squat, dispiriting hovel of a hotel, one story, roof of chipped red tiles in which weeds were growing. Not even the ubiquitous bougainvillea and the great clay urns overflowing with dazzling geraniums diminished its ugliness. Cucaracha Hilton indeed, Halperin thought dourly. She said, "This is the place. You can park on the side."

The parking lot was empty. "Are you and I the only guests?" he asked.

"So it seems."

"Guzmán was supposed to be here. Smooth-looking man, bald shiny head, dresses like a financier."

"I haven't seen him," she said. "Maybe his car broke down."

They got out, and a slouching fourteen-year-old mozo came to get Halperin's luggage. He indicated his single bag and followed Ellen into the hotel. She moved in a sleek, graceful way that kindled in him the idea that she and he might get something going in this forlorn place. But as soon as the notion arose, he felt it fizzling: she was friendly, she was good-looking, but she radiated an offputting vibe, a noli-me-tangere sort of thing, that was unmistakable and made any approach from him inappropriate. Too bad. Halperin liked the company of women and fell easily and uncomplicatedly into liaisons with them wherever he traveled, but this one puzzled him. Was she a lesbian? Usually he could tell, but he had no reading on her except that she meant him to keep his distance. At least for the time being.

The hotel was grim, a string of lopsided rooms arranged around a weedy courtyard that served as a sort of lobby. Some hens and a rooster were marching about, and a startling green iguana, enormous, like a miniature dinosaur, was sleeping on a branch of a huge yellow-flowered hibiscus just to the left of the entrance. Everything was falling apart in the usual haphazard tropical way. Nobody seemed to be in charge. The mozo put Halperin's suitcase down in front of a room on the far side of the courtyard and went away without a word. "You've got the one next to mine," Ellen said. "That's the dining room over there and the cantina next to it. There's a shower out in back and a latrine a little further into the jungle."

"Wonderful."

"The food isn't bad. You know enough to watch out for the water. There are bugs but no mosquitoes."

"How long have you been here?" Halperin asked.

"Centuries," she said. "I'll see you in an hour and we'll have dinner, okay?"

His room was a whitewashed irregular box, smelling faintly of disinfectant, that contained a lumpy narrow bed, a sink, a massive mahogany chest of drawers that could have come over with the Spaniards, and an ornate candlestick. The slatted door did not lock and the tile-rimmed window that gave him an unsettling view of thick jungle close outside was without glass, an open hole in the wall. But there was a breathtaking mask mounted above the bed, an armadillo-faced man with a great gaping mouth, and next to the chest of drawers was a weatherbeaten but extraordinary helmet mask, a long-nosed man with an owl for one ear and a coyote for another, and over the bed was a double mask, owl and pig, that was finer than anything he had seen in any museum. Halperin felt such a rush of possessive zeal that he began to sweat. The sour acrid scent of it filled the room. Could he buy these masks? From whom? The dull-eyed mozo? He had done all his collecting through galleries; he had no idea how to go about acquiring masks from natives. He remembered Guzmán's warning about not trying to buy from them. But these masks must no longer be sacred if they were mere hotel decorations. Suppose, he thought, I just *take* that owl-pig when I check out, and leave three thousand pesos on the sink. That must be a fortune here. Five thousand, maybe. Could they find me? Would there be trouble when I was leaving the country? Probably. He put the idea out of his mind. He was a collector, not a thief. But these masks were gorgeous.

He unpacked and found his way outside to the shower—a cubicle of braided ropes, a creaking pipe, yellowish tepid water—and then he put on clean clothes and knocked at Ellen's door. She was ready for dinner. "How do you like your room?" she asked.

"The masks make up for any little shortcomings. Do they have them in every room?"

"They have them all over," she said.

He peered past her shoulder into her room, which was oddly bare, no luggage or discarded clothes lying around, and saw two masks on the wall, not as fine as his but fine enough. But she did not invite him to take a close look, and closed the door behind her. She led him to the dining room. Night had fallen some time ago, and the jungle was alive with sounds, chirpings and rachetings and low thunking booms and something that sounded the way the laughter of a jaguar might sound. The dining room, oblong and lit by candles, had three tables and more masks on the wall, a devil face with a lizard for a nose, a crudely carved mermaid, and a garish tiger-hunter mask. He wandered around studying them in awe, and said to her, "These aren't local. They've been collected from all over Guerrero."

"Maybe your friend Guzmán sold them to the owner," she suggested. "Do you own many?"

"Dozens. I could bore you with them for hours. Do you know San Francisco at all? I've got a big old three-story Victorian in Noe Valley and there are masks in every room. I've collected all sorts of primitive art, but once I discovered Mexican masks they pushed everything else aside, even the Northwest Indian stuff. You collect too, don't you?"

"Not really. I'm not an acquirer. Of things, at any rate. I travel, I look, I learn, I move on. What do you do when you aren't collecting things?"

"Real estate," he said. "I buy and sell houses. And you?"

"Nothing worth talking about," she said.

The mozo appeared, silently set their table, brought them, unbidden, a bottle of red wine. Then a tureen of albóndigas soup, and afterward tortillas, tacos, a decent turkey molé. Without a word, without a change of expression.

"Is that kid the whole staff?" Halperin asked.

"His sister is the chambermaid. I guess his mother is the cook. The patrón is Filiberto, the father, but he's busy getting the fiesta set up. He's one of the important dancers. You'll meet him. Shall we get more wine?"

"I've had plenty," he said.

They went for a stroll after dinner, skirting the jungle's edge and wandering through a dilapidated residential area. He heard music and handclapping coming from the plaza but felt too tired to see what was happening there. In the darkness of the tropical night he might easily have reached for Ellen and drawn her against him, but he was too tired for that, too, and she was still managing to be amiable, courteous, but distant. She was a mystery to him. Moneyed, obviously. Divorced, widowed young, gay, what? He did not precisely mistrust her, but nothing about her seemed quite to connect with anything else.

About nine-thirty he went back to his room, toppled down on the ghastly bed, and dropped at once into a deep sleep that carried him well past dawn. When he woke, the hotel was deserted except for the boy. *"Cómo se llama?"* Halperin asked, and got an odd smouldering look, probably for mocking a mere mozo by employing the formal construction. *"Elustesio,"* the boy muttered. Had Elustesio seen the *Norteamericano señorita?* Elustesio hadn't seen anyone. He brought Halperin some fruit and cold tortillas for breakfast and disappeared. Afterward Halperin set out on a slow stroll into town.

Though it was early, the plaza and surrounding marketplace were already crowded. Again Halperin got the visiting-Martian treatment from the townsfolk—fishy stares, surreptitious whispers, the occasional shy and tentative grin. He did not see Ellen. Alone among these people once more, he felt awkward, intrusive, vulnerable; yet he preferred that, he realized, to the curiously unsettling companionship of the Florida woman.

The shops now seemed to be stocking little except Day of the Dead merchandise, charming and playful artifacts that Halperin found irresistible. He had long been attracted to the imagery of brave defiance of death that this Mexican version of Halloween, so powerful in the inner life of the country, called forth. Halperin bought a yellow papier-mâché skull with brilliant flower-eyes and huge teeth, an elegant little guitar-playing skeleton and a bag of grisly, morbid marzipan candies. He stared at the loaves of bread decorated with skulls and saints in a bakery window. He smiled at a row of sugar coffins with nimble skeletons clambering out of them. There was some extraordinary lacquer work on sale too, trays and gourds decorated with gleaming red-and-black patterns. By mid-morning he had bought so much that carrying it was a problem, and he returned to the hotel to drop off his purchases.

A blue Toyota van was parked next to his car and Guzmán, looking just as dapper in khakis as he always did in his charcoal gray suits, was rearranging a mound of bundles in it. "Are you enjoying yourself?" he called to Halperin.

"Very much. I thought I'd find you in town when I got here yesterday."

"I came and I went again, to Tlacotepec, and I returned. I have bought good things for the gallery." He nodded toward Halperin's armload of toy skulls and skeletons. "I see you are buying too. Good. Mexico needs your help."

"I'd rather buy one of the masks that's hanging in my room," Halperin said. "Have you seen it? Pig and owl, and carved like—"

"Patience. We will get masks for you. But think of this trip as an experience, not as a collecting expedition, and you will be happier. Acquisitions will happen of their own accord if you don't try to force them, and if you enjoy the favor of *amo tokinwan* while you are here."

Halperin was staring at some straw-wrapped wooden statuettes in the back of the van. "*Amo tokinwan?* Who's that?"

"The Lords of the Animals," said Guzmán. "The protectors of the village. Perhaps protectors is not quite the right word, for protectors are benevolent, and *amo tokinwan* often are not. Quite dangerous sometimes, indeed."

Halperin could not decide how serious Guzmán was. "How so?"

"Sometimes at fiesta time they enter the village and mingle. They look like anyone else and attract no special attention, and they have a way of making the villagers think that they belong here. Can you imagine that, seeing a stranger and believing you have known him all your life? Beyond doubt they are magical."

"And they are what? Guardians of the village?"

"In a sense. They bring the rain; they ward off the lightning; they guard the crops. But sometimes they do harm. No one can predict their whims. And so the dancing, to propitiate them. Beyond doubt they are magical. Beyond doubt they are something very other. *Amo tokinwan.*"

"What does that mean?" Halperin asked.

"In Nahuatl it means, 'Not our brother,' of different substance.

Alien. Supernatural. I think I have met them, do you know? You stand in the plaza watching the dancers, and there is a little old woman at your elbow or a boy or a pregnant woman wearing a fine rebozo, and everything seems all right, but you get a little too close and you feel the chill coming from them, as though they were statues of ice. So you back away and try to think good thoughts." Guzmán laughed. "Mexico! You think I am civilized because I have a Rolex on my wrist? Even I am not civilized, my friend. If you are wise you will not be too civilized while you are here, either. They are not our brother, and they do harm. I told you you will see the real Mexico here, eh?"

"I have a hard time believing in spirits," Halperin said. "Good ones and evil ones alike."

"These are both at once. But perhaps they will not bother you." Guzmán slammed shut the door of the van. "In town they are getting ready to unlock the masks and dust them and arrange them for the fiesta. Would you like to be there when that is done? The mayordomo is my friend. He will admit you."

"I'd like that very much. When?"

"After lunch." Guzmán touched his hand lightly to Halperin's wrist. "One word, first. Control your desire to collect. Where we go today is not a gallery."

The masks of San Simón were kept in a locked storeroom of the municipal building. Unlocking them turned out to be a solemn and formal occasion. All the town's officials were there, Guzmán whispered: the alcalde, the five alguaciles, the regidores, and Don Luis Gutiérrez, the mayordomo, an immense mustachioed man whose responsibility it was to maintain the masks from year to year, to rehearse the dancers and to stage the fiesta. There was much bowing and embracing. Most of the conversation was in Nahuatl, which Halperin did not understand at all, and he was able to follow very little of the quick, idiosyncratic Spanish they spoke either, though he heard Guzmán introduce him as an important *Norteamericano* scholar and tried thereafter to look important and scholarly. Don Luis produced an enormous old-fashioned key, thrust it with a flourish into the door and led the way down a narrow, musty corridor to a large white-walled storeroom with a ceiling of heavy black beams. Masks were stacked everywhere, on the floor, on shelves, in cupboards. The place was a museum. Halperin, who could claim a certain legitimate scholarly expertise by now in this field, recognized many of the masks as elements in familiar dances of the region, the ghastly faces of the Diablo Macho Dance, the heavy-bearded elongated Dance of the Moors and Christians masks, the ferocious cat-faces of the Tigre Dance. But there were many that were new and astounding to him, the Bat Dance masks, terrifying bat-winged heads that all were minglings of bat characters and other animals, bat-fish, bat-coyote, bat-owl, bat-squirrel, and some that were unidentifiable except for the weird outspread rubbery wings, bats hybridized with creatures of another world, perhaps. One by one the masks were lifted, blown clean of dust, admired, passed around, though not to Halperin. He trembled with amazement at the power and beauty of these bizarre wooden effigies. Don Luis drew a bottle of mescal from a niche and handed it to the alcalde, who took a swig and passed it on; the bottle came in time to Halperin, and without a thought for the caterpillar coiled in the bottom of the bottle he gulped the fiery liquor. Things were less formal now. The high officials of the town were laughing, shuffling about in clumsy little dance steps, picking up gourd rattles from the shelves and shaking them. They called out in Nahuatl, all of it lost on Halperin, though the words *amo tokinwan* at one point suddenly stood out in an unintelligible sentence, and someone shook rattles with curious vehemence. Halperin stared at the masks but did not dare go close to them or try to touch them. This is not a gallery, he reminded himself. Even when things got so uninhibited that Don Luis and a couple of the others put masks on and began to lurch about the room in a weird lumbering polka, Halperin remained tense and controlled. The mescal bottle came to him again. He drank, and this time his discipline eased; he allowed himself to pick up a wondrous bat mask, phallic and with great staring eyes. The carving was far finer than on the superb one he had seen at Guzmán's gallery. He ran his fingers lovingly over the gleaming wood, the delicately outlined ribbed wings. Guzmán said, "In some villages the Bat Dance was a Christmas dance, the animals paying homage to little Jesus. But here it is a fertility rite, and therefore the bat is phallic. You would like that mask, no?" He grinned broadly. "So would I, my friend. But it will never leave San Simón."

Just as the ceremony appeared to be getting rowdy, it came to an end: the laughter ceased, the mescal bottle went back to its niche, the officials grew solemn again and started to file out. Halperin, in schoolboy Spanish, thanked Don Luis for permitting him to attend, thanked the alcalde, thanked the alguaciles and the regidores. He felt flushed and excited as he left the building. The cache of masks mercilessly stirred his acquisitive lust. That they were unattainable made them all the more desirable, of course. It was as though the storeroom were a gallery in which the smallest trifle cost a million dollars.

Halperin caught sight of Ellen Chambers on the far side of the plaza, sitting outside a small café. He waved to her and she acknowledged it with a smile.

Guzmán said, "Your traveling companion?"

"No. She's a tourist down from Taxco. I met her yesterday."

"I did not know any other Americans were here for the fiesta. It surprises me." He was frowning. "Sometimes they come, but very rarely. I thought you would be the only *extranjero* here this year."

"It's all right," said Halperin. "We gringos get lonely for our own sort sometimes. Come on over and I'll introduce you."

Guzmán shook his head. "Another time. I have business to attend to. Commend me to your charming friend and offer my regrets."

He walked away. Halperin shrugged and crossed the plaza to Ellen, who beckoned him to the seat opposite her. He signaled the waiter. "Two margaritas," he said.

She smiled. "Thank you, no."

"All right. One."

"Have you been busy today?" she asked.

"Seeing masks. I salivate for some of the things they have in this town. I find myself actually thinking of stealing some if they won't sell to me. That's shocking. I've never stolen anything in my life. I've always paid my own way."

"This would be a bad place to begin, then."

"I know that. They'd put the curse of the mummy on me, or the black hand, or God knows what. The sign of Moctezuma. I'm not serious about stealing masks. But I do want them. Some of them."

"I can understand that," she said. "But I'm less interested in the masks than in what they represent. The magic character, the transformative power. When they put the masks on, they *become* the otherworldly beings they represent. That fascinates me. That the mask dissolves the boundary between our world and *theirs*."

"*Theirs?*"

"The invisible world. The world the shaman knows, the world of the were-jaguars and were-bats. A carved and painted piece of wood becomes a gateway into that world and brings the benefits of the supernatural. That's why the masks are so marvelous, you know. It isn't just an aesthetic thing."

"You actually believe what you've just said?" Halperin asked.

"Oh, yes. Yes, definitely."

He chose not to press the point. People believed all sorts of things, pyramid power, yoghurt as a cure for cancer, making your plants grow by playing Bach to them. That was all right with him. Just now he found her warmer, more accessible, than she had been before, and he had no wish to offend her. As they strolled back to the hotel, he asked her to have dinner with him, imagining hopefully that that might lead somewhere tonight, but she said she would not be eating at the hotel this evening. That puzzled him—where else around here could she get dinner, and with whom?—but of course he did not probe.

He dined with Guzmán. The distant sound of music could be heard, shrill, alien. "They are rehearsing for the fiesta," Guzmán explained. The hotel cook outdid herself, preparing some local freshwater flatfish in a startlingly delicate sauce that would have produced applause in Paris. Filiberto, the patrón, came into the dining room and greeted Guzmán with a bone-crushing *abrazo*. Guzmán introduced Halperin once again as an important *Norteamericano* scholar. Filiberto, tall and very dark-skinned, with cheekbones like blades, showered Halperin with effusive courtesies.

"I have been admiring the masks that decorate the hotel," Halperin said, and waited to be invited to buy whichever one took his fancy, but Filiberto merely offered a dignified bow of thanks. Praising individual ones, the owl-pig, the lizard-nose, also got nowhere. Filiberto presented Guzmán with a chilled bottle of a superb white wine from Michoacán, crisp and deliciously metallic on the tongue; he spoke briefly with Guzmán in Nahuatl; then, saying he was required at the rehearsal, he excused himself. The music grew more intense.

Halperin said, "Is it possible to see the rehearsal after dinner?"

"Better to wait for the actual performance," said Guzmán.

Halperin slept poorly that night. He listened for the sound of Ellen Chambers entering the room next door, but either he was asleep when she came in or she was out all night.

And now finally the fiesta was at hand. Halperin spent the day watching the preparations: the stringing of colored electric lights around the plaza, the mounting of huge papier-mâché images of monsters and gods and curious spindly-legged clowns, the closing down of the shops and the clearing away of the tables that displayed their merchandise. All day long the town grew more crowded. No doubt people were filtering in from the outlying districts, the isolated jungle farms, the little remote settlements on the crest of the sierra. Through most of the day he saw nothing of Guzmán or Ellen, but that was all right. He was quite accustomed now to being here, and the locals seemed to take him equally for granted. He drank a good deal of mescal at one cantina or another around the plaza and varied it with the occasional bottle of the excellent local beer. As the afternoon waned, the crowds in the plaza grew ever thicker and more boisterous, but nothing particular seemed to be happening, and Halperin wondered whether to go back to the hotel for dinner. He had another mescal instead. Suddenly the fiesta lights were switched on, gaudy, glaring, reds and yellows and greens, turning everything into a psychedelic arena, and then at last Halperin heard music, the skreeing bagpipy sound of bamboo flutes, the thump of drums, the whispery, dry rattle of tambourines, the harsh punctuation of little clay whistles. Into the plaza came ten or fifteen boys, leaping, dancing cartwheels, forming impromptu human pyramids that promptly collapsed, to general laughter. They wore no masks. Halperin, disappointed and puzzled, looked around as though to find an explanation and discovered Guzmán, suave and elegant in charcoal gray, almost at his elbow. "No masks?" he said. "Shouldn't they be masked?"

"This is only the beginning," said Guzmán.

Yes, just the overture. The boys cavorted until they lost all discipline and went pell-mell across the plaza and out of sight. Then a little old man, also unmasked, tugged three prancing white goats caparisoned with elaborate paper decorations into the center of the plaza and made them cavort, too. Two stilt-walkers fought a mock duel. Three trumpeters played a hideous discordant fanfare and got such cheers that they played it again and again. Guzmán was among those who cheered. Halperin, who had not eaten, was suddenly captured by the aroma from a stand across the way where an old woman was grilling tacos on a brazier and a tin griddle. He headed toward her, but paused on the way for a tequila at an improvised cantina someone had set up on the streetcorner, using a big wooden box as the bar. He saw Ellen Chambers in the crowd on the far side of the plaza and waved, but she did not appear to see him, and when he looked again he could not find her.

The music grew wilder and now, at last, the first masked dancers appeared. A chill ran through him at the sight of the nightmare figures marching up the main avenue, bat-faced ones, skull-faced ones, grinning devils, horned creatures, owls, jaguars. Some of the masks were two or three feet high and turned their wearers into malproportioned dwarfs. They advanced slowly, pausing often to backtrack, circling one another, kicking their legs high, madly waving their arms. Halperin, sweating, alert, aroused, realized that the dancers must have been drinking heavily, for their movements were jerky, ragged, convulsive. As they came toward the plaza he saw that they were herding four figures in white robes and pale human-faced masks before them, and were chanting something repetitively in Nahuatl. He caught that phrase again, *amo tokinwan*. Not our brother.

To Guzmán he said, "What are they saying?"

"The prayer against the *amo tokinwan*. To protect the fiesta, in case any of the Lords of the Animals actually are in the plaza tonight."

Those around Halperin had taken up the chant now.

"Tell me what it means," Halperin said.

Guzmán said, chanting the translation in a rhythm that matched the voices around them: *"They eat us!" They are—not our brother. They are worms, wild beasts. Yes!"*

Halperin looked at him strangely. "They eat us?" he said. "Cannibal gods?"

"Not literally. Devourers of souls."

"And these are the gods of these people?"

"No, not gods. Supernatural beings. They lived here before there were people, and they naturally retain control over everything important here. But not gods as Christians understand gods. Look, here come the bats!"

*They eat us,* Halperin thought, shivering in the warm humid night. A new phalanx of dancers was arriving now, half a dozen bat-masked ones. He thought he recognized the long legs of Filiberto in their midst. Darkness had come and the dangling lights cast an eerier, more brilliant glow. Halperin decided he wanted another tequila, a mescal, a cold cerveza, whatever he could find quickest. *Not our brother.* He excused himself vaguely to Guzmán and started through the crowd. *They are worms, wild beasts.* They were still chanting it. The words meant nothing to him, except *amo tokinwan*, but from the spacing, the punctuation, he knew what they were saying. *They eat us.* The crowd had become something fluid now, oozing freely from place to place; the distinction between dancers and audience was hard to discern. *Not our brother.* Halperin found one of the little curbside cantinas and asked for mescal. The proprietor splashed some in a paper cup and would not take his pesos. A gulp and Halperin felt warm again. He tried to return to Guzmán but no longer saw him in the surging, frenzied mob. The music was louder. Halperin began to dance—it was easier than walking—and found himself face to face with one of the bat-dancers, a short man whose elegant mask showed a bat upside down, in its resting position, ribbed wings folded like black shrouds. Halperin and the dancer, pushed close together in the press, fell into an inadvertent pas de deux. "I wish I could buy that mask," Halperin said. "What do you want for it? Five thousand pesos? Ten thousand? *Habla usted Español?* No? Come to the hotel with the mask tomorrow. You follow? *Venga mañana.*" There was no reply. Halperin was not even certain he had spoken the words aloud.

He danced his way back across the plaza. Midway he felt a hand catch his wrist. Ellen Chambers. Her khaki blouse was open almost to the waist and she had nothing beneath it. Her skin gleamed with sweat, as if it had been oiled. Her eyes were wide and rigid. She leaned close to him and said, "Dance! Everybody dances! Where's your mask?"

"He wouldn't sell it to me. I offered him ten thousand pesos, but he wouldn't—"

"Wear a different one," she said. "Any mask you like. How do you like mine?"

"Your mask?" He was baffled. She wore no mask.

"Come! Dance!" She moved wildly. Her breasts were practically bare and now and then a nipple flashed. Halperin knew that that was wrong, that the villagers were cautious about nudity and a *gringa* especially should not be exhibiting herself. Drunkenly he reached for her blouse, hoping to button one or two of the buttons, and to his chagrin his hand grazed one of her breasts. She laughed and pushed herself against him. For an instant she was glued to him from knees to chest, with his hand wedged stupidly between their bodies. Then he pulled back, confused. An avenue seemed to have opened around them. He started to walk stumblingly to some quieter part of the plaza, but she caught his wrist again and

grinned a tiger-grin, all incisors and tongue. "Come on!" she said
harshly.

He let her lead him. Past the taco stands, past the cantinas, past
a little brawl of drunken boys, past the church, on whose steps the
dancer in the phallic bat mask was performing, juggling pale green
fruits and now and then batting one out into the night with the
phallus that jutted from his chin. Then they were on one of the side
streets, blind crumbling walls hemming them on both sides and
cold moonlight the only illumination. Two blocks, three, his heart
pounding, his lungs protesting. Into an ungated courtyard of what
looked like an abandoned house, shattered tumbledown heaps of
masonry everywhere and a vining night-blooming cactus growing
over everything like a tangle of terrible green snakes. The cactus
was in bloom and its vast white trumpetlike flowers emitted a
sickly sweet perfume, overpoweringly intense. He wanted to gag
and throw up, but Ellen gave him no time, for she was embracing
him, pressing herself fiercely against him, forcing him back
against a pile of shattered adobe bricks. In the strange moonlight
her skin glistened and then seemed to become transparent, so that
he could see the cage of her ribs, the flat long plate of her breast-
bone, the throbbing purplish heart behind it. She was all teeth and
bones, a Day of the Dead totem come to life. He did not understand
and he could not resist. He was without will. Her hands roamed
him, so cold they burned his skin, sending up puffs of steam as her
icy fingers caressed him. Something was flowing from him to her,
his warmth, his essence, his vitality, and that was all right. The
mescal and the beer and the tequila and the thick musky fragrance
of the night-blooming cereus washed through his soul and left it
tranquil. From far away came the raw dissonant music, the flutes
and drums, and the laughter, the shouts, the chants. *They eat us.*
Her breath was smoke in his face. *They are worms, wild beasts.* As
they embraced one another, he imagined that she was insubstantial, a column of mist, and he began to feel misty himself, growing
thinner and less solid as his life-force flowed toward her. Now for
the first time he was seized by anguish and fright. As he felt himself being pulled from his body, his soul rushing forth and out and
out and out, helpless, drawn, his drugged calm gave way to panic.
*They are—not our brother.* He struggled, but it was useless. He
was going out swiftly, the essence of him quitting his body as
though she were reeling it in on a line. Bats fluttered above him,
their faces streaked with painted patterns, yellow and green and

brilliant ultramarine. The sky was a curtain of fiery bougainvillea. He was losing the struggle. He was too weak to resist or even to care. He could no longer hear himself breathe. He drifted freely, floating in the air, borne on the wings of the bats.

Then there was confusion, turmoil, struggle. Halperin heard voices speaking sharply in Spanish and in Nahuatl, but the words were incomprehensible to him. He rolled over on his side and drew his knees to his chest and lay shivering with his cheek against the warm wet soil. Someone was shaking him. A voice said in English, "Come back. Wake up. She is not here."

Halperin blinked and looked up. Guzmán was crouched above him, pale, stunned-looking, his teeth chattering. His eyes were wide and tensely fixed.

"Yes," Guzmán said. "Come back to us. Here. Sit up, let me help you."

The gallery-owner's arm was around his shoulders. Halperin was weak and trembling, and he realized Guzmán was trembling too. Halperin saw figures in the background—Filiberto from the hotel and his son Elustesio, the mayordomo Don Luis, the alcalde, one of the alguaciles.

"Ellen?" he said uncertainly.

"She is gone. *It* is gone. We have driven it away."

"It?"

"*Amo tokinwan.* Devouring your spirit."

"No," Halperin muttered. He stood up, still shaky, his knees buckling. Don Luis offered him a flask; Halperin shook it away, then changed his mind, reached for it, took a deep pull. Brandy. He walked four or five steps, getting his strength back. The reek of the cactus-flowers was nauseating. He saw the bare ribs again, the pulsating heart, the sharp white teeth. "No," he said. "It wasn't anything like that. I had too much to drink—maybe ate something that disagreed with me—the music, the scent of the flowers—"

"We saw," Guzmán said. His face was bloodless. "We were just in time. You would have been dead."

"She was from Miami—she said she knew San Francisco—"

"These days they take any form they like. The woman from Miami was here two years ago, for the fiesta. She vanished in the night, Don Luis says. And now she has come back. Perhaps next year there will be one who looks like you and talks like you and sniffs around studying the masks like you, and we will know it is

151

not you, and we will keep watch. Eh? You should come back to the hotel now. You need to rest."

Halperin walked between them down the walled streets. The fiesta was still in full swing, masked figures capering everywhere, but Guzmán and Don Luis and Filiberto guided him around the plaza and toward the hotel. He thought about the woman from Miami, and remembered that she had had no car and there had been no luggage in her room. *They eat us.* Such things are impossible, he told himself. *They are worms, wild beasts.* And next year would there be a diabolical counterfeit Halperin haunting the fiesta? *They are—not our brother.* He did not understand.

Guzmán said, "I promised you you would see the real Mexico. I did not think you would see as much of it as this."

Halperin insisted on inspecting her hotel room. It was empty and looked as if it had not been occupied for months. He stretched out on his bed fully clothed, but he did not particularly want to be left alone in the darkness, and so Guzmán and Filiberto and the others took turns sitting up with him through the night while the sounds of the fiesta filled the air. Dawn brought a dazzling sunrise. Halperin and Guzmán stepped out into the courtyard. The world was still.

"I think I'll leave here now," Halperin said.

"Yes. That would be wise. I will stay another day, I think."

Filiberto appeared, carrying the owl-pig mask from Halperin's room. "This is for you," he said. "Because that you were troubled here, that you will think kindly of us. Please take it as our gift."

Halperin was touched by that. He made a little speech of gratitude and put the mask in his car.

Guzmán said, "Are you well enough to drive?"

"I think so. I'll be all right once I leave here." He shook hands with everyone. His fingers were quivering. At a very careful speed he drove away from the hotel, through the plaza, where sleeping figures lay sprawled like discarded dolls, and mounds of paper streamers and other trash were banked high against the curb. At an even more careful speed he negotiated the cactus-walled road out of town. When he was about a kilometer from San Simón Zuluaga he glanced to his right and saw Ellen Chambers sitting next to him in the car. If he had been traveling faster, he would have lost control of the wheel. But after the first blinding moment of terror came a rush of annoyance and anger. "No," he said. "You don't belong in here. Get the hell out of here. Leave me alone." She laughed lightly. Halperin felt like sobbing. Swiftly and unhesitatingly he seized Filiberto's owl-pig mask, which lay on the seat beside him, and scaled it with a flip of his wrist past her nose and out the open car window. Then he clung tightly to the wheel and stared forward. When he could bring himself to look to the right again, she was gone. He braked to a halt and rolled up the window and locked the car door.

It took him all day to reach Acapulco. He went to bed immediately, without eating, and slept until late the following afternoon. Then he phoned the Aeromexico office.

Two days later he was home in San Francisco. The first thing he did was call a Sacramento Street dealer and arrange for the sale of all his masks. Now he collects Japanese netsuke, Hopi kachina dolls, and Navaho rugs. He buys only through galleries and does not travel much any more.

# JAMES TIPTREE, JR.

## "Beyond the Dead Reef"

*James Tiptree, Jr. was the best-known pseudonym of psychologist Alice Sheldon (1915-1987). Not surprisingly, much of the ground-breaking science fiction she began publishing in 1968 is concerned with gender roles and sexual identity. She is the author of two novels, the galaxy-spanning* Up the Walls of the World, *and* Brightness Falls from the Air, *a dark meditation on the significance of death. Her short fiction is her most highly regarded work. She won the Hugo Award for "The Girl Who Was Plugged In" and both the Hugo and Nebula for "Houston, Houston, Do You Read?" Collections of her stories include* Ten Thousand Light Years From Home, Warm Worlds and Otherwise, Star Songs of an Old Primate, Out of the Everywhere and Other Extraordinary Visions, *and the retrospective* Her Smoke Rose Up Forever. *"Beyond the Dead Reef" was collected in* Tales of the Quintana Roo, *a trilogy of fantasy stories based on legends of the Yucatan.*

# Beyond the Dead Reef

## by James Tiptree, Jr.

y informant was, of course, spectacularly unreliable.

The only character reference I have for him comes from the intangible nuances of a small restaurant-owner's remarks, and the only confirmation of his tale lies in the fact that an illiterate fishing-guide appears to believe it. If I were to recount all the reasons why no sane mind should take it seriously, we could never begin. So I will only report the fact that today I found myself shuddering with terror when a perfectly innocent sheet of seaworn plastic came slithering over my snorkeling-reef, as dozens have done for years—and get on with the story.

I met him one evening this December at the Cozumel *Buzo*, on my first annual supply trip. As usual, the *Buzo*'s outer rooms were jammed with tourist divers and their retinues and gear. That's standard. *El Buzo* means, roughly, The Diving, and the *Buzo* is their place. Marcial's big sign in the window reads "DIVVERS UEL-COME! BRING YR FISH WE COK WITH CAR. FIRST DRINK FREE!"

Until he went in for the "Divvers," Marcial's had been a small quiet place where certain delicacies like stone-crab could be at least semi-legally obtained. Now he did a roaring trade in snappers and groupers cooked to order at outrageous fees, with a flourishing sideline in fresh fish sales to the neighborhood each morning.

The "roaring" was quite literal. I threaded my way through a crush of burly giants and giantesses of all degrees of nakedness, hairiness, age, proficiency, and inebriation—all eager to share

155

their experiences and plans in voices powered by scuba-deafened ears and Marcial's free drink, beneath which the sound-system could scarcely be heard at full blast. (Marcial's only real expense lay in first-drink liquor so strong that few could recall whether what they ultimately ate bore any resemblance to what they had given him to cook.) Only a handful were sitting down yet, and the amount of gear underfoot and on the walls would have stocked three sports shops. This was not mere exhibitionism; on an island chronically short of washers, valves, and other spare parts the diver who lets his gear out of his sight is apt to find it missing in some vital.

I paused to allow a young lady to complete her massage of the neck of a youth across the aisle who was deep in talk with three others, and had time to notice the extraordinary number of heavy spear-guns racked about. Oklahomans, I judged, or perhaps South Florida. But then I caught clipped New England from the center group. Too bad; the killing mania seems to be spreading yearly, and the armament growing ever more menacing and efficient. When I inspected their platters, however, I saw the usual array of lavishly garnished lobsters and common fish. At least they had not yet discovered what to eat.

The mermaiden blocking me completed her task—unthanked— and I continued on my way in the little inner sanctum Marcial keeps for his old clientele. As the heavy doors cut off the uproar, I saw that this room was full too—three tables of dark-suited Mexican businessmen and a decorous family of eight, all quietly intent on their plates. A lone customer sat at the small table by the kitchen door, leaving an empty seat and a child's chair. He was a tall, slightly balding Anglo some years younger than I, in a very decent sports jacket. I recalled having seen him about now and then on my banking and shopping trips to the island.

Marcial telegraphed me a go-ahead nod as he passed through laden with more drinks, so I approached.

"Mind if I join you?"

He looked up from his stone-crab and gave me a slow, owlish smile.

"Welcome. A *diverse* welcome," he enunciated carefully. The accent was vaguely British, yet agreeable. I also perceived that he was extremely drunk, but in no common way.

"Thanks."

As I sat down I saw that he was a diver too, but his gear was stowed so unobtrusively I hadn't noticed it. I tried to stack my own modest snorkel outfit neatly, pleased to note that, like me, he seemed to carry no spear-gun. He watched me attentively, blinking once or twice, and then returned to an exquisitely exact dissection of his stone-crab.

When Marcial brought my own platter of crab—unasked—we engaged in our ritual converse. Marcial's English is several orders of magnitude better than my Spanish, but he always does me the delicate courtesy of allowing me to use his tongue. How did I find my rented *casita* on the coco ranch this year? Fine. How goes the tourist business this year? Fine. I learn from Marcial: the slight pause before his answer in a certain tone, meant that in fact the tourist business was lousy so far, but would hopefully pick up; I used the same to convey that in fact my *casa* was in horrible shape but reparable. I tried to cheer him by saying that I thought the *Buzo* would do better than the general *turismo*, because the diving enthusiasm was spreading in the States. "True," he conceded. "So long as they don't discover the other places—like Bélizé." Here he flicked a glance at my companion, who gave his solemn blink. I remarked that my country's politics were in disastrous disarray, and he conceded the same for his; the *Presidente* and his pals had just made off with much of the nation's treasury. And I expressed the hope that Mexico's new oil would soon prove a great boon. "Ah, but it will be a long time before it gets to the little people like us," said Marcial, with so much more than his normal acerbity that I refrained from my usual joke about his having a Swiss bank account. The uproar from the outer rooms had risen several decibels, but just before Marcial had to leave he paused and said in a totally different voice, "My grandson Antonito Vincente has four teeth!"

His emotion was so profound that I seized his free hand and shook it lightly, congratulating him in English. And then he was gone, taking on his "Mexican waiter" persona quite visibly as he passed the inner doors.

As we resumed our attention to the succulence before us, my companion said in his low, careful voice, "Nice chap, Marcial. He likes you."

"It's mutual," I told him between delicate mouthfuls. Stone-crab is not to be gulped. "Perhaps because I'm old enough to respect the limits where friendship ends and the necessities of life take over."

"I say, that's rather good," my companion chuckled. "Respect for the limits where friendship ends and the necessities of life take over, eh? Very few Yanks do, you know. At least the ones we see down here."

His speech was almost unslurred, and there were no drinks before him on the table. We chatted idly a bit more. It was becoming apparent that we would finish simultaneously and be faced with the prospect of leaving together, which could be awkward, if he, like me, had no definite plans for the evening.

The dilemma was solved when my companion excused himself momentarily just as Marcial happened by.

I nodded to his empty chair. "Is he one of your old customers, Señor Marcial?"

As always Marcial understood the situation at once. "One of the oldest," he told me, and added low-voiced, "*muy buenes gentes*—a really good guy. *Un poco de dificultades*—" he made an almost imperceptible gesture of drinking—"but *controlado*. And he has also *negocios*—I do not know all, but some are important for his country. —So you really like the crab?" he concluded in his normal voice. "We are honored."

My companion was emerging from the rather dubious regions that held the *excusado*.

Marcial's recommendation was good enough for me. Only one puzzle remained: what was his country? As we both refused *dulce* and coffee, I suggested that he might care to stroll down to the marina with me and watch the sunset.

"Good thought."

We paid up Marcial's outrageous bills and made our way through the exterior Bedlam, carrying our gear. One of the customers was brandishing his spear-gun as he protested his bill. Marcial seemed to have lost all his English except the words "Police," and cooler heads were attempting to calm the irate one. "All in a night's work," my companion commented as we emerged into a blaze of golden light.

The marina to our left was a simple L-shaped *muelle*, or pier, still used by everything from dinghies to commercial fishermen and baby yachts. It will be a pity when and if the town decides to separate the sports tourist-trade from the more interesting working craft. As we walked out toward the pier in the last spectacular color of the tropic sunset over the mainland, the rigging lights of a cruise ship standing out in the channel came on, a fairyland illusion over the all-too-dreary reality.

"They'll be dumping and cleaning out their used bunkers

tonight," my companion said, slurring a trifle now. He had a conge-
nial walking gait, long-strided but leisurely. I had the impression
that his drunkenness had returned slightly; perhaps the fresh air.
"Damn crime."

"I couldn't agree more," I told him. "I remember when we used to
start snorkeling and scuba diving right off the shore here—you
could almost wade out to untouched reefs. And now—"

There was no need to look; one could smell it. The effluvia of half
a dozen hotels and the town behind ran out of pipes that were
barely covered at low tide; on a few parrot fish, who can stand anything, remained by the hotel-side restaurants to feed on the crusts
the tourists threw them from their tables. And only the very igno-
rant would try out—once—the dilapidated Sunfish and water-ski
renters who plied the small stretches of beach between hotels.

We sat down on one of the near benches to watch a commercial
trawler haul net. I had been for some time aware that my companion, while of largely British culture, was not completely Cau-
casian. There was a minute softness to the voice, a something not
quite dusky about hair and fingernails—not so much as to be what
in my youth was called "A touch of tarbrush," but nothing that
originated in Yorkshire, either. Nor was it the obvious Hispano-
Indian. I recollected Marcial's earlier speech and enlightenment
came.

"Would I be correct in taking Marcial's allusions to mean that
you are a British Honduran—forgive me, I mean a Bélizéian, or
Bélizan?"

"Nothing to forgive, old chap. We haven't existed long enough to
get our adjectives straight."

"May god send you do." I was referring to the hungry maws of
Guatemala and Honduras, the little country's big neighbors, who
had the worst of intentions toward her. "I happen to be quite a fan
of your country. I had some small dealings there after independence which involved getting all my worldly goods out of your customs on a national holiday, and people couldn't have been finer to
me."

"Ah yes. Bélizé the blessed, where sixteen nationalities live in
perfect racial harmony. The odd thing is, they do."

"I could see that. But I couldn't quite count all sixteen."

"My own grandmother was a Burmese—so called. I think it was
the closest grandfather could come to Black. Although the mix *is*
extraordinary."

"My factor there was a very dark Hindu with red hair and a Scottish accent, named Robinson. I had to hire him in seven minutes. He was a miracle of efficiency. I hope he's still going."

"Robinson . . . Used to work for customs?"

"Why, yes, now you recall it."

"He's fine. . . . Of course, we felt it when the British left. Among other things, half the WCs in the hotels broke down the first month. But there are more important things in life than plumbing."

"That I believe. . . . But you know, I've never been sure how much help the British would have been to you. Two years before your independence I called the British Embassy with a question about your immigration laws, and believe it or not I couldn't find one soul who even knew there *was* a British Honduras, let alone that they owned it. One child finally denied it flatly and hung up. And this was their main embassy in Washington, D.C. I realized then that Britain was not only sick, but crazy."

"Actually denied our existence, eh?" My companion's voice held a depth and timbre of sadness such as I have heard only from victims of better-known world wrongs. Absently his hand went under his jacket, and he pulled out something gleaming.

"Forgive me." It was a silver flask, exquisitely plain. He uncapped and drank, a mere swallow, but, I suspected, something of no ordinary power. He licked his lips as he recapped it, and sat up straighter while he put it away.

"Shall we move along out to the end?"

"With pleasure."

We strolled on, passing a few late sports-boats disgorging hungry divers.

"I'm going to do some modest exploring tomorrow," I told him. "A guide named Jorge—" in Spanish it's pronounced Horhay— "Jorge Chuc is taking me out to the end of the north reef. He says there's a pretty little untouched spot out there. I hope so. Today I went south, it was so badly shot over I almost wept. Cripples—and of course shark everywhere. Would you believe I found a big she-turtle, trying to live with a steel bolt through her neck? I managed to catch her, but all I could do for her was pull it out. I hope she makes it."

"Bad . . . Turtles are tough, though. If it wasn't vital you may have saved her. But did you say that Jorge Chuc is taking you to the end of the north reef?"

"Yes, why? Isn't it any good?"

"Oh, there is one pretty spot. But there's some very bad stuff there too. If you don't mind my advice, don't go far from the boat. I mean, a couple of meters. And don't follow anything. And above all be very sure it *is* Jorge's boat."

His voice had become quite different, with almost military authority.

"A couple of meters!" I expostulated. "But—"

"I know, I know. What I don't know is why Chuc is taking you there at all." He thought for a moment. "You haven't by any chance offended him, have you? In any way?"

"Why, no—we were out for a long go yesterday, and had a nice chat on the way back. Yes . . . although he is a trifle changeable, isn't he? I put it down to fatigue, and gave him some extra *dinero* for being only one party."

My companion made an untranslatable sound, compounded of dubiety, speculation, possible enlightenment, and strong suspicion.

"Did he tell you the name of that part of the reef? Or that it's out of sight of land?"

"Yes, he said it was far out. And that part of it was so poor it's called dead."

"And you chatted—forgive me, but was your talk entirely in Spanish?"

I chuckled deprecatingly. "Well, yes—I know my Spanish is pretty horrible, but he seemed to get the drift."

"Did you mention his family?"

"Oh, yes—I could draw you the whole Chuc family tree."

"Hmmm . . ." My companion's eyes had been searching the pierside where the incoming boats were being secured for the night.

"Ah. There's Chuc now. This is none of my business, you understand—but do I have your permission for a short word with Jorge?"

"Why, yes. If you think it necessary."

"I do, my friend. I most certainly do."

"Carry on."

His long-legged stride had already carried him to Chuc's big skiff, the *Estrellita*. Chuc was covering his motors. I had raised my hand in greeting but he was apparently too busy to respond. Now he greeted my companion briefly, but did not turn when he clambered into the boat uninvited. I could not hear the interchange. But presently the two men were standing, faces somewhat averted from each other as they conversed. My companion made rather a long speech, ending with questions. There was little response from Chuc until a sudden outburst from him took me by surprise. The odd dialogue went on for some time after that; Chuc seemed to calm down. Then the tall Bélizan waved me over.

"Will you say exactly what I tell you to say?"

"Why—" But his expression stopped me. "If you say it's important."

"It is. Can you say in Spanish, 'I ask your pardon, Mr. Chuc. I mistook myself in your language. I did not say anything of what you thought I said. Please forgive my error. And please let us be friends again.' "

"I'll try."

I stumbled through the speech, which I will not try to reproduce here, as I repeated several phrases with what I thought was better accent, and I'm sure I threw several verbs into the conditional future. Before I was through, Chuc was beginning to grin. When I came to the "friends" part he had relaxed, and after a short pause, said in very tolerable English, "I see, so I accept your apology. We will indeed be friends. It was a regrettable error. . . . And I advise you, do not again speak in Spanish."

We shook on it.

"Good," said my companion. "And he'll take you out tomorrow, but not the Dead Reef. And keep your hands off your wallet tonight, but I suggest liberality tomorrow eve."

We left Chuc to finish up, and paced down to a bench at the very end of the *muelle*. The last colors of evening, peaches and rose shot with unearthly green, were set off by a few low-lying clouds already in grey shadow, like sharks of the sky passing beneath a sentimental vision of bliss.

"Now what was all *that* about!" I demanded of my new friend. He was just tucking the flask away again, and shuddered lightly.

"I don't wish to seem overbearing, but *that* probably saved your harmless life, my friend. I repeat Jorge's advice—stay away from that Spanish of yours unless you are absolutely sure of being understood."

"I know it's ghastly."

"That's not actually the problem. The problem is that it isn't ghastly enough. Your pronunciation is quite fair, and you've mastered some good idioms, so people who don't know you think you speak more fluently than you do. In this case the trouble came from your damned rolled *rrr*s. Would you mind saying the words for 'but' and 'dog'?"

"*Pero . . . perro.* Why?"

"The difference between a rolled and a single *r*, particularly in Maya Spanish, is very slight. The upshot of it was that you not only insulted his boat in various ways, but you ended by referring to his mother as a dog. . . . He was going to take you out beyond the Dead Reef and leave you there."

"*What?*"

"Yes. And if it hadn't been I who asked—he knows I know the story—you'd never have understood a thing. Until you turned up as a statistic."

"Oh, Jesus Christ . . ."

"Yes," he said dryly.

"I guess some thanks are in order," I said finally. "But words seem a shade inadequate. Have you any suggestions?"

My companion suddenly turned and gave a highly concentrated look.

"You were in World War Two, weren't you? And afterwards you worked around quite a bit." He wasn't asking me, so I kept quiet. "Right now, I don't see anything," he went on. "But just possibly I might be calling on you," he grinned, "with something you may not like."

"If it's anything I can do from a wheelchair, I won't forget."

"Fair enough. We'll say no more about it now."

"Oh yes, we will," I countered. "You may not know it, but you owe *me* something. I can smell a story when one smacks me in the face. What I want from you is the story behind this Dead Reef business, and how it is that Jorge knows you know something special about it. If I'm not asking too much? I'd really like to end our evening with your tale of the Dead Reef."

"Oho. My error—I'd forgotten Marcial telling me you wrote. . . . Well, I can't say I enjoy reliving it, but maybe it'll have a salutary effect on your future dealings in Spanish. The fact is, I was the one it happened to, and Jorge was driving a certain boat. You realize, though, there's not a shred of proof except my own word? And my own word—" he tapped the pocket holding his flask "—is only as good as you happen to think it is."

"It's good enough for me."

"Very well, then. Very well," he said slowly, leaning back. "It happened about three, no, four years back—by god, you know this is hard to tell, though there's not much to it." He fished in another pocket, and took out, not a flask, but the first cigarette I'd seen him smoke, a *Petit Caporal*. "I was still up to a long day's scuba then, and, like you, I wanted to explore north. I'd run into this nice, strong, young couple who wanted the same thing. Their gear was good, they seemed experienced and sensible. So we got a third tank apiece, and hired a trustable boatman—not Jorge, Victor Camul— to take us north over the worst of the reef. It wasn't so bad then, you know.

"We would be swimming north with the current until a certain point, where if you turn east, you run into a long reverse eddy that makes it a lot easier to swim back to Cozumel. And just to be extra safe, Victor was to start out up the eddy in two hours sharp to meet us and bring us home. I hadn't one qualm about the arrangements. Even the weather cooperated—not a cloud, and the forecast perfect. Of course, if you miss up around here, the next stop is four hundred miles to Cuba, but you know that; one gets used to it. . . . By the way, have you heard they're still looking for that girl who's been gone two days on a Sunfish with no water?"

I said nothing.

"Sorry." He cleared his throat. "Well, Victor put us out well in sight of shore. We checked watches and compasses and lights. The plan was for the lad Harry to lead, Ann to follow, and me to bring up the rear. Harry had Day Glo-red shorts you could see a mile, and Ann was white-skinned with long black hair and a brilliant neon-blue-and-orange bathing suit on her little rump—you could have seen her in a mine at midnight. Even I got some yellow safety-tape and tied it around my arse and tanks.

"The one thing we didn't have then was a radio. At the time they didn't seem worth the crazy cost, and were unreliable besides. I had no way of guessing I'd soon give my life for one—and very nearly did.

"Well, when Victor let us out and we got organized and started north single file over the dead part of the reef, we almost surfaced and yelled for him to take us back right then. It was purely awful. But we knew there was better stuff ahead, so we stuck it out and flippered doggedly along—actually doing pretty damn fair time, with the current—and trying not to look too closely at what lay below.

"Not only was the coral dead, you understand—that's where the name got started. We think now it's from oil and chemical wash, such as that pretty ship out there is about to contribute—but there was tons and tons of litter, *basura* of all description, crusted there. It's everywhere, of course—you've seen what washes onto the mainland beach—but here the current and the reef produce a particularly visible concentration. Even quite large heavy things—bedsprings, auto chassis—in addition to things you'd expect, like wrecked skiffs. Cozumel, *Basurero del Caribe!"*

He gave a short laugh, mocking the Gem-of-the-Caribbean ads, as he lit up another *Caporal*. The most polite translation of *basurero* is garbage can.

"A great deal of the older stuff was covered with that evil killer algae—you know, the big coarse red-brown hairy kind, which means that nothing else can ever grow there again. But some of the heaps were too new.

"I ended by getting fascinated and swimming lower to look, always keeping one eye on that blue-and-orange rump above me with her white legs and black flippers. And the stuff—I don't mean just Clorox and *detergente* bottles, beer cans and netting—but weird things like about ten square meters of butchered pink plastic baby-dolls—arms and legs wiggling, and rosebud mouths—it looked like a babies' slaughter-house. Syringes, hypos galore. Fluorescent tubes on end, waving like drowned orchestra conductors. A great big red sofa with a skeletonized banana-stem or *something* sitting on it—when I saw that, I went back up and followed right behind Ann.

"And then the sun dimmed unexpectedly, so I surfaced for a look. The shoreline was fine, we had plenty of time, and the cloud was just one of a dozen little thermals that form on a hot afternoon like this. When I went back down Ann was looking at me, so I gave her the All's Fair sign. And with that we swam over a pair of broken dories and found ourselves in a different world—the beauty patch we'd been looking for.

"The reef was live here—whatever had killed the coral hadn't reached yet, and the damned *basura* had quit or been deflected, aside from a beer bottle or two. There was life everywhere; anemones, sponges, conches, fans, stars—and fish, oh my! No one ever came here, you see. In fact, there didn't seem to have been any spearing, the fish were as tame as they used to be years back.

"Well, we began zig-zagging back and forth, just reveling in it. And every time we'd meet head-on we'd make the gesture of putting our fingers to our lips, meaning, Don't tell anyone about this, ever!

"The formation of the reef was charming, too. It broadened into a sort of big stadium, with allées and cliffs and secret pockets, and there were at least eight different kinds of coral. And most of it was shallow enough so the sunlight brought out the glorious colors—those little black-and-yellow fish—butterflies, I forget their proper name—were dazzling. I kept having to brush them off my mask, they wanted to look in.

"The two ahead seemed to be in ecstasies; I expect they hadn't seen much like this before. They swam on and on, investigating it all—and I soon realized there was real danger of losing them in some coral pass. So I stuck tight to Ann. But time was passing. Presently I surfaced again to investigate—and, my god, the shoreline was damn near invisible and the line-up we had selected for our turn marker was all but passed! Moreover, a faint hazy overcast was rising from the west.

"So I cut down again, intending to grab Ann and start, which Harry would have to see. So I set off after the girl. I used to be a fair sprint swimmer, but I was amazed how long it took me to catch her. I recall vaguely noticing that the reef was going a bit bad again, dead coral here and there. Finally I came right over her, signed to her to halt, and kicked up in front of her nose for another look.

"To my horror the shoreline was gone and the overcast had overtaken the sun. We would have to swim east by compass, and swim hard. I took a moment to hitch my compass around where I could see it well—it was the old-fashioned kind—and then I went back down for Ann. And the damn fool girl wasn't there. It took me a minute to locate that blue bottom and white legs; I assumed she'd gone after Harry, having clearly no idea of the urgency of our predicament.

"I confess the thought crossed my mind that I could cut out of there, and come back for them later with Victor, but this was playing a rather iffy game with someone else's lives. And if they were truly unaware, it would be fairly rotten to take off without even warning them. So I went after Ann again—my god, I can still see that blue tail and the white limbs and black feet and hair with the light getting worse every minute and the bottom now gone really rotten again. And as bad luck would have it she was going in just the worst line—north-north-west.

"Well, I swam and I swam and I *swam*. You know how a chase takes you, and somehow being unable to overtake a mere girl made it worse. But I was gaining, age and all, until just as I got close enough to sense something was wrong, she turned sidewise above two automobile tires—and I saw it wasn't a girl at all.

"I had been following a goddamned great fish—a fish with a bright blue-and-orange band around its belly, and a thin white body ending in a black flipperlike tail. Even its head and nape were black, like her hair and mask. It had a repulsive catfishlike mouth, with barbels.

"The thing goggled at me and then swam awkwardly away, just as the light went worse yet. But there was enough for me to see that it was no normal fish, either, but a queer archaic thing that looked more tacked together than grown. This I can't swear to, because I was looking elsewhere by then, but it was my strong impression that as it went out of my line of sight its whole tail broke off.

"But as I say, I was looking elsewhere. I had turned my light on, although I was not deep but only dim, because I had to ready my watch and compass. It had just dawned on me that I was very probably a dead man. My only chance, if you can call it that, was to swim east as long as I could, hoping for that eddy and Victor. And when my light came on, the first thing I saw was the girl, stark naked and obviously stone cold dead, lying in a tangle of nets and horrid stuff on the bottom ahead.

"Of Harry or anything human there was no sign at all. But there was a kind of shining, like a pool of moonlight, around her, which was so much stronger than my lamp that I clicked it off and swam slowly toward her, through the nastiest mess of *basura* I had yet seen. The very water seemed vile. It took longer to reach her than I had expected, and soon I saw why.

"They speak of one's blood running cold with horror, y'know. Or people becoming numb with horror piled on horrors. I believe I experienced both those effects. It isn't pleasant, even now." He lit a third *Caporal*, and I could see that the smoke column trembled. Twilight had fallen while he'd been speaking. A lone mercury lamp came on at the shore end of the pier; the one near us was apparently out, but we sat in what would ordinarily have been a pleasant tropic evening, sparkling with many moving lights—whites, reds, and green, of late-moving incomers, and the rainbow lighting from the jewel-lit cruise ship ahead, all cheerfully reflected in the unusually calm waters.

"Again I was mistaken, you see. It wasn't Ann at all; but the rather more distant figure of a young woman, of truly enormous size. All in this great ridge of graveyard luminosity, of garbage in phosphorescent decay. The current was carrying me slowly, inexorably, right toward her—as it had carried all that was there now. And perhaps I was also a bit hypnotized. She grew in my sight meter by meter as I neared her. I think six meters—eighteen feet—was about it, at the end. . . . I make that guess later, you understand, as an exercise in containing the unbearable—by recalling the size of known items in the junkpile she lay on. One knee, for example, lay alongside an oil drum. At the time she simply filled my world. I had no doubt she was dead, and very beautiful. One of her legs seemed to writhe gently.

"The next stage of horror came when I realized that she was not a gigantic woman at all—or rather, like the fish, she was a woman-shaped construction. The realization came to me first, I think, when I could no longer fail to recognize that her 'breasts' were two of those great net buoys with their blue knobs for nipples.

"After that it all came with a rush—that she was a made-up body—all sorts of pieces of plastic, rope, styrofoam, netting, crates, and bolts—much of it clothed with that torn translucent white polyethylene for skin. Her hair was a dreadful tangle of something, and her crotch was explicit and unspeakable. One hand was a torn, inflated rubber glove, and her face—well, I won't go into it except that one eye was a traffic reflector and her mouth was partly a rusted can.

"Now you might think this discovery would have brought some relief, but quite the opposite. Because simultaneously I had realized the very worst thing of all—

"She was alive."

He took a long drag on his cigarette.

"You know how things are moved passively in water? Plants waving, a board seesawing and so on? Sometimes enough almost to give an illusion of mobile life. What I saw was nothing of this short.

"It wasn't merely that as I floated over, her horrible eyes 'opened' and looked at me and her rusted-can mouth *smiled*. Oh, no.

"What I mean is that as she smiled, first one whole arm, shedding junk, stretched up and reached for me *against the current*, and then the other did the same.

"And when I proved to be out of reach, this terrifying figure, or creature, or unliving life, actually sat up, again *against the current*, and reached up toward me with both arms at full extension.

"And as she did so, one of her 'breasts'—the right one—came loose and dangled by some tenuous thready stuff.

"All this seemed to pass in slow motion—I even had time to see that there were other unalive yet living things moving near her on the pile. Not fish, but more what I should have taken, on land, for rats or vermin—and I distinctly recall the paper-flat skeleton of something like a chicken, running and pecking. And other moving things like nothing in this world. I have remembered all this very carefully, y'see, from what must have been quick glimpses, because in actual fact I was apparently kicking like mad in a frenzied effort to get away from those dreadful reaching arms.

"It was not till I shot to the surface with a mighty splash that I came somewhere near my senses. Below and behind me I could still see faint cold light. Above was twilight and the darkness of an oncoming small storm.

"At that moment the air in my last tank gave out—or rather that splendid Yank warning buzz, which means you have just time to get out of your harness, sounded off.

"I had, thank god, practiced the drill. Despite being a terror-paralysed madman, habit got me out of the harness before the tanks turned into lethal deadweight. In my panic, of course, the headlight went down too. I was left unencumbered in the night, free to swim toward Cuba, or Cozumel, and to drown as slow or fast as fate willed.

"The little storm had left the horizon stars free. I recall that pure habit made me take a sight on what seemed to be Canopus, which should be over Cozumel. I began to swim in that direction. I was appallingly tired, and as the adrenalin of terror which had brought me this far began to fade out of my system, I realized I could soon be merely drifting, and would surely die in the next day's sun if I survived till then. Nevertheless it seemed best to swim whilst I could.

"I rather resented it when some time after a boat motor passed nearby. It forced me to attempt to yell and wave, nearly sinking myself. I was perfectly content when the boat passed on. But someone had seen—a spotlight wheeled blindingly, motors reversed, I was forcibly pulled from my grave and voices from what I take to be your Texas demanded, roaring with laughter,"—here he gave quite a creditable imitation—" 'Whacha doin' out hyar, boy, this time of night? Ain't no pussy out hyar, less'n ya'all got a date with a mermaid.' They had been trolling for god knows what, mostly beer.

"The driver of that boat claimed me as a friend and later took me home for the night, where I told him—and to him alone—the whole story. He was Jorge Chuc.

"Next day I found that the young couple, Harry and Ann, had taken only a brief look at the charming unspoiled area, and then started east, exactly according to plan, with me—or something very much like me—following behind them all the way. They had been a trifle surprised at my passivity and uncommunicativeness, and more so when, on meeting Victor, I was no longer to be found. But they had taken immediate action, even set a full-scale search in progress—approximately seventy kilometers from where I then was. As soon as I came to myself I had to concoct a wild series of lies about cramps and heart trouble to get them in the clear and set their minds at ease. Needless to say, my version included no mention of diver-imitating fish-life."

He tossed the spark of his cigarette over the rail before us.

"So now, my friend, you know the whole story of all I know of what is to be found beyond the Dead Reef. It may be that others know of other happenings and developments there. Or of similar traps elsewhere. The sea is large. . . . Or it may be that the whole yarn comes from neuroses long abused by stuff like this."

I had not seen him extract his flask, but he now took two deep, shuddering swallows.

I sighed involuntarily, and then sighed again. I seemed to have been breathing rather inadequately during the end of his account.

"Ordinary thanks don't seem quite appropriate here," I finally said. "Though I do thank you. Instead I am going to make two guesses. The second is that you might prefer to sit quietly here alone, enjoying the evening, and defer the mild entertainment I was about to offer you to some other time. I'd be glad to be proved wrong . . . ?"

"No. You're very perceptive, I welcome the diverse—the deferred offer." His tongue stumbled a bit now, more from fatigue than anything he'd drunk. "But what was your first guess?"

I rose and slowly paced a few meters to and fro, remembering to pick up my absurd snorkel bag. Then I turned and gazed out to the sea.

"I can't put it into words. It has something to do with the idea that the sea is still, well, strong. Perhaps it can take revenge? No, that's too simple. I don't know. I have only a feeling that our ordinary ideas of what may be coming on us may be—oh—not deep, or broad enough. I put this poorly. But perhaps the sea, or nature, will not die passively at our hands . . . perhaps death itself may turn or return in horrible life upon us, besides the more mechanical dooms. . . ."

"Our thoughts are not so far apart," the tall Bélizan said. "I welcome them to my night's agenda."

"To which I now leave you, unless you've changed your mind?"

He shook his head. I hoisted his bag to the seat beside him. "Don't forget this. I almost left mine."

"Thanks. And don't you forget about dogs and mothers," he grinned faintly.

"Goodnight."

My footsteps echoed on the now deserted *muelle* left him sitting there. I was quite sure he was no longer smiling.

Nor was I.

# WILLIAM F. WU

# "Wong's Lost and Found Emporium"

*The stories of William F. Wu are heady blends of fantasy and science fiction, often steeped in the lore and legends of China. His first novel,* Masterplay, *is set in a fantasy wargaming world, and his cyberwestern,* Hong on the Range, *is based on the exploits of his series character Hong, a Chinese-American gunslinger. He has written young-adult novels in Isaac Asimov's "Robots in Time" series and Robert Silverberg's "Time Travels" series. His short fiction has appeared in numerous anthologies, including* Pulphouse. *The Hugo, Nebula and World Fantasy Award-nominated "Wong's Lost and Found Emporium" is the title story of his first collection of short fiction.*

# Wong's Lost and Found Emporium

*by William F. Wu*

---

he sharp clicking of high heels echoed in the dark shop. The brisk footsteps on the unpolished wooden floor slowed and became irregular and uncertain as my new visitor saw some of the stuff on the shelves. They always did that.

I was on a different aisle. The shop was very big, though crammed with all kinds of objects to the point where every shelf was crowded and overflowing. Most of the stuff was inanimate, or at least dead. However, many of the beasties still stirred when adequately provoked. The inanimate objects included everything from uncut diamonds to nailclippers to bunny bladders. Still more of the sealed crates and boxes and bottles contained critters, or other things, that might or might not be counted among the living. I had no idea and didn't care, either. For instance, whoever had hung big wooden crates from the ceiling—and there were plenty, up where they couldn't endanger anybody—must have had a good reason.

The edges of the shop were a little mysterious. I tried not to go too far down any of the aisles except the two big perpendicular corridors that ended in doors to the outside. They formed a cross in the center of the shop. The farther from the middle I went in any direction, the darker the place became, and colder. On a few occasions, I had had to go out to shelf space on the fringe that was mostly empty, and in almost complete darkness. All the edges were like that, except for the four doors at each end of those main corridors.

I didn't dare venture into the real darkness, where nothing was visible. Cold stale air seemed to be all it contained, but I wasn't going to investigate. I also had a suspicion that the shop kept growing of its own accord, outward into that nothingness. I had seen for myself that new stuff spontaneously appeared on all the shelves; but if the shop had been finite in size, it would have been absolutely crammed to the ceiling. Instead, I guessed, it simply extended its aisles and plain wooden shelves outward somehow, always providing just enough new empty space to avoid total chaos. The place was weird enough where I was; I didn't see any need to wander off the edge of the world or something.

I was seeking my destiny in this world, or at least I had been hoping to when I first came in here. My visitor was probably doing the same right now.

I came around the corner into one of the two main corridors, where the light was a little better. For a second, I thought I heard someone in one of the aisles, but that sort of thing happened all the time. Some of the live beings thumped and slithered in their containers occasionally.

My customer was a woman with snow-white hair, slender and well-dressed with a good tan. She wore a peach-colored suit and four gold chains around her neck. One hand with long, peach-colored fingernails clutched a small handbag. She looked like a shrivelled peach in a light snowfall.

"Oh—uh, I'm looking for Mr. Wong, I guess." She smiled cautiously.

"That's me," I said, walking forward briskly. After I had been here a while, I had put my signs on the four doors, saying **Wong's Lost and Found Emporium.**

She looked me over in some surprise; they always seemed to expect a doddering old geezer with a wispy white beard and an opium pipe, muttering senilities to the spirit world. I wore a blue T-shirt, fading Levi's, and Adidas indoor track shoes. After all, I'd only been here a few months, though time was different in here than on the outside. This was that kind of place.

"Oh, I'm sorry." She smiled apologetically, fidgeting now with all ten peach fingernails scratching at her purse.

"The name is Wong," I said casually, "but you can call me Mr. Double-you for short."

She didn't get the joke—they never do.

"Thank you. I, uh, was told that . . . this is an unusual shop? Where one can find something . . . she lost?"

"If you lost it, I got it." Like most of the others, she needed more encouragement. I waited for her to ask.

"I mean . . . well, I suppose this will sound silly, but . . . I'm not looking for a thing, exactly, not a solid object, I don't suppose you have a . . . second chance?" She forced herself to laugh, a little, like it was a joke. "Well, no, I'm sorry. I really just need a restroom, and—"

"Of course I have it," I said. "If you lost a chance at something, it's here. Follow me."

I looked around the floor and pointed to the little blue throw rug. "Have to watch out for this. It slips."

She smiled politely, but I could see her shaking with anticipation.

I glanced around the shelves, looking for the little spot of white. "What's your name?" It didn't matter, but asking made me sound official.

"I'm Mrs. Barbara Patricia Whitford and I live here in Boca. Um—I was born in New York in 1926. I grew up . . ."

I didn't care. A bit of white light was shining on a shoulder-high shelf across the main corridor from me. "This way," I said, signalling over my shoulder. She shut up and followed me.

As we walked, the light moved ahead of us toward the object she wanted to recover. I had no idea how it worked—I had figured it out by trial and error, or I might say by accident. I had come in here myself looking for something I had lost, but the place had had no one in it. Now, I was waiting for the proprietor, but everyone else who came in thought I was in charge. So I was.

"What kind of chance was it?" I asked over my shoulder, like it was shoe size or something. It might be a long walk.

"Well," she said, just a little breathless behind me. "I always wanted to be an artist—a painter. I didn't get started until fifteen years ago, when I started taking lessons in acrylics. And even oils. I got pretty good, even if I do say so. Several of my paintings sold at art fairs and I was just getting a few exhibited, even. I got discouraged, though. It was so hard to keep going."

The white light turned down another aisle, more cramped and dimly lit then the last. The light was brighter in these shadows, but she couldn't see it. Only I could. I had tested that on earlier customers. Unfortunately, I couldn't see my own.

A shadow shifted in the corner of my eye that was not mine or hers, but I ignored it. If something large was loose in here, it was apparently shy. It was nothing new.

"Six or seven years ago," she continued, "all of my friends were going back to school. It was easier than painting—I went for my Master's; and since I was just going to go, I didn't really have to hurry, or worry about grades. It was the thing to do, and so much easier than painting. Only, I didn't care about it." Her voice caught, and she paused to swallow. "I do care about my painting. Now, well, I just would like to have the chance I missed, when my skills were still sharp and I had more time and business connections. It—I know it sounds small. But it's the only thing I've ever accomplished. And I don't have time to start over."

She started crying.

I nodded. The white light had come to a stop, playing across a big open wooden box on an upper shelf. "Just a moment. I'll get it. It's very important to get exactly the right one, because if you get the wrong object, you're still stuck with it."

She nodded, watching me start to climb up the wooden shelves.

"For instance, if I gave you someone else's lost chance to work a slow freighter to Sakhalin Island, why, it would just happen. You'd have to go."

"I would? . . . oh. Well, be careful." She sniffled. "No, uh, glove cleaner or anything like that. If you know what I mean."

The shelves were dusty and disgusting. My fingers caught cobwebs and brushed against small feathery clumps that were unidentifiable in the shadowy aisle. Tiny feet scurried away from me on the shelves as I climbed, prodding aside old jars with my feet. Faint shuffling noises came from inside some of them.

I finally got my head up to the shelf with the little light. It was now sitting on a transparent cylindrical container inside the wooden box. Inside, ugly brown lumps swirled around in a thick, emerald-green solution.

The box had several similar containers and a lot of miscellaneous junk. I grabbed one of the smaller pieces at random and stuck it in my pants pocket. Then I tucked the swirling green cylinder under one arm and started down.

When I had reached the floor, I held it up. Her eyes grew wide when she saw the liquid spinning inside. "Okay," I said. "When you open this, the contents will evaporate very quickly. You have to breathe in the vapor before it disappears, or the chance is lost forever." I had done this before.

She took it from me, glowing like a half-lit wino.

"You can do it here if you want," I said, "but the light's better in the main corridors."

She nodded and followed me as close as one dog behind another.

We turned along the main corridor, and I walked at a good clip back toward my beat-up steel desk and battered piano stool. They were near the junction of the main corridors. This was her business.

Before I got there, I heard a slight gasp behind me and turned around. She had slipped on the throw rug and as I turned, her slender legs were struggling for balance. Her arms reflexively made a sharp upward movement and her precious transparent cylinder was tossed out to one side.

The woman let out a wail as it sailed away and smashed on the hard floorboards. She clattered after it clumsily in her high heels. When she finally reached it, she bent over and started sniffling around like a bowser at a barbeque.

I got up stiffly and walked over.

"Did I get it? Did I get it?" She whimpered frantically.

"Doubt it," I said, sniffing around. If the stuff had lingered long enough for her to inhale it, I would have smelled some residual scent.

"Oh, no—I . . . uh . . . but, but—" She started to cry.

Criers bore into me. I had a vague sense that I was expected to be sympathetic, but I had lost that ability. That's what I was here for, in fact.

"Wait a minute," I said, tapping her on the shoulder. I reached into my pocket for the other lost object I had taken from her box. It was a metal ring with four or five keys on it and a leather circle with "BPW" stamped in gold. The keys looked fairly new; I figured she had lost them some time in the decade or so. "Here," I said. "You lost these, too."

"What?" She looked up between sobs.

I gave her the keys. "I'm glad you came. Have a nice day."

"What?" She stared at the keys. "It was the *only* thing I ever accomplished," she whimpered. "Ever." She turned away, in shock, her wide eyes fixed blankly on her old car keys. "It was my very last chance." She squeaked in a high, tiny voice.

"That way." I took her shoulders and aimed her down the corridor that led to a shopping mall in Florida.

She staggered away, snuffling.

I sat down disgustedly on a nearby stool. My time was almost up. I had to leave soon in order to get any sleep at home and then show up at work tomorrow. Without savings, I couldn't afford to leave my job, even for something as important as this. If the proprietor had been coming back, then he, she, or it would probably have returned by now. The dual passages of time in here and outside meant that I had spent over two months here, and I had only spent one week of sick days and vacation days back in New York, on the other side of one of the doors.

I had even taken my job on a loading dock in Chinatown just to be near this shop. That was why I had moved to New York. When a friend had first told me about this establishment, she had warned me of the trickiest part—the doors could not always be located. Different people could find them at their own times, sometimes. The door in New York appeared, when it did, in the back hall of a small, second-story Chinatown restaurant. Most of the time, the hall ended in two restroom doors. For a select few, though, it occasionally had three, and now the mystic third door bore my sign.

I had checked the spot often; and when I had found the door, I had phoned in immediately for a week off, begging an emergency. It had taken some arguing, but I had managed. The presence of the restaurant had allowed me to stay so long, since I sneaked food out when night fell in New York. Naturally, the shop had a few misplaced refrigerators and other appliances; a few even worked.

Once I left this place, I might not find the door again for years—if ever.

I kicked in annoyance at a random bit of crud on the floor. It unfolded five legs and scurried away under a nearby shelf. Well, I had left a mark; the doors all bore my handmade signs, minor amusement though they were.

At least my stay had been eventful. My first customer after I had figured out how the place worked had been a tall slender Chinese guy from the San Francisco corridor. The door there was in the back of a porno shop. He had been in his fifties and wore a suit that had been in style in 1961, when it was last pressed. Something about him suggested Taiwan.

He had come looking for the respect of his children, which he had of course lost. I found him a box with five frantic mice in it:

what he had to do was pet them until they calmed down. However, while he was gingerly poking at them, a boa constrictor glided silently out of the shadows unnoticed. It ate all the mice and then quietly slithered away. The guy got hysterical. I almost pointed out that snakes have to eat, too, but actually I didn't care about the snake, either. I'm strictly neutral.

My youngest visitor had been a little boy, maybe about ten, who came in through the boarded-up gas station in Bosworth, Missouri. It was a one-stoplight town that didn't send me much company. The kid wore jeans and a blue Royals baseball cap. He was looking for a dog whistle he had lost. I found it for him. Nothing happened to him or it. That was okay with me, too.

I sighed and stood up. No one else would be coming in. As I rose, I saw a large shadow out of the corner of my eye and glanced toward it, expecting it to slide away among the shelves as usual. Instead, it stayed where it was. I was looking at a young woman of Asian descent, wrapped up in a long white crocheted shawl. She also wore a denim skirt and striped knee socks.

"You're sickening." She spoke with elegant disgust, in New York accent.

I knew that, but I didn't like hearing it. "You've been here a while, haven't you?"

"I think about two days." She brushed back her hair with one hand. It was cut short and blunt. "You were asleep when I came in."

That was a relief. She didn't belong here any more than I did. On the other hand, she had apparently been watching me.

"Where've you been sleeping?" I asked out of curiosity. On my first day, I had spent several hours locating a sleeping bag.

"I found an air mattress," she said, still angrily. "I just meant to sleep until you woke up, but you had a—a client when I got up. After I saw the way you treated him—and all the rest of them—I decided not to approach you at all. Don't you have any feelings for them? When something goes wrong? You could at least try to help them."

"I don't sabotage anybody. Whatever happens, happens—good or bad or indifferent."

She tossed her short hair, probably less to move it than for the disdain it conveyed. "I can't stand it. Why are you so callous?"

I shrugged. "What do you care? Anyhow, some go away happy."

"*What?*" She looked astonished. "Can't you even understand sim-

179

ple—" She stopped and shook her head. "Maybe you'll understand selfishness. Suppose *I* want what I came for. I can't get any help from you if I have trouble."

"Well, I guess that's logi—"

I stopped when she reached for a big stoppered metal bottle, on the shelf next to her. She heaved it at me, and I only had time to spin around. It hit my shoulder blade, hard, and bounced unharmed to the floor.

I whirled back toward her, ready to grab it and throw it back at her, but she was already striding quickly toward me.

"What's *wrong* with you?" She demanded. "I want to know! Why are you so callous?" She snatched up the metal container from the floor in front of me and held it wrapped in her shawl. "Tell me *now!*" she screamed, right in front of me.

I leaned forward and spoke, glaring into her eyes. "*I* came in here looking for my compassion. I lost it years ago, bit by bit. I lost it when I was eight, and other kids chased me around the playground for no visible reason—and they weren't playing. When I started junior high and got beat up in gym class because the rest of the school was white, like my grade school. When I ran for student congress and had my posters covered with swastikas and **KKK** symbols. And that was *before* I got out into the world on my own. You want to hear about my *adult* life?"

I paused to catch my breath. She backed away from me.

"I've lost more of my compassion every year of my life for every year I can remember, until I don't have any more. Well, it's here, but I can't find it."

She stood speechless in front of me. Letting her have it all at once accomplished that much, at least.

"Maybe you were in the wrong town," she muttered.

"You think I *like* being like this? Hating the memories of my life and not caring what happens to anybody? I said I've lost my compassion, not my conscience."

She walked back and put the metal bottle back in its place on the shelf. "I can find it," she said quietly.

"What?"

"I've been watching you. When you get something for someone, you follow the little white light that appears."

"You can see that?"

"Of course I can—anybody can. You think you're special? We just can't see our own. *I* figured that out."

"Well . . . so did I," I said lamely.

"So, I could get your compassion for you."

"Yeah?" I didn't think she would, considering all she'd said.

"Only you have to get what I want, first."

"You don't trust me, remember?"

She smiled smugly. It looked grotesque, as though she hadn't smiled in ages. "I can trust you. Because you know that if you don't give me what I want, I won't give you your compassion. Besides, if all goes well, your lack of compassion won't make any difference."

"Well, yeah. I guess so." I hadn't considered a deal with another customer before. Until now, I had just been waiting for the no-show proprietor, and then given up even on that.

"Well?" she demanded, still with that weird forced smile.

"Uh—yeah, okay." It was my last chance. I glanced around and found her spot of white light behind me on a lower shelf. "This way."

She walked next to me, watching me carefully as the white light led us down the crowded aisle. A large porcelain vase emitted guttural mutterings on an upper shelf as we passed. Two small lizards from the Florida corridor and something resembling a T-bone steak with legs were drinking at a pool of shiny liquid in the middle of the floor. The viscous liquid was oozing slowly out of a cracked green bottle. We stepped over it and kept going.

The light finally stopped on the cork of a long-necked blue bottle at the back of a bottom shelf. I stopped and looked down at it, wondering if this deal had an angle I hadn't figured.

"Well?" She forced herself to smile again. It gave her a sort of tortured visage.

"What is it, anyway?" I tried to sound casual.

"You don't need to know, I know that, too."

"Suppose I don't get it till you tell me."

"I won't tell you. And you won't get what you want."

She couldn't have known I had to leave soon, but she was still my last chance. I would be getting home late as it was. Besides, she was the sort who might really want more compassion in the world.

"Hurry up," she said.

I knelt down and looked at the bottle. She might have guessed what I had focused on; but with all the other junk jammed around it, she couldn't be sure. Well, I knew she had compassion herself, already. She wouldn't want to regain any lost tendencies that were nasty, like cruelty or vengefulness, so I was not in personal danger.

I took the bottle by the long neck and stood up. "It's in here, whatever it is. If it's a material object, you just open the bottle and spill it out. If it's a chance, or a personal trait, you have to uncork the bottle and inhale the fumes as they come out."

She was already taking the bottle from me, carefully in both hands. I backed away as she sank her teeth into the cork and yanked it out with a pop. White vapor issued from the bottle. She started taking deep breaths in through her nose, with her eyes closed.

I backed away, smelling something like rotten lettuce mixed with wet gerbil fur.

She kept on breathing until the vapors ran out. Then she re-corked the bottle and smiled at me, looking relaxed and natural. "Well! You're still sickening, but that was it, all right." She laughed gently. "Wow, that stuff stunk. Smelled like rotting cabbage and wet cat fur, didn't it?"

"Wha—?" I laughed, surprised at her sudden good humor. "It sure did."

"Okay, brown eyes. I see your little spot of light. Follow the swaying rear." She sashayed past me and walked casually down another dark aisle, humming to herself.

At one point, something on a shelf caught her eye and she stopped to giggle at it. It was a large brown and white snake, shoved into a jar of some kind of clear solution. She paused to make a face, imitating the snake's motionless expression. Here, of course, one never knew if a pickled snake was really pickled snake or something else temporarily in that guise. Anyway, she made a funny face and then laughed delightedly. After that, we pushed on.

When she stopped again, she was looking up at a shelf just within her reach. "There it is." She chuckled, without moving to take anything.

"Yeah?" I was suddenly afraid of that laugh.

She looked at me and laughed again.

"What's so funny?"

She shook her head and reached up on tiptoe with both hands. When she came down, she was cradling four sealed containers in her arms. One was a short-necked brown bottle encrusted with dry sand. Two were sealed jars of smoky glass and the last was a locked wooden box engraved with smile faces. She squatted on the floor Asian style and set them down.

"One of these holds your lost compassion." She looked up and laughed. "Guess which one."

My stomach tightened. I could not be sure of getting my compassion back this way. After my general insensitivity to people here, I didn't think I would ever be allowed back in, either.

"We have a deal," I said weakly. "You were going to give it to me."

"I have; it's right here. Besides, you should talk. And remember—if you inhale someone else's lost chance to wrestle an alligator or something, you'll wrestle it." She clapped her hands and laughed.

I stared at her. Maybe I deserved it, but I couldn't figure out what had happened to her. She had been concerned and compassionate before I had given her the long-necked bottle, and she certainly didn't seem angry or righteous now. I wondered what she had regained.

"Well?" She giggled at me and stood up. "One of them is it. That's a better chance than you gave anyone."

I looked down at the containers. She had no more idea what was in three of them than I did. "I have no intention of opening any of these," I said.

She shrugged, still grinning. "Have it your way, brown eyes. I'm leaving." She started strolling away.

"Wait."

She turned and walked away backwards, facing me. "What?"

"Uh—" I couldn't think of anything.

"Bye!"

"No—uh, hey, what *did* I give back to you, anyway?"

"Oh!" She laughed. "My sense of humor." She was still backpedaling.

"I'll do it! Wait a minute."

She stopped and folded her arms. "You'll really do it?"

"Come on. Come on back here while I do this." I wasn't sure why I wanted company, but I did.

She came back, grinning. "If you got the guts, brown eyes, you can open 'em all."

I smiled weakly. "They could all be good."

She smirked. "Sure—it's possible."

I looked down at the four containers. The wooden box seemed more likely to hold a tangible object than a lost quality. Though this place had few reliable rules, I decided to leave the box alone. The brown bottle with the short neck had such a heavy layer of sand that its contents were hidden. I knelt down and looked over the two smoky jars.

"Come on, sweetie." She started tapping her foot.

Quickly, before I could reconsider, I grabbed both jars, stood, and smashed them down on the floor. The glass shattered and two small billows of blue-gray smoke curled upward.

She stepped back.

I leaned forward, waited for the smoke to reach me, and inhaled. One strand smelled like charcoal-broiled Kansas City steak; the other, like the inside of a new car. I breathed both in, again and again, until the vapors were gone.

After a moment, I blinked and looked around. "I don't feel any different."

"Sure you do." She smiled. "Just go on as normal, and it'll come clear."

"Okay." I bent down and picked up the box and the bottle. "Where were these? I'll put 'em back. There's a broom—"

"You?" She laughed gaily. "Well, that's something. You mean you're actually going to straighten up this place?"

"No, I—well, I've been in charge; I suppose I should do something. . . ." I replaced the items where she pointed.

"Integrity."

"What?"

"You've got your integrity back, for one."

"Oh, I don't know. . . ." I looked at her for a moment and then gazed up the dark aisle toward the light from one of the main corridors. "I guess I did lose that, too. . . . Otherwise, I couldn't have been so cruel to people, even without compassion. They trusted me." I started walking up the aisle.

She followed, watching me closely. "So what are you going to do?"

"I guess I'll stay and run the shop." It just came out naturally. I hadn't even realized I was going to say it. "The . . . other thing I got back is kind of minor. For a long time, I used to try to remember the details of a fishing trip in the mountains my family went on, back when I was little. I knew I had a great time, but that was all. Now, all of a sudden, I can remember it completely."

She cocked her head to one side. "Was it still really wonderful?"

I considered my new memories a moment. "Yeah."

"Aw . . ." She looked at me, smiling. "I can't help it, brown eyes. I give in. It's in that brown thing, with the sand all over it."

Excitement surged in my chest. *"Thanks!"* I reached up with trembling fingers and snatched it off the shelf.

"Careful—"

I fumbled it away. It hit my shoulder, bounced to the floor, and cracked. It rolled, and before I could bend down to grab it, it was under a bottom shelf. I dropped to the floor and slid my face under the shelf. The cracked bottle was hissing in the darkness as the special vapors escaped. I couldn't smell anything. It was too far from me.

I reached for it with one hand. It was wedged against something and stuck. I could touch it, but I couldn't get enough of a hold to pull it back.

I remained on the floor, inhaling frantically, motionless until the hissing stopped. Then, suddenly feeling heavy all over, I managed to stand up.

"What happened?" She smiled hopefully.

"It's gone," I muttered. "It . . . sure was over quick." I hesitated, then added, "Thanks anyhow." Stunned, I eased past her and started walking. I could hear her follow me.

We came out into the main corridor. I picked up the little blue throw rug and hung it on a nearby hook. Then I turned, all the way around, surveying my shop. "Maybe it was no accident."

"You were nervous, that's all—"

"I don't mean that. I mean my finding the door to this place when I most needed it, and staying until . . . someone came in to find my stuff."

"You think your new integrity adds up to something, it sounds like."

"My destiny."

She laughed, then tapered off when I looked at her calmly. "You serious?"

I shrugged. "This place is mine. I knew that, somehow, when I put my signs up. And now I owe this shop my best attention."

"With integrity."

I shrugged again. Taking care of the shop and its customers was important; the reasons I felt that way were not.

"I . . . think I got news for you, brown eyes."

"I don't want any news." I was still in shock from disappointment. It was justice of a sort, but it wasn't pleasant.

*185*

"You have your compassion back. I'm sure of it. You can't help it."

"But you said it was in the bottle I broke—"

"It was, as a separate quality. Only, I think your integrity comes with a little compassion in a package deal. Forces it on you."

I looked up at her, hopeful. "Really?"

"You could try it." She pointed down the Florida corridor.

"What'shername, the peach-colored former artist lady, had never made it out the door. She was sitting near it, slumped on the floor, an incongruous position for a woman of her age and dignity. The skirt of her suit was smudged and rumpled under her, exposing more of her legs than it was supposed to.

"This is your shop now," said my companion. She put a hand on my shoulder.

I didn't say anything.

"You can't just let a customer sit there, can you?"

"No—not anymore. A matter of—integrity."

"In this case, it's the same as compassion. I don't see how you can help her, but if you try—"

"I know how."

"Huh?"

"I lost one chance to help her." I smiled, suddenly understanding the true potential of this place. "If you'll go down the aisles and find it, we can fix up that customer after all."

She winked. "You got it, brown eyes."

# HARLAN ELLISON

## "Laugh Track"

*Harlan Ellison (1934- ) published his first science fiction story in 1956 and became one of the leading writers of science fiction's New Wave in the 1960s with such provocative and controversial stories "I Have no Mouth and I Must Scream," " 'Repent, Harlequin!' Said the Ticktockman" and "A Boy and His Dog." He is best known for his short stories, and his collections* Approaching Oblivion, Deathbird Stories, Angry Candy *and the retrospective volume* The Essential Ellison *gathers most of his distinguished fantasy and science fiction tales. His credits as an editor include the groundbreaking anthologies* Dangerous Visions *and* Again, Dangerous Visions. *He has made a name for himself in television through his contributions to "The Outer Limits," "Star Trek," and the revived "The Twilight Zone." Ellison is also an insightful and perceptive critic and some of his best essays and reviews can be found in* The Glass Teat, The Other Glass Teat, Sleepless Nights in the Procrustean Bed, *and* An Edge in My Voice. *He has won nearly every award possible in the fantasy, horror and science fiction fields, and is a recipient of the World Fantasy Award for lifetime achievement.*

# Laugh Track

## by *Harlan Ellison*

loved my Aunt Babe for three reasons. The first was that even though I was only ten or eleven, she flirted with me as she did with any male of any age who was lucky enough to pass through the heat of her line-of-sight. The second was her breasts—I knew them as "titties"—which left your arteries looking like the Holland Tunnel at rush hour. And the third was her laugh. Never before and never since, in the history of this planet, including every species of life-form extant or extinct, has there been a sound as joyous as my Aunt Babe's laugh which I, as a child, imagined as the sound of the Toonerville Trolley clattering downhill. If you have never seen a panel of that long-gone comic strip, and have no idea what the Toonerville Trolley looked like, forget it. It was some terrific helluva laugh. It could pucker your lips.

My Aunt Babe died of falling asleep and not waking up in 1955, when I was twelve years old.

I first recognized her laugh while watching a segment of *Leave It to Beaver* in November of 1957. It was on the laugh track they'd dubbed in after the show had been shot, but I was only fourteen and thought those were real people laughing at Jerry Mathers's predicament. I yelled for my mother to come quickly, and she came running from the kitchen, her hands all covered with wax from putting up the preserves, and she thought I'd hurt myself or something.

"No . . . no, I'm okay . . . listen!"

She stood there, listening. "Listen to what?" she said after a minute.

"Wait . . . wait . . . *there!* You hear that? It's Aunt Babe. She isn't dead, she's at that show."

My mother looked at me just the way your mother would look at you if you said something like that, and she shook her head, and she said something in Italian my grandmother had no doubt said while shaking her head at *her*, long ago; and she went back to imprisoning boysenberries. *I* sat there and watched The Beav and Eddie Haskell and Whitey Whitney, and broke up every time my Aunt Babe laughed at their antics.

I heard my Aunt Babe's laugh on *The Real McCoys* in 1958; on *Hennessey* and *The Many Loves of Dobie Gillis* in 1959; on *The Andy Griffith Show* in 1960; on *Car 54, Where Are You?* in 1962; and in the years that followed I laughed along with her at *The Dick Van Dyke Show, The Lucy Show, My Favorite Martian, The Addams Family, I Dream of Jeannie,* and *Get Smart!*

In 1970 I heard my Aunt Babe laughing at *Green Acres,* which—though I always liked Eddie Albert and Alvy Moore—I thought was seriously lame; and it bothered me that her taste had deteriorated so drastically. Also, her laugh seemed a little thin. Not as ebulliently Toonerville Trolley going downhill any more.

By 1972 I knew something was wrong because Aunt Babe was convulsing over *Me and the Chimp* but not a sound from her for *My World . . . And Welcome To It.*

By 1972 I was almost thirty, I was working in television, and because I had lived with the sound of my Aunt Babe's laughter for so long, I never thought there was anything odd about it; and I never again mentioned it to anyone.

Then, one night, sitting with a frozen pizza and a Dr. Brown's cream soda, watching an episode of the series I was writing, a sitcom you may remember called *Misty Malone,* I heard my Aunt Babe laughing at a line that the story editor had not understood, that he had rewritten. At that moment, bang! comes the light bulb burning in my brain, comes the epiphany, comes the rude awakening, and I hear myself say, "This is crazy. Babe's been dead and buried lo these seventeen years, and there is strictly *no way* she can be laughing at this moron line that Bill Tidy rewrote from my golden prose, and this is weirder than shit, and *what the hell is going on here!?*"

Besides which, Babe's laugh was now sounding a lot like a 1971

Pinto without chains trying to rev itself out of a snowy rut into which cinders had been shoveled.

And I suppose for the first time I understood that Babe was not alive at the taping of all those shows over the years, but was merely on an old laugh track. At which point I remembered the afternoon in 1953 when she'd taken me to the Hollywood Ranch Market to go shopping, and one of those guys had been standing there handing out tickets to the filming of tv shows, and Babe had taken two tickets to *Our Miss Brooks*, and she'd gone with some passing fancy she was dating at the time, and told us later that she thought Eve Arden was funnier than Lucille Ball.

The laugh track from that 1953 show was obviously still in circulation. Had been, in fact, in circulation for twenty years. And for twenty years my Aunt Babe had been forced to laugh at the same old weary sitcom minutiae, over and over and over. She'd had to laugh at the salt instead of the sugar in Fred MacMurray's coffee; at Granny Clampett sending Buddy Ebsen out to shoot a possum in Beverly Hills; at Bob Cummings trying to conceal Julie Newmar's robot identity; at The Fonz *almost* running a comb through his pompadour; at all the mistaken identities, all the improbable last-minute saves of hopeless situations, all the sophomoric pratfalls from Gilligan to Gidget. And I felt just terrible for her.

Native Americans, what we used to be allowed to call Indians when I was a kid, have a belief that if someone takes their picture with a camera, the box captures their soul. So they shy away from photographers. AmerInds seldom become bank robbers: there are cameras in banks. There was no graduation picture of Cochise in his high school yearbook.

What if—I said to myself—sitting there with that awful pizza growing cold on my lap—what if my lovely Aunt Babe, who had been a Ziegfeld Girl, and who had loved my Uncle Morrie, and who had had such wonderful titties and never let on that she knew *exactly* what I was doing when I'd fall asleep in the car on the way home and snuggle up against them, *what if* my dear Aunt Babe's soul, like her laugh, had been trapped on that goddam track?

And what if she was in there, in there forever, doomed to laugh endlessly at imbecilic shit rewritten by ex-hairdressers, instead of roaming around Heaven, flirting with the angels, which I was certain should have been her proper fate, being that she was such a swell person? What if?

It was the sort of thinking that made my head hurt a lot.

And it made me feel even lower, the more I thought about it, because I didn't know what I could do about it. I just knew that that was what had happened to my Aunt Babe; and there she was in there, condemned to the stupidest hell imaginable. In some arcane way, she had been doomed to an eternity of electronic restimulation. In speech therapy they have a name for it: cataphasia: verbal repetition. But I could tell from the frequency with which I was now hearing Babe, and from the indiscriminate use to which her laugh was being put—not just on *M\*A\*S\*H* and *Maude*, but on yawners like *The Sandy Duncan Show* and a mid-season replacement with Larry Hagman called *Here We Go Again*, which didn't—and the way her laugh was starting to slur like an ice skating elephant, that she wasn't having much fun in there. I began to believe that she was like some sort of beanfield slave, every now and then being goosed electronically to laugh. She was a video galley slave, one of the pod people, a member of some ghastly high-frequency chain gang. Cataphasia, but worse. Oh, how I wanted to save her; to drag her out of there and let her tormented soul bound free like a snow rabbit, to vanish into great white spaces where the words *Laverne and Shirley* had never trembled in the lambent mist.

Then I went to bed and didn't think about it again until 1978.

By September of 1978 I was working for Bill Tidy again. In years to come I would refer to that pox-ridden period as the Season I Stepped In a Pile of Tidy.

Each of us has one dark eminence in his or her life who somehow has the hoodoo sign on us. Persons so cosmically loathsome that we continually spend our time when in their company silently asking ourselves *What the hell, what the bloody hell, what the everlasting Technicolor hell am I doing sitting here with this ambulatory piece of offal? This is the worst person who ever got born, and someone ought to wash out his life with a bar of Fels-Naptha.*

But there you sit, and the next time you blink, there you sit again. It was probably the way Catherine the Great felt on her dates with Rasputin.

Bill Tidy had that hold over me.

In 1973 when I'd been just a struggling sitcom writer, getting his first breaks on *Misty Malone*, Tidy had been the story editor.

An authoritarian Fascist with all the creative insight of a sump pump. But now, a mere five years later, things were a great deal different: I had created a series, which meant I was a struggling sitcom writer with my name on a parking slot at the studio; and Bill Tidy, direct lineal descendant of The Blob that tried to eat Steve McQueen, had swallowed up half the television industry. He was now the heavy-breathing half of Tidy-Spellberg Production, in partnership with another ex-hairdresser named Harvey Spellberg, whom he'd met during a metaphysical retreat to Reno, Nevada. They'd become corporate soul-mates while praying over the crap tables and in just a few years had built upon their unerring sense of how much debasement the American television-viewing audience could sustain (a much higher gag-reflex level than even the experts had postulated, thereby paving the way for *Three's Company*), to emerge as "prime suppliers" of gibbering lunacy for the three networks.

Bill Tidy was to Art as Pekin, North Dakota is to wild nightlife.

But he was the fastest money in town when it came to marketing a series idea to one of the networks, and my agent had sent over the prospectus for *Ain't It the Truth*, without my knowing it; and before I had a chance to scream, "Nay, nay, my liege! There are some things mere humans were never meant to know, Doctor Von Frankenstein!" the network had made a development deal with the Rupert Murdoch of mindlessness, and of a sudden I was—as they so aptly put it—in bed with Bill Tidy again.

This is the definition of ambivalence: to have struggled in the ditches for five years, to have created something that was guaranteed to get on the air, and to have that creation masterminded by a toad with the charm of a charnel house and the intellect of a lead of lettuce. I thought seriously of moving to Pekin, North Dakota, where the words *coaxial cable* are as speaking-in-tongues to the simple, happy natives; where the blight of Jim Nabors has never manifested itself; where I could open a grain and feed store and never have to sit in the same room with Bill Tidy as he picked his nose and surreptitiously examined the findings.

But I was weak, and even if the series croaked before the season ran its course, I would have a credit that could lead to bigger things. So I pulled down the covers, plumped the pillows, straightened the rubber pishy-pad, and got into bed with Bill Tidy.

By September, I was a raving lunatic. I spent much of my time dreaming about biting the heads off chickens. The deranged wind of network babble and foaming Tidyism blew through the haunted cathedral of my brain. What little originality and invention I'd brought to the series concept—and at best what we're talking about here is primetime network situation comedy, not a PBS tour conducted by Alistair Cooke through the Library of Alexandria—was steadily and firmly leached out of the production by Bill Tidy. Any time a line or a situation with some charm or esthetic value dared to peek its head out of the *merde* of the scripts, Tidy as Grim Reaper would lurch onto the scene swinging the scythe of his demented bad taste, and intellectual decapitation instantly followed.

I developed a hiatic hernia, I couldn't hold down solid food and took to subsisting on strained mung from Gerber's inexhaustible and vomitous larder, I snapped at everyone, sex was a concept whose time had come and gone for me, and I saw my gentle little offering to the Gods of Comedy turned into something best suited for a life under mossy stones.

Had I known that on the evening of Thursday, September 14, 1978 *Ain't It the Truth* was to premiere opposite a new ABC show called *Mork & Mindy*, and that within three weeks a dervish named Robin Williams would be dining on Nielsen rating shares the way sharks devour entire continents, I might have been able to hold onto enough of my sanity to weather the Dark Ages. And I wouldn't have gotten involved with Wally Modisett, the phantom sweetener, and I wouldn't have spoken into the black box, and I wouldn't have found the salvation for my dead Aunt Babe's soul.

But early in September Williams had not yet uttered his first *Nanoonanoo* (except on a spinoff segment of *Happy Days* and who the hell watched *that*?) and we had taped the first three segments of *Ain't It the Truth* before a live audience at the Burbank Studios, if you can call those who voluntarily go to tapings of sitcoms as "living," and late one night the specter of Bill Tidy appeared in the doorway of my office, his great horse face looming down at me like the demon that emerges from the *Night on Bald Mountain* section of Disney's *Fantasia*; and his sulphurous breath reached across the room and made all the little hairs in my nostrils curl up and try to pull themselves out so they could run away and hide in the back of my head somewhere; and the two reflective puddles of Vegemite he called eyes smoldered at me, and this is what he said. First he said:

"That fuckin' fag cheese-eater director's never gonna work

again. He's gonna go two days over, mark my words. I'll see the putzola never works again."

Then he said:

"I bought another condo in Phoenix. Solid gold investment. Better than Picassos."

Then he said:

"I heard it at lunch today. A cunt is just a clam that's wearin' a frightwig. Good, huh?"

Then he said:

"I want you to stay late tonight. I can't trust anyone else. Guy'll show up here about eight. He'll find you. Just stay put till he gets here. Never mind a name. He'll make himself known to you. Take him over to the mixing studio, run the first three shows for him. Nobody else gets in, *kapeesh, paisan?*"

I was having such a time keeping my gorge from becoming buoyant that I barely heard his directive. Bill Tidy gave new meaning to the words King of the Pig People. The only groups he had failed to insult in the space of thirteen seconds were blacks, Orientals, paraplegics, and Doukhobors, and if I didn't quickly agree to his demands, he'd no doubt round on them, as well. "Got it, Bill. Yessiree, you can count on me. Uh-huh, absolutely, right-on, dead-center, I hear ya talkin', I'm your boy, I loves workin' foah ya Massa' Tidy-suh, you can bank on me!"

He gave me a look. "You know, Angelo, you are gettin' stranger and stranger, like some kind of weird insect."

And he turned and he vanished, leaving me all alone there in the encroaching darkness, just tuning my antennae and rubbing my hind legs together.

I was slumped down on my spine, eyes closed, in the darkened office with just the desk lamp doing its best to rage against the dying of the light, when I heard someone whisper huskily, "Turn off the light."

I opened my eyes. The room was empty. I looked out the window behind my desk. It was night. I was three flights up in the production building. No one was there.

"The light. Turn off the light, can you hear what I'm telling you?"

I strained forward toward the open door and the dark hallway beyond. "You talking to me?" Nothing moved out there.

"The light. Slow; you're a very slow person."

Being Catholic, I respond like a Pavlovian dog to guilt. I turned out the light.

From the deeper darkness of the hallway I saw something shadowy detach itself and glide into my office. "Can I keep my eyes open," I said, "Or would a blindfold serve to palliate this unseemly paranoia of yours?"

The shadowy form snorted disdainfully. "At these prices you can use words even bigger than that and I don't give a snap." I heard fingers snap. "You care to take me over to the mixing booth?"

I stood up. Then I sat down. "Don't wanna play." I folded my arms.

The shadowy figure got a petulant tone in his voice. "Okay, c'mon now. I've got three shows to do, and I haven't got all night. The world keeps turning. Let's go."

"Not in the cards, Lamont Cranston. I've been ordered around a lot these last few days; and since I don't know you from a stubborn stain, I'm digging in my heels. Remember the Alamo. Millions for defense, not one cent for tribute. The only thing we have to fear is fear itself. Forty-four forty or fight."

"I think that's fifty-four forty or fight," he said.

We thought about that for a while. Then after a long time I said, "Who the hell are you, and what is it you do that's so illicit and unspeakable that first of all Bill Tidy would hire you to do it, which puts you right on the same level as me, which is the level of graverobbers, dog catchers, and horse-dopers; and second, which is so furtive and vile that you have to do it in the dead of night, coming in here wearing garb fit only for a commando raid? Answer in the key of C#."

He chuckled. It was a nice chuckle. "You're okay, kid," he said. And he dropped into the chair on the other side of my desk where writers pitching ideas for stories sat; and he turned on the desk lamp.

"Wally Modisett," he said, extending a black-gloved hand. "Sound editor." I took the hand and shook. "Free-lance," he said.

That didn't sound so ominous. "Why the Creeping Phantom routine?" Then he said the word no one in Hollywood says. He looked intently at all of my face, particularly around the mouth, where lies come from, and he said: "Sweetening."

If I'd had a silver crucifix, I'd have thrust it at him at arm's-length. *Be still my heart*, I thought.

There are many things of which one does not speak in the television industry. One does not repeat the name of the NBC executive who was making women writers give him blowjobs in his office in exchange for writing assignments, even though he's been pensioned off with a lucrative production deal at a major studio and the network paid for his psychiatric counseling for several years. One does not talk about the astonishing Digital Dance done by the royalty numbers in a major production company's ledgers, thereby fleecing several superstar participants out of their "points" in the profits, even though it made a large stink on the *World News Tonight* and everybody scampered around trying to settle out of court while *TV Guide* watched. One does not talk about how the studio frightened a buxom ingenue who had become an overnight national sensation into modifying her demands for triple salary in the second season her series was on the air, not even to hint knowingly of a kitchen chair with nails driven up through the seat from the underside.

And one never, never, no never ever talks about the phantom sweeteners.

*This show was taped before a live studio audience!*

If you've heard it once, you've heard it at least twice. And so when those audiences break up and fall on the floor and roll around and drum their heels and roar so hard they have to clutch their stomachs and tears of hilarity blind them and their noses swell from crying too much and they sound as if they're all genetically selected high-profile tickleables, you fall right in with them because that ain't canned laughter, it's a live audience, onaccounta *This show was taped before a live studio audience.*

While high in the fly loft of the elegant opera house, the Phantom Sweetener looks down and chuckles smugly.

They're legendary. For years there was only Charlie Douglas, a name never spoken. A laugh man. A sound technician. A sweetener. They say he still uses laughs kidnapped off radio shows from the Forties and Fifties. Golden laughs. Unduplicable originals. Special, rich laughs that blend and support and lift and build a resonance that punches your subliminal buttons. Laughs from *The Jack Benny Show*, from segments of *The Fred Allen Show* down in Allen's Alley, from *The Chase & Sanborn Hour* with Edgar Bergen and Charlie McCarthy (one of the shows on which Charlie mixed it up with W.C. Fields). The laughs that Ed Wynn got, that Goodman and Jane Ace got, that Fanny Brice got. Rich, teak-colored laughs from a time in this country when humor wasn't produced by slugs like Bill Tidy. For along time Charlie Douglas was all alone as the man who would make even dull thuds go over boffola.

But no one knew how good he was. Except the IRS, which took note of his underground success in the industry by raking in vast amounts of his hard-earned cash.

Using the big Spotmaster cartridges—carts that looked like eight-track cassettes, with thirty cuts per cart—twelve or fourteen per job—Charlie Douglas became a hired gun of guffaws, a highwayman of hee-haws, Zorro of zaniness; a troubleshooter working extended overtime in a specialized craft where he was a secret weapon with a never-spoken code-name.

Carrying with him from studio to studio the sounds of great happy moments stolen from radio signals long-since on their way to Proxima Centauri.

And for a long time Charlie Douglas had it all to himself, because it was a closely-guarded secret; not one of the open secrets perhaps unknown in Kankakee or Key West, like Merv Griffin or Ida Lupino or Roger Moore; but common knowledge at the Polo Lounge and Chasen's.

But times got fat and the industry grew and there was more work, and more money, than one Phantom Sweetener could handle.

So the mother of invention called forth more audio soldiers of fortune: Carroll Pratt and Craig Porter and Tom Kafka and two silent but sensational guys from Tokyo and techs at Glen Glenn Sound and Vidtronics. And you never mention their names or the shows they've sweetened, lest you get your buns run out of the industry. It's an open secret, closely-held by the community. The networks deny their existence, the production company executives would let you nail them hands and feet to their office doors before they'd cop to having their shows shot before a live studio audience sweetened. In the dead of night by the phantoms.

Of whom Wally Modisett is the most mysterious.

And here I sat, across from him. He wore a black turtleneck sweater, jeans, and gloves. And he placed on the desk the legendary black box. I looked at it. He chuckled.

"That's it," he said.

"I'll be damned," I said.

I felt as if I were in church.

In sound editing, the key is equalization. Bass, treble, they can isolate a single laugh, pull it off the track, make a match even twenty years later. They put them on "endless loops" and then lay the show over to a multi-track audio machine, and feed in one laugh on a separate track, meld it, blend it in, punch it up, put that special button-punch giggle right in there with the live studio audience track. They do it, they've always done it, and soon now they'll be able to do it with digital encoding. And he sat right there in front of me with the legendary black box. Legendary, because Wally Modisett was an audio genius, an electronics Machiavelli who had built himself a secret system to do it all through that little black box that he took to the studios in the dead of night when everyone was gone, right into the booth at the mixing room, and he didn't need a multi-track.

If it weren't something to be denied to the grave, the *mensches* and moguls of the television industry would have Wally Modisett's head right up there on Mt. Rushmore in the empty space between Teddy Roosevelt and Abe Lincoln.

What took twenty-two tracks for a combined layering on a huge machine, Wally Modisett carried around in the palm of his hand. And looking at his long, sensitive face, with the dark circles under his eyes, I guess I saw a foreshadowing of great things to come. There was laughter in his eyes.

I sat there most of the night, running the segments of *Ain't It the Truth*. I sat down below in the screening room while the Phantom Sweetener locked himself up in the booth. *No one*, he made it clear, watched him work his magic.

And the segments played, with the live audience track, and he used his endless loops from his carts—labeled "Single Giggle 1" and "Single Giggle 2" and slightly larger "Single Giggle 3" and the dreaded "Titter/Chuckle" and the ever-popular "Rim Shot"—those loops of his own design, smaller than those made by Spotmaster, and he built and blended and sweetened the hell out of that laugh track till even I chuckled at moronic material Bill Tidy had bastardized to a level that only the Jukes and Kallikaks could have found uproarious.

And then, on the hundredth playback, after Modisett had added another increment of hilarity, I heard my dead Aunt Babe. I sat straight up in the plush screening room chair, and I slapped the switch on the console that fed into the booth, and I yelled, "Hey! That last one! That last laugh . . . what was that . . . ?"

He didn't answer for a moment. Then, tinnily, through the console intercom, he said, "I call it a wonky."

"Where'd it come from?"

Silence.

"C'mon, man, where'd you get that laugh?"

"Why do you want to know?"

I sat there for a second, then I said, "Listen, either you've got to come down here, or let me come up there. I've got to talk to you."

Silence. Then after a moment, "Is there a coffee machine around here somewhere?"

"Yeah, over near the theater."

"I'll be down in fifteen minutes. We'll have a cup of coffee. Think you can hold out that long?"

"If you nail a duck's foot down, does he walk in circles?"

It took me almost an hour to convince him. Finally, he decided I was almost as bugfuck as he was, and the idea was so crazy it might be fun to try and work it out. I told him I was glad he'd decided to try it because if he hadn't I'd have followed him to his secret lair and found some way to blackmail him into it, and he said, "Yeah, I can see you'd do that. You're not a well person."

"Try working with Bill Tidy sometime," I said. "It's enough to turn Mother Teresa into a hooker."

"Give me some time," he said. "I'll get back to you."

I didn't hear from him for a year and a half. *Ain't It the Truth* had gone to the boneyard to join *The Chicago Teddy Bears* and *Angie* and *The Dumplings*. Nobody missed it, not even its creator. Bill Tidy had wielded his scythe with skill.

Then just after two A.M. on a summer night in Los Angeles, my phone rang, and I fumbled the receiver off the cradle and found my face somehow, and a voice said, "I've got it. Come." And he gave me an address; and I went.

The warehouse was large, but all his shit was jammed into one corner. Multi-tracks and oscilloscopes and VCRs and huge 3-mil thick Mylar foam speakers that looked like the rear seats of a 1933 Chevy. And right in the middle of the floor was a larger black box.

"You're kidding?" I said.

He was like a ten-year-old kid. "Would I shit you? I'm telling you, fellah, I've gone where no man has gone before. I has done did it! Jonas Salk and Marie Curie and Lee De Forest and all the rest of them have got to move over, slide aside, get to the back of the bus." And he leaped around, howling, *"I am the king!"*

When I was able to peel him off the catwalks that made a spiderweb tracery above us, he started making some sense. Not a *lot* of sense, because I didn't understand half of what he was saying, but enough sense for me to begin to believe that this peculiar obsession of mine might have some toe in the world of reality.

"The way they taped shows back in 1953, when your aunt went to that *Our Miss Brooks*, was they'd use a 1/4" machine, reel-to-reel. They'd have directional mikes above the audience, to separate individual laughs. One track for the program, and another track for the audience. They they'd just pick up what they want, equalize, and sock it onto one track for later use. Sweetened as need be."

He went to a portable fridge and pulled out a Dr. Pepper and looked in my direction. I shook my head. I was too excited for junk food. He popped the can, took a swig and came back to me.

"The first thing I had to do was find the original tape, the master. Took me a long time. It was in storage with . . . well, you don't need to know that. It was in storage. I must have gone through a thousand old masters. But I found her. Then I had to pull her out. But not just the *sound* of her laugh. The actual laugh itself. The electronic impulses. I used an early model of this to do it." He waved a hand at the big black box.

"She'd started sounding weak to me, over the years," I said. "Slurred sometimes. Scratchy."

"Yeah, yeah, yeah." Impatient to get on with the great revelation. "That was because she was being diminished by fifth, sixth, twentieth generation re-recording. No, I got her at full strength, and I did what I call 'deconvolving.' "

"Which is?"

"Never mind."

"You going to say 'never mind' every time I ask what the hell you did to make it work?"

"As Groucho used to say to contestants, 'You bet your ass.' "

I shrugged. It was his fairy tale.

"Once I had her deconvolved, I put her on an endless loop. But not just *any* kind of normal standard endless loop. You want to know what kind of endless loop I put her on?"

I looked at him. "You going to tell me to piss off?"

"No. Go ahead and ask."

"All right already: I'm asking. What the hell kind of endless loop did you put her on?"

"A moebius loop."

He looked at me as if he'd just announced the birth of a two-headed calf. I didn't know what the hell he was talking about. That didn't stop me from whistling through my two front teeth, loud enough to cause echoes in the warehouse, and I said, "No shit?!?"

He seemed pleased, and went on faster than before. "Now I feed her into the computer, digitally encode her so she never diminishes. Slick, right? Then I feed in a program that says harmonize and synthesize her, get a simulation mapping for the instrument that produced that sound; in other words, your aunt's throat and tongue and palate and teeth and larynx and alla that. Now comes the tricky part. I build a program that postulates an actual physical *situation*, a terrain, a *place* where that voice exists. And I send the computer on a search to bring me back everything that composes that place."

"Hold hold *hold* it, Lamont. Are you trying to tell me that you went in search of the Land of Oz, using that loop of Babe's voice?"

He nodded about a hundred and sixteen times.

"How'd you do *that*? I know: piss off. But that's some kind of weird metaphysical shit. It can't be done."

"Not by drones, fellah. But *I* can do it. I *did* it." He nodded at the black box.

"The tv sitcom land where my dead Aunt Babe is trapped, it's in there, in that cube?"

"Ah calls it a *simularity matrix*," he said, with an accent that could get him killed in SouthCentral L.A.

"You can call it rosewater if you like, Modisett, but it sounds like the foothills of Bandini Mountain to me."

His grin was the mutant offspring of a sneer and a smirk. I'd seen that kind of look only once, on the face of a failed academic at a collegiate cocktail party. Later that evening the guy used the smirk ploy once too often and a little tweety-bird of an English prof gave him high cause to go see a periodontal reconstructionist.

"I can reconstruct her like a clone, right in the machine," he said.

"How do you know? Tried it yet?"

"It's your aunt, not mine," he said. "I told you I'd get back to you. Now I'm back to you, and I'm ready to run the showboat out to the middle of the river."

So he turned on a lot of things on the big board he had, and he moved a lot of slide-switches up the gain slots, and he did this, and he did that, and a musical hum came from the Quad speakers, and he looked over his shoulder at me, across the tangle of wires and cables that disappeared into the black box, and he said, "Wake her up."

I said, "What?"

He said, "Wake her. She's been an electronic code for almost twenty-five years. She's been asleep. She's an amputated frog leg. Send the current through her."

"How?"

"Call her. She'll recognize your voice."

"How? It's been a long time. I don't sound like the kid I was when she died."

"Trust me," he said. "Call her."

I felt like a goddam fool. "Where do I speak?"

"Just speak, asshole. She'll hear you."

So I stood there in the middle of that warehouse and I said, "Aunt Babe?" There was nothing.

"A little louder. Gentle, but louder. Don't startle her."

"You're outta your . . ." His look silenced me. I took a deep breath and said, a little louder, "Hey, Aunt Babe? You in there? It's me, Angelo."

I heard something. At first it sounded like a mouse running toward me across a long blackboard, a blackboard maybe a hundred miles long. Then there was something like the wind you hear in thick woods in the autumn. Then the sound of somebody unwrapping Christmas presents. Then the sound of water, like surf, pouring into a cave at the base of a cliff, and then draining out again. Then the sound of a baby crying and the sound suddenly getting very deep as if it were a three hundred pound killer baby that wanted to be fed parts off a freshly-killed dinosaur. This kind of torrential idiocy went on for a while, and then, abruptly, out of nowhere, I heard my Aunt Babe clearing her throat, as if she were getting up in the morning. That phlegmy throat-clearing that sounds like quarts of yogurt being shoveled out of a sink.

"Angelo . . . ?"

I crossed myself about eleven times, ran off a few fast Hail

Mary's and Our Father's, swallowed hard and said, "Yeah, Aunt Babe, it's me. How are you?"

"Let me, for a moment here, let me get my bearings." It took more than a moment. She was silent for a few minutes, though she did once say, "I'll be right with you, *mio caro*."

And finally, I heard her say, "I am really fit to be tied. Do you have any idea what they have put me through? Do you have even the *faintest* idea how many times they've made me watch *The Partridge Family*? Do you have any *idea* how much I hate that kind of music? Never Cole Porter, never Sammy Cahn, not even a little Gus Edwards; I'd settle for Sigmund Romberg after those squalling children. *Caro nipote, quanto mi sei mancato!* Angelo . . . *bello bello*. I want you to tell me everything that's happened, because as soon as I get a chance, I'm going to make a stink you're not going to believe!"

It *was* Babe. My dearest Aunt Babe. I hadn't heard that wonderful mixture of pungent English and lilting Italian with its show biz Yiddish resonances in almost thirty years. I hadn't *spoken* any Italian in nearly twenty years. But I heard myself saying to the empty air, *"Come te la sei passata?"* How've you been?

*"Ti voglio bene—bambino caro.* I feel just fine. A bit fuzzy, I've been asleep a while but *come sta la famiglia? Anche quelli che non posso sopportare."*

So I told her all about the family, even the ones she couldn't stand, like Uncle Nuncio with breath like a goat, and Carmine's wife, Giuletta, who'd always called Babe a floozy. And after a while she had me try to explain what had happened to her, and I did the best I could, to which she responded, *"Non mi sento come un fantasma."*

So I told her she didn't feel like a ghost because she *wasn't*, strictly speaking a ghost. More like a random hoot in the empty night. Well, that didn't go over too terrific, because in an instant she'd grasped the truth that if she wasn't going where it is that dead people go, she'd never meet up with my Uncle Morrie again; and that made her very sad, *"Oh, dio!"* and she started crying.

So I tried to jolly her out of it by talking about all the history that had transpired since 1955, but it turned out she knew most of it anyhow. After all, hadn't she been stuck there, inside the biggest blabbermouth the world had ever known? Even though she'd been in something like an alpha state of almost-sleep, her essence had been *saturated* with news and special reports, docudramas and public service announcements, talk shows and panel discussions, network extra alerts and hour-by-hour live coverage of fast-breaking events.

Eventually I got around to explaining how I'd gotten in touch with her, about Modisett and the big black box, about how the Phantom Sweetener had deconvolved her, and about Bill Tidy.

She was not unfamiliar with the name.

After all, hadn't she been stuck there, inside the all-talking, all-singing, all-dancing, electromagnetic pimp for Tidy's endless supply of brain-damaged, insipid persiflage?

I painted Babe a loving word-portrait of my employer and our unholy liaison. She said, *"Stronzo! Figlio di una mignotta! Mascalzone!"* She also called him *bischero*, by which I'm sure she meant the word in its meaning of goof, or simpleton, rather than literally: "man with erection."

Modisett, who spoke no Italian, stared wildly at me, seeming to bask in the unalloyed joy of having tapped a line into some Elsewhere. Yet even he could tell from the tone of revulsion in Babe's disembodied voice that she had suffered long under the exquisite tortures of swimming in a sea of Tidy product.

What Tidy had been doing to me seemed to infuriate her. She was still my loving Aunt Babe.

So I spent all that night, and the next day, and the next night— while Modisett mostly slept and emptied Dr. Pepper down his neck—chatting at leisure with my dead Aunt Babe.

You'll never know how angry someone can get from prolonged exposure to Gary Coleman.

The Phantom Sweetener can't explain what followed. He says it defies the rigors of Boolean logic, whatever the hell that means. He says it transcends the parameters of Maxwell's Equation, which ought to put Maxwell in a bit of a snit. He says (and with more than a touch of the gibber in his voice) it deflowers, rapes, & pillages, breaks & enters Minkowski's Covariant Tensor. He says it is enough to start Philo T. Farnsworth spinning so hard in his grave that he would carom off Vladimir K. Zworykin in his. He says it would get Marvin Minsky up at M.I.T. speaking in tongues. He says—and this one *really* turned me around and opened my eyes—he says it (wait for it), "Distorts Riemannian geometry." To which I said, "You have *got* to be shitting me! Not Riemannian gefuckingometry!?!"

This is absolute babble to me, but it's got Modisett down on all fours, foaming at the mouth and sucking at the electrical outlets.

Apparently, Babe has found pathways in the microwave comm-system. The Phantom Sweetener says it might have happened because of what he calls "print-through," that phenomenon that occurs on audio tape when one layer magnetizes the next layer, so you hear an echo of the word or sound that is next to be spoken. He says if the tape is wound "heads out" and is stored that way, then the signal will jump. The signal that is my dead Aunt Babe has jumped. And keeps jumping. She's loose in the comm-system and she ain't asking where's the beef: *she knows*! And Modisett says the reason they can't catch her and wipe her is that old tape *always* bleeds through. Which is why, when Bill Tidy's big multi-million dollar sitcom aired last year, instead of audience roaring with laughter, there was the voice of this woman shouting above the din, "That's stupid! Worse than stupid! That's *bore*-ing! Ka-ka! C'mon folks, let's have a good old-fashioned Bronx cheer for crap-ola like this! Let's show 'em what we *really* think of this flopola!"

And then, instead of augmented laughter, instead of yoks, came a raspberry that could have floated the Titanic off the bottom.

Well, they pulled the tape, and they tried to find her, but she was gone, skipping off across the simularity matrix like Bambi, only to turn up the next night on another Tidy-Spellberg abomination.

Well, there was no way to stop it, and the networks got very leery of Tidy and Company, because they couldn't even use the millions of billions of dollars worth of shitty rerun shows they'd paid billions and millions for syndication rights to, and they sued the hell out of Bill Tidy, who went crazy as a soup sandwich not too long ago, and I'm told he's trying to sell ocean-view lots in some place like Pekin, North Dakota, and living under the name Silas Marner or somesuch because half the civilized world is trying to find him to sue his ass off.

And I might have a moment of compassion for the creep, but I haven't the time. I have three hit shows running at the moment, one each on ABC, NBC, and CBS.

They are big hits because somehow, in a way that no one seems able to figure out, there are all these little subliminal buttons being pushed by my shows, and they just soar to the top of the Nielsen ratings.

And I said to Aunt Babe, "Listen, don't you want to go to

Heaven, or wherever it is? I mean, don't you want out of that limbo existence?"

And with love, because she wanted to protect her *bambino caro*, because she wanted to make up for the fact that I didn't have her wonderful bosom to fall asleep on anymore, she said, "Get out of here, Angelo, my darling? What . . . and leave show business?"

The Author would like to thank Franco & Carol Betti, Jody Clark, Bart Di Grazia, Tom Kafka, Alan Kay, Ann Knight, Gil Lamont, Michele D. Malamud, and the Grand Forks, North Dakota Public Library reference staff for invaluable assistance in getting the details of this story written accurately.

# GREG BEAR

## "Dead Run"

*Greg Bear (1951- ) began publishing science fiction in 1967 and quickly established a reputation as writer of inventive hard science fiction. His novel* Blood Music *is considered one of the best fictional treatments of the themes of nanotechnology and genetic engineering. In his trilogy* Eon, Eternity *and* Legacy, *a basic space opera premise serves as the springboard for insightful explorations of alien cultures, the interplay of politics and science, and the technological future of mankind. He has also written a fantasy diptych comprised of the novels* The Infinity Concerto *and* The Serpent Mage, *and the Nebula Award-winning* Moving Mars, *a profound speculation on the ramifications of contemporary social attitudes toward science. His Hugo and Nebula Award-winning short fiction has been collected in* The Wind from a Burning Woman *and* Tangents.

# Dead Run

### *by Greg Bear*

---

There aren't many hitchhikers on the road to Hell.

I noticed this dude from four miles away. He stood where the road is straight and level, crossing what looks like desert except it has all these little empty towns and motels and shacks. I had been on the road for about six hours, and the folks in the cattle trailers behind me had been quiet for the last three—resigned, I guess—so my nerves had settled a bit and I decided to see what the dude was up to. Maybe he was one of the employees. That would be interesting, I thought.

Truth to tell, once the wailing settled down, I got pretty bored.

The dude was on the right-hand side of the road, thumb out. I piano-keyed down the gears, and the air brakes hissed and squealed at the tap of my foot. The semi slowed and the big diesel made that gut-deep dinosaur-belch of shuddered-downness. I leaned across the cab as everything came to a halt and swung the door open.

"Where you heading?" I asked.

He laughed and shook his head, then spit on the soft shoulder. "I don't know," he said. "Hell, maybe." He was thin and tanned with long, greasy black hair and blue jeans and a vest. His straw hat was dirty and full of holes, but the feathers around the crown were bright and new-looking, pheasant, if I was any judge. A worn gold chain hung out of his vest going into his watch pocket. He wore old Frye boots with the toes turned up and soles thinner than my spare's retread. He looked an awful lot like I had when I hitch-hiked out of Fresno, broke and unemployed, looking for work.

"Can I take you there?" I asked.

"Sho'." He climbed in and eased the door shut behind him, took out a kerchief and mopped his forehead, then blew his long nose and stared at me with bloodshot sleepless eyes. "What you haul-ing?" he asked.

"Souls," I said. "Whole shitload of them."

"What kind?" He was young, not more than twenty-five. He wanted to sound nonchalant, but I could hear the nerves.

"Usual kind," I said. "Human. Got some Hare Krishnas this time. Don't look too close anymore."

I coaxed the truck along, wondering if the engine was as bad as it sounded. When we were up to speed—eighty, eighty-five, no smokies on *this* road—he asked, "How long you been hauling?"

"Two years."

"Good pay?"

"It'll do."

"Benefits?"

"Union like everyone else."

"I heard about that," he said. "In that little dump about two miles back."

"People live there?" I asked. I didn't think anything lived along the road.

"Yeah. Real down folks. They said Teamster bosses get carried in limousines when they go."

"Don't really matter how you get there, I suppose. The trip's short, and forever is a long time."

"Getting there's all the fun?" he asked, trying to grin. I gave him a shallow one.

"What're you doing out here?" I asked a few minutes later. "You aren't dead, are you?" I'd never heard of dead folks running loose or looking quite as vital as he did, but I couldn't imagine anyone else being on the road. Dead folks—and drivers.

"No," he said. He was quiet for a bit. Then, slow, as if it embar-rassed him, "I came to find my woman."

"Yeah?" Not much surprised me, but that was a new twist. "There ain't no returning, you know."

"Sherill's her name, spelled like sheriff but with two L's."

"Got a cigarette?" I asked. I didn't smoke, but I could use them later. He handed me the last three in a crush-proof pack, not just one but all, and didn't say anything.

"Haven't heard of her," I said. "But then, I don't get to converse with everybody I haul. And there are lots of trucks, lots of drivers."

"I know," he said. "But I heard about them benefits."

He had a crazy kind of sad look in his eye when he glanced at me, and that made me angry. I tightened my jaw and stared straight ahead.

"You know," he said, "back in that town they tell some crazy stories. About how they use old trains for China and India, and in Russia there's a tramline. In Mexico it's old buses along roads, always at night—"

"Listen, I don't use all the benefits," I said. "I know some do, but I don't."

"Sure, I got you," he said, nodding that exaggerated goddamn young folks' nod, his whole neck and shoulders moving along, it's all right everything's cool.

"How you gonna find her?" I asked.

"I don't know. Do the road, ask the drivers."

"How'd you get in?"

He didn't answer for a moment. "I'm coming here when I die. That's pretty sure. It's not so hard for folks like me to get in beforehand. And . . . my daddy was a driver. He told me the route. By the way, my name's Bill."

"Mine's John," I said.

"Glad to meet you."

We didn't say much after that for a while. He stared out the right window and I watched the desert and faraway shacks go by. Soon the mountains came looming up—space seems compressed on the road, especially once past the desert—and I sped up for the approach. There was some noise from the back.

"What'll you do when you get off work?" Bill asked.

"Go home and sleep."

"Nobody knows?"

"Just the union."

"That's the way it was with Daddy, until just before the end. Look, I didn't mean to make you mad or nothing. I'd just heard about the perks, and I thought . . ." He swallowed, his Adam's apple bobbing. "Thought you might be able to help. I don't know how I'll ever find Sherill. Maybe back in the annex . . ."

"Nobody in their right minds goes into the yards by choice," I said. "And you'd have to look over everybody that's died in the last four months. They're way backed up."

Bill took that like a blow across the face, and I was sorry I'd said it. "She's only been gone a week," he said.

"Well," I said.

"My mom died two years ago, just before Daddy."

"The High Road," I said.

"What?"

"Hope they both got the High Road."

"Mom, maybe. Yeah. She did. But not Daddy. He knew." Bill hawked and spit out the window. "Sherill, she's here—but she don't belong."

I couldn't help but grin.

"No, man, I mean it, I belong but not her. She was in this car wreck couple of months back. Got pretty badly messed up. I'd dealed her dope at first and then fell in love with her, and by the time she landed in the hospital, she was, you know, hooked on about four different things."

My arms stiffened on the wheel.

"I tried to tell her when I visited that it wouldn't be good for her to get anything, no more dope, but she begged me. What could I do? I loved her." He wasn't looking out the window now. He was looking down at his worn boots and nodding. "She begged me, man. So I brought her stuff. I mean she took it all when they weren't looking. She just took it *all*. They pumped her out, but her insides were just gone. I didn't hear about her being dead until two days ago, and that really burned me. I was the only one who loved her and they didn't even tell me. I had to go up to her room and find her bed empty. Jesus. I hung out at Daddy's union hall. Someone talked to someone else and I found her name on a list. The Low Road."

I hadn't known it was that easy to find out; but then, I'd never traveled in dopers' territory. Dope can loosen a lot of lips.

"I don't use any of those perks," I said, just to make it clear I couldn't help him. "Folks in back got enough trouble without me. I think the union went too far there."

"Bet they felt you'd get lonely, need company," Bill said quietly, looking at me. "It don't hurt the folks back there. Maybe give them another chance to, you know, think things over. Give 'em relief for a couple of hours, a break from the mash—"

"Listen, a couple of hours don't mean nothing in relation to eternity. I'm not so sure I won't be joining them someday, and if that's the way it is, I want it smooth, nobody pulling me out of a trailer and putting me back in."

"Yeah," he said. "Got you, man. I know where that's at. But she might be back there right now, and all you'd have to—"

"Bad enough I'm driving this rig in the first place." I wanted to change the subject.

"Yeah. How'd that happen?"

"Couple of accidents. Hot-rodding with an old fart in a Triumph. Nearly ran over some joggers on a country road. My premiums went up to where I couldn't afford payments and finally they took my truck away."

"You coulda gone without insurance."

"Not me," I said. "Anyway, some bad word got out. No companies would hire me. I went to the union to see if they could help. They told me I was a dead-ender, either get out of trucking or . . ." I shrugged. "This. I couldn't leave trucking. It's bad out there, getting work. Lots of unemployed. Couldn't see myself pushing a hack in some big city."

"No, man," Bill said, giving me that whole-body nod again. He cackled sympathetically.

"They gave me an advance, enough for a down payment on my rig." The truck was grinding a bit but maintaining. Over the mountains, through a really impressive pass like from an old engraving, and down in a rugged rocky valley, was the City. I'd deliver my cargo, get my slip, and take the rig (with Bill) back to Baker. Park it in the yard next to my cottage after letting him out someplace sane.

Get some sleep.

Start over again next Monday, two loads a week.

"I don't think I'd better go on," Bill said. "I'll hitch with some other rig, ask around."

"Well, I'd feel better if you rode with me back out of here. Want my advice?" Bad habit. "Go home—"

"No," Bill said. "Thanks anyway. I can't go home. Not without Sherill. She don't belong here." He took a deep breath. "I'll try to work up a trade. I stay, she goes to the High Road. That's the way the game runs down here, isn't it?"

I didn't tell him otherwise. I couldn't be sure he wasn't right. He'd made it this far. At the top of the pass I pulled the rig over and let him out. He waved at me, I waved back, and we went our separate ways.

Poor rotten doping son of a bitch. I'd screwed up my life half a dozen different ways—three wives, liquor, three years at Tehachapi—but I'd never done dope. I felt self-righteous just listening to the dude. I was glad to be rid of him, truth be told.

The City looks a lot like a county full of big white cathedrals. Casting against type. High wall around the perimeter, stretching as far as my eye can see. No horizon but a vanishing point, the wall looking like an endless highway turned on its side. As I geared the truck down for the decline, the noise in the trailers got irritating again. They could smell what was coming, I guess, like pigs stepping up to the man with the knife.

I pulled into the disembarkation terminal and backed the first trailer up to the holding pen. Employees let down the gates and used some weird kind of prod to herd them. These people were past mortal.

Employees unhooked the first trailer and I backed in the second.

I got down out of the cab and an employee came up to me, a big fellow with red eyes and brand-new coveralls. "Good ones this load?" he asked. His breath was like the end of a cabbage, bean and garlic dinner.

I shook my head and held a cigarette out for a light. He pressed his fingernail against the tip. The tip flared and settled down to a steady glow. He looked at it with pure lust.

"Listen," I said. "You had anyone named Sherill through here?"

"Who's asking?" he grumbled, still eyeing the cigarette. He started to do a slow dance.

"Just curious. I heard you guys knew all the names."

"So?" He stopped. He had to walk around, otherwise his shoes melted the asphalt and got stuck. He came back and stood, lifting one foot, twisting a bit, then putting it down and lifting the other.

"So," I said, with as much sense.

"Like Cherry with an L?"

"No. Sherill, like sheriff but with two L's."

"Couple of Cheryls. No Sherills," he said. "Now . . ."

I handed him the cigarette. They loved the things. "Thanks," I said. I pulled another out of the pack and gave it to him. He popped both of them into his mouth and chewed, bliss pushing over his seamed face. Tobacco smoke came out his nose and he swallowed. "Nothing to it," he said, and walked on.

The road back is shorter than the road in. Don't ask how. I'd have thought it was the other way around, but barriers are what's important, not distance. Maybe we all get our chances so the road to Hell is long. But once we're there, there's no returning. You have to save on the budget somewhere.

I took the empties back to Baker. Didn't see Bill. Eight hours later I was in bed, beer in hand, paycheck on the bureau, my eyes wide open.

Shit, I thought. Now my conscience was working. I could have sworn I was past that. But then, I didn't use the perks. I wouldn't drive without insurance.

I wasn't really cut out for the life.

There are no normal days and nights on the road to Hell. No matter how long you drive, it's always the same time when you arrive as when you left, but it's not necessarily the same time from trip to trip.

The next trip, it was cool dusk, and the road didn't pass through desert and small, empty towns. Instead, it crossed a bleak flatland of skeletal trees, all the same uniform gray as if cut from paper. When I pulled over to catch a nap—never sleeping more than two hours at a stretch—the shouts of the damned in the trailers bothered me even more than usual. Silly things they said, like:

"You can take us back, mister! You really can!"

"Can he?"

"Shit no, mofuck pig."

"You can let us out! We can't hurt you!"

That was true enough. Drivers were alive, and the dead could never hurt the living. But I'd heard what happened when you let them out. There were about ninety of them in back, and in any load there was always one would make you want to use your perks.

I scratched my itches in the narrow bunk, looking at the Sierra Club calendar hanging just below the fan. The Devil's Postpile. The load became quieter as the voices gave up, one after the other. There was one last shout—some obscenity—then silence.

It was then I decided I'd let them out and see if Sherill was there, or if anyone knew her. They mingled in the annex, got their last socializing before the City. Someone might know. Then I saw Bill again—

What? What could I do to help him? He had screwed Sherill up royally, but then, she'd had a hand in it too, and that was what Hell was all about. Poor stupid sons of bitches.

I swung out of the cab, tucking in my shirt and pulling my straw hat down on my crown. "Hey!" I said, walking alongside the trailers. Faces peered at me from the two inches between each white slat. "I'm going to let you out. Just for a while. I need some information."

"Ask!" someone screamed. "Just ask, goddammit!"

"You know you can't run away. You can't hurt me. You're all dead. Understand?"

"We know," said another voice, quieter.

"Maybe we can help."

"I'm going to open the gates one trailer at a time." I went to the rear trailer first, took out my keys and undid the Yale padlock. Then I swung the gates open, standing back a little like there was some kind of infected wound about to drain.

They were all naked, but they weren't dirty. I'd seen them in the annex yards and at the City; I knew they were't like concentration camp prisoners. The dead can't really be unhealthy. Each just had some sort of air about him telling why he was in Hell; nothing specific but subliminal.

Like three black dudes in the rear trailer, first to step out. Why they were going to Hell was all over their faces. They weren't in the least sorry for the lives they'd led. They wanted to keep on doing what had brought them here in the first place—scavenging, hurting, hurting *me* in particular.

"Stupid ass mofuck," one of them said, staring at me beneath thin, expressive eyebrows. He nodded and swung his fists, trying to pound the slats from the outside, but the blows hardly made them vibrate.

An old woman crawled down, hair white and neatly coifed. I couldn't be certain what she had done, but she made me uneasy. She might have been the worst in the load. And lots of others, young, old, mostly old. Quiet for the most part.

They looked me over, some defiant, most just bewildered.

"I need to know if there's anyone here named Sherill," I said, "who happens to know a fellow named Bill."

"That's my name," said a woman hidden in the crowd.

"Let me see her." I waved my hand at them. The black dudes came forward. A funny look got in their eyes and they backed away.

The others parted and a young woman walked out. "How do you spell your name?" I asked.

She got a panicked expression. She spelled it, hesitating, hoping she'd make the grade. I felt horrible already. She was a Cheryl.

"Not who I'm looking for," I said.

"Don't be hasty," she said, real soft. She wasn't trying hard to be seductive, but she was succeeding. She was very pretty with medium-sized breasts, hips like a teenager's, legs not terrific but nice. Her black hair was clipped short and her eyes were almost Oriental. I figured maybe she was Lebanese or some other kind of Middle Eastern.

I tried to ignore her. "You can walk around a bit," I told them. "I'm letting out the first trailer now." I opened the side gates on that one and the people came down. They didn't smell, didn't look hungry, they just all looked pale. I wondered if the torment had begun already, but if so, I decided, it wasn't the physical kind.

One thing I'd learned in my two years was that all the Sunday school and horror movie crap about Hell was dead wrong.

"Woman named Sherill," I repeated. No one stepped forward. Then I felt someone close to me and I turned. It was the Cheryl woman. She smiled. "I'd like to sit up front for a while," she said.

"So would we all, sister," said the white-haired old woman. The black dudes stood off separate, talking low.

I swallowed, looking at her. Other drivers said they were real insubstantial except at one activity. That was the perk. And it was said the hottest ones always ended up in Hell.

"No," I said. I motioned for them to get back into the trailers. Whatever she was on the Low Road for, it wouldn't affect her performance in the sack, that was obvious.

It had been a dumb idea all around. They went back and I returned to the cab, lighting up a cigarette and thinking about what had made me do it.

I shook my head and started her up. Thinking on a dead run was no good. "No," I said, "goddamn," I said, "good."

Cheryl's face stayed with me.

Cheryl's body stayed with me longer than the face.

Something always comes up in life to lure a man onto the Low Road, not driving but riding in the back. We all have some weakness. I wondered what reason God had to give us each that little flaw, like a chip in crystal, you press the chip hard enough, everything splits up crazy.

At least now I knew one thing. My flaw wasn't sex, not this way. What most struck me about Cheryl was wonder. She was so pretty; how'd she end up on the Low Road?

For that matter, what had Bill's Sherill done?

I returned hauling empties and found myself this time outside a small town called Shoshone. I pulled my truck into the cafe parking lot. The weather was cold and I left the engine running. It was about eleven in the morning and the cafe was half-full. I took a seat at the counter next to an old man with maybe four teeth in his head, attacking French toast with downright solemn dignity. I ordered eggs and hash browns and juice, ate quickly, and went back to my truck.

Bill stood next to the cab. Next to him was an enormous young woman with a face like a bulldog. She was wrapped in a filthy piece of plaid fabric that might have been snatched from a trash dump somewhere. "Hey," Bill said. "Remember me?"

"Sure."

"I saw you pulling up. I thought you'd like to know . . . This is Sherill. I got her out of there." The woman stared at me with all the expression of a brick. "It's all screwy. Like a power failure or something. We just walked out on the road and nobody stopped us."

Sherill could have hid any number of weirdnesses beneath her formidable looks and gone unnoticed by ordinary folks. But I didn't have any trouble picking out the biggest thing wrong with her: she was dead. Bill had brought her out of Hell. I looked around to make sure I was in the World. I was. He wasn't lying. Something serious had happened on the Low Road.

"Trouble?" I asked.

"Lots." He grinned at me. "Pan-demon-ium." His grin broadened.

"That can't happen," I said. Sherill trembled, hearing my voice.

"He's a *driver*, Bill," she said. "He's the one takes us there. We should git out of here." She had that soul-branded air and the look of a pig that's just escaped slaughter, seeing the butcher again. She took a few steps backward. Gluttony, I thought. Gluttony and buried lust and a real ugly way of seeing life, inner eye pulled all out of shape by her bulk.

Bill hadn't had much to do with her ending up on the Low Road. "Tell me more," I said.

"There's folks running all over down there, holing up in them towns, devils chasing them—"

"Employees," I corrected.

"Yeah. Every which way."

Sherill tugged on his arm. "We got to go, Bill."

"We got to go," he echoed. "Hey, man, thanks. I found her!" He nodded his whole-body nod and they were off down the street, Sherill's plaid wrap dragging in the dirt.

I drove back to Baker, wondering if the trouble was responsible for my being rerouted through Shoshone. I parked in front of my little house and sat inside with a beer while it got dark, checking my calendar for the next day's run and feeling very cold. I can take so much supernatural in its place, but now things were spilling over, smudging the clean-drawn line between my work and the World. Next day I was scheduled to be at the annex and take another load.

Nobody called that evening. If there was trouble on the Low Road, surely the union would let me know, I thought.

I drove to the annex early in the morning. The crossover from the World to the Low Road was normal; I followed the route and the sky muddied from blue to solder-color and I was on the first leg to the annex. I backed the rear trailer up to the yard's gate and unhitched it, then placed the forward trailer at a ramp, all the while keeping my ears tuned to pick up interesting conversation.

The employees who work the annex look human. I took my invoice from a red-faced old guy with eyes like billiard balls and looked at him like I was in the know but could use some updating. He spit smoking saliva on the pavement, returned my look slantwise and said nothing. Maybe it was all settled. I hitched up both full trailers and pulled out.

I didn't even mention Sherill and Bill. Like in most jobs, keeping one's mouth shut is good policy. That and don't volunteer.

It was the desert again this time, only now the towns and tumbledown houses looked bomb-blasted, like something big had come through flushing out game with a howitzer.

Eyes on the road. Push that rig.

Four hours in, I came to a roadblock. Nobody on it, no employees, just big carved-lava barricades cutting across all lanes, and beyond them a yellow smoke which, the driver's unwritten instructions advised, meant absolutely no entry.

I got out. The load was making noises. I suddenly hated them. Nothing beautiful there—just naked Hell-bounders shouting and screaming and threatening like it wasn't already over for them.

They'd had their chance and crapped out and now they were still bullshitting the World.

Least they could do was go with dignity and spare me their misery.

That's probably what the engineers on the trains to Auschwitz thought. Yeah, yeah, except I was the fellow who might be hauling those engineers to their just deserts.

Crap, I just couldn't be one way or the other about the whole thing. I could feel mad and guilty and I could think Jesus, probably I'll be complaining just as much when my time comes. Jesus H. Twentieth Century Man Christ.

I stood by the truck, waiting for instructions or some indication what I was supposed to do. The load became quieter after a while, but I heard noises off the road, screams mostly and far away.

"There isn't anything," I said to myself, lighting up on of Bill's cigarettes even though I don't smoke and dragging deep, *"anything* worth this shit."* I vowed I would quit after this run.

I heard something come up behind the trailers and I edged closer to the cab steps. High wisps of smoke obscured things at first, but a dark shape three or four yards high plunged through and stood with one hand on the top slats of the rear trailer. It was covered with naked people, crawling all over, biting and scratching and shouting obscenities. It made little grunting noises, fell to its knees, then stood again and lurched off the road. Some of the people hanging on saw me and shouted for me to come help.

"Help us get this son of a bitch down!"

"Hey, you! We've almost got 'im!"

"He's a driver—"

"Fuck 'im, then."

I'd never seen an employee so big before, nor in so much trouble. The load began to wail like banshees. I threw down my cigarette and ran after it.

Workers will tell you. Camaraderie extends even to those on the job you don't like. If they're in trouble, it's part of the mystique to help out. Besides, the unwritten instructions were very clear on such things, and I've never knowingly broken a job rule—not since getting my rig back—and couldn't see starting now.

Through the smoke and across great ridges of lava, I ran until I spotted the employee about ten yards ahead. It had shaken off the naked people and was standing with one in each hand. Its shoulders smoked and scales stood out at all angles. They'd really done a job on the bastard. Ten or twelve of the dead were picking themselves off the lava, unscraped, unbruised. They saw me.

The employee saw me.

Everyone came at me. I turned and ran for the truck, stumbling, falling, bruising and scraping myself everywhere. My hair stood on end. People grabbed me, pleading for me to haul them out, old, young, all fawning and screeching like whipped dogs.

Then the employee swung me up out of reach. Its hand was cold and hard like iron tongs kept in a freezer. It grunted and ran toward my truck, opening the door wide and throwing me roughly inside. It made clear with huge, wild gestures that I'd better turn around and go back, that waiting was no good and there was no way through.

I started the engine and turned the rig around. I rolled up my window and hoped the dead weren't substantial enough to scratch paint or tear up slats.

All rules were off now. What about the ones in my load? All the while I was doing these things, my head was full of questions, like how could souls fight back and wasn't there some inflexible order in Hell that kept such things from happening? That was what had been implied when I hired on. Safest job around.

I headed back down the road. My load screamed like no load I'd ever had before. I was afraid they might get loose, but they didn't. I got near the annex and they were quiet again, too quiet for me to hear over the diesel.

The yards were deserted. The long, white-painted cement platforms and whitewashed wood-slat loading ramps were unattended. No souls in the pens.

The sky was an indefinite gray. An out-of-focus yellow sun gleamed faintly off the stark white employees' lounge. I stopped the truck and swung down to investigate.

There was no wind, only silence. The air was frosty without being particularly cold. What I wanted to do most was unload and get out of there, go back to Baker or Barstow or Shoshone.

I hoped that was still possible. Maybe all exits had been closed. Maybe the overseers had closed them to keep any more souls from getting out.

I tried the gate latches and found I could open them. I did so and returned to the truck, swinging the rear trailer around until it was flush with the ramp. Nobody made a sound. "Go on back," I said. "Go on back. You've got more time here. Don't ask me how."

"Hello, John." That was behind me. I turned and saw an older man without any clothes on. I didn't recognize him at first. His eyes finally clued me in.

"Mr. Martin?" My high school history teacher. I hadn't seen him in maybe twenty years. He didn't look much older, but then, I'd never seen him naked. He was dead, but he wasn't like the others. He didn't have that look that told me why he was here.

"This is not the sort of job I'd expect one of my students to take," Martin said. He laughed the smooth laugh he was famous for, the laugh that seemed to take everything he said in class and put it in perspective.

"You're not the first person I'd expect to find here," I responded.

"The cat's away, John. The mice are in charge now. I'm going to try to leave."

"How long you been here?" I asked.

"I died a month ago, I think," Martin said, never one to mince words.

"You can't leave," I said. Doing my job even with Mr. Martin. I felt the ice creep up my throat.

"Team player," Martin said. "Still the screwball team player, even when the team doesn't give a damn what you do."

I wanted to explain, but he waked away toward the annex and the road out. Looking back over his shoulder, he said, "Get smart, John. Things aren't what they seem. Never have been."

"Look!" I shouted after him. "I'm going to quit, honest, but this load is my responsibility." I thought I saw him shake his head as he rounded the corner of the annex.

The dead in my load had pried loose some of the ramp slats and were jumping off the rear trailer. Those in the forward trailer were screaming and carrying on, shaking the whole rig.

Responsibility, shit, I thought. As the dead followed after Mr. Martin, I unhitched both trailers. Then I got in the cab and swung away from the annex, onto the incoming road. "I'm going to quit," I said. "Sure as anything, I'm going to quit."

The road out seemed awfully long. I didn't see any of the dead, surprisingly, but then, maybe they'd been shunted away. I was taking a route I'd never been on before, and I had no way of knowing if it would put me where I wanted to be. But I hung in there for two hours, running the truck dead-out on the flats.

The air was getting grayer like somebody turning down the contrast on a TV set. I switched on the high beams, but they didn't help. By now I was shaking in the cab and saying to myself, Nobody deserves this. Nobody deserves going to Hell no matter what they did. I was scared. It was getting colder.

Three hours and I saw the annex and yards ahead of me again. The road had looped back. I swore and slowed the rig to a crawl. The loading docks had been set on fire. Dead were wandering around with no idea what to do or where to go. I sped up and drove over the few that were on the road. They'd come up and the truck's bumper would hit them and I wouldn't feel a thing, like they weren't there. I'd see them in the rearview mirror, getting up after being knocked over. Just knocked over. Then I was away from the loading docks and there was no doubt about it this time.

I was heading straight for Hell.

The disembarkation terminal was on fire, too. But beyond it, the City was bright and white and untouched. For the first time I drove past the terminal and took the road into the City.

It was either that or stay on the flats with everything screwy. Inside, I thought maybe they'd have things under control.

The truck roared through the gate between two white pillars maybe seventy or eighty feet thick and as tall as the Washington Monument. I didn't see anybody, employees or the dead. Once I was through the pillars—and it came as a shock—

There was no City, no walls, just the road winding along and countryside in all directions, even behind.

The countryside was covered with shacks, houses, little clusters and big clusters. Everything was tight-packed, people working together on one hill, people sitting on their porches, walking along paths, turning to stare at me as the rig barreled on through. No employees—no monsters. No flames. No bloody lakes or rivers.

This must be the outside part, I thought. Deeper inside it would get worse.

I kept on driving. The dog part of me was saying let's go look for authority and ask some questions and get out. But the monkey was saying let's just go look and find out what's going on, what Hell is all about.

Another hour of driving through that calm, crowded landscape and the truck ran out of fuel. I coasted to the side and stepped down from the cab, very nervous.

Again I lit up a cigarette and leaned against the fender, shaking a little. But the shaking was running down and a tight kind of calm was replacing it.

The landscape was still condensed, crowded, but nobody looked tortured. No screaming, no eternal agony. Trees and shrubs and grass hills and thousands and thousands of little houses.

It took about ten minutes for the inhabitants to get around to investigating me. Two men came over to my truck and nodded cordially. Both were middle-aged and healthy-looking. They didn't look dead. I nodded back.

"We were betting whether you're one of the drivers or not," said the first, a black-haired fellow. He wore a simple handwoven shirt and pants. "I think you are. That so?"

"I am."

"You're lost, then."

I agreed. "Maybe you can tell me where I am?"

"Hell," said the second man, younger by a few years and just wearing shorts. The way he said it was just like you might say you came from Los Angeles or Long Beach. Nothing big, nothing dramatic.

"We've heard rumors there's been problems outside," a woman said, coming up to join us. She was about sixty and skinny. She looked like she should be twitchy and nervous, but she acted rock-steady. They were all rock-steady.

"There's some kind of strike," I said. "I don't know what it is, but I'm looking for an employee to tell me."

"They don't usually come this far in," the first man said. "We run things here. Or rather, nobody tells us what to do."

"You're alive?" the woman asked, a curious hunger in her voice. Others came around to join us, a whole crowd. They didn't try to touch. They stood their ground and stared and talked.

"Look," said an old black fellow. "You ever read about the Ancient Mariner?"

I said I had in school.

"Had to tell everybody what he did," the black fellow said. The woman beside him nodded slowly. "We're all Ancient Mariners here. But there's nobody to tell it to. Would you like to know?" The way he asked was pitiful. "We're sorry. We just want everybody to know how sorry we are."

"I can't take you back," I said. "I don't know how to get there myself."

"We can't go back," the woman said. "That's not our place."

More people were coming and I was nervous again. I stood my

ground, trying to seem calm, and the dead gathered around me, eager.

"I never thought of anybody but myself," one said. Another interrupted with, "Man, I fucked my whole life away, I hated everybody and everything. I was burned out—"

"I thought I was the greatest. I could pass judgment on everybody—"

"I was the stupidest goddamn woman you ever saw. I was a sow, a pig. I farrowed kids and let them run wild, without no guidance. I was stupid and cruel, too. I used to hurt things—"

"Never cared for anyone. Nobody ever cared for me. I was left to rot in the middle of a city and I wasn't good enough not to rot."

"Everything I did was a lie after I was about twelve years old—"

"Listen to me, mister, because it hurts, it hurts so bad—"

I backed up against my truck. They were lining up now, organized, not like any mob. I had a crazy thought they were behaving better than any people on Earth, but these were the damned.

I didn't hear or see anybody famous. An ex-cop told me about what he did to people in jails. A Jesus-freak told me that knowing Jesus in your heart wasn't enough. "Because I should have made it, man, I should have made it."

"A time came and I was just broken by it all, broke myself really. Just kept stepping on myself and making all the wrong decisions—"

They confessed to me, and I began to cry. Their faces were so clear and so pure, yet here they were, confessing, and except maybe for specific things—like the fellow who had killed Ukrainians after the Second World War in Russian camps—they didn't sound any worse than the crazy sons of bitches I called friends who spent their lives in trucks or bars or whorehouses.

They were all recent. I got the impression the deeper into Hell you went, the older the damned became, which made sense; Hell, just got bigger, each crop of damned got bigger, with more room on the outer circles.

"We wasted it," someone said. "You know what my greatest sin was? I was dull. Dull and cruel. I never saw beauty. I saw only dirt. I loved the dirt, and the clean just passed me by."

Pretty soon my tears were uncontrollable. I kneeled down beside the truck, hiding my head, but they kept on coming and confessing. Hundreds must have passed, talking quietly, gesturing with their hands.

Then they stopped. Someone had come and told them to back

away, that they were too much for me. I took my face out of my hands and a very young-seeming fellow stood looking down on me. "You all right?" he asked.

I nodded, but my insides were like broken glass. With every confession I had seen myself, and with every tale of sin, I had felt an answering echo.

"Someday, I'm going to be here. Someone's going to drive me in a cattle car to Hell," I mumbled. The young fellow helped me to my feet and cleared a way around my truck.

"Yeah, but not now," he said. "You don't belong here yet." He opened the door to my cab and I got back inside.

"I don't have any fuel," I said.

He smiled that sad smile they all had and stood on the step, up close to my ear. "You'll be taken out of here soon anyway. One of the employees is bound to get around to you." He seemed a lot more sophisticated than the others. I looked at him maybe a little queerly, like there was some explaining in order.

"Yeah, I know all that stuff," he said. "I was a driver once. Then I got promoted. What are they all doing back there?" He gestured up the road. "They're really messing things up now, ain't they?"

"I don't know," I said, wiping my eyes and cheeks with my sleeve.

"You go back, and you tell them that all this revolt on the outer circles, it's what I expected. Tell them Charlie's here and that I warned them. Word's getting around. There's bound to be discontent.

"Word?"

"About who's in charge. Just tell them Charlie knows and I warned them. I know something else, and you shouldn't tell anybody about this . . ." He whispered an incredible fact into my ear then, something that shook me deeper than what I had already been through.

I closed my eyes. Some shadow passed over. The young fellow and everybody else seemed to recede. I felt rather than saw my truck being picked up like a toy.

Then I suppose I was asleep for a time.

In the cab in the parking lot of a truck stop in Bakersfield, I jerked awake, pulled my cap out of my eyes and looked around. It was about noon. There was a union hall in Bakersfield. I checked and my truck was full of diesel, so I started her up and drove to the union hall.

I knocked on the door of the office. I went in and recognized the fat old dude who had given me the job in the first place. I was tired and I smelled bad, but I wanted to get it all done with now.

He recognized me but didn't know my name until I told him. "I can't work the run anymore," I said. The shakes were on me again. "I'm not the one for it. I don't feel right driving them when I know I'm going to be there myself, like as not."

"Okay," he said, slow and careful, sizing me up with a knowing eye. "But you're out. You're busted then. No more driving, no more work for us, no more work for any union we support. It'll be lonely."

"I'll take that kind of lonely any day," I said.

"Okay." That was that. I headed for the door and stopped with my hand on the knob.

"One more thing," I said. "I met Charlie. He says to tell you word's getting around about who's in charge, and that's why there's so much trouble in the outer circles."

The old dude's knowing eye went sort of glassy. "You're the fellow got into the City?"

I nodded.

He got up from his seat real fast, jowls quivering and belly doing a silly dance beneath his work blues. He flicked one hand at me, come 'ere. "Don't go. Just you wait a minute. Outside in the office."

I waited and heard him talking on the phone. He came out smiling and put his hand on my shoulder. "Listen, John, I'm not sure we should let you quit. I didn't know you were the one who'd gone inside. Word is, you stuck around and tried to help when everybody else ran. The company appreciates that. You've been with us a long time, reliable driver, maybe we should give you some incentive to stay. I'm sending you to Vegas to talk with a company man . . ."

The way he said it, I knew there wasn't much choice and I better not fight it. You work union long enough and you know when you keep your mouth shut and go along.

They put me up in a motel and fed me, and by late morning I was on my way to Vegas, arriving about two in the afternoon. I was in a black union car with a silent driver and air conditioning and some *Newsweeks* to keep me company.

The limo dropped me off in front of a four-floor office building, glass and stucco, with lots of divorce lawyers and a dentist and small companies with anonymous names. White plastic letters on a ribbed felt background in a glass case. There was no name on the office number I had been told to go to, but I went up and knocked anyway.

I don't know what I expected. A district supervisor opened the door and asked me a few questions and I said what I'd said before. I was adamant. He looked worried. "Look," he said. "It won't be good for you now if you quit."

I asked him what he meant by that, but he just looked unhappy and said he was going to send me to somebody higher up.

That was in Denver, nearer my God to thee. The same black car took me there, and Saturday morning, bright and early, I stood in front of a very large corporate building with no sign out front and a bank on the bottom floor. I went past the bank and up to the very top.

A secretary met me, pretty but her hair done up very tight and her jaw grimly square. She didn't like me. She let me into the next office, though.

I swear I'd seen the fellow before, but maybe it was just a passing resemblance. He wore a narrow tie and a tasteful but conservative gray suit. His shirt was pastel blue and there was a big Rembrandt Bible on his desk, sitting on the glass top next to an alabaster pen holder. He shook my hand firmly and perched on the edge of the desk.

"First, let me congratulate you on your bravery. We've had some reports from the . . . uh . . . field, and we're hearing nothing but good about you." He smiled like that fellow on TV who's always asking the audience to give him some help. Then is face got sincere and serious. I honestly believe he was sincere; he was also well trained in dealing with not-very-bright people. "I hear you have a report for me. From Charles Frick."

"He said his name was Charlie." I told him the story. "What I'm curious about, what did he mean, this thing about who's in charge?"

"Charlie was in Organization until last year. He died in a car accident. I'm shocked to hear he got the Low Road." He didn't look shocked. "Maybe I'm shocked but not surprised. To tell the truth, he was a bit of a troublemaker." He smiled brightly again and his eyes got large and there was a little too much animation in his face. He had on these MacArthur wire-rimmed glasses too big for his eyes.

"What did he mean?"

"John, I'm proud of all our drivers. You don't know how proud we all are of you folks down there doing the dirty work."

"What did Charlie mean?"

"The abortionists and pornographers, the hustlers and muggers and murderers. Atheists and heathens and idol-worshippers. Surely there must be some satisfaction in keeping the land clean. Sort of a giant sanitation squad, you people keep the scum away from the good folks. The plain good folks. Now, we know that driving's maybe the hardest job we have in the company, and that not everyone can stay on the Low Road indefinitely. Still, we'd like you to stay on. Not as a driver—unless you really wish to continue. For the satisfaction of a tough job. No, if you want to move up—and you've earned it by now, surely—we have a place for you here. A place where you'll be comfortable and—"

"I've already said I want out. You're acting like I'm hot stuff and I'm just shit. You know that, I know that. What is going on?"

His face hardened on me. "It isn't easy up here, either, buster." The "buster" bit tickled me. I laughed and got up from the chair. I'd been in enough offices, and this fancy one just made me queasy. When I stood, he held up his hand and pursed his lips as he nodded. "Sorry. There's incentive, there's certainly a reason why you should want to work here. If you're so convinced you're on your way to the Low Road, you can work it off here, you know."

"How can you say that?"

Bright smile. "Charlie told you something. He told you about who's in charge here."

Now I could smell something terribly wrong, like with the union boss. I mumbled, "He said that's why there's trouble."

"It comes every now and then. We put it down gentle. I tell you where we really need good people, compassionate people. We need them to help with the choosing."

"Choosing?"

"Surely you don't think the Boss does all the choosing directly?"

I couldn't think of a thing to say.

"Listen, the Boss . . . let me tell you. A long time ago, the Boss decided to create a new kind of worker, one with more decision-making ability. Some of the supervisors disagreed, especially when the Boss said the workers would be around for a long, long time—that they'd be indestructible. Sort of like nuclear fuel, you know. Human souls. The waste builds up after a time, those who turn out bad, turn out to be chronically unemployable. They don't go along with the scheme, or get out of line. Can't get along with their fellow workers. You know the type. What do you do with them? Can't just let them go away—they're indestructible, and that ain't no joke, so—"

"Chronically unemployable?"

"You're a union man. Think of what it must feel like to be out of work . . . *forever*. Damned. Nobody will hire you."

I knew the feeling, both the way he meant it and the way it had happened to me.

"The Boss feels the project half succeeded, so He doesn't dump it completely. But He doesn't want to be bothered with all the pluses and minutes, the bookkeeping."

"*You're* in charge," I said, my blood cooling.

And I knew where I had seen him before.

On television.

God's right-hand man.

And human. Flesh and blood.

*We* ran Hell.

He nodded. "Now, that's not the sort of thing we'd like to get around."

"You're in charge, and you let the drivers take their perks on the loads, you let—" I stopped, instinct telling me I would soon be on a rugged trail with no turnaround.

"I'll tell you the truth, John. I have only been in charge here for a year, and my predecessor let things get out of hand. He wasn't a religious man, John, and he thought this was a job like any other, where you could compromise now and then. I know that isn't so. There's no compromise here, and we'll straighten out those inequities and bad decisions very soon. You'll help us, I hope. You may know more about the problems than we do."

"How do you . . . how do you qualify for a job like this?" I asked. "And who offered it to you?"

"Not the Boss, if that's what you're getting at, John. It's been kind of traditional. You may have heard about me. I'm the one, when there was all this talk about after-death experiences and everyone was seeing bright light and beauty, I'm the one who wondered why no one was seeing the other side. I found people who had almost died and had seen Hell, and I turned their lives around. The management in the company decided a fellow with my ability could do good work here. And so I'm here. And I'll tell you, it isn't easy. I sometimes wish we had a little more help from the

Boss, a little more guidance, but we don't, and somebody has to do it. Somebody has to clean out the stables, John." Again the smile.

I put on my mask. "Of course," I said. I hoped a gradual increase in piety would pass his sharp-eyed muster.

"And you can see how this all makes you much more valuable to the organization."

I let light dawn slowly.

"We'd hate to lose you now, John. Not when there's security, so much security, working for us. I mean, here we learn the real ins and outs of salvation."

I let him talk at me until he looked at his watch, and all the time I nodded and considered and tried to think of the best ploy. Then I eased myself into a turnabout. I did some confessing until his discomfort was stretched too far—I was keeping him from an important appointment—and made my concluding statement.

"I just wouldn't feel right up here," I said. "I've driven all my life. I'd just want to keep on, working where I'm best suited."

"Keep your present job?" he said, tapping his shoe on the side of the desk.

"Lord, yes," I said, grateful as could be.

Then I asked him for his autograph. He smiled real big and gave it to me, God's right-hand man, who had prayed with presidents.

The next time out, I thought about the incredible thing that Charlie Frick had told me. Halfway to Hell, on the part of the run that he had once driven, I pulled the truck onto the gravel shoulder and walked back, hands in pockets, squinting at the faces. Young and old. Mostly old, or in their teens or twenties. Some were clearly bad news . . . But I was looking more closely this time, trying to discriminate. And sure enough, I saw a few that didn't seem to belong.

The dead hung by the slats, sticking their arms through, beseeching. I ignored as much of that as I could. "You," I said, pointing to a pale, thin fellow with a listless expression. "Why are you here?"

They wouldn't lie to me. I'd learned that inside the City. The dead don't lie.

"I kill people," the man said in a high whisper. "I kill children."

That confirmed my theory. I had *known* there was something wrong with him. I pointed to an old woman, plump and white-haired, lacking any of the signs. "You. Why are you going to Hell?"

She shook her head. "I don't know," she said. "Because I'm bad, I suppose."

"What did you do that was bad?"

"I don't know!" she said, flinging her hands up. "I really don't know. I was a librarian. When all those horrible people tried to take books out of my library, I fought them. I tried to reason with them . . . They wanted to remove Salinger and Twain and Baum . . ."

I picked out another young man. "What about you?"

"I didn't think it was possible," he said. "I didn't believe that God hated me, too."

"What did you do?" These people *didn't need to confess*.

"I loved God. I loved Jesus. But, dear Lord, I couldn't help it. I'm gay. I never had a choice. God wouldn't send me here just for being gay, would he?"

I spoke to a few more, until I was sure I had found all I had in this load. "You, you, you and you, out," I said, swinging open the rear gate. I closed the gate after them and led them away from the truck. Then I told them what Charlie Frick had told me, what he had learned on the road and in the big offices.

"Nobody's really sure where it goes," I said. "But it doesn't go to Hell, and it doesn't go back to Earth."

"Where, then?" the old woman asked plaintively. The hope in her eyes made me want to cry, because I just wasn't sure.

"Maybe it's the High Road," I said. "At least it's a chance. You light out across this stretch, go back of that hill, and I think there's some sort of trail. It's not easy to find, but if you look carefully, it's there. Follow it."

The young man who was gay took my hand. I felt like pulling away, because I've never been fond of homos. But he held on and he said, "Thank you. You must be taking a big risk."

"Yes, thank you," the librarian said. "Why are you doing it?"

I had hoped they wouldn't ask. "When I was a kid, one of my Sunday school teachers told me about Jesus going down to Hell during the three days before he rose up again. She told me Jesus went to Hell to bring out those who didn't belong. I'm certainly no Jesus, I'm not even much of a Christian, but that's what I'm doing. She called it Harrowing Hell." I shook my head. "Never mind. Just go," I said. I watched them walk across the gray flats and around the hill, then I got back into my truck and took the rest into the annex. Nobody noticed. I suppose the records just aren't that important to the employees.

None of the folks I've let loose have ever come back.

I'm staying on the road. I'm talking to people here and there, being cautious. When it looks like things are getting chancy, I'll take my rig back down to the City. And then I'm not sure what I'll do.

I don't want to let everybody loose. But I want to know who's ending up on the Low Road who shouldn't be. People unpopular with God's right-hand man.

My message is simple.

The crazy folks are running the asylum. We've corrupted Hell.

If I get caught, I'll be riding in back. And if you're reading this, chances are you'll be there, too.

Until then, I'm doing my bit. How about you?

# NANCY SPRINGER

# "The Boy Who Plaited Manes"

*Early in her writing career, Nancy Springer (1948- ) established a
reputation as a specialist in imaginary world fantasy. Between
1977 and 1985, she wrote* The Book of Suns *and four more novels
set in the world of Isle, a magical realm built from elements of
Celtic lore and inhabited by both human characters and anthropo-
morthized creatures of legend. Her Sea King trilogy includes the
quest romances* Madbond, Mindbond *and* Godbond. *She has also
written the dark fantasies* Apocalypse *and* Dambanna, *and several
fantasy novels for young readers, including* A Horse to Love *and*
Red Wizard. *Her short fiction and poetry has been collected in*
Chance: And Other Gestures of the Hand of Fate. *"The Boy Who
Plaited Manes" is perhaps her most highly regarded short story,
and was nominated for the Nebula and World Fantasy Awards.*

# The Boy Who Plaited Manes

*by Nancy Springer*

---

The boy who plaited the manes of horses arrived, fittingly enough, on the day of the Midsummer Hunt: when he was needed worst, though Wald the head groom did not yet know it. The stable seethed in a muted frenzy of work, as it had done since long before dawn, every groom and apprentice vehemently polishing. The lord's behest was that all the horses in his stable should be brushed for two hours every morning to keep the fine shine and bloom on their flanks, and this morning could be no different. Then there was also all the gear to be tended to. Though old Lord Robley of Auberon was a petty manor lord, with only some hundred of horses and less than half the number of grooms to show for a lifetime's striving, his lowly status made him all the more keen to present himself and his retinue grandly before the more powerful lords who would assemble for the Hunt. Himself and his retinue and his lovely young wife.

Therefore it was an eerie thing when the boy walked up the long stable aisle past men possessed with work, men so frantic they did not look up to glance at the stranger, up the aisle brick-paved in chevron style until he came to the stall where the lady's milk-white palfrey stood covered withers to croup with a fitted sheet tied on to keep the beast clean, and the boy swung open the heavy stall door and walked in without fear, as if he belonged there, and went up to the palfrey to plait its mane.

He was an eerie boy, so thin that he seemed deformed, and of an

234

age difficult to guess because of his thinness. He might have been ten, or he might have been seventeen with something wrong about him that made him beardless and narrow-shouldered and thin. His eyes seemed too gathered for a ten-year-old, gray-green and calm yet feral, like woodland. His hair, dark and shaggy, seemed to bulk large above his thin, thin face.

The palfrey's hair was far better cared for than his. Its silky mane, coddled for length, hung down below its curved neck, and its tail was bundled into a wrapping, to be let down at the last moment before the lady rode, when it would trail on the ground and float like a white bridal train. The boy did not yet touch the tail, but his thin fingers flew to work on the palfrey's mane.

Wald the head groom, passing nearly at a run to see to the saddling of the lord's hotblooded hunter, stopped in his tracks and stared. And to be sure it was not that he had never seen plaiting before. He himself had probably braided a thousand horses' manes, and he knew what a time it took to put even a row of small looped braids along a horse's crest, and how hard it was to get them even, and how horsehair seems like a demon with a mind of its own. He frankly gawked, and other grooms stood beside him and did likewise, until more onlookers stood gathered outside the palfrey's stall than could rightly see, and those in the back demanded to know what was happening, and those in the front seemed not to hear them, but stood as if in a trance, watching the boy's thin, swift hands.

For the boy's fingers moved more quickly and deftly than seemed human, than seemed possible, each hand by itself combing and plaiting a long, slender braid in one smooth movement, as if he no more than stroked the braid out of the mane. That itself would have been wonder enough, as when a groom is so apt that he can curry with one hand and follow after with the brush in the other, and have a horse done in half the time. A shining braid forming out of each hand every minute, wonder enough—but that was the least of it. The boy interwove them as he worked, so that they flowed into each other in a network, making of the mane a delicate shawl, a veil, that draped the palfrey's fine neck. The ends of the braids formed a silky hem curving down to a point at the shoulder, and at the point the boy spiraled the remaining mane into an uncanny horsehair flower. And all the time, though it was not tied and was by no means a cold-blooded beast, the palfrey had not moved, standing still as a stone.

Then Wald the head groom felt fear prickling at the back of his astonishment. The boy had carried each plait down to the last three hairs. Yet he had fastened nothing with thread or ribbon, but merely pressed the ends between two fingers, and the braids stayed as he had placed them. Nor did the braids ever seem to fall loose as he was working, or hairs fly out at random, but all lay smooth as white silk, shimmering. The boy, or whatever he was, stood still with his hands at his sides, admiring his work.

Uncanny. Still, the lord and lady would be well pleased. . . . Wald jerked himself out of amazement and moved quickly. "Get back to your work, you fellows!" he roared at the grooms, and then he strode into the stall.

"Who are you?" he demanded. "What do you mean coming in here like this?" It was best, in a lord's household, never to let anyone know you were obliged to them.

The boy looked at him silently, turning his head in the alert yet indifferent way of a cat.

"I have asked you a question! What is your name?"

The boy did not speak, or even move his lips. Then or thereafter, as long as he worked in that stable, he never made any sound.

His stolid manner annoyed Wald. But though the master groom could not yet know that the boy was a mute, he saw something odd in his face. A halfwit, perhaps. He wanted to strike the boy, but even worse he wanted the praise of the lord and lady, so he turned abruptly and snatched the wrapping off the palfrey's tail, letting the cloud of white hair float down to the clean straw of the stall. "Do something with that," he snapped.

A sweet, intense glow came into the boy's eyes as he regarded his task. With his fingers he combed the hair smooth, and then he started a row of small braids above the bone.

Most of the tail he left loose and flowing, with just a cluster of braids at the top, a few of them swinging halfway to the ground. And young Lady Aelynn gasped with pleasure when she saw them, and with wonder at the mane, even though she was a lord's daughter born and not unaccustomed to finery.

It did not matter, that day, that Lord Robley's saddle had not been polished to a sufficient shine. He was well pleased with his grooms. Nor did it matter that his hawks flew poorly, his hounds were unruly and his clumsy hunter stumbled and cut its knees. Lords and ladies looked again and again at his young wife on her white palfrey, its tail trailing and shimmering like her blue silk

gown, the delicate openwork of its mane as dainty as the lace kerchief tucked between her breasts or her slender gloved hand
which held the caparisoned reins. Every hair of her mount was as
artfully placed as her own honey-gold hair looped in gold-beaded
curls atop her fair young head. Lord Robley knew himself to be
the envy of everyone who saw him for the sake of his lovely wife
and the showing she made on her white mount with the plaited
mane.

And when the boy who plaited manes took his place among the
lord's other servants in the kitchen line for the evening meal, no
one gainsaid him.

Lord Robley was a hard old man, his old body hard and hale, his
spirit hard. It took him less than a day to pass from being well
pleased to being greedy for more: no longer was it enough that the
lady's palfrey should go forth in unadorned braids. He sent a servant to Wald with silk ribbons in the Auberon colors, dark blue
and crimson, and commanded that they should be plaited into the
palfrey's mane and tail. This the strange boy did with ease when
Wald gave him the order, and he used the ribbon ends to tie tiny
bows and love knots and leave a few shimmering tendrils bobbing
in the forelock. Lady Aelynn was enchanted.

Within a few days Lord Robley had sent to the stable thread of
silver and of gold, strings of small pearls, tassels, pendant jewels,
and fresh-cut flowers of every sort. All of these things the boy who
plaited manes used with ease to dress the lady's palfrey when he
was bid. Lady Aelynn went forth to the next hunt with tiny bells
of silver and gold chiming at the tip of each of her mount's dainty
ribbon-decked braids, and eyes turned her way wherever she
rode. Nor did the boy ever seem to arrange the mane and tail and
forelock twice in the same way, but whatever way he chose to plait
and weave and dress it seemed the most perfect and poignant and
heartachingly beautiful way a horse had ever been arrayed. Once
he did the palfrey's entire mane in one great, thick braid along the
crest, gathering in the hairs as he went, so that the neck seemed
to arch as mightily as a destrier's, and he made the braid drip
thick with flowers, roses and great lilies and spires of larkspur
trailing down, so that the horse seemed to go with a mane of flowers. But another time he would leave the mane loose and floating,
with just a few braids shimmering down behind the ears or in the

forelock, perhaps, and this also seemed perfect and poignant and the only way a horse should be adorned.

Nor was it sufficient, any longer, that merely the lady's milk-white palfrey should go forth in braids. Lord Robley commanded that his hotblooded hunter also should have his mane done up in stubby ribboned braids and rosettes in the Auberon colors, and the horses of his retinue likewise, though with lesser rosettes. And should his wife choose to go out riding with her noble guests, all their mounts were to be prepared like hers, though in lesser degree.

All these orders Wald passed on to the boy who plaited manes, and the youngster readily did as he was bid, working sometimes from before dawn until long after dark, and never seeming to want more than what food he could eat while standing in the kitchen. He slept in the hay and straw of the loft and did not use even a horseblanket for covering until one of the grooms threw one on him. Nor did he ask for clothing, but Wald, ashamed of the boy's shabbiness, provided him with the clothing due to a servant. The master groom said nothing to him of a servant's pay. The boy seemed content without it. Probably he would have been content without the clothing as well. Though in fact it was hard to tell what he was thinking or feeling, for he never spoke and his thin face seldom moved.

No one knew his name, the boy who plaited manes. Though many of the grooms were curious and made inquiries, no one could tell who he was or where he had come from. Or even what he was, Wald thought sourly. No way to tell if the young snip was a halfwit or a bastard or what, if he would not talk. No way to tell what sort of a young warlock he might be, that the horses never moved under his hands, even the hotblooded hunter standing like a stump for him. Scrawny brat. He could hear well enough; why would he not talk?

It did not make Wald like the strange boy, that he did at once whatever he was told and worked so hard and so silently. In particular he did not like the boy for doing the work for which Wald reaped the lord's praise; Wald disliked anyone to whom he was obliged. Nor did he like the way the boy had arrived, as if blown in on a gust of wind, and so thin that it nearly seemed possible. Nor did he like the thought that any day the boy might leave in like wise. And even disliking that thought, Wald could not bring himself to give the boy the few coppers a week which were his due, for he disliked the boy more. Wald believed there was something wrongheaded, nearly evil, about the boy. His face seemed wrong, so very thin, with the set mouth and the eyes both wild and quiet, burning like a steady candle flame.

Summer turned into autumn, and many gusts of wind blew, but the boy who plaited manes seemed content to stay, and if he knew of Wald's dislike he did not show it. In fact he showed nothing. He braided the palfrey's mane with autumn starflowers and smiled ever so slightly as he worked. Autumn turned to the first dripping and dismal, chill days of winter. The boy used bunches of bright feathers instead of flowers when he dressed the palfrey's mane, and he did not ask for a winter jerkin, so Wald did not give him any. It was seldom enough, anyway, that the horses were used for pleasure at this season. The thin boy could spend his days huddled under a horseblanket in the loft.

Hard winter came, and the smallpox season.

Lady Aelynn was bored in the wintertime, even more so than during the rest of the year. At least in the fine weather there were walks outside, there were riding and hunting and people to impress. It would not be reasonable for a lord's wife, nobly born (though a younger child, and female), to wish for more than that. Lady Aelynn knew full well that her brief days of friendships and courtships were over. She had wed tolerably well, and Lord Robley counted her among his possessions, a beautiful thing to be prized like his gold and his best horses. He was a manor lord, and she was his belonging, his lady, and not for others to touch even with their regard. She was entirely his. So there were walks for her in walled gardens, and pleasure riding and hunting by her lord's side, and people to impress.

But in the wintertime there were not even the walks. There was nothing for the Lady Aelynn to do but tend to her needlework and her own beauty, endlessly concerned with her clothes, her hair, her skin, even though she was so young, no more than seventeen—for she knew in her heart that it was for her beauty that Lord Robley smiled on her, and for no other reason. And though she did not think of it, she knew that her life lay in his grasping hands.

Therefore she was ardently uneasy, and distressed only for herself, when the woman who arranged her hair each morning was laid abed with smallpox. Though as befits a lady of rank, Aelynn hid her dismay in vexation. And it did not take her long to dis-

239

cover that none of her other tiring-women could serve her nearly as well.

"Mother of God!" she raged, surveying her hair in the mirror for perhaps the tenth time. "The groom who plaits the horses' manes in the stable could do better!" Then the truth of her own words struck her, and desperation made her willing to be daring. She smiled. "Bring him hither!"

Her women stammered and curtseyed and fled to consult among themselves and exclaim with the help in the kitchen. After some few minutes of this, a bold kitchen maid was dispatched to the stable and returned with a shivering waif: the boy who plaited manes.

It was not to be considered that such a beggar should go in to the lady. Her tiring-women squeaked in horror and made him bathe first, in a washbasin before the kitchen hearth, for there was a strong smell of horse and stable about him. They ordered him to scrub his own hair with strong soap and scent himself with lavender, and while some of them giggled and fled, others giggled and stayed, to pour water for him and see that he made a proper job of his ablutions. All that was demanded of him the boy who plaited manes did without any change in his thin face, any movement of his closed mouth, any flash of his feral eyes. At last they brought him clean clothing, jerkin and woolen hose only a little too large, and pulled the things as straight as they could on him, and took him to the tower where the lady waited.

He did not bow to the Lady Aelynn or look into her eyes for his instructions, but his still mouth softened a little and his glance, calm and alert, like that of a woodland thing, darted to her hair. And at once, as if he could scarcely wait, he took his place behind her and lifted her tresses in his hands. Such a soft, fine, honey-colored mane of hair as he had never seen, and combs of gold and ivory lying at hand on a rosewood table, and ribbons of silk and gold, everything he could have wanted, his for the sake of his skill.

He started at the forehead, and the lady sat as if in a trance beneath the deft touch of his hands.

Gentle, he was so gentle, she had never felt such a soft and gentle touch from any man, least of all from her lord. When Lord Robley wanted to use one of his possessions he seized it. But this boy touched her as gently as a woman, no, a mother, for no tiring-woman or maid had ever gentled her so. . . . Yet unmistakably his

was the touch of a man, though she could scarcely have told how
she knew. Part of it was power, she could feel the gentle power in
his touch, she could feel—uncanny, altogether eerie and uncanny,
what she was feeling. It was as if his quick fingers called to her
hair in soft command and her hair obeyed just for the sake of the
one quick touch, all the while longing to embrace. . . . She stayed
breathlessly still for him, like the horses.

He plaited her hair in braids thin as bluebell stems, only a wisp
of hairs to each braid, one after another with both his deft hands
as if each was as easy as a caress, making them stay with merely
a touch of two fingers at the end, until all her hair lay in a silky
cascade of them, catching the light and glimmering and swaying
like a rich drapery when he made her move her head. Some of
them he gathered and looped and tied up with the ribbons which
matched her dress, blue edged with gold. But most of them he left
hanging to her bare back and shoulders. He surveyed his work
with just a whisper of a smile when he was done, then turned and
left without waiting for the lady's nod, and she sat as if under a
spell and watched his thin back as he walked away. Then she
tossed her head at his lack of deference. But the swinging of her
hair pleased her.

She had him back to dress her hair the next day, and the next,
and many days thereafter. And so that they would not have to be
always bathing him, her tiring-women found him a room within
the manorhouse doors, and a pallet and clean blankets, and a
change of clothing, plain course clothing, such as servants wore.
They trimmed the heavy hair that shadowed his eyes, also, but he
looked no less the oddling with his thin, thin face and his calm,
burning glance and his mouth that seemed scarcely ever to move.
He did as he was bid, whether by Wald or the lady or some kitchen
maid, and every day he plaited Lady Aelynn's hair differently.
One day he shaped it all into a bright crown of braids atop her
head. On other days he would plait it close to her head so that the
tendrils caressed her neck, or in a haughty crest studded with
jewels, or in a single soft feathered braid at one side. He always
left her tower chamber at once, never looking at the lady to see if
he had pleased her, as if he knew that she would always be
pleased.

Always, she was.

Things happened. The tiring-woman who had taken smallpox
died of it, and Lady Aelynn did not care, not for the sake of her

cherished hair and most certainly not for the sake of the woman herself. Lord Robley went away on a journey to discipline a debtor vassal, and Lady Aelynn did not care except to be glad, for there was a sure sense growing in her of what she would do.

When even her very tresses were enthralled by the touch of this oddling boy, longing to embrace him, could she be otherwise?

When next he had plaited her mane of honey-colored hair and turned to leave her without a glance, she caught him by one thin arm. His eyes met hers with a steady, gathered look. She stood— she was taller than he, and larger, though she was as slender as any maiden. It did not matter. She took him by one thin hand and led him to her bed, and there he did as he was bid.

Nor did he disappoint her. His touch—she had never been touched so softly, so gently, so deftly, with such power. Nor was he lacking in manhood, for all that he was as thin and hairless as a boy. And his lips, after all, knew how to move, and his tongue. But it was the touch of his thin hands that she hungered for, the gentle, tender, potent touch that thrilled her almost as if—she were loved . . .

He smiled at her afterward, slightly, softly, a whisper of a smile in the muted half-light of her curtained bed, and his lips moved.

"You are swine," he said, "all of you nobles."

And he got up, put on his plain, coarse clothing and left her without a backward glance.

It terrified Lady Aelynn, that he was not truly a mute. Terrified her even more than what he had said, though she burned with mortified wrath whenever she thought of the latter. He, of all people, a mute, to speak such words to her and leave her helpless to avenge herself . . . Perhaps for that reason he would not betray her. She had thought it would be safe to take a mute as her lover. . . . Perhaps he would not betray her.

In fact, it was not he who betrayed her to her lord, but Wald.

Her tiring-women suspected, perhaps because she had sent them on such a long errand. She had not thought they would suspect, for who would think that such a wisp of a beardless boy could be a bedfellow? But perhaps they also had seen the wild glow deep in his gray-green eyes. They whispered among themselves and with the kitchen maids, and the bold kitchen maid giggled with the grooms, and Wald heard.

Even though the boy who plaited manes did all the work, Wald considered the constant plaiting and adorning of manes and tails a great bother. The whole fussy business offended him, he had decided, and he had long since forgotten the few words of praise it had garnered from the lord at first. Moreover, he disliked the boy so vehemently that he was not thinking clearly. It seemed to him that he could be rid of the boy and the wretched onus of braids and rosettes all in one stroke. The day the lord returned from his journey, Wald hurried to him, begged private audience, bowed low and made his humble report.

Lord Robley heard him in icy silence, for he knew pettiness when he saw it; it had served him often in the past, and he would punish it if it misled him. He summoned his wife to question her. But the Lady Aelynn's hair hung lank, and her guilt and shame could be seen plainly in her face from the moment she came before him.

Lord Robley's roar could be heard even to the stables.

He strode over to her where she lay crumpled and weeping on his chamber floor, lifted her head by its honey-gold hair and slashed her across the face with his sword. Then he left her screaming and stinging her wound with fresh tears, and he strode to the stable with his bloody sword still drawn. Wald fleeing before him all the way; when the lord burst in all the grooms were scattering but one. The boy Wald had accused stood plaiting the white palfrey's mane.

Lord Robley hacked the palfrey's head from its braid-bedecked neck with his sword, and the boy who plaited manes stood by with something smoldering deep in his unblinking gray-green eyes, stood calmly waiting. If he had screamed and turned to flee, Lord Robley would with great satisfaction have given him a coward's death from the back. But it unnerved the lord that the boy awaited his pleasure with such mute—what? Defiance? There was no servant's bow in this one, no falling to the soiled straw, no groveling. If he had groveled he could have been kicked, stabbed, killed out of hand. . . . But this silent, watchful waiting, like the alertness of a wild thing—on the hunt or being hunted? It gave Lord Robley pause, like the pause of the wolf before the standing stag or the pause of the huntsman before the thicketed boar. He held the boy at the point of his sword—though no such holding was necessary, for the prisoner had not moved even to tremble— and roared for his men-at-arms to come take the boy to the dungeon.

There the nameless stranger stayed without water or food, and aside from starving him Lord Robley could not decide what to do with him.

At first the boy who plaited manes paced in his prison restlessly—he had that freedom, for he was so thin and small that the shackles were too large to hold him. Later he lay in a scant bed of short straw and stared narrow-eyed at the darkness. And yet later, seeing the thin cascades of moonlight flow down through the high, iron-barred window and puddle in moon-glades on the stone floor, he got up and began to plait the moonbeams.

They were far finer than any horsehair, moonbeams, finer even than the lady's honey-colored locks, and his eyes grew wide with wonder and pleasure as he felt them. He made them into braids as fine as silk threads, flowing together into a lacework as close as woven cloth, and when he had reached as high as he could, plaiting, he stroked as if combing a long mane with his fingers and pulled more moonlight down out of sky—for this stuff was not like any other stuff he had ever worked with, it slipped and slid worse than any hair, there seemed to be no beginning or end to it except the barriers that men put in its way. He stood plaiting the fine, thin plaits until he had raised a shimmering heap on the floor, and then he stepped back and allowed the moon to move on. His handiwork he laid carefully aside in a corner.

The boy who plaited moonbeams did not sleep, but sat waiting for the dawn, his eyes glowing greenly in the darkened cell. He saw the sky lighten beyond the high window and waited stolidly, as the wolf waits for the gathering of the pack, as a wildcat waits for the game to pass along the trail below the rock where it lies. Not until the day had neared its mid did the sun's rays, thrust through narrow spaces between the high bars, wheel their shafts down to where he could reach them. Then he got up and began to plait the sunlight.

Guards were about, or more alert, in the daytime, and they gathered at the heavy door of his prison, peering in between the iron bars of its small window, gawking and quarreling with each other for turns. They watched his unwavering eyes, saw the slight smile come on his face as he worked, though his thin hands glowed red as if seen through fire. They saw the shining mound he raised on the floor, and whispered among themselves and did not know what to do, for none of them dared to touch it or him. One of them requested a captain to come look. And the captain summoned the steward, and the steward went to report to the lord. And from outside, cries began to sound that the sun was standing still.

After the boy had finished, he stood back and let the sun move on, then tended to his handiwork, then sat resting on his filthy straw. Within minutes the dungeon door burst open and Lord Robley himself strode in.

Lord Robley had grown weary of mutilating his wife, and he had not yet decided what to do with his other prisoner. Annoyed by the reports from the prison, he expected that an idea would come to him when he saw the boy. He entered with drawn sword. But all thoughts of the thin young body before him were sent whirling away from his mind by what he saw laid out on the stone floor at his feet.

A mantle, a kingly cloak—but no king had ever owned such a cloak. All shining, the outside of it silver and the inside gold—but no, to call it silver and gold was to insult it. More like water and fire, flow and flame, shimmering as if it moved, as if it were alive, and yet it had been made by hands, he could see the workmanship, so fine that every thread was worth a gasp of pleasure, the outside of it somehow braided and plaited to the lining, and all around the edge a fringe of threads like bright fur so fine that it wavered in the air like flame. Lord Robley had no thought but to settle the fiery gleaming thing on his shoulders, to wear that glory and be finer than any king. He seized it and flung it on—

And screamed as he had not yet made his wife scream, with the shriek of mortal agony. His whole hard body glowed as if in a furnace. His face contorted, and he fell dead.

The boy who plaited sunbeams got up in a quiet, alert way and walked forward, as noiseless on his feet as a lynx. He reached down and took the cloak off the body of the lord, twirled it and placed it on his own shoulders, and it did not harm him. But in that cloak he seemed insubstantial, like something moving in moonlight and shadow, something nameless roaming in the night. He walked out of the open dungeon door, between the guards clustered there, past the lord's retinue and the steward, and they all shrank back from him, flattened themselves against the stone walls of the corridor so as not to come near him. No one dared take hold of him or try to stop him. He walked out through the courtyard, past the stable, and out the manor gates with the settled air of one whose business is done. The men-at-arms gathered atop the wall and watched him go.

Wald the master groom lived to an old age sweating every night with terror, and died of a weakened heart in the midst of a nightmare. Nothing else but his own fear harmed him. The boy who plaited—mane of sun, mane of moon—was never seen again in that place, except that children sometimes told the tale of having glimpsed him in the wild heart of a storm, plaiting the long lashes of wind and rain.

# URSULA K. LE GUIN

## "Buffalo Gals, Won't You Come Out Tonight"

*Much of the writing of Ursula K. Le Guin is informed by anthropological speculations on alien and human cultures. Her Hugo and Nebula Award-winning novel* The Left Hand of Darkness *brilliantly explodes sexual stereotypes through its portrayal of a planet whose natives can assume the roles of both male and female in their lifetimes. Prior to its publication, she had published* Rocannon's World, Planet of Exile, *and* City of Illusions, *novels in her Hainish sequence that deal with the problems human beings and aliens face adapting to new environments. She is also the author of the multiple award-winning* The Dispossessed, *and* The Lathe of Heaven, *an eerie exploration of the intersection of dreams and reality that was successfully adapted for television. Le Guin's four-volume Earthsea saga, which includes the Nebula Award-winning* Tehanu: The Last Book of Earthsea, *is a coming-of-age saga about an apprentice magician that reflects her interest in mythopoesis. Her essays have been collected in several volumes, among them* The Language of the Night: Essays on Fantasy and Science Fiction. *Most of her short fiction can be found in* The Winds Twelve Quarters, *and* Buffalo Gals, Won't You Come Out Tonight. *"Buffalo Gals, Won't You Come Out Tonight" was nominated for the Nebula Award and won the Hugo and World Fantasy Awards.*

# Buffalo Gals, Won't You Come Out Tonight

*by Ursula K. Le Guin*

## 1

*Y*ou fell out of the sky," coyote said.

Still curled up tight, lying on her side, her back pressed against the overhanging rock, the child watched the coyote with one eye. Over the other eye she kept her hand cupped, its back on the dirt.

"There was a burned place in the sky, up there alongside the rimrock, and then you fell out of it," the coyote repeated, patiently, as if the news was getting a bit stale. "Are you hurt?"

She was all right. She was in the plane with Mr. Michaels, and the motor was so loud she couldn't understand what he said even when he shouted, and the way the wind rocked the wings was making her feel sick, but it was all right. They were flying to Canyonville. In the plane.

She looked. The coyote was still sitting there. It yawned. It was a big one, in good condition, its coat silvery and thick. The dark tear line back from its long yellow eye was as clearly marked as a tabby cat's.

She sat up slowly, still holding her right hand pressed to her right eye.

"Did you lose an eye?" the coyote asked, interested.

"I don't know," the child said. She caught her breath and shivered. "I'm cold."

"I'll help you look for it," the coyote said. "Come on! If you move around, you won't have to shiver. The sun's up."

Cold, lonely brightness lay across the falling land, a hundred miles of sagebrush. The coyote was trotting busily around, nosing under clumps of rabbitbrush and cheatgrass, pawing at a rock. "Aren't you going to look?" it said, suddenly sitting down on its haunches and abandoning the search. "I knew a trick once where I could throw my eyes way up into a tree and see everything from up there, and then whistle, and they'd come back into my head. But that goddamn bluejay stole them, and when I whistled, nothing came. I had to stick lumps of pine pitch into my head so I could see anything. You could try that. But you've got one eye that's O.K.; what do you need two for? Are you coming, or are you dying there?"

The child crouched, shivering.

"Well, come if you want to," said the coyote, yawned again, snapped at a flea, stood up, turned, and trotted away among the sparse clumps of rabbitbrush and sage, along the long slope that stretched on down and down into the plain streaked across by long shadows of sagebrush. The slender gray-yellow animal was hard to keep in sight, vanishing as the child watched.

She struggled to her feet and—without a word, though she kept saying in her mind, "Wait, please wait"—she hobbled after the coyote. She could not see it. She kept her hand pressed over the right eye socket. Seeing with one eye, there was no depth; it was like a huge, flat picture. The coyote suddenly sat in the middle of the picture, looking back at her, its mouth open, its eyes narrowed, grinning. Her legs began to steady, and her head did not pound so hard, though the deep black ache was always there. She had nearly caught up to the coyote, when it trotted off again. This time she spoke. "Please wait!" she said.

"O.K.," said the coyote, but it trotted right on. She followed, walking downhill into the flat picture that at each step was deep.

Each step was different underfoot; each sage bush was different, and all the same. Following the coyote, she came out from the shadow of the rimrock cliffs, and the sun at eye level dazzled her left eye. Its bright warmth soaked into her muscles and bones at once. The air, which all night had been so hard to breathe, came sweet and easy.

The sage bushes were pulling in their shadows, and the sun was hot on the child's back when she followed the coyote along the rim of a gully. After a while the coyote slanted down the undercut slope, and the child scrambled after, through scrub willows to the thin creek in its wide sand bed. Both drank.

The coyote crossed the creek, not with a careless charge and splashing like a dog, but single foot and quiet like a cat; always it carried its tail low. The child hesitated, knowing that wet shoes make blistered feet, and then waded across in as few steps as possible. Her right arm ached with the effort of holding her hand up over her eye. "I need a bandage," she said to the coyote. It cocked its head and said nothing. It stretched out its forelegs and lay watching the water, resting but alert. The child sat down nearby on the hot sand and tried to move her right hand. It was glued to the skin around her eye by dried blood. At the little tearing-away pain, she whimpered; though it was a small pain, it frightened her. The coyote came over close and poked its long snout into her face. Its strong, sharp smell was in her nostrils. It began to lick the awful, aching blindness, cleaning and cleaning with its curled, precise, strong, wet tongue, until the child was able to cry a little with relief, being comforted. Her head was bent close to the gray-yellow ribs, and she saw the hard nipples, the whitish belly fur. She put her arm around the she-coyote, stroking the harsh coat over back and ribs.

"O.K.," the coyote said, "let's go!" And set off without a backward glance. The child scrambled to her feet and followed. "Where are we going?" she said, and the coyote, trotting on down along the creek, answered, "On down along the creek. . . ."

There must have been a time while she was asleep that she walked because she felt like she was waking up, but she was walking along only in a different place. They were still following the creek, though the gully had flattened out to nothing much, and there was still sagebrush range as far as the eye could see. The eye—the good one—felt rested. The other one still ached, but not so sharply, and there was no use thinking about it. But where was the coyote?

She stopped. The pit of cold into which the plane had fallen reopened, and she fell. She stood falling, a thin whimper making itself in her throat.

"Over here!"

The child turned.

She saw a coyote gnawing at the half-dried-up carcass of a crow, black feathers sticking to the black lips and narrow jaw.

She saw a tawny-skinned woman kneeling by a campfire, sprinkling something into a conical pot. She heard the water boiling in the pot, though it was propped between rocks, off the fire. The woman's hair was yellow and gray, bound back with a string. Her feet were bare. The upturned soles looked as dark and hard as shoe soles, but the arch of the foot was high, and the toes made two neat curving rows. She wore blue jeans and an old white shirt. She looked over at the girl. "Come on, eat crow!" she said.

The child slowly came toward the woman and the fire, and squatted down. She had stopped falling and felt very light and empty; and her tongue was like a piece of wood stuck in her mouth.

Coyote was now blowing into the pot or basket or whatever it was. She reached into it with two fingers, and pulled her hand away, shaking it and shouting, "Ow! Shit! Why don't I ever have any spoons?" She broke off a dead twig of sagebrush, dipped it into the pot, and licked it. "Oh boy," she said. "Come on!"

The child moved a little closer, broke off a twig, dipped. Lumpy pinkish mush clung to the twig. She licked. The taste was rich and delicate.

"What is it?" she asked after a long time of dipping and licking.

"Food. Dried salmon mush," Coyote said. "It's cooling down." She stuck two fingers into the mush again, this time getting a good load, which she ate very neatly. The child, when she tried, got mush all over her chin. It was like chopsticks: it took practice. She practiced. They ate turn and turn until nothing was left in the pot but three rocks. The child did not ask why there were rocks in the mush pot. They licked the rocks clean. Coyote licked out the inside of the pot-basket, rinsed it once in the creek, and put it onto her head. It fit nicely, making a conical hat. She pulled off her blue jeans. "Piss on the fire!" she cried, and did so, standing straddling it. "Ah, steam between the legs!" she said. The child, embarrassed, thought she was supposed to do the same thing, but did not want to, and did not. Bareassed, Coyote danced around the dampened fire, kicking her long, thin legs out and singing:

> *Buffalo gals, won't you come out tonight*
> *Come out tonight, come out tonight,*
> *Buffalo gals, won't you come out tonight,*
> *And dance by the light of the moon?*

She pulled her jeans back on. The child was burying the remains of the fire in the creek sand, heaping it over, seriously, wanting to do right. Coyote watched her.

"Is that you?" she said. "A Buffalo Gal? What happened to the rest of you?"

"The rest of me?" The child looked at herself, alarmed.

"All your people."

"Oh. Well, Mom took Bobbie—he's my little brother—away with Uncle Norm. He isn't really my uncle or anything. So Mr. Michaels was going there anyway, so he was going to fly me over to my real father, in Canyonville. Linda—my stepmother, you know—she said it was O.K. for the summer anyhow if I was there, and then we could see. But the plane."

In the silence the girl's face became dark red, then grayish white. Coyote watched, fascinated. "Oh," the girl said, "oh—oh— Mr. Michaels—he must be—Did the—"

"Come on!" said Coyote, and set off walking.

The child cried, "I ought to go back—"

"What for?" said Coyote. She stopped to look round at the child, then went on faster. "Come on, Gal!" She said it as a name; maybe it was the child's name, Myra, as spoken by Coyote. The child, confused and despairing, protested again, but followed her. "Where are we going? Where *are* we?"

"This is my country," Coyote answered with dignity, making a long, slow gesture all around the vast horizon. "I made it. Every goddamn sagebrush."

And they went on. Coyote's gait was easy, even a little shambling, but she covered the ground; the child struggled not to drop behind. Shadows were beginning to pull themselves out again from under the rocks and shrubs. Leaving the creek, Coyote and the child went up a long, low, uneven slope that ended away off against the sky in rimrock. Dark trees stood one here, another way over there; what people called a juniper forest, a desert forest, one with a lot more between the trees than trees. Each juniper they passed smelled sharply—cat-pee smell the kids at school called it—but the child liked it; it seemed to go into her mind and wake her up. She picked off a juniper berry and held it in her mouth, but after a while spat it out again. The aching was coming back in huge black waves, and she kept stumbling. She found that she was sitting down on the ground. When she tried to get up, her legs shook and would not go under her. She felt foolish and frightened, and began to cry.

"We're home!" Coyote called from way on up the hill.

The child looked with her one weeping eye, and saw sagebrush, juniper, cheatgrass, rimrock. She heard a coyote yip far off in the dry twilight.

She saw a little town up under the rimrock: board houses, shacks, all unpainted. She heard Coyote call again, "Come on, pup! Come on, Gal, we're home!"

She could not get up, so she tried to go on all fours, the long way up the slope to the houses under the rimrock. Long before she got there, several people came to meet her. They were all children, she thought at first, and then began to understand that most of them were grown people, but all were very short; they were broad-bodied, fat, with fine, delicate hands and feet. Their eyes were bright. Some of the women helped her stand up and walk, coaxing her. "It isn't much farther, you're doing fine." In the late dusk, lights shone yellow-bright through doorways and through unchinked cracks between boards. Woodsmoke hung sweet in the quiet air. The short people talked and laughed all the time, softly. "Where's she going to stay?"—"Put her in with Robin, they're all asleep already!"— "Oh, she can stay with us."

The child asked hoarsely, "Where's Coyote?"

"Out hunting," the short people said.

A deeper voice spoke: "Somebody new has come into town?"

"Yes, a new person," one of the short men answered.

Among these people the deep-voiced man bulked impressive; he was broad and tall, with powerful hands, a big head, a short neck. They made way for him respectfully. He moved very quietly, respectful of them also. His eyes when he stared down at the child were amazing. When he blinked, it was like the passing of a hand before a candle flame.

"It's only an owlet," he said. "What have you let happen to your eye, new person?"

"I was—We were flying—"

"You're too young to fly," the big man said in his deep, soft voice. "Who brought you here?"

"Coyote."

And one of the short people confirmed: "She came here with Coyote, Young Owl."

"Then maybe she should stay in Coyote's house tonight," the big man said.

"It's all bones and lonely in there," said a short woman with fat cheeks and a striped shirt. "She can come with us."

That seemed to decide it. The fat-cheeked woman patted the

child's arm and took her past several shacks and shanties to a low, windowless house. The doorway was so low even the child had to duck down to enter. There were a lot of people inside, some already there and some crowding in after the fat-cheeked woman. Several babies were fast asleep in cradleboxes in the corner. There was a good fire, and a good smell, like toasted sesame seeds. The child was given food and ate a little, but her head swam, and the blackness in her right eye kept coming across her left eye, so she could not see at all for a while. Nobody asked her name or told her what to call them. She heard the children call the fat-cheeked woman Chipmunk. She got up courage finally to say, "Is there somewhere I can go to sleep, Mrs. Chipmunk?"

"Sure, come on," one of the daughters said, "in here," and took the child into a back room, not completely partitioned off from the crowded front room, but dark and uncrowded. Big shelves with mattresses and blankets lined the walls. "Crawl in!" said Chipmunk's daughter, patting the child's arm in the comforting way they had. The child climbed onto a shelf, under a blanket. She laid down her head. She thought, "I didn't brush my teeth."

<u>2</u>

She woke; she slept again. In Chipmunk's sleeping room it was always stuffy, warm, and half dark, day and night. People came in and slept and got up and left, night and day. She dozed and slept, got down to drink from the bucket and dipper in the front room, and went back to sleep and doze.

She was sitting up on the shelf, her feet dangling, not feeling bad anymore, but dreamy, weak. She felt in her jeans pocket. In the left front one was a pocket comb and a bubble gum wrapper; in the right front, two dollar bills and a quarter and a dime.

Chipmunk and another woman—a very pretty, dark-eyed, plump one—came in. "So you woke up for your dance!" Chipmunk greeted her, laughing, and sat down by her with an arm around her.

"Jay's giving you a dance," the dark woman said. "He's going to make you all right. Let's get you all ready!"

There was a spring up under the rimrock, which flattened out into a pool with slimy, reedy shores. A flock of noisy children splashing in it ran off and left the child and the two women to bathe. The water was warm on the surface, cold down on the feet and legs. All naked, the two soft-voiced, laughing women, their round bellies and breasts, broad hips and buttocks gleaming warm in the late-afternoon light, sluiced the child down, washed and stroked her limbs and hands and hair, cleaned around the cheek-bone and eyebrow of her right eye with infinite softness, admired her, sudsed her, rinsed her, splashed her out of the water, dried her off, dried each other off, got dressed, dressed her, braided her hair, braided each other's hair, tied feathers on the braid-ends, admired her and each other again, and brought her back down into the little straggling town and to a kind of playing field or dirt parking lot in among the houses. There were no streets, just paths and dirt; no lawns and gardens, just sagebrush and dirt. Quite a few people were gathering or wandering around the open place, looking dressed up, wearing colorful shirts, bright dresses, strings of beads, earrings. "Hey there, Chipmunk, Whitefoot!" they greeted the women.

A man in new jeans, with a bright blue velveteen vest over a clean, faded blue work shirt, came forward to meet them, very handsome, tense, and important. "All right, Gal!" he said in a harsh, loud voice, which startled among all these soft-speaking people. "We're going to get that eye fixed right up tonight! You just sit down here and don't worry about a thing." He took her wrist, gently despite his bossy, brassy manner, and led her to a woven mat that lay on the dirt near the middle of the open place. There, feeling very foolish, she had to sit down, and was told to stay still. She soon got over feeling that everybody was looking at her, since nobody paid her more attention than a checking glance or, from Chipmunk or Whitefoot and their families, a reassuring wink. Every now and then, Jay rushed over to her and said something like, "Going to be as good as new!" and went off again to organize people, waving his long blue arms and shouting.

Coming up the hill to the open place, a lean, loose, tawny figure—and the child started to jump up, remembered she was to sit still, and sat still, calling out softly, "Coyote! Coyote!"

Coyote came lounging by. She grinned. She stood looking down at the child. "Don't let that Bluejay fuck you up, Gal," she said, and lounged on.

The child's gaze followed her, yearning.

People were sitting down now over on one side of the open place, making an uneven half circle that kept getting added to at the ends until there was nearly a circle of people sitting on the dirt around the child, ten or fifteen paces from her. All the people wore the kind of clothes the child was used to—jeans and jeans jackets, shirts, vests, cotton dresses—but they were all barefoot; and she thought they were more beautiful than the people she knew, each in a different way, as if each one had invented beauty. Yet some of them were also very strange: thin black shining people with whispery voices, a long-legged woman with eyes like jewels. The big man called Young Owl was there, sleepy-looking and dignified, like Judge McCown who owned a sixty-thousand acre ranch. And beside him was a woman the child thought might be his sister, for like him she had a hook nose and big, strong hands; but she was lean and dark, and there was a crazy look in her fierce eyes. Yellow eyes, but round, not long and slanted like Coyote's. There was Coyote sitting yawning, scratching her armpit, bored. Now somebody was entering the circle: a man, wearing only a kind of kilt and a cloak painted or beaded with diamond shapes, dancing to the rhythm of the rattle he carried and shook with a buzzing fast beat. His limbs and body were thick yet supple, his movements smooth and pouring. The child kept her gaze on him as he danced past her, around her, past again. The rattle in his hand shook almost too fast to see; in the other hand was something thin and sharp. People were singing around the circle now, a few notes repeated in time to the rattle, soft and tuneless. It was exciting and boring, strange and familiar. The Rattler wove his dancing closer and closer to her, darting at her. The first time, she flinched away, frightened by the lunging movement and by his flat, cold face with narrow eyes, but after that she sat still, knowing her part. The dancing went on, the singing went on, till they carried her past boredom into a floating that could go on forever.

Jay had come strutting into the circle and was standing beside her. He couldn't sing, but he called out, "Hey! Hey! Hey! Hey!" in his big, harsh voice, and everybody answered from all round, and the echo came down from the rimrock on the second beat. Jay was holding up a stick with a ball on it in one hand, and something like a marble in the other. The stick was a pipe: he got smoke into his mouth from it and blew it in four directions and up and down and then over the marble, a puff each time. Then the rattle stopped suddenly, and everything was silent for several breaths. Jay squatted down and looked intently into the child's face, his head cocked to one side. He reached forward, muttering something in time to

256

the rattle and the singing that had started up again louder than before; he touched the child's right eye in the black center of the pain. She flinched and endured. His touch was not gentle. She saw the marble, a dull yellow ball like beeswax, in his hand; then she shut her seeing eye and set her teeth.

"There!" Jay shouted. "Open up. Come on! Let's see!"

Her jaw clenched like a vise, she opened both eyes. The lid of the right one stuck and dragged with such a searing white pain that she nearly threw up as she sat there in the middle of everybody watching.

"Hey, can you see? How's it work? It looks great!" Jay was shaking her arm, railing at her. "How's it feel? Is it working?"

What she saw was confused, hazy, yellowish. She began to discover, as everybody came crowding around peering at her—smiling, stroking and patting her arms and shoulders—that if she shut the hurting eye and looked with the other, everything was clear and flat; if she used them both, things were blurry and yellowish, but deep.

There, right close, was Coyote's long nose and narrow eyes and grin. "What is it, Jay?" she was asking, peering at the new eye. "One of mine you stole that time?"

"It's pine pitch," Jay shouted furiously. "You think I'd use some stupid secondhand coyote eye? I'm a doctor!"

"Ooooh, ooooh, a doctor," Coyote said. "Boy, that is one ugly eye. Why didn't you ask Rabbit for a rabbit dropping? That eye looks like shit." She put her lean face yet closer, till the child thought she was going to kiss her; instead, the thin, firm tongue once more licked accurately across the pain, cooling, clearing. When the child opened both eyes again, the world looked pretty good.

"It works fine," she said.

"Hey!" Jay yelled. "She says it works fine! It works fine; she says so! I told you! What'd I tell you?" He went off waving his arms and yelling. Coyote had disappeared. Everybody was wandering off.

The child stood up, stiff from long sitting. It was nearly dark; only the long west held a great depth of pale radiance. Eastward, the plains ran down into night.

Lights were on in some of the shanties. Off at the edge of town, somebody was playing a creaky fiddle, a lonesome chirping tune.

A person came beside her and spoke quietly: "Where will you stay?"

"I don't know," the child said. She was feeling extremely hungry. "Can I stay with Coyote?"

"She isn't home much," the soft-voiced woman said. "You were staying with Chipmunk, weren't you? Or there's Rabbit, or Jackrabbit; they have families. . . ."

"Do you have a family?" the girl asked, looking at the delicate, soft-eyed woman.

"Two fawns," the woman answered, smiling. "But I just came into town for the dance."

"I'd really like to stay with Coyote," the child said after a pause, timid but obstinate.

"O.K., that's fine. Her house is over here." Doe walked along beside the child to a ramshackle cabin on the high edge of town. No light shone from inside. A lot of junk was scattered around the front. There was no step up to the half-open door. Over a battered pine board, nailed up crooked, said: "Bide-A-Wee."

"Hey, Coyote? Visitors," Doe said. Nothing happened.

Doe pushed the door farther open and peered in. "She's out hunting, I guess. I better be getting back to the fawns. You going to be O.K.? Anybody else here will give you something to eat—you know. . . . O.K.?"

"Yeah. I'm fine. Thank you," the child said.

She watched Doe walk away through the clear twilight, a severely elegant walk, small steps, like a woman in high heels, quick, precise, very light.

Inside Bide-A-Wee it was too dark to see anything, and so cluttered that she fell over something at every step. She could not figure out where or how to light a fire. There was something that felt like a bed, but when she lay down on it, it felt more like a dirty-clothes pile, and smelled like one. Things bit her legs, arms, neck, and back. She was terribly hungry. By smell, she found her way to what had to be a dead fish hanging from the ceiling in one corner. By feel, she broke off a greasy flake and tasted it. It was smoked, dried salmon. She ate one succulent piece after another until she was satisfied, and licked her fingers clean. Near the open door, starlight shone on water in a pot of some kind; the child smelled it cautiously, tasted it cautiously, and drank just enough to quench her thirst, for it tasted of mud and was warm and stale. Then she went back to the bed of dirty clothes and fleas, and lay down. She could have gone to Chipmunk's house, or other friendly households; she thought of that as she lay forlorn in Coyote's dirty bed. But she did not go. She slapped at fleas until she fell asleep.

Along in the deep night, somebody said, "Move over, pup," and was warm beside her.

Breakfast, eaten sitting in the sun in the doorway, was dried-salmon-powder mush. Coyote hunted, morning and evenings, but what they ate was not fresh game but salmon, and dried stuff, and any berries in season. The child did not ask about this. It made sense to her. She was going to ask Coyote why she slept at night and waked in the day like humans, instead of the other way round like coyotes, but when she framed the question in her mind, she saw at once that night is when you sleep and day when you're awake; that made sense, too. But one question she did ask, one hot day when they were lying around slapping fleas.

"I don't understand why you all look like people," she said.

"We are people."

"I mean, people like me, humans."

"Resemblance is in the eye," Coyote said. "How is that lousy eye, by the way?"

"It's fine. But—like you wear clothes—and live in houses—with fires and stuff—"

"That's what *you* think. . . . If that loudmouth Jay hadn't horned in, I could have done a really good job."

The child was quite used to Coyote's disinclination to stick to any one subject, and to her boasting. Coyote was like a lot of kids she knew, in some respects. Not in others.

"You mean what I'm seeing isn't true? Isn't real—like TV or something?"

"No," Coyote said. "Hey, that's a tick on your collar." She reached over, flicked the tick off, picked it up on one finger, bit it, and spat out the bits.

"Yecch!" the child said. "So?"

"So, to me, you're basically grayish yellow and run on four legs. To that lot"—she waved disdainfully at the warren of little houses next down the hill—"you hop around twitching your nose all the time. To Hawk, you're an egg, or maybe getting pinfeathers. See? It just depends on how you look at things. There are only two kinds of people."

"Humans and animals?"

"No. The kind of people who say, 'There are two kinds of people,'

and the kind of people who don't." Coyote cracked up, pounding her
thighs and yelling with delight at her joke. The child didn't get it,
and waited.

"O.K.," Coyote said. "There's the first people, and then the others. Those're the two kinds."

"The first people are—?"

"Us, the animals . . . and things. All the old ones. You know. And
you pups, kids, fledglings. All first people."

"And the—others?"

"Them," Coyote said. "You know. The others. The new people.
The ones who came." Her fine, hard face had gone serious, rather
formidable. She glanced directly, as she seldom did, at the child, a
brief gold sharpness. "We are here," she said. "We are always here.
We are always here. Where we are is here. But it's their country
now. They're running it. . . . Shit, even I did better!"

The child pondered and offered a word she had used to hear a
good deal: "They're illegal immigrants."

"Illegal!" Coyote said, mocking, sneering. "Illegal is a sick bird.
What the fuck's illegal mean? You want a code of justice from a coyote? Grow up kid!"

"I don't want to."

"You don't want to grow up?"

"I'll be the other kind if I do."

"Yeah. So," Coyote said, and shrugged. "That's life." She got up
and went around the house, and the child heard her pissing in the
backyard.

A lot of things were hard to take about Coyote as a mother.
When her boyfriends came to visit, the child learned to go stay
with Chipmunk or the Rabbits for the night, because Coyote and
her friend wouldn't even wait to get on the bed, but would start
doing that right on the floor or even out in the yard. A couple of
times, Coyote came back late from hunting with a friend, and the
child had to lie up against the wall in the same bed and hear and
feel them doing that right next to her. It was something like fighting and something like dancing, with a beat to it, and she didn't
mind too much except that it made it hard to stay asleep. Once she
woke up and one of Coyote's friends was stroking her stomach in a
creepy way. She didn't know what to do, but Coyote woke up and
realized what he was doing, bit him hard, and kicked him out of
bed. He spent the night on the floor, and apologized next morn-

ing—"Aw, hell, Ki, I forgot the kid was there; I thought it was you—"

Coyote, unappeased, yelled, "You think I don't got any standards? You think I'd let some coyote rape a kid in my *bed*?" She kicked him out of the house, and grumbled about him all day. But a while later he spent the night again, and he and Coyote did that three or four times.

Another thing that was embarrassing was the way Coyote peed anywhere, taking her pants down in public. But most people here didn't seem to care. The thing that worried the child most, maybe, was when Coyote did number two anywhere and then turned around and talked to it. That seemed so awful. As if Coyote were—the way she often seemed, but really wasn't—crazy.

The child gathered up all the old dry turds from around the house one day while Coyote was having a nap, and buried them in a sandy place near where she and Bobcat and some of the other people generally went and did and buried their number twos.

Coyote woke up, came lounging out of Bide-A-Wee, rubbing her hands through her thick, fair, grayish hair and yawning, looked all round once with those narrow eyes, and said, "Hey! Where are they?" Then she shouted, "Where are you? Where are you?"

And a faint chorus came from over in the draw: "Mommy! We're here!"

Coyote trotted over, squatted down, raked out every turd, and talked with them for a long time. When she came back, she said nothing, but the child, red-faced and heart pounding, said, "I'm sorry I did that."

"It's just easier when they're all around close by," Coyote said, washing her hands (despite the filth of her house, she kept herself quite clean, in her own fashion).

"I kept stepping on them," the child said, trying to justify her deed.

"Poor little shits," said Coyote, practicing dance steps.

"Coyote," the child said timidly. "Did you ever have any children? I mean real pups?"

"Did I? Did I have children? Litters! That one that tried feeling you up, you know? That was my son. Pick of the litter. . . . Listen, Gal. Have daughters. When you have anything, have daughters. At least they clear out."

## 3

The child thought of herself as Gal, but also sometimes as Myra. So far as she knew, she was the only person in town who had two names. She had to think about that, and about what Coyote had said about the two kinds of people; she had to think about where she belonged. Some persons in town made it clear that as far as they were concerned, she didn't and never would belong there. Hawk's furious stare burned through her; the Skunk children made audible remarks about what she smelled like. And though Whitefoot and Chipmunk and their families were kind, it was the generosity of big families, where one more or less simply doesn't count. If one of them, or Cottontail, or Jackrabbit, had come upon her in the desert lying lost and half blind, would they have stayed with her, like Coyote? That was Coyote's craziness, what they called her craziness. She wasn't afraid. She went between the two kinds of people; she crossed over. Buck and Doe and their beautiful children were really afraid, because they lived so constantly in danger. The Rattler wasn't afraid, because he was so dangerous. And yet maybe he was afraid of her, for he never spoke, and never came close to her. None of them treated her the way Coyote did. Even among the children, her only constant playmate was one younger than herself, a preposterous and fearless little boy called Horned Toad Child. They dug and built together, out among the sagebrush, and played at hunting and gathering and keeping house and holding dances, all the great games. A pale, squatty child with fringed eyebrows, he was a self-contained but loyal friend; and he knew a good deal for his age.

"There isn't anybody else like me here," she said as they sat by the pool in the morning sunlight.

"There isn't anybody much like me anywhere," said Horned Toad Child.

"Well, you know what I mean."

"Yeah. . . . There used to be people like you around, I guess."

"What were they called?"

"Oh—people. Like everybody. . . ."

"But where do *my* people live? They have towns. I used to live in one. I don't know where they are, is all. I ought to find out. I don't know where my mother is now, but daddy's in Canyonville. I was going there when. . . ."

"Ask Horse," said Horned Toad Child sagaciously. He had moved away from the water, which he did not like and never drank, and was plaiting rushes.

"I don't know Horse."

"He hangs around the butte down there a lot of the time. He's waiting till his uncle gets old and he can kick him out and be the big honcho. The old man and the women don't want him around till then. Horses are weird. Anyway, he's the one to ask. He gets around a lot. And his people came here with the new people; that's what they say, anyhow."

Illegal immigrants, the girl thought. She took Horned Toad's advice, and one long day when Coyote was gone on one of her unannounced and unexplained trips, she took a pouchful of dried salmon and salmonberries and went off alone to the flat-topped butte miles away in the southwest.

There was a beautiful spring at the foot of the butte, and a trail to it with a lot of footprints on it. She waited there under willows by the clear pool, and after a while Horse came running, splendid, with copper-red skin and long, strong legs, deep chest, dark eyes, his black hair whipping his back as he ran. He stopped, not at all winded, and gave a snort as he looked at her. "Who are you?"

Nobody in town asked that—ever. She saw it was true: Horse had come here with her people, people who had to ask each other who they were.

"I live with Coyote," she said cautiously.

"Oh sure, I heard about you," Horse said. He knelt to drink from the pool. Long, deep drafts, his hands plunged in the cool water. When he had drunk, he wiped his mouth, sat back on his heels, and announced, "I'm going to be king."

"King of the horses?"

"Right! Pretty soon now. I could lick the old man already, but I can wait. Let him have his day," said Horse, vainglorious, magnanimous. The child gazed at him, in love already, forever.

"I can comb your hair, if you like," she said.

"Great!" said Horse, and sat still while she stood behind him, tugging her pocket comb through his coarse, black, shining, yard-long hair. It took a long time to get it smooth. She tied it in a massive ponytail with willow bark when she was done. Horse bent over the pool to admire himself. "That's great," he said. "That's really beautiful!"

"Do you ever go . . . where the other people are?" she asked in a low voice.

He did not reply for long enough that she thought he wasn't going to; then he said, "You mean the metal places, the glass places. The holes? I go around them. There are all the walls now. There didn't used to be so many. Grandmother said there didn't use to be any walls. Do you know Grandmother?" he asked naively, looking at her with his great, dark eyes.

"Your grandmother?"

"Well, yes—Grandmother—you know. Who makes the web. Well, anyhow. I know there're some of my people, horses, there. I've seen them across the walls. They act really crazy. You know, we brought the new people here. They couldn't have got here without us: they have only two legs, and they have those metal shells. I can tell you that whole story. The king has to know the stories."

"I like stories a lot."

"It takes three nights to tell it. What do you want to know about them?"

"I was thinking that maybe I ought to go there. Where they are."

"It's dangerous. Really dangerous. You can't go through—they'd catch you."

"I'd just like to know the way."

"I know the way," Horse said, sounding for the first time entirely adult and reliable; she knew he did know the way. "It's a long run for a colt." He looked at her again. "I've got a cousin with different-color eyes," he said, looking from her right to her left eye. "One brown and one blue. But she's an Appaloosa."

"Bluejay made the yellow one," the child explained. "I lost my own one. In the . .. when . . . You don't think I could get to those places?"

"Why do you want to?"

"I sort of feel like I have to."

Horse nodded. He got up. She stood still.

"I could take you, I guess," he said.

"Would you? When?"

"Oh, now, I guess. Once I'm king I won't be able to leave, you know. Have to protect the women. And I sure wouldn't let my people get anywhere near those places!" A shudder ran right down his magnificent body, yet he said, with a toss of his head, "They couldn't catch *me*, of course, but the others can't run like I do. . . ."

"How long would it take us?"

Horse thought for a while. "Well, the nearest place like that is over the red rocks. If we left now, we'd be back here around tomorrow noon. It's just a little hole."

She did not know what he meant by "a hole," but did not ask. "You want to go?" Horse said, flipping back his ponytail. "O.K.," the girl said, feeling the ground go out from under her. "Can you run?"

She shook her head. "I walked here, though."

Horse laughed, a large, cheerful laugh. "Come on," he said, and knelt and held his hands back-turned like stirrups for her to mount to his shoulders. "What do they call you?" he teased, rising easily, setting right off at a jog trot. "Gnat? Fly? Flea?"

"Tick, because I stick!" the child cried, gripping the willow bark tie of the black mane, laughing with delight at being suddenly eight feet tall and traveling across the desert without even trying, like the tumbleweed, as fast as the wind.

Moon, a night past full, rose to light the plains for them. Horse jogged easily on and on. Somewhere deep in the night, they stopped at a Pygmy Owl camp, ate a little, and rested. Most of the owls were out hunting, but an old lady entertained them at her campfire, telling them tales about the ghost of a cricket, about the great invisible people, tales that the child heard interwoven with her own dreams as she dozed and half woke and dozed again. Then Horse put her up on his shoulders, and on they went at a tireless, slow lope. Moon went down behind them, and before them the sky paled into rose and gold. The soft night wind was gone; the air was sharp, cold, still. On it, in it, there was a faint, sour smell of burning. The child felt Horse's gait change, grow tighter, uneasy.

"Hey, Prince!"

A small, slightly scolding voice: the child knew it, and placed it as soon as she saw the person sitting by a juniper tree, neatly dressed, wearing an old black cap.

"Hey, Chickadee!" Horse said, coming round and stopping. The child had observed, back in Coyote's town, that everybody treated Chickadee with respect. She didn't see why. Chickadee seemed an ordinary person, busy and talkative like most of the small birds, nothing so endearing as Quail or so impressive as Hawk or Great Owl.

"You're going on that way?" Chickadee asked Horse.

"The little one wants to see if her people are living there," Horse said, surprising the child. Was that what she wanted?

Chickadee looked disapproving, as she often did. She whistled a few notes thoughtfully, another of her habits, and then got up. "I'll come along."

"That's great," Horse said thankfully.

"I'll scout," Chickadee said, and off she went, surprisingly fast, ahead of them, while Horse took up his steady, long lope.

The sour smell was stronger in the air.

Chickadee halted, way ahead of them on a slight rise, and stood still. Horse dropped to a walk, and then stopped. "There," she said in a low voice.

The child stared. In the strange light and slight mist before sunrise, she could not see clearly, and when she strained and peered, she felt as if her left eye were not seeing at all. "What is it?" she whispered.

"One of the holes. Across the wall—see?"

It did seem there was a line, a straight, jerky line drawn across the sagebrush plain, and on the far side of it—nothing? Was it mist? Something moved there—

"It's cattle!" she said.

Horse stood silent, uneasy. Chickadee was coming back toward them.

"It's a ranch," the child said. "That's a fence. There're a lot of Herefords." The words tasted like iron, like salt in her mouth. The things she named wavered in her sight and faded, leaving nothing—a hole in the world, a burned place like a cigarette burn. "Go closer!" she urged Horse. "I want to see."

And as if he owed her obedience, he went forward, tense but unquestioning.

Chickadee came up to them. "Nobody around," she said in her small, dry voice, "but there's one of those fast turtle things coming."

Horse nodded but kept going forward.

Gripping his broad shoulders, the child stared into the blank, and as if Chickadee's words had focused her eyes, she saw again: the scattered whitefaces, a few of them looking up with bluish, rolling eyes—the fences—over the rise a chimneyed house roof and a high barn—and then in the distance, something moving fast, too fast, burning across the ground straight at them at terrible speed. "Run!" she yelled to Horse. "Run away! Run!" As if released from bonds, he wheeled and ran, flat out, in great reaching strides, away from sunrise, the fiery burning chariot, the smell of acid, iron, death. And Chickadee flew before them like a cinder on the air of dawn.

## 4

"Horse?" Coyote said. "That prick? Cat food!"

Coyote had been there when the child got home to Bide-A-Wee, but she clearly hadn't been worrying about where Gal was, and maybe hadn't even noticed she was gone. She was in a vile mood, and took it all wrong when the child tried to tell her about where she had been.

"If you're going to do damn fool things, next time do 'em with me; at least I'm an expert," she said, morose, and slouched out the door. The child saw her squatting down, poking an old white turd with a stick, trying to get it to answer some questions she kept asking it. The turd lay obstinately silent. Later in the day the child saw two coyote men, a young one and a mangy-looking older one loitering around near the spring, looking over at Bide-A-Wee. She decided it would be a good night to spend somewhere else.

The thought of the crowded rooms of Chipmunk's house was not attractive. It was going to be a warm night again tonight, and moonlit. Maybe she would sleep outside. If she could feel sure some people wouldn't come around, like the Rattler. . . . She was standing indecisively halfway through town when a dry voice said, "Hey, Gal."

"Hey, Chickadee."

The trim, black-capped woman was standing on her doorstep shaking out a rug. She kept her house neat, trim like herself. Having come back across the desert with her, the child now knew, though she still could not have said, why Chickadee was a respected person.

"I thought maybe I'd sleep out tonight," the child said, tentative.

"Unhealthy," said Chickadee. "What are nests for?"

"Mom's kind of busy," the child said.

"Tsk!" went Chickadee, and snapped the rug with disapproving vigor. "What about her little friend? At least they're decent people."

"Horny-toad? His parents are so shy. . . ."

"Well. Come in and have something to eat, anyhow," said Chickadee.

The child helped her cook dinner. She knew now why there were rocks in the mush pot.

"Chickadee," she said, "I still don't understand; can I ask you? Mom said it depends who's seeing it, but still; I mean, if I see you wearing clothes and everything like humans, then how come you cook this way, in baskets, you know, and there aren't any—any of the things like they have—there where we were with Horse this morning?"

"I don't know," Chickadee said. Her voice indoors was quite soft and pleasant. "I guess we do things the way they always were done, when your people and my people lived together, you know. And together with everything else here. The rocks, you know. The plants and everything." She looked at the basket of willow bark, fern root, and pitch, at the blackened rocks that were heating in the fire. "You see how it all goes together. . . ."

"But you have fire—That's different—"

"Ah!" said Chickadee, impatient, "you people! Do you think you invented the sun?"

She took up the wooden tongs, plopped the heated rocks into the water-filled basket with a terrific hiss and steam and loud bubblings. The child sprinkled in the pounded seeds and stirred.

Chickadee brought out a basket of fine blackberries. They sat on the newly shaken-out rug and ate. The child's two-finger scoop technique with mush was now highly refined.

"Maybe I didn't cause the world," Chickadee said, "but I'm a better cook than Coyote."

The child nodded, stuffing.

"I don't know why I made Horse go there," she said after she had stuffed. "I got just as scared as he did when I saw it. But now I feel again like I have to go back there. But I want to stay here. With my friends, with Coyote, I don't understand."

"When we lived together, it was all one place," Chickadee said in her slow, soft home-voice. "But now the others, the new people, they live apart. And their places are so heavy. They weigh down on our place, they press on it, draw it, suck it, eat it, eat holes in it, crowd it out. . . . Maybe after a while longer, there'll be only one place again, their place. And none of us here. I knew Bison, out over the mountains. I knew Antelope right here. I knew Grizzly and Graywolf, up west there. Gone. All gone. And the salmon you eat at Coyote's house, those are the dream salmon, those are the true food; but in the rivers, how many salmon now? The rivers that were red with them in spring? Who dances, now, when the First Salmon offers himself? Who dances by the river? Oh, you should ask Coyote about all this. She knows more than I do! But she forgets . . . She's hopeless, worse than Raven; she has to piss on every post; she's a terrible housekeeper. . . ." Chickadee's voice had sharpened. She whistled a note or two, and said no more.

After a while the child asked very softly, "Who is Grandmother?"

"Grandmother," Chickadee said. She looked at the child and ate several blackberries thoughtfully. She stroked the rug they sat on. "If I built the fire on the rug, it would burn a hole in it," she said. "Right? So we build the fire on sand, on dirt. . . . Things are woven together. So we call the weaver the Grandmother." She whistled four notes, looking up the smoke hole. "After all," she added, "maybe all this place—the other places, too—maybe they're all only one side of the weaving. I don't know. I can look with one eye at a time; how can I tell how deep it goes?"

Lying that night rolled up in a blanket in Chickadee's backyard, the child heard the wind soughing and storming in the cotton-woods down in the draw, and then slept deeply, weary from the long night before. Just at sunrise she woke. The eastern mountains were a cloudy dark red as if the level light shone through them as through a hand held before the fire. In the tobacco patch—the only farming anybody in this town did was to raise a little wild tobacco—Lizard and Beetle were singing some kind of growing song or blessing song, soft and desultory, *huh*-huh-huh-huh, *huh*-huh-huh-huh, and as she lay warm-curled on the ground, the song made her feel rooted in the ground, cradled on it and in it, so where her fingers ended and the dirt began, she did not know, as if she were dead—but she was wholly alive; she was the earth's life. She got up dancing, left the blanket folded neatly on Chickadee's nest and already empty bed, and danced up the hill to Bide-A-Wee. At the half-open door, she sang:

> *Danced with a gal with a hole in her stocking*
> *And her knees kept a knocking and her toes kept a rocking.*
> *Danced with a gal with a hole in her stocking.*
> *Danced by the light of the moon!*

Coyote emerged, tousled and lurching, and eyed her narrowly. "Sheeeoot," she said. She sucked her teeth and then went to splash water all over her head from the gourd by the door. She shook her head, and the water drops flew. "Let's get out of here," she said. "I have had it. I don't know what got into me. If I'm pregnant again, at my age, oh shit. Let's get out of town. I need a change of air."

In the foggy dark of the house, the child could see at least two coyote men sprawled snoring away on the bed and floor.

Coyote walked over to the old white turd and kicked it. "Why didn't you stop me?" she shouted.

"I *told* you," the turd muttered sulkily.

"Dumb shit," Coyote said. "Come on, Gal. Let's go. Where to?" She didn't wait for an answer. "I know. Come on!"

And she set off through town at that lazy-looking, rangy walk that was so hard to keep up with. But the child was full of pep, and came dancing, so that Coyote began dancing, too, skipping and pirouetting and fooling around all the way down the long slope to the level plains. There she slanted their way off northeastward. Horse Butte was at their backs, getting smaller in the distance.

Along near noon the child said, "I didn't bring anything to eat."

"Something will turn up," Coyote said. "Sure to." And pretty soon she turned aside, going straight to a tiny gray shack hidden by a couple of half-dead junipers and a stand of rabbitbrush. The place smelled terrible. A sign on the door said: Fox. Private. No Trespassing!—but Coyote pushed it open, and trotted right back out with half a small smoked salmon. "Nobody home but us chickens," she said, grinning sweetly.

"Isn't that stealing?" the child asked, worried.

"Yes," Coyote answered, trotting on.

They ate the fox-scented salmon by a dried-up creek, slept a while, and went on.

Before long the child smelled the sour burning smell, and stopped. It was as if a huge, heavy hand had begun pushing her chest, pushing her away, and yet at the same time as if she had stepped into a strong current that drew her forward, helpless.

"Hey, getting close!" Coyote said, and stopped to piss by a juniper stump.

"Close to what?"

"Their town. See?" She pointed to a pair of sage-spotted hills. Between them was an area of grayish blank.

"I don't want to go there."

"We won't go all the way in. No way! We'll just get a little closer and look. It's fun," Coyote said, putting her head on one side, coaxing. "They do all these weird things in the air."

The child hung back.

Coyote became businesslike, responsible. "We're going to be very careful," she announced. "And look out for big dogs, O.K.? Little dogs I can handle. Make a good lunch. Big dogs, it goes the other way. Right? Let's go, then."

Seemingly as casual and lounging as ever, but with a tense alertness in the carriage of her head and the yellow glance of her eyes, Coyote led off again, not looking back; and the child followed.

All around them the pressures increased. It was as if the air itself were pressing on them, as if time were going too fast, too hard, not flowing but pounding, pounding, pounding, faster and harder till it buzzed like Rattler's rattle. "Hurry, you have to hurry!" everything said. "There isn't time!" everything said. Things rushed past screaming and shuddering. Things turned, flashed, roared, stank, vanished. There was a boy—he came into focus all at once, but not on the ground: he was going along a couple of inches above the ground, moving very fast, bending his legs from side to side in a kind of frenzied, swaying dance, and was gone. Twenty children sat in rows in the air, all singing shrilly, and then the walls closed over them. A basket, no, a pot, no, a can, a garbage can, full of salmon smelling wonderful, no, full of stinking deer hides and rotten cabbage stalks—keep out of it. Coyote! Where was she?

"Mom!" the child called. "Mother!"—standing a moment at the end of an ordinary small-town street near the gas station, and the next moment in a terror of blanknesses, invisible walls, terrible smells and pressures and the overwhelming rush of Time straightforward rolling her helpless as a twig in the race above a waterfall. She clung, held on trying not to fall—"Mother!"

Coyote was over by the big basket of salmon, approaching it, wary but out in the open, in the full sunlight, in the full current. And a boy and a man borne by the same current were coming down the long, sage-spotted hill behind the gas station, each with a gun, red hats—hunters; it was killing season. "Hey, will you look at that damn coyote in broad daylight big as my wife's ass," the man said, and cocked, aimed, shot—all as Myra screamed and ran against the enormous drowning current. Coyote fled past her yelling, "Get out of here!" She turned and was borne away.

Far out of sight of that place, in a little draw among low hills, they sat and breathed air in searing gasps until, after a long time, it came easy again.

"Mom, that was *stupid*," the child said furiously.

"Sure was," Coyote said. "But did you see all that food!"

"I'm not hungry," the child said sullenly. "Not till we get all the way away from here."

"But they're your folks," Coyote said. "All yours. Your kith and kin and cousins and kind. Bang! Pow! There's Coyote! Bang! There's my wife's ass! Pow! There's anything—BOOOOM! Blow it away, man! BOOOOOOM!"

"I want to go home," the child said.

"Not yet," said Coyote. "I got to take a shit." She did so, then turned to the fresh turd, leaning over it. "It says I have to stay," she reported, smiling.

"It didn't say anything. I was listening!"

"You know who to understand? You hear everything, Miss Big Ears? Hears all—See all with her crummy, gummy eye—"

"You have pine-pitch eyes, too! You told me so!"

"That's a story," Coyote snarled. "You don't even know a story when you hear one! Look, do what you like; it's a free country. I'm hanging around here tonight. I like the action." She sat down and began patting her hands on the dirt in a soft four-four rhythm and singing under her breath, one of the endless, tuneless songs that kept time from running too fast, that wove the roots of trees and bushes and ferns and grass in the web that held the stream in the streambed and the rock in the rock's place and the earth together. And the child lay listening.

"I love you," she said.

Coyote went on singing.

Sun went down the last slope of the west and left a pale green clarity over the desert hills.

Coyote had stopped singing. She sniffed. "Hey," she said. "Dinner." She got up and moseyed along the little draw. "Yeah," she called back softly. "Come on!"

Stiffly, for the fear-crystals had not yet melted out of her joints, the child got up and went to Coyote. Off to one side along the hill was one of the lines, a fence. She didn't look at it. It was O.K. They were outside it.

"Look at that!"

A smoked salmon, a whole chinook, lay on a little cedar-bark mat.

"An offering! Well, I'll be darned!" Coyote was so impressed she didn't even swear. "I haven't seen one of these for years! I thought they'd forgotten!"

"Offering to whom?"

"Me! Who else? Boy, *look* at that!"

The child looked dubiously at the salmon.

"It smells funny."

"How funny?"

"Like burned."

"It's smoked, stupid! Come on."

"I'm not hungry."

"O.K. It's not your salmon anyhow. It's mine. My offering, for me. Hey, you people! You people over there! Coyote thanks you! Keep it up like this, and maybe I'll do some good things for you, too!"

"Don't, don't yell, Mom! They're not that far away—"

"They're all my people," said Coyote with a great gesture, and then sat down cross-legged, broke off a big piece of salmon, and ate.

Evening Star burned like a deep, bright pool of water in the clear sky. Down over the twin hills was a dim suffusion of light, like a fog. The child looked away from it, back at the star.

"Oh," Coyote said. "Oh shit."

"What's wrong?"

"That wasn't so smart, eating that," Coyote said, and then held herself and began to shiver, to scream, to choke—her eyes rolled up; her long arms and legs flew out jerking and dancing; foam spurted out between her teeth. Her body arched tremendously backward, and the child, trying to hold her, was thrown violently off by the spasms of her limbs. The child scrambled back and held the body as it spasmed again, twitched, quivered, went still.

By moonrise, Coyote was cold. Till then there had been so much warmth under the tawny coat that the child kept thinking maybe she was alive, maybe if she just kept holding her, keeping her warm, Coyote would recover, she would be all right. The child held her close, not looking at the black lips drawn back from the teeth, the white balls of the eyes. But when the cold came through the fur as the presence of death, the child let the slight, stiff corpse lie down on the dirt.

She went nearby and dug a hole in the stony sand of the draw, a shallow pit. Coyote's people did not bury their dead; she knew that. But her people did. She carried the small corpse to the pit, laid it down, and covered it with her blue and white bandanna. It was not large enough; the four stiff paws stuck out. The child heaped the body over with sand and rocks and a scurf of sagebrush and tumbleweed held down with more rocks. She also heaped dirt and rocks over the poisoned salmon carcass. Then she stood up and walked away without looking back.

At the top of the hill, she stood and looked across the draw toward the misty glow of the lights of the town lying in the pass between the twin hills.

"I hope you all die in pain," she said aloud. She turned away and walked down into the desert.

## 5

It was Chickadee who met her, on the second evening, north of Horse Butte.

"I didn't cry," the child said.

"None of us do," said Chickadee. "Come with me this way now. Come into Grandmother's house."

It was underground, but very large, dark and large, and the Grandmother was there at the center, at her loom. She was making a rug or blanket of the hills and the black rain and the white rain, weaving in the lightning. As they spoke, she wove.

"Hello, Chickadee. Hello, New Person."

"Grandmother," Chickadee greeted her.

The child said, "I'm not one of them."

Grandmother's eyes were small and dim. She smiled and wove. The shuttle thrummed through the warp.

"Old Person, then," said Grandmother. "You'd better go back there now, Granddaughter. That's where you live."

"I lived with Coyote. She's dead. They killed her."

"Oh, don't worry about Coyote!" Grandmother said with a little huff of laughter. "She gets killed all the time."

The child stood still. She saw the endless weaving.

"Then I—Could I go back home—to her house—?"

"I don't think it would work," Grandmother said. "Do you, Chickadee?"

Chickadee shook her head once, silent.

"It would be dark there now, and empty, and fleas. . . . You got outside your people's time, into our place; but I think that Coyote was taking you back, see. Her way. If you go back now, you can still live with them. Isn't your father there?"

The child nodded.

"They've been looking for you."

"They have?"

"Oh yes. Ever since you fell out of the sky. The man was dead, but you weren't there—they kept looking."

"Serves him right. Served them all right," the child said. She put her hands up over her face and began to cry terribly, without tears.

"Go on, little one, Granddaughter," Spider said. "Don't be afraid. You can live well there. I'll be there, too, you know. In your dreams, in your ideas, in dark corners in the basement. Don't kill me, or I'll make it rain. . . ."

"I'll come around," Chickadee said. "Make gardens for me."

The child held her breath and clenched her hands until her sobs stopped and let her speak.

"Will I ever see Coyote?"

"I don't know," the Grandmother replied.

The child accepted this. She said, after another silence, "Can I keep my eye?"

"Yes. You can keep your eye."

"Thank you, Grandmother," the child said. She turned away then and started up the night slope toward the next day. Ahead of her in the air of dawn for a long way, a little bird flew, black-capped, light-winged.

# ANDRE NORTON

## "The Dowry of the Rag Picker's Daughter"

*Andre Norton (1912- ) began writing science fiction in 1947 as Andrew North, almost two decades after the start of her professional fiction-writing career. Although greatly varied in their themes and approaches to science fiction, the scores of novels she wrote after* Starman's Son, 2250 A.D.—*including* Sargasso of Space, The Beast Merchants, Judgment on Janus, Time Traders *and the different miniseries spun from them—integrate to form a vivid tapestry of pangalactic future history. Since 1963, and the publication of her novel* Witch World, *Norton has devoted most of her abundant energy to the* Witch World *saga, a loosely organized science-fantasy series that meld elements of space opera and sword-and-sorcery and has served as the backdrop of several shared world anthologies. Her many non-series novels include* Night of Masks. *Her short fiction can be found in* Garan the Eternal, High Sorcery, The Many Worlds of Andre Norton, *and* Perilous Dreams.

# The Dowry of the Rag Picker's Daughter

*by Andre Norton*

---

The Way of the Limping Camel was six houses long and one wide—if mounds of tumbled earthen bricks could still be termed houses. Yet they were indeed inhabited by the very least and lowest of those who vowed allegiance to Caliph Ras el Fada, whose own dwelling at the other side of the city proudly showed a blazing watchtower striped with gold leaf.

The least of the houses on the way had been claimed by the rag picker Muledowa. He was always careful to thank the Great One of the Many Names for his great luck in finding it when his former roof had nearly landed on his head and had put an end to two ragged hens which were the care of his daughter Zoradeh. Well had he used his cane on her, too, for not foreseeing such a catastrophe and being prepared against it.

He sighed as he slip-slapped along on his worn sandals, for no one looking upon Zoradeh's unveiled face would ever come brideseeking—nor could he ever put her up for sale in the Market of Slaves, for again her djinn-given face would put an end to any hope of sale.

Deliberately he pushed Zoradeh out of his mind as he wished he could pull the whole of her misbegotten face and skinny body out of his life as well. At least this day the Compassionate and All-Powerful had smiled in his direction. His grip about the edge of the collection bag tightened as he trudged along.

\*　　\*　　\*

Caliph Ras el Fada might be the ruler of Nid and at least ten surrounding territories. But he was not the ruler of his own harem; and he frowned blackly every time he thought about that. He too had a daughter, the veriest rose of a daughter, in whose person and face no man could find fault. The trouble was no longer hidden—and it was one often found among women—love of power and a hot temper. Better such a one be bagged and left in the waste to trouble mankind no more, than introduced into the company of any foolish man. For Jalnar had a strong will and a sharp mind of her own. All smiling eyes and cooing lips could she be until she got her will—then, like some warrior female of the djinn, she became a force with whom no man could deal. Willing indeed was Caliph Ras ready to get rid of her. However, gossip was gossip and spread from the harem even into the marketplace. Since rumor had near a thousand tongues he could not cut out every one of them.

Also there was the matter of the future rule of his town. Though he had taken four wives, and been served by a variety of eager and willing concubines, he had unaccountably no other child who had lived past the fifth year save Jalnar. So he could not leave any heir save her husband—and he had yet to find one willing to accept, no matter how large a dowry he might offer; none for three years at least, until now. He ran his fingers through his beard, trying to put out of mind all else about this self-styled wizard Kamar, save the fact he had not only made an offer for Jalnar but had already gifted her with one of the dresses for her bridal viewing—all of silvery stuff, so sewn with pearls as to be worth a fortune.

The caliph clapped hands and summoned his favorite mamluk, sending him to the harem with a message for the head eunuch. But still he was too ill at ease to retire to his gold-embroidered cushions, and his hand gave such a hard tug to his beard that the tweak brought smarting tears to his eyes and words to his lips which were hardly those of a sublime ruler and respected Commander of the Faithful.

Down the Way of the Limping Camel came Muledowa. Zoradeh moved closer to the wall, waited to feel his digging stick laid hard about her shoulders, though she could remember no recent fault which would arouse her father's ire. To her great surprise he

278

squirmed past the tall pile of broken mud bricks which served as a door without any greeting curse. To her even greater astonishment, he stooped to gather up the chunk of crumbling masonry which sealed the door and thumped it home, keeping his gathering bag still tight-pressed to him under his other arm. For the first time she could recall, there was an upturn to his lips within the thick beard which might be almost taken for a smile.

The shadow smile still lingered as he looked at her.

"Fortune sometimes aids the worthy man after all." With great care he placed the bag on the pavement between them. "I am at a turning of the road now, and soon I shall mount a fine she-mule and have a slave to run before me. Nor shall I grub among foul things for bread to fill the mouth."

She eyed him warily, afraid to ask any questions for fear he might well slide back into that other whom she had always known. But he had gone down on his knees and was tugging at the fastening of the bag. Still paying her no attention, he brought out something which caused her to cry out when she saw it.

Creased, and possessing a ragged tear down the front as if its last wearer had ripped it or had it torn from her body, was such a dress as she could not believe ever existed except in some tale. It was silver, shimmering, seeming to reflect the light here and there; and there were small and large pearls cunningly sewn in pattern on it. It was such a garment as only an houri would wear.

Her father was holding it up to the light, turning it carefully. He lifted the torn portion and held it in its place. Then for the first time he spoke to her. "Loathsome thou art, but still there is some use for you. Bring out your needle and the right kind of thread and make this as perfect as can be done. And"—he looked to the bucket of water she had brought from the well in the street—"wash your hands twice—thrice, before you lay hand on this. A princess' ransom might be in your hold."

Zoradeh reached out a hand to the shimmering pile of beauty. Then she leaned far forward and kissed the dusty pavement at her father's feet.

"On my head and hands be this done," she said as she gathered the bag around the treasure. She had myriad questions but dared voice none of them. She could only fear in silence that her father had in some manner stolen the robe.

"Aye, on your head, your hands, and your eyes." He went back to the broken door before he turned with infinite malice in both the look he directed at her and in his voice as he answered, "Good fortune seldom pays two visits to a man, and this is mine!"

He looked back at the shimmering heap and then went out. Zoradeh listened to the slap of his worn sandals. He was going down the street toward the small inn where he would drink minted tea and strive to outlie his two rivals for the rest of the afternoon.

She followed orders and washed her hands three times, daring to put in the rinse water of the last immersion a bit of well-shaved cinnamon bark, so that its fragrance warred against all the other, fouler odors in the wash that had once been a courtyard. Then, taking up the bag that was still half-wrapped about the wonder her father had brought home, she scrambled up to the part of the house which she had made her own, her father not choosing to follow her over the loose brick which often started sliding under one's feet. Once this must have been the harem of a noble house, for there were still fading pictures painted in flaring designs on the wall, or what was left of it. But now it was Zoradeh's own place of hiding. She spread out the bag as far as she could and stood up to shake free the robe.

Carefully the girl examined the tear across the front of the robe. It was a jagged opening apparently made by a knife, and, as she moved, pearls dripped from broken threads. Hastily she folded it tear-side-up and explored the bag and the floor about until she had near a full palm of the gleaming gems. How many had been lost along the way, or still lay near to where her father had found it? Find it he must have done, for Muledowa was the last man in the city to put his right hand into jeopardy for theft.

Ofttimes before she had mended thrown-away things her father had found in the trash and done so well that he was able to sell them to a dealer in old clothes in the market. But she had never set fingers to such as this before. Bringing forth her packet of needles, she chose the smallest, and, using ravellings of the material itself, she set to work.

In the tree-shadowed court of the harem which formed nearly a third of the Caliph's palace, Jalnar lay soft and at ease on a pile of silken rugs while a slave rubbed her feet and ankles with sweet-smelling cream. She held up her silver hand mirror and studied her reflection in the polished surface critically. Nor did she turn her head as she spoke to the blowsy bundle of shawls and faceveil who squatted a few feet away.

"They say that there be only two lots for a woman—marriage or the grave. To me it seems that these be equal choices and there should be a third—a hidden rule, which we will find within the hour. You did as was told to you, Mirza? The thing will never again see the light of day?"

"Hearing was doing, Flower of All Flowers. It was thrust deep amid the foul refuse of the city—no one would go delving for profit there."

"In a way, Old One, it is a pity, for I have never seen its like. But then I have never been courted by a wizard before, and who knows what tricks of magic he bound around it—what tricks he might use against me when I went among his womenfolk. Wizards claim great powers, and they may be right. Better not yield to such a one.

"It is the duty of the caliph to provide me with at least seven bride dresses so that when I am shown to my lord, he sees me in full beauty. Why should this Kamar present one, thus breaking custom? Perhaps he would so bind me to some ifrit who would be ever with me that I may not in anything have my will."

The bundle of shawls shook. "Precious as Water in the Desert, speak not of such horrors. It is said that some may be summoned merely by thinking on them. It could well be that the wizard wishes only to do you honor, and that such affairs are arranged differently in his country. I have heard it ever said that foreigners have queer customs."

Jalnar slapped down the fan on her knee and kicked out at one of the girls who were soothing her feet. "Be gone, it is done as well as your awkward hands can do so. And you, Mirza, forget such foolishness. Has not the mighty Orban himself laid upon this castle and all it contains a protecting shell? All have heard of Orban—who has raised a voice to cry aloud the deeds of Kamar? Only by his own words do we know that he claims to be a wizard at all.

"If he is one, and has striven to burden me with some fate of his own devising—well, we have taken care of that, have we not, Old One?"

"Hearing and obeying, Great Lady," came her servant's answer, so softly that Jalnar had to strain to hear it, and her ears were the keenest ever known in Nid.

"Go now, all of you, I would sleep away the hot hours that I may appear at my best at the second showing—"

There was a grunt from the shawls and Jalnar laughed.

"So it has been said that Kamar wanted his gift shown tonight. Now *you* will whisper in the halls and kitchen that he misjudged my size—that my workers of needlecraft need to make some changes in it. Since he cannot come into the harem to search and ask, he needs must accept my words for that if he ask outright. You may tell all your old gossips that I shall wear it on the seventh night when the contract is to be signed, which will make me one to answer his slightest whim. That will bring us time and we can plan—" Her voice slid down into a hissing whisper as she waved all those with her away.

Zoradeh had feared the task her father had set her, for the stuff of its making was so fragile she thought that even handling might bring more destruction. Yet her needle slipped through the gauzy material as if there were holes there already awaiting it. She made fast each pearl with interweaving. It would seem that the rent was less than it looked at first, and she finished well before sundown. Standing up on the scrap of wall left to the house she allowed the faint breeze tug it out to the full. Truly a robe for a princess. How had her father come upon such a thing?

She held it close to her and wondered how it would feel to go so bravely clad through the days with maids aplenty, eunuchs and mamluks to obey and guard her. Now she looked carefully down along the street and then it was but a moment's work to undo her trousers which were patch upon patch, and her faded, much-mended shirt. Over her head went the robe; and it settled down about her, seeming to cling to her as might another, fairer skin. Zoradeh drew a deep breath and brought forward the water pail, waiting for the slopping of its contents to end so that she could use it as a mirror. Then she whipped the end of the headveil worn modestly about the lower part of her djinn-given face and looked.

Ah! with her face thus covered she looked like someone out of a fair dream and she straightened her back, aching from many hours of being bent above a task, giving her head a proud little toss. . . . princess! So did clothes make the woman. Were she to venture forth with some guards and a bevy of maids, would her passage not have them talking about a princess very quickly indeed?

"Pearl among Pearls!" The voice startled her so that she nearly lost her precarious footing and fell down into the courtyard. There was a man in the outer lane, mounted on a fine black horse which seemed to dance with eagerness under his hand. And he wore the red scarf of the caliph's own guard looped about the rim of his helm.

"Fortune's Own Daughter!" He smiled gaily and raised his spear in salute. "Foolish is your lord to allow such a treasure to be seen. How came you here to glow like a lily under the full moon, but set in a marsh of muck so hard to reach and pluck forth—"

She must rid herself of this stranger before the return of her father, and what better way to do so than to prove to him what ugliness could be seen as a woman's face? Deliberately she jerked the wedge of the shawl from the veiling of her face, and waited for him to show distaste and dislike of the tooth-gnashing wrinkled mask as all the rest had done. Yet he did not turn away his head, spit out some charm against ifrit or demon. Instead he brought his horse closer to the crumbling wall and called up to her.

"Are you wed, Pearl of Great Price? If this be so I shall search out your husband and ask him to try blade against blade with me—and I am counted a mighty swordsman. If the Uniter of Souls has decreed that you are not so tied to another, tell me then your name and that of your father that I may make him an offer—"

She had backed away from the edge of the wall. Now sure that she spoke with a man whose wits were awry, she answered:

"Master, why do you make me the butt of your cruel pleasure? You see me clearly—and so seeing you view what no man would bargain for." Then she scrambled down the rude pile of bricks that led from her perch, not listening to aught he called after her, rubbing the tears from her eyes. So she stayed in hiding until she heard him ride away, and was able to reach for her own clothing and fold away the mended pearl dress in the bag.

She could hope that he might forget his foolishness and that he could not indeed set forth on a hunt for Muledowa, for the latter would indeed deem the guard mad—as would any in this quarter hearing him speak so of the rag picker's daughter, easily the most foul of countenance of any who drew water from the public well and went openly unveiled, for who would do *her* any dishonor? She wrapped the dress carefully in her father's collection bag and hid it under his sleep mat, hoping he would take it away soon. For within her, long-buried hope awakened; and she would not be so hurt again.

In the palace of the caliph there was much to do, for the seventh-day bride feast had yet three nights to go. Jalnar bathed and then had her smooth, pale skin anointed with a scent made of many herbs, so that it would seem that a whole garden had broken into the bathing chamber. Her dark hair was smoothed until there was the look of fine satin to its length; and the maid had just finished with that when Mirza scurried into the room and bent her shoulder the more so that she might kiss the ground before her mistress's feet.

There was such a look on her much-wrinkled face as made Jalnar wave her attendants away and lean towards her with a whisper for a voice.

"Old One, what trouble does Fate or ifrit lay upon us? You look like one on the way to the beheading block, with no chance of any mercy at the end of that journey."

"Well, my lady, do you choose such a description." Plainly there was both fear and anger to make her voice like the croak of carrion crown. "Our caliph, the great lord, the Prophet-descended one, has given an order—already he must be close to the guarded doorway—and he said with all men hearing him that this night you shall do proper honor to Kamar after the fashion of his own people, and wear for his viewing the robe which he brought—"

"It is too tight, too small, it was damaged in the chest in which it came to me—I would do him greater honor if I wear it on the final night after it is repaired."

Mirza began to shake her head—first slowly, and then with greater vigor. "Lady, the Companion of djinn will see through such excuses, even if it is you who speak them."

Jalnar caught a lock of her hair and held it between her teeth. The plan she had thought was so simple—how could she have hoped to use it against a wizard?

"What shall I do then, Mother of Maids?"

"You have the robe brought forth and then perhaps it may be repaired in time. For those at the banquet sit long over such delicacies as your honored father has set before him. He is, thank the Compassionate, one who is not easily disturbed from any meal."

"There is wisdom in your speech, Old One. Go and have out that rag, and my best sewing maid, to whom the All-Seeing has given a great gift with the needle, shall see what she can do. It might be well that I wear the robe from the far eastern nation which was gifted to me three years ago, and then have the wizard's rag brought in to show and say that I would keep the honor of its wearing to the last night of all, when my father gives me to this hunter of stars and teller of strange tales, despite all his present urging."

"To hear is to obey," mumbled Mirza. She once more padded away. But when she sought the hole into which she had thrust the robe there was nothing there—save a number of date seeds, and the rind of a melon. For a moment or two she looked about her wildly, thinking surely she must have been mistaken. Only, she remembered so well other points of reference to that hidey-hole and they were still about.

"Grub you for the kitchen leavings, Old One?" A boy who wore only a ragged loincloth and who was grey with the grime of the dump looked down upon her from a neighboring mound of refuse. "There will be naught worth the having there, for old Muledowa has already been here. Though his bones may be so old he cannot scramble around well, he has never lost what may bring him any sort of a bargain. Even the ifrit would welcome such skill as he has."

"Muledowa?" Mirza raised her voice a little. "He is known to you, quick one, and he has been here today?"

"As the sun weighs upon us with its heat, so it is true. Also his find here must have been a fine one, for he turned and went toward his home, looking no more this day. I strove to see what he held, but he rolled it so quickly into his collecting bag that I got no sight of it, and when I asked him a question he spat at me as if we were strange cats made foes over a choice morsel of baked camel."

Jalnar twisted the lock of hair fiercely between her hands upon Mirza's return, as she said,

"Go you to Raschman of the guard and say to him that one of my maids stole out at night and buried something among the rubbish where it was later found by this Muledowa and taken away—that it must be a plot between the two of them, and"—she hesitated a moment and then added—"say that it was Dalikah who did this—for all know that I have had her beaten for breaking my bottle of scent and she has good reason so to play, having ill thoughts against me. Tell the guardsman that you have heard of this rag picker who lives in the refuse of the town, and to send there to obtain the bag. Only warn him not to open it or look upon its contents, for it is doubtless true that it has been overlooked and magicked by the djinn."

"And Muledowa and those who live under his roof, who may have already seen what lies within that bag, my lady? What do we with them?"

"I do not think," Jalnar replied with a small cruel smile, "that he will have shared such a secret with many—they would be on him as a hawk upon a desert snake if he had. But if he does have other of his own blood—let that one or all others be brought also."

Mirza struck her head three times against the floor at the princess's feet. "Hearing is doing, lady."

So she left Jalnar to be swathed in the green gown of her choice and slipped away through the gates, for all the guards knew her well and she often ran errands for this or that of the ladies of the inner rooms.

Though she had never invaded this before she went to the outer palace, where she huddled by the door of the guards' room, trying to catch the eye of the man who was making swooping motions in the air and talking loudly.

"—fair as the moon in full glory, she moves like swallows a-wing, her skin like the softest satin such as those in the forbidden palace lie upon for sleeping. Ah, I have seen beauties a-many in my day—"

Two of the listeners laughed and the man's hand went to his sword hilt, his face frowning in warning.

"Brother by the sword," one of the listeners spoke. "Is it not true that many times you have seen maids of surpassing beauty, only later to find some irredeemable flaw in them? Let us go then to the ruin by the outer wall and test whether your story be right or whether some djinni has ensorcelled your eyes—"

But the young man had already seen Mirza, and now he came to her with some relief in his expression. "Why do you seek us out, Mother?" he asked with some respect and a tone of courtesy.

"My lady has been grievously despoiled of a treasure." She told her story quickly. "One of the slave girls took ill her punishment for a fault and stole a robe of great price. She hid this in the mound of refuse beyond the palace and there it was picked up by one Muledowa, a picker of rags, and carried home. My lady would have back her belongings and with them the rag picker and all else under his roof who might have seen this thing—for she fears it all be a piece of sport by those ifrits who dislike all mankind. Of this she wishes to be sure before she tells her father of it—lest he, too, be drawn into some devlish sorcery."

He touched his turban-wreathed helm with both hands and said,

"Having heard, it is as done."

Zoradeh was kneeling in the ruined courtyard of her home, washing her father's feet and listening with growing fear to his mumbling speech, for he was talking, if not to her, then to some djinni who had accompanied him.

"Orbasan will pay me much for this treasure." He stretched out an arm so he could finger the bag which held the robe. "Then I shall buy a donkey and, with the aid of that creature, be able to carry twice as much from the refuse heaps. For I am an old man and now it hurts my back to stretch and strain, to kneel and stand erect again all for some bit I may take. There is much greater profit to be made with things I cannot carry. Eh, girl," for the first time he looked directly at her with a cruel snarl twisting his lips, "how then has the work gone? Let me look upon your handiwork. If you have erred then you shall taste of my stick until each breath shall cost you sore—"

Zoradeh brought the bag quickly and spread it out before him, taking care that she not touch the wondrous thing with her own hands, damp and dusty as they were. For a long moment her father stared down at the fine silk and the moonlike pearls. His hand went out as if to touch and then he drew it back quickly with a deep-drawn breath.

"Aye, worth a wazir's ransom at least, that must be. We shall get but a third, a fifth, nearly an eighth portion of its price in gain. Yet I know no one else—" His hand went to his beard as he ran his nails through the crisp, age-sullied grey of it. "No," he added as one who had just made a decision of great import, "not yet shall I go to Orbasan with this. We shall put it away in secret and think more of the matter—"

But even as he spoke, they heard the clatter of horse hooves on the uneven pavement without, and Zoradeh clasped the robe tightly; while her father lost all his sly, cunning look in a rush of fear—for no one rode horses within the city save the guard of the caliph or that protector of the city himself. Her father got swiftly to his feet and hissed at her:

"Get you inside with that and put it upon you; they will think it is some foreign trash discarded by a trader. Best stay in open sight and not try to conceal it lest it show that we believe ourselves at fault!"

She hurried into the single of the lower rooms which was walled and ceilinged and so might be considered a home. There she tore hurriedly out of her own rags, wondering the while if her father had lost his wits—or was pulled into some djinni's plot and did as his master bade him. The robe slid easily across her body and she had just given the last fastening to a breast buckle when her father's voice, raised high, reached her ears.

"Come, my daughter, and show this brave rider what manner of luck I did have this morning—"

She pulled the throat scarf up about her chin, though that would in no way hide better her devil face, and made herself walk out into the wrecked courtyard of the building. There her father stood in company with three of the guard—one of those being the young officer who had so teased her earlier in the day. All three stood silent, facing her as if she were some evil ifrit ready to suck the flesh from their bones.

"Lady—where got you this robe of great beauty?" The captain found his tongue first and she, believing only the truth might save them from whatever vengeance might strike now, dared to say in return:

"Lord, my father brought it and it was torn and of no value to any. See—do you see here the stitches I, myself, set to make it whole again?"

Hurriedly she gathered up a portion of the skirt and held it out—though so perfect had been her repairs that none might see the work and swear an oath that it was indeed secondhand goods, that which was thrown away because it was damaged.

"That is my lady's robe," grated a sour voice from the door as Mirza pushed through the opening to join them. She was panting and red-faced from her effort to join them. "These are thieves whom that misbegotten she-ass of my lady's following got to come to her aid."

Muledowa had fallen to his knees, and now he gathered up a palmful of sand to throw over his dirty headcloth.

"Lord of Many, Commander of Archers, I have made no pact with any—woman or ifrit or djinni. It is my way of life to sift out that which others have thrown away—things which can be resold in the Second Market which our great lord, the caliph himself, has decreed be established for those of lean purses. This I found torn asunder and thrust into the pile of refuse before the Gate of the Nine-Headed Naga at the palace."

Mirza came forward a step or two, thrusting her face close to Muledowa, and spat forth her words as might a cat who finds another within its hunting place. "Find it you did, provider of filth and evil. But first you had notice of the place from Dalikah, who has already tasted of my lady's justice." She turned to the guardsmen. "Take you this fool of a thief and also his ugly daughter to the left wing of the palace where lies the screen through which my peerless lady views the world. Since this crime was committed against her she would have the judging of it."

Thus with a rope around his throat, fastened to the saddle of a guardsman, Muledowa was pulled at a pace hard for his old bones to make. Mirza took off the topmost of her swathing of grimy and too-well-worn shawls which she tugged around Zoradeh, forcing the girl's arms against her body as tightly as if they were bound, and keeping the head veil well over her head.

So they set off across the city, while behind them gathered a crowd of idlers and lesser merchants and craftsmen who were all agog to see and hear what must be the story behind such a sight.

They came into the courtyard that Mirza had described, but to Mirza's discomfort she found there the caliph himself and the wizard Kamar who had come to see the fair white pigeons which were one of the joys of the caliph's heart.

Seeing the caliph and thinking that perhaps one fate might be better than another, for the Lord of Many Towers was reputed to discern truth from lies when spoken before him, the ragpicker jerked on the rope about his neck and fell upon his knees, giving forth that wail with which the honest meet with misfortune. The caliph made a gesture with his hand so that the guards left Muledowa alone.

"Wretched man," he said, "what misfortune or ill wish by an ifrit brought you to this place, and in such a sorry state?"

"Only the lawful enterprise of my business, Great One." Muledowa upon his knees reached forward to touch the pavement before the caliph three times with his dust-covered lips. "I have no evil within me which wishes danger to you or any under this roof. It was this way—" and with one word tumbling over the other in his eagerness he told his story.

"Now that be a marvelous tale," the caliph commented when he was done. "Child"—he beckoned to Zoradeh—"stand forth and let us see this treasure which your father found."

Trembling, and with shaking hands, Zoradeh dropped the shawl from her shoulders and stood in the bright sunlight of the courtyard, her head hanging and her hands knotted together before her.

"Where is this tear over which so much has been made?" asked the caliph.

Timidly she passed her hand over that part which she had so laboriously stitched and rewoven. Then Kamar, who had stood silent all the while, looking first to those gathered in the courtyard and then at the pierced marble screen as if he knew who sheltered behind that, spoke:

"You have a deft needle, girl," he commented. "She who is to wear this will thank you. My lord," he turned to the Caliph then and said: "My lord, as you know this robe was gifted to me by the Fira Flowers. Let her who lightens this city now put it on and I shall pronounce on both robe and the enhanced beauty of she who rightly wears it such a spell as will never more part them."

The Caliph considered for a moment and then answered: "Let it be as you will, Kamar. It seems that by odd chance alone it has been returned to us. You"—he pointed to Mirza—"do you take this maiden behind the screen and let her change garments again—this time with that flower of my house—Jalnar."

The tall lady wearing the shimmering green was not the only one waiting behind the screen. There was also a gaggle of maids reaching into the shadows behind her, and it seemed to Zoradeh that every time one of those moved, if only for so little, there followed a breeze of the finest scent set wandering. She gasped, but Mirza had already dragged the face veil from her and now she waited to see the disgust of the princess and the loathing of her maidens rise. Yet, and she marveled at this, they had gathered around her at a distance and none of them showed the old loathing her djinn-like face had always roused in all she met.

Two of the maids hurried to disrobe the princess while Mirza's dry and leathery hands were busied about her own body. The shimmering robe of moonlike pearls was handled by the old hag, while in turn she took a dull grey slave robe and threw it to Zoradeh, leaving her to fasten it about her as best she could.

But the princess—!

Zoradeh gasped and heard a cry of fright from one of the maids, while another knelt before the princess holding up a mirror of burnished silver so that she might look at herself. The robe covered her skin as tightly as it had Zoradeh, but she had not yet raised the face veil. And—

"Djinn-face—now she bears such—the teeth which are tusks— the skin of old leather," whispered Zoradeh under her breath, glancing quickly about to make sure none had heard her. For if Jalnar was in truth not a djinna, her features were twisted in the same ugliness Zoradeh's had shown all her life long.

The princess screamed and, putting her hands to her face, rubbed hard as if to tear loose a close-fitting mask. At the sound of her cry two armed eunuchs burst in upon them, but seeing the princess they both shivered and drew back, like wise men not daring to question those who have other powers.

But that cry not only brought the eunuchs. For the first time there were visitors to the inner harem which custom and law denied them. The caliph, his curved sword in his hands, was well in the fore of that invasion, but close indeed to his very heels came the guardsmen, one of them still dragging Muledowa on his restraining rope with him. And they halted, too, even as the eunuch guards had done.

For the princess stood a little apart from them all, shaking her misshapen head from side to side and moaning piteously.

"My daughter!" The caliph looked to Kamar, who was the only one who had not drawn a weapon. "Wizard—what has happened to my daughter, who was as the full moon in all its glory and now wears the face of a djinna—even of an ifrit. There is weighty magic here, and to my eyes, it is evil." Without warning he swung his sword at the wizard, but before the blade touched Kamar, it seemed to melt, as if it had passed through some fire, and the blade dripped down to form a hook.

"My Lord." Kamar wore no armament which could be seen, yet he appeared totally unaware of the swords now pointed at him.

Zoradeh thought that surely they would attack him, yet he had no fear at all. "My Lord, this robe was my gift and it has powers of its own. It draws the inner soul into the light." He came a little more forward then and looked to the princess, instead of the men who stood ready to deliver his death.

"What," Kamar asked then as if speaking to all of them, "what does a man wish the most in a bride? Fairness of face sometimes fades quickly, and also it makes its owner proud, vain, and thoughtless of those who serve her. You—" He made a pounce forward and caught at the mirror which the maid had left on the floor. Turning, he held that before Zoradeh and she cried out a plea to save herself from looking at what hung here.

Only she did not see a djinna's twisted face above the grey garment they had given her. Instead—she drew a deep breath of wonder and glanced shyly at the wizard for some answer to this.

"You are also a maid marriageable by age, but none came to seek you out. Is that not so?"

"I was—I had the face of a djinna," she said in a voice hardly above a whisper. "My father is too poor to find me a dowry—thus even a hump-backed beggar did not desire me under his roof. But"—she rubbed her hands down the smooth flesh of her face— "what has happened to me, lord?"

"You have met with truth and it has set you free. Lord of Many Towers," he spoke to the caliph now, "I came hither to have me a wife. I have found the one that fate, which is the great weapon of the All-Compassionate, intended should rule my inner household—"

He held out his hand to Zoradeh, and she, greatly daring, for the first time in her life, allowed her fingers to lie on the rein-callused palm of a man.

"But, my daughter—" The caliph looked at Jalnar.

"In time," answered Kamar, "the Compassionate may bring to her her will and desire, but they must be by her earning and not because she dwelt before her own mirror in admiration for what she sees therein."

Jalnar let out a wail as deep with feeling as that of a newly-made widow, and then, her hands covering her face, she rushed from the room of the screen, her maids following in disorder.

Kamar went now to Muledowa who sat staring as if he did not believe what he had seen. Kamar took a heavy purse from his sash and dropped it before the bound man.

"Let this one go free, Lord of many mercies," he said to the caliph. "For he shall live under my protection from this day forth and what troubles him also troubles me. Now, my lady, we shall go—"

She flung her neck scarf over her head and shoulders, veiling a face which even now she could not believe was hers, and followed Kamar from the room.

It is said among the tellers of tales that they lived long past the lifetimes of others, and that the Divider of Souls and the Archer of the Dark did not come to them in any of the years that those living have tale of. But of Jalnar—ah, there lies another tale.

# MICHAEL SWANWICK

## "The Edge of the World"

*Michael Swanwick's (1950- ) first four novels*—In the Drift, Vacuum Flowers, Griffin's Egg, *and the Nebula Award-winning* Stations of the Tide—*turn the traditional science fiction themes of
alternate history, artificial intelligence, and nuclear holocaust into
grist for thoughtful dramas on the adaptability of individuals and
societies to complicated futures. His most recent novel,* The Iron
Dragon's Daughter, *is a hard fantasy with science fiction overtones
that ranks among the best exercises in contemporary mythmaking.
His short fiction is collected in* Gravity's Angels. *"The Edge of the
World" was nominated for the Hugo and World Fantasy Award
and won the Theodore Sturgeon Memorial Award.*

# The Edge of the World

## by Michael Swanwick

The day that Donna and Piggy and Russ went to see the Edge of the World was a hot one. They were sitting on the curb by the gas station that noontime, sharing a Coke and watching the big Starlifters lumber up into the air, one by one, out of Toldenarba AFB. The sky rumbled with their passing. There'd been an incident in the Persian Gulf, and half the American forces in the Twilight Emirates were on alert.

"My old man says when the Big One goes up, the base will be the first to go," Piggy said speculatively. "Treaties won't allow us to defend it. One bomber comes in high and *whaboom*"—he made soft nuclear explosion noises—"it's all gone." He was wearing camouflage pants and a khaki T-shirt with an iron-on reading: KILL 'EM ALL AND LET GOD SORT 'EM OUT. Donna watched as he took off his glasses to polish them on his shirt. His face went slack and vacant, then livened as he put them back on again, as if he were playing with a mask.

"You should be so lucky," Donna said. "Mrs. Khashoggi is still going to want that paper done on Monday morning, Armageddon or not."

"Yeah, can you believe her?" Piggy said. "That weird accent! And all that memorization! Cut me some slack. I mean, who cares whether Ackronnion was part of the Mezentian Dynasty?"

"You ought to care, dipshit," Russ said. "Local history's the only decent class the school's got." Russ was the smartest boy Donna had ever met, never mind the fact that he was flunking out. He had soulful eyes and a radical haircut, short on the sides with a

295

dyed-blond punklock down the back of his neck. "Man, I opened the *Excerpts from Epics* text that first night, thinking it was going to be the same old bullshit, and I stayed up 'til dawn. Got to school without a wink of sleep, but I'd managed to read every last word. This is one weird part of the world; its history is full of dragons and magic and all kinds of weird monsters. Do you realize that in the eighteenth century three members of the British legation were eaten by demons? That's in the historical record!"

Russ was an enigma to Donna. The first time they'd met, hanging with the misfits at an American School dance, he'd tried to put a hand down her pants, and she'd slugged him good, almost breaking his nose. She could still hear his surprised laughter as blood ran down his chin. They'd been friends ever since. Only there were limits to friendship, and now she was waiting for him to make his move and hoping he'd get down to it before her father was rotated out.

In Japan she'd known a girl who had a taken a razor blade and carved her boyfriend's name in the palm of her hand. How could she do that, Donna had wanted to know? Her friend had shrugged, said, "As long as it gets me noticed." It wasn't until Russ that Donna understood.

"Strange country," Russ said dreamily. "The sky beyond the Edge is supposed to be full of demons and serpents and shit. They say that if you stare into it long enough, you'll go mad."

They all three looked at one another.

"Well, hell," Piggy said. "What are we waiting for?"

The Edge of the World lay beyond the railroad tracks. They bicycled through the American enclave into the old native quarter. The streets were narrow here, the sideyards crammed with broken trucks, rusted-out buses, even yachts up in cradles with staved-in sides. Garage doors were black mouths hissing and spitting welding sparks, throbbing to the hammered sound of worked metal. They hid their bikes in a patch of scrub apricot trees where the railroad crossed the industrial canal and hiked across.

Time had altered the character of the city where it bordered the Edge. Gone were the archers in their towers, vigilant against a threat that never came. Gone were the rose quartz palaces with their thousand windows, not a one of which overlooked the Edge. The battlements where blind musicians once piped up the dawn now survived only in Mrs. Khashoggi's texts. Where they had been was now a drear line of weary factory buildings, their lower windows cinderblocked or bricked up and those beyond reach of vandals' stones painted over in patchwork squares of gray and faded blue.

A steam whistle sounded and lines of factory workers shambled back inside, brown men in chinos and white shirts, Syrian and Lebanese laborers imported to do work no native Toldenarban would touch. A shredded net waved forlornly from a basketball hoop set up by the loading dock.

There was a section of hurricane fence down. They scrambled through.

As they cut across the grounds, a loud whine arose from within the factory building. Down the way another plant lifted its voice in a solid wham-wham-wham as rhythmic and unrelenting as a headache. One by one the factories shook themselves from their midday drowse and went back to work. "Why do they locate these things along the Edge?" Donna asked.

"It's so they can dump their chemical waste over the Edge," Russ explained. "These were all erected before the Emir nationalized the culverts that the Russian Protectorate built."

Behind the factory was a chest-high concrete wall, rough-edged and pebbly with the slow erosion of cement. Weeds grew in clumps at its foot. Beyond was nothing but sky.

Piggy ran ahead and spat over the Edge. "Hey, remember what Nixon said when he came here? *It is indeed a long way down.* What a guy!"

Donna leaned against the wall. A film of haze tinted the sky gray, intensifying at the focal point to dirty brown, as if a dead spot were burned into the center of her vision. When she looked down, her eyes kept grabbing for ground and finding more sky. There were a few wispy clouds in the distance and nothing more. No serpents coiled in the air. She should have felt disappointed but, really, she hadn't expected better. This was of a piece with all the natural wonders she had ever seen, the waterfalls, geysers and scenic vistas that inevitably included power lines, railings and parking lots absent from the postcards. Russ was staring intently ahead, hawklike, frowning. His jaw worked slightly, and she wondered what he saw.

"Hey, look what I found!" Piggy whooped. "It's a stairway!"

They joined him at the top of an institutional-looking concrete and iron stairway. It zigzagged down the cliff toward an infinitely distant and nonexistent Below, dwindling into hazy blue. Quietly, as if he'd impressed himself, Piggy said, "What do you suppose is down there?"

"Only one way to find out, isn't there?" Russ said.

Russ went first, then Piggy, then Donna, the steps ringing dully under their feet. Graffiti covered the rocks, worn spraypaint letters in yellow and black and red scrawled one over the other and faded by time and weather into mutual unreadability, and on the iron railings, words and arrows and triangles had been markered onto or dug into the paint with knife or nail: JURGEN BIN SCHEIS-SKOPF. MOTLEY CRUE. DEATH TO SATAN AMERICA IMPERIALIST. Seventeen steps down, the first landing was filthy with broken brown glass, bits of crumbled concrete, cigarette butts, soggy, half-melted cardboard. The stairway folded back on itself and they followed it down.

"You ever had *fugu*?" Piggy asked. Without waiting for an answer, he said, "It's Japanese poisonous blowfish. It has to be prepared very carefully—they license the chefs—and even so, several people die every year. It's considered a great delicacy."

"Nothing tastes that good," Russ said.

"It's not the flavor," Piggy said enthusiastically. "It's the poison. Properly prepared, see, there's a very small amount left in the sashimi and you get a threshold dose. Your lips and the tips of your fingers turn cold. Numb. That's how you know you're having the real thing. That's how you know you're living right on the edge."

"I'm already living on the edge," Russ said. He looked startled when Piggy laughed.

A fat moon floated in the sky, pale as a disk of ice melting in blue water. It bounced after them as they descended, kicking aside loose soda bottles in styrofoam sleeves, crushed Marlboro boxes, a scattering of carbonized spark plugs. On one landing they found a crumpled shopping cart, and Piggy had to muscle it over the railing and watch it fall. "Sure is a lot of crap here," he observed. The landing smelled faintly of urine.

"It'll get better farther down," Russ said. "We're still near the top, where people can come to get drunk after work." He pushed on down. Far to one side they could see the brown flow from the industrial canal where it spilled into space, widening and then slowly dispersing into rainbowed mist, distance glamoring its beauty.

"How far are we planning to go?" Donna asked apprehensively.
"Don't be a weak sister," Piggy sneered. Russ said nothing.

The deeper they went, the shabbier the stairway grew, and the spottier its maintenance. Pipes were missing from the railing. Where patches of paint had fallen away the bolts anchoring the stair to the rock were walnut-sized lumps of rust.

Needle-clawed marsupials chittered warningly from niches in the rock as they passed. Tufts of grass and moth-white gentians grew in the loess-filled cracks.

Hours passed. Donna's feet and calves and the small of her back grew increasingly sore, but she refused to be the one to complain. By degrees she stopped looking over the side and out into the sky, and stared instead at her feet flashing in and out of sight while one hand went slap-grab-tug on the rail. She felt sweaty and miserable.

Back home she had a half-finished paper on the Three Days Incident of March, 1810, when the French Occupation, by order of Napoleon himself, had fired cannonade after cannonade over the Edge into nothingness. They had hoped to make rainstorms of devastating force that would lash and destroy their enemies, and created instead only a gunpowder haze, history's first great failure in weather control. This descent was equally futile, Donna thought, an endless and wearying exercise in nothing. Just the same as the rest of her life. Every time her father was reposted, she had resolved to change, to be somebody different this time around, whatever the price, even if—no, especially if—it meant playacting something she was not. Last year in Germany when she'd gone out with that local boy with the Alfa Romeo and instead of jerking him off had used her mouth, she had thought: Everything's going to be different now. But no.

Nothing ever changed.

"Heads up!" Russ said. "There's some steps missing here!" He leaped, and the landing gonged hollowly under his sneakers. Then again as Piggy jumped after.

Donna hesitated. There were five steps gone and a drop of twenty feet before the stairway cut back beneath itself. The cliff bulged outward here, and if she slipped she'd probably miss the stairs altogether.

She felt the rock draw away from her to either side, and was suddenly aware that she was connected to the world by the merest speck of matter, barely enough to anchor her feet. The sky wrapped itself about her, extending to infinity, depthless and absolute. She could extend her arms and fall into it forever. What would happen to her then, she wondered. Would she die of thirst and starvation, or would the speed of her fall grow so great that the oxygen would be sucked from her lungs, leaving her to strangle in a sea of air? "Come on Donna!" Piggy shouted up at her. "Don't be a pussy!"

"Russ—" she said quaveringly.

But Russ wasn't looking her way. He was frowning downward, anxious to be going. "Don't push the lady," he said. "We can go on by ourselves."

Donna choked with anger and hurt and desperation all at once. She took a deep breath and, heart scudding, leaped. Sky and rock wheeled over her head. For an instant she was floating, falling, totally lost and filled with a panicky awareness that she was about to die. Then she crashed onto the landing. It hurt like hell, and at first she feared she'd pulled an ankle. Piggy grabbed her shoulders and rubbed the side of her head with his knuckles. "I knew you could do it, you wimp."

Donna knocked away his arm. "Okay, wise-ass. How are you expecting to get us back up?"

The smile disappeared from Piggy's face. His mouth opened, closed. His head jerked fearfully upward. An acrobat could leap across, grab the step and flip up without any trouble at all. "I—I mean, I—"

"Don't worry about it," Russ said impatiently. "We'll think of something." He started down again.

It wasn't natural, Donna realized, his attitude. There was something obsessive about his desire to descend the stairway. It was like the time he'd brought his father's revolver to school along with a story about playing Russian roulette that morning before breakfast. "Three times!" he'd said proudly.

He'd had that same crazy look on him, and she hadn't the slightest notion then or now how she could help him.

Russ walked like an automaton, wordlessly, tirelessly, never hurrying up or slowing down. Donna followed in concerned silence, while Piggy scurried between them, chattering like somebody's pet Pekingese. This struck Donna as so apt as to be almost allegorical: the two of them together yet alone, the distance between filled with noise. She thought of this distance, this silence, as the sun passed behind the cliff and the afternoon heat lost its edge.

The stairs changed to cement-jacketed brick with small buttresses cut into the rock. There was a pile of stems and cherry pits on one landing, and the railing above them was white with bird droppings. Piggy leaned over the rail and said, "Hey, I can see seagulls down there. Flying around."

"Where?" Russ leaned over the railing, then said scornfully, "Those are pigeons. The Ghazoddis used to release them for rifle practice."

As Piggy turned to follow Russ down again, Donna caught a glimpse into his eyes, liquid and trembling with helplessness and despair. She'd seen that fear in him only once before, months ago when she'd stopped by his house on the way to school, just after the Emir's assassination.

The living room windows were draped and the room seemed unnaturally gloomy after being out in the morning sun. Blue television light flickered over shelves of shadowy ceramic figurines: Dresden milkmaids, Chantilly Chinamen, Meissen pug-dogs connected by a gold chain held in their champed jaws, naked Delft nymphs dancing.

Piggy's mother sat in a limp dressing gown, hair unbrushed, watching the funeral. She held a cup of oily-looking coffee in one hand. Donna was surprised to see her up so early. Everyone said that she had a bad problem with alcohol, that even by service wife standards she was out of control.

"Look at them," Piggy's mother said. On the screen were solemn processions of camels and Cadillacs, sheikhs in jellaba, keffigeh and mirrorshades, European dignitaries with wives in tasteful gray Parisian fashions. "They've got their nerve."

"Where did you put my lunch?" Piggy said loudly from the kitchen.

"Making fun of the Kennedys like that!" The Emir's youngest son, no more than four years old, salaamed his father's casket as it passed before him. "That kid's bad enough, but you should see the mother, crying as if her heart were broken. It's enough to turn your stomach. If I were Jackie, I'd—"

Donna and Piggy and Russ had gone bowling the night the Emir was shot. This was out in the ruck of cheap joints that surrounded the base, catering almost exclusively to servicemen. When the

Muzak piped through overhead speakers was interrupted for the news bulletin, everyone had stood up and cheered. *Up we go*, someone had begun singing, and the rest had joined in, *into the wild blue yonder*. . . . Donna had felt so sick with fear and disgust she had thrown up in the parking lot. "I don't think they're making fun of anyone," Donna said. "They're just—"

"Don't talk to her!" The refrigerator door slammed shut. A cupboard door slammed open.

Piggy's mother smiled bitterly. "This is exactly what you'd expect from these ragheads. Pretending they're white people, deliberately mocking their betters. Filthy brown animals."

"*Mother*! Where is my fucking lunch?"

She looked at him then, jaw tightening. "Don't you use that kind of language on me, young man."

"All right!" Piggy shouted. "All right, I'm going to school without lunch! Shows how much you care!"

He turned to Donna and in the instant before he grabbed her wrist and dragged her out of the house, Donna could no longer hear the words, could only see that universe of baffled futility haunting Piggy's eyes. That same look she glimpsed today.

The railings were wooden now, half the posts rotting at their bases, with an occasional plank missing, wrenched off and thrown over the side by previous visitors. Donna's knees buckled and she stumbled, almost lurching into the rock. "I have to stop," she said, hating herself for it. "I cannot go one more step."

Piggy immediately collapsed on the landing. Russ hesitated, then climbed up to join them. They three sat staring out into nothing, legs over the Edge, arms clutching the rail.

Piggy found a Pepsi can, logo in flowing Arabic, among the rubble. He held it in his left hand and began sticking holes in it with his butterfly knife, again and again, cackling like a demented sex criminal. "Exterminate the brutes!" he said happily. Then, with absolutely no transition he asked, "How are we ever going to get back up?" so dolorously Donna had to bite back her laughter.

"Look, I just want to go on down a little bit more," Russ said.

"Why?" Piggy sounded petulant.

"So I can get down enough to get away from this garbage." He gestured at the cigarette butts, the broken brown glass, sparser than above but still there. "Just a little further, okay guys?" There was an edge to his voice, and under that the faintest hint of a plea.

Donna felt helpless before those eyes. She wished they were alone, so she could ask him what was wrong.

Donna doubted that Russ himself knew what he expected to find down below. Did he think that if he went down far enough, he'd never have to climb back? She remembered the time in Mr. Herriman's algebra class when a sudden tension in the air had made her glance across the room at Russ, and he was, with great concentration, tearing the pages out of his math text and dropping them one by one on the floor. He'd taken a five-day suspension for that, and Donna had never found out what it was all about. But there was a kind of glorious arrogance to the act; Russ had been born out of time. He really should have been a medieval prince, a Medici or one of the Sabakan pretenders.

"Okay," Donna said, and Piggy of course had to go along.

Seven flights farther down the modern stairs came to an end. The wooden railing of the last short, septambic flight had been torn off entire, and laid across the steps. They had to step carefully between the uprights and the rails. But when they stood at the absolute bottom, they saw that there were stairs beyond the final landing, steps that had been cut into the stone itself. They were curving swaybacked things that millennia of rain and foot traffic had worn so uneven they were almost unpassable.

Piggy groaned. "Man, you *can't* expect us to go down that thing."

"Nobody's asking you," Russ said.

They descended the old stairway backwards and on all fours. The wind breezed up, hitting them with the force of an expected shove first to one side and then the other. There were times when Donna was so frightened she thought she was going to freeze up and never move again. But at last the stone broadened and became a wide, even ledge, with caves leading back into the rock.

The cliff face here was green-white with lichen, and had in ancient times been laboriously smoothed and carved. Between each cave (their mouths alone left in a natural state, unaltered) were heavy-thighed women—goddesses, perhaps, or demons or sacred dancers—their breasts and faces chipped away by the image-hating followers of the Prophet at a time when Mohammed yet lived. Their hands held loops of vines in which were entangled moons, cycling from new through waxing quarter and gibbous to full and then back through gibbous and waning quarter to dark. Piggy was gasping, his face bright with sweat, but he kept up his blustery front. "What the fuck is all this shit, man?"

"It was a monastery," Russ said. He walked along the ledge dazedly, a wondering half smile on his lips. "I read about this." He stopped at a turquoise automobile door someone had flung over the Edge to be caught and tossed by fluke winds, the only piece of trash that had made it down this far. "Give me a hand."

He and Piggy lifted the door, swung it back and forth three times to build up momentum, then lofted it over the lip of the rock. They all three lay down on their stomachs to watch it fall away, turning end over end and seeming finally to flicker as it dwindled smaller and smaller, still falling. At last it shrank below the threshold of visibility and became one of a number of shifting motes in the downbelow, part of the slow, mazy movement of dead blood cells in the eyes' vitreous humors. Donna turned over on her back, drew her head back from the rim, stared upward. The cliff seemed to be slowly tumbling forward, all the world inexorably, dizzyingly leaning down to crush her.

"Let's go explore the caves," Piggy suggested.

They were empty. The interiors of the caves extended no more than thirty feet into the rock, but they had all been elaborately worked, arched ceilings carved with thousands of *faux tesserae*, walls adorned with bas-relief pillars. Between the pillars the walls were taken up with long shelves carved into the stone. No artifacts remained, not so much as a potsherd or a splinter of bone. Piggy shone his pocket flash into every shadowy niche. "Somebody's been here before us and taken everything," he said.

"The Historic Registry people, probably." Russ ran a hand over one shelf. It was the perfect depth and height for a line of three-pound coffee cans. "This is where they stowed the skulls. When a monk grew so spiritually developed he no longer needed the crutch of physical existence, his fellows would render the flesh from his bones and enshrine his skull. They poured wax in the sockets, then pushed in opals while it was still warm. They slept beneath the faintly gleaming eyes of their superiors."

When they emerged it was twilight, the first stars appearing from behind a sky fading from blue to purple. Donna looked down on the moon. It was as big as a plate, full and bright. The rilles, dry seas, and mountain chains were preternaturally distinct. Somewhere in the middle was Tranquility Base, where Neil Armstrong had planted the American flag.

"Jeez, it's late," Donna said. "If we don't start home soon, my mom is going to have a cow."

"We still haven't figured a way to get back up," Piggy reminded her. Then, "We'll probably have to stay here. Learn to eat owls and grow crops sideways on the cliff face. Start our own civilization. Our only serious problem is the imbalance of sexes, but even that's not insurmountable." He put an arm around Donna's shoulders, grabbed at her breast. "You'd pull the train for us, wouldn't you, Donna?"

Angrily she pushed him away and said, "You keep a clean mouth! I'm so tired of your juvenile talk and behavior."

"Hey, calm down, it's cool." That panicky look was back in his eyes, the forced knowledge that he was not in control, could never be in control, that there was no such thing as control. He smiled weakly, placatingly.

"No, it is not. It is most emphatically not 'cool.'" Suddenly she was white and shaking with fury. Piggy was a spoiler. His simple presence ruined any chance she might have had to talk with Russ, find out just what was bugging him, get him to finally, really notice her. "I am sick of having to deal with your immaturity, your filthy language, and your crude behavior."

Piggy turned pink and began stuttering.

Russ reached a hand into his pocket, pulled out a chunk of foil-wrapped hash, and a native tin pipe with a carved coral bowl. The kind of thing the local beggar kids sold for twenty-nine cents. "Anybody want to get stoned?" he asked suavely.

"You bastard!" Piggy laughed. "You told me you were out!"

Russ shrugged. "I lied." He lit the pipe carefully, drew in, passed it to Donna. She took it from his fingers, felt how cold they were to her touch, looked up over the pipe and saw his face, thin and ascetic, eyelids closed, pale and Christlike through the blue smoke. She loved him intensely in that instant and wished she could sacrifice herself for his happiness. The pipe's stem was overwarm, almost hot, between her lips. She drew in deep.

The smoke was raspy in her throat, then tight and swirling in her lungs. It shot up into her head, filled it with buzzing harmonics: the air, the sky, the rock behind her back all buzzing, ballooning her skull outward in a visionary rush that forced wide-open first her eyes and then her mouth. She choked and spasmodically coughed. More smoke than she could imagine possibly holding in her lungs gushed out into the universe.

"Hey, watch that pipe!" Piggy snatched it from her distant fingers. They tingled with pinpricks of pain like tiny stars in the darkness of her flesh. "You were spilling the hash!" The evening light was abuzz with energy, the sky swarming up into her eyes. Staring out into the darkening air, the moon rising below her and the stars as close and friendly as those in a children's book illustration, she felt at peace, detached from worldly cares. "Tell us about the monastery, Russ," she said, in the same voice she might have used a decade before to ask her father for a story.

"Yeah, tell us about the monastery, Uncle Russ," Piggy said, but with jeering undertones. Piggy was always sucking up to Russ, but there was tension there too, and his sarcastic little challenges were far from rare. It was classic beta male jealousy, straight out of Primate Psychology 101.

"It's very old," Russ said. "Before the Sufis, before Mohammed, even before the Zoroastrians crossed the gulf, the native mystics would renounce the world and go to live in cliffs on the Edge of the World. They cut the steps down, and once down, they never went back up again."

"How did they eat then?" Piggy asked skeptically.

"They wished their food into existence. No, really! It was all in their creation myth: In the beginning all was Chaos and Desire. The world was brought out of Chaos—by which they meant unformed matter—by Desire, or Will. It gets a little inconsistent after that, because it wasn't really a religion, but more like a system of magic. They believed that the world wasn't complete yet, that for some complicated reason it could never be complete. So there's still traces of the old Chaos lingering just beyond the Edge, and it can be tapped by those who desire it strongly enough, if they have distanced themselves from the things of the world. These mystics used to come down here to meditate against the moon and work miracles.

"This wasn't sophisticated stuff like the Tantric monks in Tibet or anything, remember. It was like a primitive form of animism, a way to force the universe to give you what you wanted. So the holy men would come down here and they'd wish for . . . like riches, you know? Filigreed silver goblets with rubies, mounds of moonstones, elfinbone daggers sharper than Damascene steel. Only once they got them they weren't supposed to want them. They'd just throw them over the Edge. There were those monasteries all along the cliffs. The farther from the world they were, the more spiritually advanced."

"So what happened to the monks?"

"There was a king—Althazar? I forget his name. He was this real greedhead, started sending his tax collectors down to gather up everything the monks brought into existence. Must've figured, hey, the monks weren't using them. Which as it turned out was like a real major blasphemy, and the monks got pissed. The boss mystics, all the real spiritual heavies, got together for this big confab. Nobody knows how. There's one of the classics claims they could run sideways on the cliff just like it was the ground, but I don't know. Doesn't matter. So one night they all of them, every monk in the world, meditated at the same time. They chanted together, saying, it is not enough that Althazar should die, for he has blasphemed. He must suffer a doom such as has been visited on no man before. He must be unmade, uncreated, reduced to less than has ever been. And they prayed that there be no such king as Althazar, that his life and history be unmade, so that there never had been such king as Althazar.

"And he was no more.

"But so great was their yearning for oblivion that when Althazar ceased to be, his history and family as well, they were left feeling embittered and did not know why. And not knowing why, their hatred turned upon themselves, and their wish for destruction, and they too all of a single night, ceased to be." He fell silent.

At last Piggy said, "You believe that crap?" Then, when there was no answer, "It's none of it true, man! Got that? There's no magic, and there never was." Donna could see that he was really angry, threatened on some primal level by the possibility that someone he respected could even begin to believe in magic. His face got pink, the way it always did when he lost control.

"No, it's all bullshit," Russ said bitterly. "Like everything else."

They passed the pipe around again. Then Donna leaned back, stared straight out, and said, "If I could wish for anything, you know what I'd wish for?"

"Bigger tits?"

She was so weary now, so pleasantly washed out, that it was easy to ignore Piggy. "I'd wish I knew what the situation was."

"What situation?" Piggy asked. Donna was feeling langorous, not at all eager to explain herself, and she waved away the question. But he persisted. "What situation?"

"Any situation. I mean, all the time, I find myself talking with people and I don't know what's really going on. What games they're playing. Why they're acting the way they are. I wish I knew what the situation was."

The moon floated before her, big and fat and round as a griffin's egg, shining with power. She could feel that power washing through her, the background radiation of decayed chaos spread across the sky at a uniform three degrees Kelvin. Even now, spent and respent, a coin fingered and thinned to the worn edge of nonexistence, there was power out there, enough to flatten planets.

Staring out at that great fat boojum snark of a moon, she felt the flow of potential worlds, and within the cold silver disk of that jester's skull, rank with magic, sensed the invisible presence of Russ's primitive monks, men whose minds were nowhere near comprehensible to her, yet vibrated with power, existing as matrices of patterned stress, no more actual than Donald Duck, but no less powerful either. She was caught in a waking fantasy, in which the sky was full of power and all of it accessible to her. Monks sat empty-handed over their wishing bowls, separated from her by the least fictions of time and reality. For an eternal instant all possibilities fanned out to either side, equally valid, no one more real than any other. Then the world turned under her, and her brain shifted back to realtime.

"Me," Piggy said, "I just wish I knew how to get back up the stairs."

They were silent for a moment. Then it occurred to Donna that here was the perfect opportunity to find out what was bugging Russ. If she asked cautiously enough, if the question hit him just right, if she were just plain lucky, he might tell her everything. She cleared her throat. "Russ? What do you wish?"

In the bleakest voice imaginable, Russ said, "I wish I'd never been born."

She turned to ask him why, and he wasn't there.

"Hey," Donna said. "Where'd Russ go?"

Piggy looked at her oddly. "Who's Russ?"

It was a long trip back up. They carried the length of wooden railing between them, and every now and then Piggy said, "Hey, wasn't this a great idea of mine? This'll make a swell ladder."

"Yeah, great," Donna would say, because he got mad when she

didn't respond. He got mad, too, whenever she started to cry, but there wasn't anything she could do about that. She couldn't even explain why she was crying, because in all the world—of all his friends, acquaintances, teachers, even his parents—she was the only one who remembered that Russ had ever existed.

The horrible thing was that she had no specific memories of him, only a vague feeling of what his presence had been like, and a lingering sense of longing and frustration.

She no longer even remembered his face.

"Do you want to go first or last?" Piggy had asked her.

When she'd replied, "Last. If I go first, you'll stare at my ass all the way up," he'd actually blushed. Without Russ to show off in front of, Piggy was a completely different person, quiet and not at all abusive. He even kept his language clean. But that didn't help, for just being in his presence was enough to force understanding on her: that his bravado was fueled by his insecurities and aspirations, that he masturbated nightly and with self-loathing, that he despised his parents and longed in vain for the least sign of love from them. That the way he treated her was the sum and total of all of this and more.

She knew exactly what the situation was.

Dear God, she prayed, let it be that I won't have this kind of understanding when I reach the top. Or else make it so that situations won't be so painful up there, that knowledge won't hurt like this, that horrible secrets won't lie under the most innocent word.

They carried their wooden burden upward, back toward the world.

# ORSON SCOTT CARD

## "Lost Boys"

*Orson Scott Card (1951- ) won the John W. Campbell Award for best new science fiction writer in 1978 and made science fiction history when his novel* Ender's Game *(based on his first published story) and its sequel* Speaker for the Dead *each won the Hugo and Nebula Awards, respectively, in 1985 and 1986. He has since extended the Ender series into a trilogy with* Xenocide. *A prolific writer who works in a variety of genres, he is the author of the fantasy novel* Hart's Hope, *the historical tale* A Woman of Destiny, *and the multi-volume Worthing Chronicle sequence, which splices fantasy elements into a science fiction scenario. His epic Tales of Alvin Maker saga, which includes* Seventh Son, Red Prophet, *and* Prentice Alvin, *is set in an alternative American past in which magic works. "Lost Boys," a nominee for both the Hugo and Nebula Awards, is an unusual foray into dark fantasy that Card later expanded into a novel of the same name. Much of his short fiction has been gathered into the omnibus* Maps in a Mirror: The Short Fiction of Orson Scott Card.

# Lost Boys

*by Orson Scott Card*

I've worried for a long time about whether to tell this story as fiction or fact. Telling it with made-up names would make it easier for some people to take. Easier for me, too. But to hide my own lost boy behind some phony made-up name would be like erasing him. So I'll tell it the way it happened, and to hell with whether it's easy for either of us.

Kristine and the kids and I moved to Greensboro on the first of March, 1983. I was happy enough about my job—I just wasn't sure I wanted a job at all. But the recession had the publishers all panicky, and nobody was coming up with advances large enough for me to take a decent amount of time writing a novel. I suppose I could whip out 75,000 words of junk fiction every month and publish them under a half dozen pseudonyms, or something, but it seemed to Kristine and me that we'd do better in the long run if I got a job to ride out the recession. Besides, my Ph.D. was down the toilet. I'd been doing good work at Notre Dame, but when I had to take out a few weeks in the middle of a semester to finish *Hart's Hope*, the English Department was about as understanding as you'd expect from people who prefer their authors dead or domesticated. Can't feed your family? So sorry. You're a writer? Ah, but not one that anyone's written a scholarly essay about. So long, boy-oh!

So sure, I was excited about my job, but moving to Greensboro also meant that I had failed. I had no way of knowing that my career as a fiction writer wasn't over. Maybe I'd be editing and writing books about computers for the rest of my life. Maybe fiction was just a phase I had to go through before I got a *real* job.

Greensboro was a beautiful town, especially to a family from the western desert. So many trees that even in winter you could hardly tell there was a town at all. Kristine and I fell in love with it at once. There were local problems, of course—people bragged about Greensboro's crime rate and talked about racial tension and what-not—but we'd just come from a depressed northern industrial town with race riots in the high schools, so to us this was Eden. There was rumors that several child disappearances were linked to some serial kidnapper, but this was the era when they started putting pictures of missing children on milk cartons—those stories were in every town.

It was hard to find decent housing for a price we could afford. I had to borrow from the company against my future earnings just to make the move. We ended up in the ugliest house on Chinqua Drive. You know the house—the one with cheap wood siding in a neighborhood of brick, the one-level rambler surrounded by split-levels and two-stories. Old enough to be shabby, not old enough to be quaint. But it had a big fenced yard and enough bedrooms for all the kids and for my office, too—because we hadn't given up on my writing career, not yet, not completely.

The little kids—Geoffrey and Emily—thought the whole thing was really exciting, but Scotty, the oldest, he had a little trouble with it. He'd already had kindergarten and half of first grade at a really wonderful private school down the block from our house in South Bend. Now he was starting over in mid-year, losing all his friends. He had to ride a school bus with strangers. He resented the move from the start, and it didn't get better.

Of course, *I* wasn't the one who saw this. *I* was at work—and I very quickly learned that success at Compute! Books meant giving up a few little things like seeing your children. I had expected to edit books written by people who couldn't write. What astonished me was that I was editing books about computers written by people who couldn't *program*. Not all of them, of course, but enough that I spent far more time rewriting programs so they made sense—so they even *ran*—than I did fixing up people's language. I'd get to work at 8:30 or 9:00, then work straight through till 9:30 or 10:30 at night. My meals were Three Musketeers bars and potato chips from the machine in the employee lounge. My exercise was typing. I met deadlines, but I was putting on a pound a week and my muscles were all atrophying and I saw my kids only in the mornings as I left for work.

Except Scotty. Because he left on the school bus at 6:45 and I rarely dragged out of bed until 7:30, during the week I never saw Scotty at all.

The whole burden of the family had fallen on Kristine. During my years as a freelancer from 1978 to 1983, we'd got used to a certain pattern of life, based on the fact that Daddy was *home*. She could duck out and run some errands, leaving the kids, because I was home. If one of the kids was having discipline problems, I was there. Now if she had her hands full and needed something from the store; if the toilet clogged; if the xerox jammed, then she had to take care of it herself, somehow. She learned the joys of shopping with a cartful of kids. Add to this the fact that she was pregnant and sick half of the time, and you can understand why sometimes I couldn't tell whether she was ready for sainthood or the funny farm.

The finer points of child-rearing just weren't within our reach at that time. She knew that Scotty wasn't adapting well at school, but what could she do? What could I do?

Scotty had never been the talker Geoffrey was—he spent a lot of time just keeping to himself. Now, though, it was getting extreme. He would answer in monosyllables, or not at all. Sullen. As if he were angry, and yet if he was, he didn't know it or wouldn't admit it. He'd get home, scribble out his homework (did they give homework when *I* was in first grade?), and then just mope around.

If he had done reading, or even watched TV, then we wouldn't have worried so much. His little brother Geoffrey was already a compulsive reader at age five, and Scotty used to be. But now Scotty'd pick up a book and set it down again without reading it. He didn't even follow his mom around the house or anything. She'd see him sitting in the family room, go in and change the sheets on the beds, put away a load of clean clothes, and then come back in and find him sitting in the same place, his eyes open, staring at *nothing*.

I tried talking to him. Just the conversation you'd expect:

"Scotty, we know you didn't want to move. We had no choice."

"Sure. That's O.K."

"You'll make new friends in due time."

"I know."

"Aren't you ever happy here?"

"I'm O.K."

Yeah, right.

But we didn't have *time* to fix things up, don't you see? Maybe if we'd imagined this was the last year of Scotty's life, we'd have done more to right things, even if it meant losing the job. But you never know that sort of thing. You always find out when it's too late to change anything.

And when the school year ended, things *did* get better for a while.

For one thing, I saw Scotty in the mornings. For another thing, he didn't have to go to school with a bunch of kids who were either rotten to him or ignored him. And he didn't mope around the house all the time. Now he moped around outside.

At first Kristine thought he was playing with our other kids, the way he used to before school divided them. But gradually she began to realize that Geoffrey and Emily always played together, and Scotty almost never played with them. She'd see the younger kids with their squirtguns or running through the sprinklers or chasing the wild rabbit who lived in the neighborhood, but Scotty was never with them. Instead, he'd be poking a twig into the tent-fly webs on the trees, or digging around at the open skirting around the bottom of the house that kept animals out of the crawl space. Once or twice a week he'd come in so dirty that Kristine had to heave him into the tub, but it didn't reassure her that Scotty was acting normally.

On July 28th, Kristine went to the hospital and gave birth to our fourth child. Charlie Ben was born having a seizure, and stayed in intensive care for the first weeks of his life as the doctors probed and poked and finally figured out that they didn't know what was wrong. It was several months later that somebody uttered the words "cerebral palsy," but our lives had already been transformed by then. Our whole focus was on the child in the greatest need—that's what you *do*, or so we thought. But how do you measure a child's need? How do you compare those needs and decide who deserves the most?

When we finally came up for air, we discovered that Scotty had made some friends. Kristine would be nursing Charlie Ben, and Scotty'd come in from outside and talk about how he'd been playing army with Nicky or how he and the guys had played pirate. At first she thought they were neighborhood kids, but then one day when he talked about building a fort in the grass (I didn't get many chances to mow), she happened to remember that she'd seen him building that fort all by himself. Then she got suspicious and started asking questions. Nicky who? I don't know, Mom. Just Nicky. Where does he live? Around. I don't know. Under the house.

In other words, imaginary friends.

How long had he known them? Nicky was the first, but now there were eight names—Nicky, Van, Roddy, Peter, Steve, Howard, Rusty, and David. Kristine and I had never heard of anybody having more than one imaginary friend.

"The kid's going to be more successful as a writer than I am," I said. "Coming up with eight fantasies in the same series."

Kristine didn't think it was funny. "He's so *lonely*, Scott," she said. "I'm worried that he might go over the edge."

It *was* scary. But if he was going crazy, what then? We even tried taking him to a clinic, though I had no faith at all in psychologists. Their fictional explanations of human behavior seemed pretty lame, and their cure rate was a joke—a plumber or barber who performed at the same level as a psychotherapist would be out of business in a month. I took time off work to drive Scotty to the clinic every week during August, but Scotty didn't like it and the therapist told us nothing more than what we already knew—that Scotty was lonely and morose and a little bit resentful and a little bit afraid. The only difference was that she had fancier names for it. We were getting a vocabulary lesson when we needed help. The only thing that seemed to be helping was the therapy we came up with ourselves that summer. So we didn't make another appointment.

Our homegrown therapy consisted of keeping him from going outside. It happened that our landlord's father, who had lived in our house right before us, was painting the house that week, so that gave us an excuse. And I brought home a bunch of videogames, ostensibly to review them for *Compute!*, but primarily to try to get Scotty involved in something that would turn his imagination away from these imaginary friends.

It worked. Sort of. He didn't complain about not going outside (but then, he never complained about anything), and he played the videogames for hours a day. Kristine wasn't sure she loved *that*, but it was an improvement—or so we thought.

Once again, we were distracted and didn't pay much attention to Scotty for a while. We were having insect problems. One night Kristine's screaming woke me up. Now, you've got to realize that when Kristine screams, that means everything's pretty much O.K.

When something really terrible is going on, she gets cool and quiet and *handles* it. But when it's a little spider or a huge moth or a stain on a blouse, then she screams. I expected her to come back into the bedroom and tell me about this monstrous insect she had to hammer to death in the bathroom.

Only this time, she didn't stop screaming. So I got up to see what was going on. She heard me coming—I was up to 230 pounds by now, so I sounded like Custer's whole cavalry—and she called out, "Put your shoes on first!"

I turned on the light in the hall. It was hopping with crickets. I went back into my room and put on my shoes.

After enough crickets have bounced off your naked legs and squirmed around in your hands you stop wanting to puke—you just scoop them up and stuff them into a garbage bag. Later you can scrub yourself for six hours before you feel clean and have nightmares about little legs tickling you. But at the time your mind goes numb and you just do the job.

The infestation was coming out of the closet in the boys' room, where Scotty had the top bunk and Geoffrey slept on the bottom. There were a couple of crickets in Geoff's bed, but he didn't wake up even as we changed his top sheet and shook out his blanket. Nobody but us even saw the crickets. We found the crack in the back of the closet, sprayed Black Flag into it, and then stuffed it with an old sheet we were using for rags.

Then we showered, making jokes about how we could have used some seagulls to eat up our invasion of crickets, like the Mormon pioneers got in Salt Lake. Then we went back to sleep.

It wasn't just crickets, though. That morning in the kitchen Kristine called me again: There were dead June bugs about three inches deep in the window over the sink, all down at the bottom of the space between the regular glass and the storm window. I opened the window to vacuum them out, and the bug corpses spilled all over the kitchen counter. Each bug made a nasty little rattling sound as it went down the tube toward the vacuum filter.

The next day the window was three inches deep again, and the day after. Then it tapered off. Hot fun in the summertime.

We called the landlord to ask whether he'd help us pay for an exterminator. His answer was to send his father over with bug spray, which he pumped into the crawl space under the house with such gusto that we had to flee the house and drive around all that Saturday until a late afternoon thunderstorm blew away the stench and drowned it enough that we could stand to come back.

Anyway, what with that and Charlie's continuing problems, Kristine didn't notice what was happening with the videogames at all. It was on a Sunday afternoon that I happened to be in the kitchen, drinking a Diet coke, and heard Scotty laughing out loud in the family room.

That was such a rare sound in our house that I went and stood in the door to the family room, watching him play. It was a great little videogame with terrific animation: Children in a sailing ship, battling pirates who kept trying to board, and shooting down giant birds that tried to nibble away the sail. It didn't look as mechanical as the usual videogame, and one feature I really liked was the fact that the player wasn't alone—there were other computer-controlled children helping the player's figure to defeat the enemy.

"Come on, Sandy!" Scotty said. "Come on!" Whereupon one of the children on the screen stabbed the pirate leader through the heart, and the pirates fled.

I couldn't wait to see what scenario this game would move to then, but at that point Kristine called me to come and help her with Charlie. When I got back, Scotty was gone, and Geoffrey and Emily had a different game in the Atari.

Maybe it was that day, maybe later, that I asked Scotty what was the name of that game about children on a pirate ship. "It was just a game, Dad," he said.

"It's got to have a name."

"I don't know."

"How do you find the disk to put it in the machine?"

"I don't know." And he sat there staring past me and I gave up.

Summer ended. Scotty went back to school. Geoffrey started kindergarten, so they rode the bus together. More important, things settled down with the newborn, Charlie—there wasn't a cure for cerebral palsy, but at least we knew the bounds of his condition. He wouldn't get *worse*, for instance. He also wouldn't get well. Maybe he'd talk and walk someday, and maybe he wouldn't. Our job was just to stimulate him enough that if it turned out he wasn't retarded, his mind would develop even though his body was so drastically limited. It was doable. The fear was gone, and we could breathe again.

Then, in mid-October, my agent called to tell me that she'd pitched my Alvin Maker series to Tom Doherty at TOR Books, and

Tom was offering enough of an advance that we could live. That plus the new contract for *Ender's Game*, and I realized that for us, at least, the recession was over. For a couple of weeks I stayed on at Compute! Books, primarily because I had so many projects going that I couldn't just leave them in the lurch. But then I looked at what the job was doing to my family and to my body, and I realized the price was too high. I gave two weeks' notice, figuring to wrap up the projects that only I knew about. In true paranoid fashion, they refused to accept the two weeks—they had me clean my desk out that afternoon. It left a bitter taste, to have them act so churlishly, but what the heck. I was free. I was home.

You could almost feel the relief. Geoffrey and Emily went right back to normal; I actually got acquainted with Charlie Ben; Christmas was coming (I start playing Christmas music when the leaves turn) and all was right with the world. Except Scotty. Always except Scotty.

It was then that I discovered a few things that I simply hadn't known. Scotty never played any of the videogames I'd brought home from *Compute!* I knew that because when I gave the games back, Geoff and Em complained bitterly—but Scotty didn't even know what the missing games *were*. Most important, that game about kids in a pirate ship wasn't there. Not in the games I took back, and not in the games that belonged to us. Yet Scotty was still playing it.

He was playing one night before he went to bed. I'd been working on *Ender's Game* all day, trying to finish it before Christmas. I came out of my office about the third time I heard Kristine say, "Scotty, go to bed *now!*"

For some reason, without yelling at the kids or beating them or anything, I've always been able to get them to obey when Kristine couldn't even get them to acknowledge her existence. Something about a fairly deep male voice—for instance, I could always sing insomniac Geoffrey to sleep as an infant when Kristine couldn't. So when I stood in the doorway and said, "Scotty, I think your mother asked you to go to bed," it was no surprise that he immediately reached up to turn off the computer.

"*I'll* turn it off," I said. "Go!"

He still reached for the switch.

"Go!" I said, using my deepest voice-of-God tones.

He got up and went, not looking at me.

I walked to the computer to turn it off, and saw the animated children, just like the ones I'd seen before. Only they weren't on a pirate ship, they were on an old steam locomotive that was speeding along a track. What a game, I thought. The single-sided Atari disks didn't even hold a 100K, and here they've got two complete scenarios and all this animation and—

And there wasn't a disk in the disk drive.

That meant it was a game that you upload and then remove the disk, which meant it was completely RAM resident, which meant all this quality animation fit into a mere 48K. I knew enough about game programming to regard that as something of a miracle.

I looked around for the disk. There wasn't one. So Scotty had put it away, thought I. Only I looked and looked and couldn't find any disk that I didn't already know.

I sat down to play the game—but now the children were gone. It was just a train. Just speeding along. And the elaborate background was gone. It was the plain blue screen behind the train. No tracks, either. And then no train. It just went blank, back to the ordinary blue. I touched the keyboard. The letters I typed appeared on the screen. It took a few carriage returns to realize what was happening—the Atari was in memo-pad mode. At first I thought it was a pretty terrific copy-protection scheme, to end the game by putting you into a mode where you couldn't access memory, couldn't do anything without turning off the machine, thus erasing the program code from RAM. But then I realized that a company that could produce a game so good, with such tight code, would surely have some kind of sign-off when the game ended. And why did it end? Scotty hadn't touched the computer after I told him to stop. I didn't touch it, either. Why did the children leave the screen? Why did the train disappear? There was no way the computer could "know" that Scotty was through playing, especially since the game *had* gone on for a while after he walked away.

Still, I didn't mention it to Kristine, not till after everything was over. She didn't know anything about computers then except how to boot up and get WordStar on the Altos. It never occurred to her that there was anything weird about Scotty's game.

It was two weeks before Christmas when the insects came again. And they shouldn't have—it was too cold outside for them to be alive. The only thing we could figure was that the crawl space under our house stayed warmer or something. Anyway, we had another exciting night of cricket-bagging. The old sheet was still wadded up in the crack in the closet—they were coming from under the bathroom cabinet this time. And the next day it was daddy-long-legs spiders in the bathtub instead of June bugs in the kitchen window.

"Just don't tell the landlord," I told Kristine. "I couldn't stand another day of that pesticide."

"It's probably the landlord's father *causing* it," Kristine told me. "Remember he was here painting when it happened the first time? And today he came and put up the Christmas lights."

We just lay there in bed chuckling over the absurdity of that notion. We had thought it was silly but kind of sweet to have the landlord's father insist on putting up Christmas lights for us in the first place. Scotty went out and watched him the whole time. It was the first time he'd ever seen lights put up along the edge of the roof—I have enough of a case of acrophobia that you couldn't get me on a ladder high enough to do the job, so our house always went undecorated except the tree lights you could see through the window. Still, Kristine and I are both suckers for Christmas kitsch. Heck, we even play the Carpenters' Christmas album. So we thought it was great that the landlord's father wanted to do that for us. "It was my house for so many years," he said. "My wife and I always had them. I don't think this house'd look *right* without lights."

He was such a nice old coot anyway. Slow, but still strong, a good steady worker. The lights were up in a couple of hours.

Christmas shopping. Doing Christmas cards. All that stuff. We were busy.

Then one morning, only about a week before Christmas, I guess, Kristine was reading the morning paper and she suddenly got all icy and calm—the way she does when something *really* bad is happening. "Scott, read this," she said.

"Just *tell* me," I said.

"This is an article about missing children in Greensboro.

I glanced at the headline: CHILDREN WHO WON'T BE HOME FOR CHRISTMAS. "I don't want to hear about it," I said. I can't read stories about child abuse or kidnappings. They make me crazy. I can't sleep afterward. It's always been that way.

"You've got to," she said. "Here are the names of the little boys who've been reported missing in the last three years. Russell De Verge, Nicholas Tyler—"

"What are you getting at?"

"Nicky. Rusty. David. Roddy. Peter. Are these names ringing a bell with you?"

I usually don't remember names very well. "No."

"Steve, Howard, Van. The only one that doesn't fit is the last one. Alexander Booth. He disappeared this summer."

For some reason the way Kristine was telling me this was making me very upset. *She* was so agitated about it, and she wouldn't get to the point. "So *what?*" I demanded.

"Scotty's imaginary friends," she said.

"Come on," I said. But she went over them with me—she had written down all the names of his imaginary friends in our journal, back when the therapist asked us to keep a record of his behavior. The names matched up, or seemed to.

"Scotty must have read an earlier article," I said. "It must have made an impression on him. He's always been an empathetic kid. Maybe he started identifying with them because he felt—I don't know, like maybe he'd been abducted from South Bend and carried off to Greensboro." It sounded really plausible for a moment there—the same moment of plausibility that psychologists live on.

Kristine wasn't impressed. "This article says that it's the first time anybody's put all the names together in one place."

"Hype. Yellow journalism."

"Scott, he got *all* the names right."

"Except one."

"I'm so relieved."

But I wasn't. Because right then I remembered how I'd heard him talking during the pirate videogame. Come on Sandy. I told Kristine. Alexander, Sandy. It was as good a fit as Russell and Rusty. He hadn't matched a mere eight out of nine. He'd matched them all.

You can't put a name to all the fears a parent feels, but I can tell you that I've never felt any terror for myself that compares to the feeling you have when you watch your two-year-old run toward the street, or see your baby go into a seizure, or realize that somehow there's a connection between kidnappings and your child. I've never been on a plane seized by terrorists or had a gun pointed to my head or fallen off a cliff, so maybe there are worse fears. But then, I've been in a spin on a snowy freeway, and I've clung to the handles of my airplane seat while the plane bounced up and down in mid-air, and still those weren't like what I felt then, reading the whole article. Kids who just disappeared. Nobody saw anybody pick up the kids. Nobody saw anybody lurking around their houses. The kids just didn't come home from school, or played outside and never came in when they were called. Gone. And Scotty knew all their names. Scotty had played with them in his imagination. How did he know who they were? Why did he fixate on these lost boys?

We watched him, that last week before Christmas. We saw how distant he was. How he shied away, never let us touch him, never stayed with a conversation. He was aware of Christmas, but he never asked for anything, didn't seem excited, didn't want to go shopping. He didn't even seem to sleep. I'd come in when I was heading for bed—at one or two in the morning, long after he'd climbed up into his bunk—and he'd be lying there, all his covers off, his eyes wide open. His insomnia was even worse than Geoffrey's. And during the day, all Scotty wanted to do was play with the computer or hang around outside in the cold. Kristine and I didn't know what to do. Had we already lost him somehow?

We tried to involve him with the family. He wouldn't go Christmas shopping with us. We'd tell him to stay inside while we were gone, and then we'd find him outside anyway. I even unplugged the computer and hid all the disks and cartridges, but it was only Geoffrey and Emily who suffered—I still came into the room and found Scotty playing his impossible game.

He didn't ask for anything until Christmas Eve.

Kristine came into my office, where I was writing the scene where Ender finds his way out of the Giant's Drink problem. Maybe I was so fascinated with computer games for children in that book because of what Scotty was going through—maybe I was just trying to pretend that computer games made sense. Anyway, I still know the very sentence that was interrupted when she spoke to me from the door. So very calm. So very frightened.

"Scotty wants us to invite some of his friends in for Christmas Eve," she said.

"Do we have to set extra places for imaginary friends?" I asked.

"They aren't imaginary," she said. "They're in the back yard, waiting."

"You're kidding," I said. "It's *cold* out there. What kind of parents would let their kids go outside on Christmas Eve?"

She didn't say anything. I got up and we went to the back door together. I opened the door.

There were nine of them. Ranging in age, it looked like, from six to maybe ten. All boys. Some in shirt sleeves, some in coats, one in a swimsuit. I've got no memory for faces, but Kristine does. "They're the ones," she said softly, calmly, behind me. "That one's Van. I remembered him."

"Van?" I said.

He looked up at me. He took a timid step toward me.

I heard Scotty's voice behind me. "Can they come in, Dad? I told them you'd let them have Christmas Eve with us. That's what they miss the most."

I turned to him. "Scotty, these boys are all reported missing. Where have they been?"

"Under the house," he said.

I thought of the crawl space. I thought of how many times Scotty had come in covered with dirt last summer.

"How did they get there?" I asked.

"The old guy put them there," he said. "They said I shouldn't tell anybody or the old guy would get mad and they never wanted him to be mad at them again. Only I said it was O.K., I could tell *you*."

"That's right," I said.

"The landlord's father," whispered Kristine.

I nodded.

"Only how could he keep them under there all this time? When does he feed them? When—"

She already knew that the old guy didn't feed them. I don't want you to think Kristine didn't guess that immediately. But it's the sort of thing you deny as long as you can, and even longer.

"They can come in," I told Scotty. I looked at Kristine. She nodded. I knew she would. You don't turn away lost children on Christmas Eve. Not even when they're dead.

Scotty smiled. What that meant to us—Scotty smiling. It had been so long. I don't think I really saw a smile like that since we moved to Greensboro. Then he called out to the boys. "It's O.K.! You can come in!"

Kristine held the door open, and I backed out of the way. They filed in, some of them smiling, some of them too shy to smile. "Go on into the living room," I said. Scotty led the way. Ushering them in, for all the world like a proud host in a magnificent new mansion. They sat around on the floor. There weren't many presents, just the ones from the kids; we don't put out the presents from the parents till the kids are asleep. But the tree was there, lighted, with all our homemade decorations on it—even the old needlepoint decorations that Kristine made while lying in bed with desperate morning sickness when she was pregnant with Scotty, even the little puff-ball animals we glued together for that first Christmas tree in Scotty's life. Decorations older than he was. And not just the tree—the whole room was decorated with red and green tassels and little wooden villages and a stuffed Santa hippo beside a wicker sleigh and a large chimney-sweep nutcracker and anything else we hadn't been able to resist buying or making over the years.

We called in Geoffrey and Emily, and Kristine brought in Charlie Ben and held him on her lap while I told the stories of the birth of Christ—the shepherds and the wise men, and the one from the Book of Mormon about a day and a night and a day without darkness. And then I went on and told what Jesus lived for. About forgiveness for all the bad things we do.

"Everything?" asked one of the boys.

It was Scotty who answered. "No!" he said. "Not killing."

Kristine started to cry.

"That's right," I said. "In our church we believe that God doesn't forgive people who kill on purpose. And in the New Testament Jesus said that if anybody ever hurt a child, it would be better for him to tie a huge rock around his neck and jump into the sea and drown."

"Well, it *did* hurt, Daddy," said Scotty. "They never told me about that."

"It was a secret," said one of the boys. Nicky, Kristine says, because she remembers names and faces.

"You should have told me," said Scotty. "I wouldn't have let him touch me."

That was when we knew, really knew, that it was too late to save him, that Scotty, too, was already dead.

"I'm sorry, Mommy," said Scotty. "You told me not to play with them anymore, but they were my friends, and I wanted to be with them." He looked down at his lap. "I can't even cry anymore. I used it all up."

It was more than he'd said to us since we moved to Greensboro in March. Amid all the turmoil of emotions I was feeling, there was this bitterness: All this year, all our worries, all our efforts to reach him, and yet nothing brought him to speak to us except death.

But I realized now it wasn't death. It was the fact that when he knocked, we opened the door, that when he asked, we let him and his friends come into our house that night. He had trusted us, despite all the distance between us during that year, and we didn't disappoint him. It was that trust that brought us one last Christmas Eve with our boy.

But we didn't try to make sense of things that night. They were children, and needed what children long for on a night like that. Kristine and I told them Christmas stories and we told about Christmas traditions we'd heard of in other countries and other times, and gradually they warmed up until every one of the boys told us all about his own family's Christmases. They were good memories. They laughed, they jabbered, they joked. Even though it was the most terrible of Christmases, it was also the best Christmas of our lives, the one in which every scrap of memory is still precious to us, the perfect Christmas in which being together was the only gift that mattered. Even though Kristine and I don't talk about it directly now, we both remember it. And Geoffrey and Emily remember it, too. They call it "the Christmas when Scotty brought his friends." I don't think they ever really understood, and I'll be content if they never do.

Finally, though, Geoffrey and Emily were both asleep. I carried each of them to bed as Kristine talked to the boys, asking them to help us. To wait in our living room until the police came, so they could help us stop the old guy who stole them away from their families and their futures. They did. Long enough for investigating officers to get there and see them, long enough for them to hear the story Scotty told.

Long enough for them to notify the parents. They came at once, frightened because the police had dared not tell them more over the phone than this: that they were needed in a matter concerning their lost boy. They came: with eager, frightened eyes they stood on our doorstep, while a policeman tried to help them understand. Investigators were bringing ruined bodies out from under the house—there was no hope. And yet if they came inside, they would see that cruel Providence was also kind, and *this* time there would be what so many other parents had longed for but never had: a chance to say good-bye. I will tell you nothing of the scenes of joy and heartbreak inside our home that night—those belong to other families, not to us.

Once their families came, once the words were spoken and the tears were shed, once the muddy bodies were laid on canvas on our lawn and properly identified from the scraps of clothing, then they brought the old man in handcuffs. He had our landlord and a sleepy lawyer with him, but when he saw the bodies on the lawn he brokenly confessed, and they recorded his confession. None of the parents actually had to look at him; none of the boys had to face him again.

But they knew. They knew that it was over, that no more families would be torn apart as theirs—as ours—had been. And so the boys, one by one, disappeared. They were there, and then they weren't there. With that the other parents left us, quiet with grief and awe that such a thing was possible, that out of horror had come one last night of mercy and of justice; both at once.

Scotty was the last to go. We sat alone with him in our living room, though by the lights and talking we were aware of the police still doing their work outside. Kristine and I remember clearly all that was said, but what mattered most to us was at the very end.

"I'm sorry I was so mad all the time last summer," Scotty said. "I knew it wasn't really your fault about moving and it was bad for me to be so angry but I just was."

For him to ask *our* forgiveness was more than we could bear. We were full of far deeper and more terrible regrets, we thought, as we poured out our remorse for all that we did or failed to do that might have saved his life. When we were spent and silent at last, he put it all in proportion for us. "That's O.K. I'm just glad that you're not mad at me." And then he was gone.

We moved out that morning before daylight; good friends took us in, and Geoffrey and Emily got to open the presents they had been looking forward to for so long. Kristine's and my parents all flew out from Utah and the people in our church joined us for the funeral. We gave no interviews to the press; neither did any of the other families. The police told only of the finding of the bodies and the confession. We didn't agree to it; it's as if everybody who knew the whole story also knew that it would be wrong to have it in headlines in the supermarket.

Things quieted down very quickly. Life went on. Most people don't even know we had a child before Geoffrey. It wasn't a secret. It was just too hard to tell. Yet, after all these years, I thought it *should* be told, if it could be done with dignity, and to people who might understand. Others should know how it's possible to find light shining even in the darkest place. How even as we learned of the most terrible grief of our lives, Kristine and I were able to rejoice in our last night with our firstborn son, and how together we gave a good Christmas to those lost boys, and they gave as much to us.

## AFTERWORD

In August 1988 I brought this story to the Sycamore Hill Writers Workshop. That draft of the story included a disclaimer at the end, a statement that the story was fiction, that Geoffrey is my oldest child and that no landlord of mine has ever done us harm. The reaction of the other writers at the workshop ranged from annoyance to fury.

Karen Fowler put it most succinctly when she said, as best as I can remember her words, "By telling this story in first person with so much detail from your own life, you've appropriated something that doesn't belong to you. You've pretended to feel the grief of a parent who has lost a child, and you don't have a right to feel that grief."

When she said that, I agreed with her. While this story had been rattling around in my imagination for years, I had only put it so firmly in first person the autumn before, at a Halloween party with the students of Watauga College at Appalachian State. Everybody was trading ghost stories that night, and so on a whim I tried out this one; on a whim I made it highly personal, partly because by telling true details from my own life I spared myself the effort of inventing a character, partly because ghost stories are most powerful when the audience half-believes they might be true. It worked better than any tale I'd ever told out loud, and so when it came time to write it down, I wrote it the same way.

Now, though, Karen Fowler's words made me see it in a different moral light, and I resolved to change it forthwith. Yet the moment I thought of revising the story, of stripping away the details of my own life and replacing them with those of a made-up character, I felt a sick dread inside. Some part of my mind was rebelling against what Karen said. No, it was saying, she's wrong, you *do* have a right to tell this story, to claim this grief.

I knew at that moment what this story was *really* about, why it had been so important to me. It wasn't a simple ghost story at all; I hadn't written it just for fun. I should have known—I never write anything just for fun. This story wasn't about a fictional eldest child named "Scotty." It was about my real-life youngest child, Charlie Ben.

Charlie, who in the five and a half years of his life has never been able to speak a word to us. Charlie, who could not smile at us until he was a year old, who could not hug us until he was four, who still spends his days and nights in stillness, staying wherever we put him, able to wriggle but not to run, able to call out but not to speak, able to understand that he cannot do what his brother and sister do, but not to ask us why. In short, a child who is not dead and yet can barely taste life despite all our love and all our yearning.

Yet in all the years of Charlie's life, until that day at Sycamore Hill, I had never shed a single tear for him, never allowed myself to grieve. I had worn a mask of calm and acceptance so convincing that I had believed it myself. But the lies we live will always be confessed in the stories that we tell, and I am no exception. A story that I had fancied was a mere lark, a dalliance in the quaint old ghost-story tradition, was the most personal, painful story of my career—and, unconsciously, I had confessed as much by making it by far the most autobiographical of all my works.

Months later, I sat in a car in the snow at a cemetery in Utah, watching a man I dearly love as he stood, then knelt, then stood again at the grave of his eighteen-year-old daughter. I couldn't help but think of what Karen had said: truly I had no right to pretend that I was entitled to the awe and sympathy we give to those who have lost a child. And yet I knew that I couldn't leave this story untold, for that would also be a kind of lie. That was when I decided on this compromise: I would publish the story as I knew it had to be written, but then I would write this essay as an afterward, so that you would know exactly what was true and what was not true in it. Judge it as you will; this is the best that I know how to do.

# LARRY NIVEN

## "The Wishing Game"

*Larry Niven (1938- ) has devoted most of his 32 years as a writer to elaborating his "Tales of Known Space," a future history of the universe that includes his well-known novel* Ringworld *and its sequel* Ringworld Engineers. *In the novels and short fiction collections it encompasses—among them* The World of Ptavvs, A Gift from Earth, Neutron Star *and* Tales of Known Space: The Universe of Larry Niven—*he has explored many classic science fiction themes. The Ringworld universe has also served as the backdrop for four shared-world volumes of* The Man-Kzin Wars. *His collaborations with Jerry Pournelle include the celebrated alien contact novel* The Mote in God's Eye, *the fantasy* Inferno, *and the disaster novel* Lucifer's Hammer. *With Steven Barnes, he has written* Dream Park, The Barsoom Project, *and* Dream Park: The Voodoo Game, *all set in a future world of government-controlled theme parks. His short fantasies are collected in* The Time of the Warlock, *and his fantasy novel* The Magic Goes Away *has inspired two shared-world anthologies,* The Magic May Return *and* More Magic.

# The Wishing Game

*by Larry Niven*

---

runching and grinding sounds brought him half-awake. He was being pulled upward through gritty sand, in jerks. Then the stopper jerked free, sudden sunlight flamed into his refuge, and the highly compressed substance that was Kreezerast the Frightener exploded into the open air.

Kreezerast attempted to gather his senses and his thoughts. He had slept for a long time . . .

A long time. A human male, an older man not in the best of shape, was standing above the bottle. There was desert all about. Kreezerast, tall as the tallest of trees and still expanding, had a good view of scores of miles of yellow sand blazing with heat and light. Far south he saw a lone pond ringed by stunted trees, the only sign of life. And this had been forest when he entered his refuge!

What of the man? He was looking up at Kreezerast, probably perceiving him as a cloud of thinning smoke. His aura was that of a magic user, though much faded from disuse. At his feet, beside Kreezerast's bottle, was a block of gold wrapped in ropes.

Gold? Gold was wild magic. It would take no spells. It drove some species mad; it made humans mad enough to value the soft, useless metal. Was that why the man had carried this heavy thing into a desert? Or had its magic somehow pointed the way to Kreezerast's refuge?

Men often wished for gold. Once upon a time Kreezerast had

given three men too much gold to carry or to hide, and watched them try to move it all, until bandits put the cap to his jest.

Loose white cloth covered most of the man's body. Knobby hands showed, and part of a sun-darkened face. Deep wrinkles surrounded the eyes. The nose was prominent, curved and sharp-edged like an eagle's beak, and sunburnt. The mouth was calm as he watched the cloud grow.

Kreezerast pulled himself together: the cloud congealed into a tremendous man. He shaped a face that was a cartoon of the other's features, wide mouth, nose like a great ax, red-brown skin, disproportionately large eyes and ears. He bellowed genially, "Make yourself known to me, my rescuer!"

"I am Clubfoot," the man said. "And you are an afright, I think."

"Indeed! I am Kreezerast the Frightener, but you need not fear me, my rescuer. How may I reward you?"

"What I—"

"Three wishes!" Kreezerast boomed. He had always enjoyed the wishing game. "You shall have three wishes if I have the power to grant them."

"I want to be healthy," Clubfoot said.

The answer had come quickly. This was no wandering yokel. Good: brighter minds made for better entertainment. "What disease do you suffer from?"

"Nothing too serious. Nothing you cannot see, Kreezerast, with your senses more powerful than human. I suffer from sunburn, from too little water, and from various symptoms of age. And there's this." The man sat; he took the slipper off his left foot. The foot was twisted inward. Callus was thick along the outer edge and side. "I was born this way."

"You could have healed yourself. There is magic, and you are a magician.

Clubfoot smiled. "There was magic."

Kreezerast nodded. His own kind were creatures of magic. Over tens of thousands of years the world's *manna*, the power that worked spells, had dwindled almost to nothing. The most powerful of magical creatures had gone mythical first. The afrights had outlived the gods. They had watched the dragons sickening, the merpeople becoming handless creatures of the sea; and they had survived that. They had watched men spread across the land, and change.

*331*

"There was magic," Kreezerast affirmed. "Why didn't you heal your foot?"

"It would have cost me half my power. That mattered, when I had power. Now I can't heal myself."

But now you have me. So! What is your wish?"

"I wish to be healthy."

Did this Clubfoot intend to be entirely healed from all the ills of mankind on the strength of one wish? The question answered itself: he did. Kreezerast said, "There are things I can't do for you—"

"Don't do them."

Was there no way to force Clubfoot to make his wish more specific, more detailed? "Total health is impossible for your kind."

"Fortunate it is, that I have not wished for total health."

The wish was well chosen. It was comprehensive. It was unambiguous. The Frightener could not claim that he could not fulfill the conditions; they were too general.

Magic was still relatively strong in this place. Kreezerast knew that he had the power to search Clubfoot's structure and heal every ill he found.

To lose the first wish was no disaster. One did like to play the game to the end. Still, Kreezerast preferred that the first wish come out a bit wrong, to give the victim warning.

Pause a bit. Think. They stood in a barren waste. What was a man doing here? His magic must had led him to Kreezerast's refuge, but—

Footprints led north: parallel lines of sandal-marks and shapeless splotches. They led to the corpse of a starved beast, not long dead, half a mile away. Here was more life: scavengers had set to work.

Saddlebags lay near the dead beast. They held (Kreezerast adjusted his eyes) only water skins. Three were quite dry; the fourth held five or six mouthfuls.

The prints blurred as he followed them farther. Dunes, more dunes . . . the prints faded, but Kreezerast's gaze followed the pathless path . . . a fleck of scarlet at the peak of a crescent dune, twelve miles north . . . and beyond that his eyes still saw, but his other senses did not. The *manna* level dropped to nothing, as if cut by a sword. The desert continued for scores of miles.

It tickled Kreezerast's fancy. Clubfoot would be obscenely healthy when he died of thirst. He would suffer no ill save for fa-

tigue and water loss and sunstroke. Of course he still had two
wishes . . . but such was the nature of the game.

"You shall be healthy," Kreezerast roared jovially. "This will
hurt."

He looked deep within Clubfoot. Spells had eased some of the
stresses that were the human lot, and other stresses due to a
twisted walk, but those spells were long gone.

First: brain and nerves had lost some sensitivity. Inert matter
had accumulated in the cells. Kreezerast removed that, carefully.
The wrinkles deepened around Clubfoot's eyes. The nerves of
youth now sensed the aches and pains of an aged half-cripple.

Next: bones. Here was arthritis, swollen joints. Kreezerast re-
shaped them. He softened the cartilage. The bones of the left foot
he straightened. The man howled and flailed aimlessly.

The callus on that foot was now wrong. Kreezerast burned it
away.

Age had dimmed the man's eyes. Kreezerast took the opacity
from the humor, tightened the irises. He was enjoying himself,
for this task challenged his skills. Arteries and veins were half-
clogged with goo, particularly around and through the heart.
Kreezerast removed it. Digestive organs were losing their function; Kreezerast repaired them, grinning in anticipation.

In a few hours Clubfoot would be as hungry as an adolescent
boy. He'd want a banquet and he'd want it *now*. It would be salty.
There would be wine, no water.

Reproductive organs had lost function; the prostate gland was
ready to clamp shut on the urethra. Kreezerast made repairs.
Perhaps the man would ask for an houri too, when glandular
juices commenced bubbling within his veins.

A few hours of pain, a few hours of pleasure. For Kreezerast to
win the game, his three wishes must leave a man (or an afright,
for they played the game among themselves) with nothing he
hadn't started with. To leave him injured or dead was acceptable
but inferior.

The man writhed with pain. His face was in the sand and he
was choking. His lungs, for that matter, had collected sixty years
of dust. Kreezerast swept them clean. He burned four skin tu-
mors away in tiny flashes.

The sunburn would heal itself. Wrinkled skin was not ill
health, nor were dead hair follicles.

Anything else?

Nothing that could be done by an afright working with insufficient *manna*.

Clubfoot sat up gasping. His breathing eased. A slow smile spread across his face. "No pain. Wait—" The smile died.

"You have lost your sense of magic," the afright said. "Of course."

"I expected that. Ugh. It's like going deaf." The man got up.

"Were you powerful?"

"I was in the Guild. I was part of the group that tried to restore magic to the world by bringing down the Moon."

"The Moon!" Kreezerast guffawed; the sand danced to the sound. He had never heard the like. "It was well you didn't succeed!"

"In the end some of us had to die to stop it. Yes, I was powerful. All things end and so will I, but you've given me a little more time, and I thank you." The man picked up his golden cube by two leather straps and settled it on his back. "My next wish is that you take me to Xyloshan Village without leaving the ground."

Kreezerast laughed a booming laugh. "Do you fear that I will drop you on Xyloshan Village from a height?" It would make a neat finale.

"Not anymore," Clubfoot said.

Here the magic was relatively strong, perhaps because the desert would not support men. Men were not powerful in magic, but there were so many! Where men were, magic disappeared rapidly. That would explain the sharp drop-off to the north. Wars did that. Opposing spells burned the *manna* out locally in a few hours, and then it was down to blades and murder.

To east and west and south, the level of power dwindled gradually. "Where is this Xyloshan Village?"

"Almost straight north," Clubfoot pointed. "Rise a mile and you'll see it easily. There are low hills around it, a big bell tower and two good roads—"

The man's level of confidence was an irritant. Struck suddenly young again, free of the ever-present pains that came with age in men, he must be feeling like the king of the world. How pleasant it would be, to puncture the man's balloon of conceit!

"Take me to Xyloshan Village without leaving the ground." Very well. Kreezerast would not leave the ground.

The Frightener didn't rise into the air; he *grew*. At a mile tall he could scan everything to the north. Xyloshan was a village of fifteen or sixteen hundred with a tall, crude bell tower, two hundred miles distant. If he hurled Clubfoot through the air in a parabola . . .

He couldn't. It was too far and he didn't have sufficient magic. Just as well. It would have ended the game early.

He still had two choices.

Clubfoot had made the wrong wish. It could not be fulfilled. The afright could simply say so. Or . . .

He laughed. He shrank to twenty feet or so. He picked up Clubfoot, tucked him under his arm and ran. He covered twelve miles in ten minutes (weak!) and stopped with a jar. He set Clubfoot down in the sand. The man lay gasping. His hands had a death-grip on the ropes that bound the gold cube.

"Here I must stop," Kreezerast said. "I must not venture where there is no *manna*."

The man's breathing gradually eased. He rolled to his knees. In a moment he'd realize that his minuscule water supply lay twelve miles behind him.

Kreezerast needled him. "And your third wish, my rescuer?"

"Whoof! That was quite a ride. Are you sure *rescuer* is the word you want?" Clubfoot stood and looked around him. He spoke as if to himself. "All right, where's the smoke? Mirandee!"

"Why should I not say *rescuer?*"

"Your kind can't tolerate boredom. You built those little bottles as refuges. When you're highly compressed and there's no light or sound, you go to sleep. You sleep until something wakes you up."

"You know us very well, do you?"

"I've read a great deal."

"What are you looking for?"

"Smoke. It isn't here. Something must have happened to Mirandee. *Mirandee!*"

"You have a companion? I can find her, if such is your wish." He had already found her. There was a patch of scarlet cloth at the top of a dune, and a small canopy pitched on the north side, two hundred paces west.

Clubfoot played the game well. He had a companion waiting just this side of the border between magic and no magic, on a line between Xyloshan Village and Kreezerast's refuge. The afright had taken him almost straight to her. And to their camp, where waited two more loadbeasts and their water supply.

A puff of wind could cover that scarlet blanket with sand . . .

An afright would have gloated over his two victories. The man merely picked up his gold and walked. In a moment he was jogging, then running flat out, testing his symmetrical feet and newly youthful legs. He bellowed, "Mirandee!" half in the joy of new youth, half in desperation. He ran straight up the side of a tall dune, spraying sand. At the top he looked about him, and favored Kreezerast with a poisonous glare. Then he was running again.

Kreezerast's little whirlwind had buried the scarlet marker. But of course: the man had failed to find it, but he'd seen a dying whirlwind.

Kreezerast followed, taking his time.

The man was in the shade of the canopy, bending over a woman. Kreezerast stopped as his highly sensitive ears picked up Clubfoot's near-whisper. "I came as quick as I could. Oh, Mirandee! Hang on, Mirandee, stay with me, we're almost there."

The Frightener could study her more thoroughly now: a very old woman, tall and still straight. An aura of magic, nearly gone. She was unconscious and days from death. The golden cube lay beside her, pushed up against her ribs. Wild magic . . . it might reinforce some old spell.

Once upon a time, a man had wished for a woman who didn't want him. Kreezerast found her and brought her to him, but he made no effort to hide where she had gone. He'd watched her relatives take their vengeance. Humans took their lusts seriously . . . but this woman did not seem a proper object for lust. She'd be thirty or forty years older then he.

The man must have thought the Frightener was out of earshot. He rubbed her knobby hand. "We got this far. The bottle was there. The afright was there. The magic was there. The first spell worked. Look at me, can you see? It worked!"

Her eyes opened. She stirred.

"Don't mind the wrinkles. I don't *hurt* anywhere. Here, feel!" He wrapped the woman's fingers around his left foot. "The second spell, he did just as we thought. I don't think we'll even need—" The man looked up. He raised his voice. "Frightener, this is Mirandee."

Kreezerast approached. "Your mate?"

"Close enough. My companion. My final wish is that Mirandee be healthy."

This was too much. "You know we hate boredom. It is discourteous of you to make two wishes that are the same."

Clubfoot picked up the gold, turned his back and walked away. "I'll remain as courteous as possible," he snarled over his shoulder. "I remind you that you carried me facing backward. Was that discourteous, or did you consider it a joke?"

"A joke. Here's another. Your . . . companion must be nearly one hundred years old. A healthy woman of that age would be dead."

"Hah hah. Nobody dead is healthy. I already know that you can fulfill my wish."

Kreezerast wondered if the man would use the gold to bribe him. *That* would be amusing. "I point out also that you are not truly my rescuer—"

"Am I not? Haven't I rescued you from boredom? Aren't you enjoying the wishing game?" Clubfoot was shouting over his shoulder across a gap of twenty paces. In fact he had walked beyond the region where magic lived, while Kreezerast was still looking for ways to twist his third wish.

That easily, he was beyond Kreezerast's vengeance. "You have bested me. I admit it, but I can limit your satisfaction. One more word from you and I kill the woman."

Clubfoot nodded. He spread a robe from the saddlebags against the side of a dune and made himself comfortable on it.

No curses, no pleading, no bribe? Kreezerast said, "Speak your one word."

"Wait."

What? "I won't hurt her. Speak."

The man's voice now showed no anger. "Our biggest danger was that we would find you to be stupid."

"Well?"

"I think we've been lucky. A stupid afright would have been very dangerous."

The man spoke riddles. Kreezerast turned to black smoke and drifted south, beaten and humiliated.

Once upon a time a man had wished to be taller. Kreezerast had lengthened his bones and left the muscles and tendons alone. Over time he'd healed. A woman had wished for beauty; Kreezerast had given her an afright's beauty. Afterward men admired her eerie, abstract loveliness, but never wished her favors . . . and she was the one who had shied from men.

But no man had ever bested him like this!

What did the magician expect? Kreezerast had watched men evolve over the thousands of years. He had watched magicians strip the land of magic, until better species died or changed. He had no reason to love men, nor to keep his promises to a lesser breed.

The bottle beckoned . . . but Kreezerast rose into the air. High, higher; three miles, ten. Was there any sign of his own kind? None at all. Patches where *manna* still glowed strong? None. Here and here were encampments, muffled men and women attended by strange misshapen beasts. Men had taken the world.

The world had changed. It would change again. Kreezerast the Frightener would wait in his refuge until something or someone dug him up. A companion would come . . . and would hear the tale. Afrights didn't lie to each other.

So be it. At least he need not confess to killing the woman out of mere spite. Let her man watch her die over the next few days. Let him tend her while his water dwindled.

The key to survival was to live only through interesting times.

Here was the bottle. Now, where . . .

Where was the stopper?

The stopper bore afright's magic. Sand would not hide it.

Gold would. Wild magic would hide the magic in the stopper. It was a box, a box!

The camp was untouched. The woman had not moved. Her breathing was labored.

Clubfoot lay against the next dune. He had gone for the beasts and the supplies in their saddlebags. He said nothing. The golden cube glowed at his feet.

Kreezerast said, "Very well. You can reach Xyloshan Village and I cannot stop you, if you are willing to abandon the woman. So. You win."

Clubfoot said, "Why do I want to talk to a liar?"

The answer was obvious enough. "For the woman."

"And why will you stoop to bargaining with a mere man?"

"For the stopper. But I can make another."

"Can you? I could never make another Mirandee." The man sat up. "We feared you would twist the third wish somehow. We never dreamed you'd refuse to grant it at all."

He would have to remake the stopper *and* bottle, for they were linked. And he could do that, but not here, nor anywhere on this *manna*-poor desert. Perhaps nowhere.

He said, "Give me the stopper and I will grant your third wish, or any other you care to make."

"But I don't trust you."

"Trust this, then. I can repair this Mirandee's nerves. In fact . . . yes." He looked deep into her body, deep into her fine structure. This one had never been crippled. She'd never born children either. Odd. It was humankind's only form of immortality.

Clear out the capillaries, clean the jugulars and carotids, repair the heart. Now she cannot die inconveniently. More blood flows to the brain. Myelin sheaths are becoming inert. Fix it.

She stirred, flung out an arm. Her breathing was faster now.

Kreezerast called, "So sensation has returned—"

She whispered, "Clubfoot?" She rolled over, and squeaked with pain. She saw the tremendous man-shape above her; studied it without blinking, then rolled to her knees and faced north. "Clubfoot. Stay there," she croaked. "Well done!" He couldn't have heard her.

"So her sensation has returned and her mind is active, too," the Frightener called. "Now she can feel and understand pain. I will give her pain. Do you trust my word?"

"Let us see if you trust mine," the man called. "I will never give the stopper to you. Never. Mirandee must do that for me. You must persuade her to do that."

Persuade? Torture! Until she begged to do him any service he asked. But then she must go and get the stopper, where magic failed . . . fool. Fool!

The Frightener shrank until he stood some seven feet tall. He said, "Woman, your paramour has wished you to be healthy. If I make you healthy, will you give me that which he holds in ransom?"

She blinked. "Yes."

"Will you also keep me company for a day?" Postpone. Delay. Wait. "Tell me stories. The world is not familiar to me anymore."

Her thoughts were slow . . . and careful. "I will do that, if you will give me food and water. As for keeping you company—"

"I speak of social intercourse," he said quickly. To show Clubfoot's woman that an afright was a better mate would have been entertaining. *If* they were lovers. She was far older than he was . . . but there were spells to keep a woman young. Had been spells. She had been a powerful magician, he saw that. In fact (that unwinking gaze, as if he were being judged by an equal!), this whole plan might have been hers.

He had lost. He was even losing his anger. They had *known* the danger. What a gamble they had taken! And Kreezerast must even be polite to this woman, and persuade her not to break her promise after she had walked beyond his reach.

He said, "Then tell me how you almost brought the Moon to Earth. But first I will heal you. This will hurt." He set to work. She screamed a good deal; and so he kept that promise too.

Bones, joints, tendons: he healed them all. Ovaries were shrunken, but not all eggs were gone; they could be brought to life. Glands. Stomach. Gut. Kreezerast continued until she was a young woman writhing and gasping, new inside and withered outside.

Clubfoot did not run to his lady to help her in her pain.

They might still make a mistake. If nothing else thwarted them, perhaps he had one last joke to play.

She'd feel the wrinkles when she touched her face! But wrinkles do not constitute ill health. But she *must* give him the stopper. Kreezerast pulled her skin smooth, face and hands and forearms (but not where cloth covers her. Hah! She'll never notice until it's too late!), legs, belly, breasts, pectoral muscles too. (She might.)

The sun had gone. He set sand afire for warmth and summoned up a king's banquet. Clubfoot stayed in his place of safety and chewed dried meat. She didn't touch the wine. Mirandee and the Frightener ate together, and talked long, while Clubfoot listened at a distance.

He told her of the tinker and his family who had wished for jewels, once upon a time. He'd given them eighty pounds of jewels. They had one horse and a travois. A hundred curious villagers were swarming to where they had seen the looming, smoky form of an afright.

But the tinker and his wife had thrown handfuls of jewels about the road and into the low bushes, and fled for a day before they stopped to hide what they kept. Forty years later their grandchildren were wealthy merchants.

Mirandee had seen the last god die, and it was a harrowing tale. She spoke of a changed world, where powerless sorcerers were becoming artists and artisans and musicians, where men learned to fish for themselves because the merpeople were gone, where war was fought with bloody blades and no magic at all.

Almost he was tempted to see more of it. But what would he see? If he ventured where the *manna* was gone, he would go mythical.

Presently he watched her sleep. Boring.

They talked the morning and afternoon away. At evening Mirandee folded the canopy and gathered the blankets and bedding and walked away with it all on her shoulders. She had been strong; she was strong again. She crossed the barrier between magic and no magic. Kreezerast could do nothing. She came back to collect food and wine left over from the banquet, and crossed again.

She and her man set up their camp. Kreezerast heard them talking and laughing. He saw Clubfoot's hands wander beneath the woman's robes, and was relieved: he had not fooled *himself*, at least. *What of the stopper?*

Neither had mentioned it at all.

He waited. He would not beg.

Mirandee took Clubfoot's golden cube. She carried it to the margin of magic. Her magical sense was gone; would she cross? No, they'd marked it. She swung the cube by the straps and hurled it several feet.

Kreezerast picked it up. The wild magic hurt his hands. There was no lid. He pulled the soft metal apart and had the stopper.

Time to sleep.

He let himself become smoke, and let the smoke thin. The humans ignored him. Perhaps they thought he had gone away; perhaps they didn't care. He hovered.

The canopy and the darkness hid their lovemaking, but it couldn't hide their surging, flashing auras. Magic was being made in that dead region. They were lovers indeed, if they had not been before. And Kreezerast grinned and turned toward his bottle.

In her youth she had chosen not to bear children.

Kreezerast had given them their health in meticulous detail. The ex-sorceress's natural lust to mate had already set their auras blazing again. She'd have a dozen children before time caught up with her, unless she chose abstinence, and abstinence would be a hardship on her.

Some human cultures considered many children a blessing. Some did not. Certainly their traveling days were over; they'd never get past that little village. And Kreezerast the Frightener crawled into his bottle and pulled the stopper after him.